A NAME LONG BURIED

The Drifter Duology
Book Two

~

C. M. Banschbach

Uncommon Universes Press LLC
1052 Cherry St.
Danville, PA 17821
www.uncommonuniverses.com

This is a work of fiction. Names, characters, businesses, places, events, and incidents are either the products of the author's imagination or used in a fictitious manner. Any resemblance to actual persons, living or dead, or actual events is purely coincidental.

Editing: A. C. Williams
Proofreading: Sarah McConahy
Formatting: Sarah Delena White

Cover Design: E. A. H. Creative Design

ISBN-13: 978-1-948896-47-4

For those with scars and cracks.
You are enough.

Dear Reader,

This book is very special to me, but it has a few things I want to gently talk about first. It opens with the characters from Then Comes a Drifter dealing with the aftermath of their choices and challenges. Broken friendships, broken hearts, and a broken world. This time we see a little more closely Dayo's alcoholism and addiction withdrawals. Gioia nudges open the door a little wider on her past sexual abuse and how it has impacted her in so many ways. Gered's latent PTSD raises its head and invades every aspect of his new life, leaving those around him feeling helpless. These things are not treated lightly. And it was important to me to portray how these traumas could impact someone in a way I've not often seen in fiction books. Gered's front and center journey with his PTSD, including at least one panic attack, is compiled from research and statements made by those dealing with their own PTSD. It's not something I wanted to treat lightly, but rather pay homage to those fighting these battles every day. Gioia's hurt does not just go away. Dayo makes a choice to face his wounds. And in the end, there's healing and the promise of continued growth, hope, and a beckoning future for every one of them.

CHAPTER ONE

"Dusting piece of—"

"Sure you don't need help?" Gered stared down over crossed arms at Laramie half-hidden under a transpo truck.

Her hand grabbed the edge and she pulled herself out on the wheeled cart, squinting a glare up at him. "I'm fine. Besides, your hands still look like crap." She disappeared again.

Gered flexed his fingers in his gloves, a faint pulling on his skin with the action. The blistering sunburn from being strung up in the desert heat over a week ago had faded to a peeling mess. But at least they were healing.

A bit of bandage around his wrist peeked out from between his dark blue jacket and the glove. The wounds from the cuffs were on their way to healing, but he'd kept the bandages on to protect them from the road dust, and—he twitched the jacket cuff—to hide the viper tattoo on his left wrist from view.

Another frustrated yell and sound of wrench hitting metal later, Laramie emerged again. Her cheerful face distorted in a scowl as she thrust the wrench up at him.

"Here," she growled. She pushed up to her feet and made room for him to settle on the wheeled cart and pull himself under the truck.

He found the problematic bolt, and one, two tugs with the wrench later, it budged free. He didn't say anything as he kept working it loose, but a faint grin tugged his lips.

A scuff, and long, blonde braid and Laramie's upside-down face appeared by his leg. "I loosened it for you."

His grin grew.

"Whatever." She lightly punched his thigh, but laughter teased her voice. "While you're down there, you might as well finish."

He didn't reply, just settled into the work. The bits of blue in his grey eyes made it easier, remnants of magic left over from before the Rifts opened up across every continent three hundred years ago and drained magic from the world except for the drops still humming in their blood.

For the first time since leaving Arrow and the med center two days ago, he relaxed a little. It was almost like it hadn't sunk in yet that he'd gotten out of Rosche's gangs. Thanks to Laramie. His sister.

Some days he didn't know which was harder to believe. That he'd escaped the brutal motorcycle gangs which had been his life for five years, or that the smart-mouthed drifter was the long-lost sister he'd thought had died sixteen years ago in the same Tlengin raids that had taken him.

"You want to find lunch here?" Her dust-covered boots shifted on the pavement as she leaned up against the truck.

He switched out tools, grabbing a rag to wipe away chunks of dust and grease. "We should probably keep riding."

"Okay," came Laramie's easy agreement.

Gered eased his arms down to his chest, taking a short breath to ease the ache already building in his ribs. That was another thing to get used to. Having his own choices.

Despite the doc at the Arrow med center discharging him, his ribs still ached, and fading streaks of bruises still lingered on his face and torso. Laramie had to help him change out bandages every night on his right thigh, chest, and arm from where the road had torn into him at the end of their fateful first attempt at running.

But the urge to keep putting as many miles as possible between them and Rosche's borders fueled every moment. Laramie had left Rosche for dead in a ravine, but the doubt lingered in the back of Gered's mind. The warlord had survived worse.

"Doing okay down there?"

He stirred, raising his arms to keep working. "Yeah."

"You better not mess up those bandages. I'm not changing them twice today."

Another smile threatened. Laramie apparently didn't do well with wounds.

"Got it, drifter."

Her snort of laughter floated down. He paused again to use his grey dustscarf to wipe sweat from his forehead. Despite the first onset of autumn, the days were still overly warm. Even more so underneath a transpo truck with the heat from the sun saturating the pavement.

A bark and skittering paws announced a new arrival. Laramie squatted down, ruffling a shaggy black-and-white dog's ears. Gered watched a moment, knuckles tight around the wrench handle until the cheery, panting face of the dog turned up at Laramie reassured him enough to turn back to work.

"Hey there," she cooed. "You're handsome, aren't you?"

Heavier boots announced the owner. "Thought I was paying

you to work on my truck?" A bit of suspicion laced the man's voice.

Gered tensed, hand clenching again. Laramie pushed back to her feet, stance widening a fraction.

"My partner's finishing up. He's got a good head for engines. You won't be disappointed." Her voice stayed easy.

The man grunted. He whistled to his dog and they both left.

"Charming," Laramie muttered.

Gered finished up and pulled himself back out from under the truck. "You were the one who took this job."

She frowned down at him a moment before extending a hand to help him carefully sit up, then stand.

"How could I not? Look at this poor truck." She pressed a hand over her heart with a sorrowful look.

Gered wiped bits of grease from his gloves and tossed the rag back into the toolbox.

"You know he's just going to dust it up again in a few weeks, right?"

Laramie shrugged, nudging her sunglasses higher on her nose. "As long as he pays up right now, who cares?"

Gered shook his head and fished out his own sunglasses, tucking them back on like a piece of armor.

Her smirk twisted up one side of her mouth. "This is life as a drifter." She leaned into the cab of the truck and started it up. They both tilted their heads, listening to the steady rumble of the engine. It had a hum of satisfaction that seemed to ripple all the way into his bones. She nodded and killed the engine.

"Perfect. Let's go get our money."

She led the way, her long blonde braid tapping the back of her olive-green jacket with every confident step. One hand tucked into a pocket, the other swung beside her leg, a tic he'd noticed to ensure one hand was close to the knives she kept strapped to both thighs.

One hand swept down to his right leg, fingers curling as they met empty air. He shoved both hands firmly inside his jacket pockets. He'd destroyed the right holster in the crash, leaving him feeling a little off-balance only having one of his twin bone-handled pistols holstered.

Laramie knocked on the frame of the tired house. Sun-dried paint peeled off the boards, weeds grew up around the base of the house, obscuring more warped boards. A deflated ball lurked beside the porch wrapping the front end of the house.

The cement pad where the man stored his transpo truck was cracked, more weeds pushing through. An oak tree sprawled in the corner of the ragged yard, the dog panting in its shadows as it watched them.

The man appeared, scratching a protruding belly through a grimy shirt. Too slow to do more than bluster if he didn't like the results of the job.

"All done," Laramie informed him.

He grunted and pushed the screen door open. The scent of smoke followed him, rising from the cigarette dangling in one hand. A brief twitch ran through Gered's hand. The slightest smell made him think of the Tlengin. Of threats all around and amplified by the bitter smoke.

"Sure it works?" The man scowled at them, taking a deep drag of the cigarette.

Laramie tilted her head back, and her jaw tightened a little. Already bristling at any implication against her skill. It made Gered almost smile and drew his attention from the smoke.

"Wouldn't be knocking on your door if it didn't."

He grunted again and turned back inside. Laramie tipped a glance back at Gered, eyebrows raised over her sunglasses. He rolled his eyes even though she couldn't see behind his glasses and she smirked.

The man pushed open the door and handed her a thin stack of bills. Laramie fanned through them and frowned.

"Seems a bit short."

The man shrugged.

Laramie pushed her sunglasses up. Gered shifted slightly, but enough to draw the man's attention to him. He didn't take his hands from his pockets, just stayed still, chin up, face blank as he stared at the man through the dark glasses.

The man blinked, darted a glance between him and Laramie, and turned back in. Laramie graciously accepted the rest of the payment without another word and tucked it away in her pockets. Gered backed away one step before turning to follow her away.

"That happen often?" he asked as they reached their motorcycles, parked just inside the chain-link fence that marked the rundown property.

Laramie swung a leg over her bike. "Been awhile. Though last time I had to punch a guy to get him to pay up."

"Doesn't surprise me." He fished out his keys.

She tossed her braid over her shoulder. "What's that supposed to mean?"

"Asks the girl who picked a fight with the most dangerous man in the lower territory."

"On your advice, as I recall."

"And then got into how many more fights?" He started up his bike.

"What?" she yelled over the revving of her engine, tilting her head as if she couldn't hear. But the smirk returned.

He shook his head and pushed toward the road.

They drove slowly down the main street, painted brick buildings lining each side. Signs for shops dangled from wrought iron poles. Brick planters abutted the street, ferns and bright flowers spilling out. They'd crossed out of the desert that morning, leaving behind the derelict towers holding remnants of magic, and the land had shaped into greener hills with sporadic spreads of trees.

Even the people walking down the even sidewalks and casting them cautious glances looked different. There was an air of civility pervading the small town, the neatly pressed lines of pants and shirts, the notable absence of dust.

He and Laramie stuck out like a tumbleweed in a patch of flowers.

Another reason to leave the town behind. They might be too memorable.

He stiffened when Laramie's head whipped to the left. She pulled over, and he hurried to follow.

"What's wrong?" He reached for his gun.

"The lack of chocolate in my bag, that's what. Be right back."

He relaxed when he finally looked up and saw the sweet shop sign above them. "Really?"

She wrinkled her nose. "Want to come in?"

Gered shook his head. Things like shopping in sweet stores were so far out of his norm, he was panicking already just thinking about it.

She studied him a minute, eyes hidden behind her glasses. "Okay. I'll be out in a sec."

He nodded even though she'd already said that. She disappeared through the door with a ring of the shop's bell. Relaxing back on the bike seat, he started automatically scanning the sidewalks and roads.

Who's going to attack? The potted plant? He gently rubbed the back of his neck so as not to disturb the bandage still there.

"Are you a drifter?"

He whipped his head up to see a young boy studying him five safe feet away.

"You're Tlengin now." The muscles in his arms tightened as the memory invaded, followed quickly by a different one of Rosche clapping him on the shoulder. *"You're a viper now. Welcome home."*

The boy still stared at him, shifting from one foot to the other. Gered swallowed hard and looked up and down the sidewalk. Did kids just wander around like this with no fear in their faces? Should he even talk to him?

"Yeah." He'd been one for two entire days, if that counted.

"Um … you can fix things, right? Mom said some drifters were in town fixing things." The boy's feet scuffed faster, and he kept one hand tucked behind his back.

Gered tensed again. *He looks like he's nine. What nine-year-old has a gun behind his back?*

Besides him at that age.

Laramie probably would have already fixed whatever it was behind the kid's back, but she was still happily trapped in the shop. Up to him, then.

"Depends. What do you have?"

The boy slid a hesitant step forward and extended a mess of gears and wires. Gered's brows drew together, not sure what he was looking at.

"It's … it's supposed to be a dog. It was my sister's, but it stopped working a long time ago, and I thought I'd try and get it to work for her birthday, but then I think I messed it up." The boy's shoulders fell.

Gered carefully took the pile, snatching a falling gear out of midair. Once it had been a thick wire figure, filled with gears and slender filaments, but it had been gutted—likely by the enterprising mechanic in front of him.

"Do you think you could fix it?" Big green eyes looked up at him, hands twisting nervously.

Oh, dust. He cleared his throat. "Yeah, I'll give it a shot."

Killing his engine, he stepped over to Laramie's bike, hesitating a second before flipping open the left saddlebag and pulling out her tool kit. Deep down he knew she wouldn't be mad, but nervousness still flitted through his fingers as he reached for it.

A glance down confirmed the boy right under his elbow, staring at the precarious hold he had on the toy. Gered sat on the curb, taken aback as the boy plopped down on his knees beside him. He tried to edge away a little, but the boy claimed the small space right back.

Trying to ignore the earnest stare, Gered set to work, sifting through pieces and setting some aside as they worked loose. He tucked his glasses up on his head to better see and pulled a slender screwdriver from the kit.

From what he could tell, the dog was meant to wind up and move around until it ran down. He shifted it around, stacking a few more pieces on the ground beside him until the pattern emerged. Nodding to himself, he set to work, and the world faded to the tools, the delicate machine, and the certainty that he could build it better than ever.

He worked until the gloves on his hands became too bulky. Using his teeth to pull them off one at a time, he flexed his fingers against the bandages' resistance once before turning back to the work. As he twisted a small screw in place, a sweeping feeling of memory crashed over him, taking him almost out of himself, and suddenly he was the boy kneeling beside someone, watching careful fingers build a clock with floral designs twisted in copper and silver wires for a grey-and-blue-eyed woman with warmth in her smile.

Gered blinked hard, and he came back to the present, but his eyes stung a little.

"Okay." He set the dog on the ground between them. "Try it."

The kid twisted the curly tail. The gears inside rotated in sync, and the dog raised its head. It trotted forward on mechanical legs, eyes flaring green as it gave a coppery bark. It made two wide circles, then came back to the kid, settling down on its haunches and into stillness.

The boy turned to Gered with an open jaw. "It never did those things before!" He peered closer at Gered, intently studying his eyes. "Do you have magic?"

Gered turned the screwdriver in his hands. The bits of blue in his eyes said he still had the gift that had made the Itan the best architects and builders in the five continents. It had kept him alive over the last sixteen years, but …

"No. Just good at building things."

And killing.

"Oh, I don't know. Maybe a little bit of magic," Laramie's voice cut in. She squatted behind them, glasses propped up on her head, a soft smile as she watched them.

The boy brushed a hand across the dog's head. "How much

do I pay you?" he blurted. "That was a lot of work, right?"

Something softened inside Gered. He nudged the toy closer to the kid.

"It's okay. I liked working on it. Just don't break it again, yeah?"

A small grin tugged the kid's face. He lurched forward and wrapped his arms around Gered's shoulders so quick all he could do was brace. Then he was gone, running down the sidewalk with the toy cradled in his arms.

Laramie laughed lightly. "You look like he was about to attack you."

Gered shifted, pulling back into himself. He tucked the screwdriver back in its spot and closed the kit. "I used your tools. Sorry."

She took it from him, head tipped slightly as she ran a thumb over the embossed surface of her name. "It's okay. You can borrow them any time, you know."

He nodded, jaw tightening as he focused on pulling his gloves back on. There was something in her voice. Not pity, but just an uncertainty again on how to act around him. His survival barriers from the Tlengin had shifted when he entered Rosche's service. But now they lay half-destroyed or whirling in confusion as he tried to figure out the first freedom he'd had in years.

"Ready to go?" Her voice pulled him back again.

He nodded and pushed to his feet, pulling his glasses back down. They started up their engines, but Laramie paused.

"That was really amazing what you did. I like getting to see that part of you." A shy half-smile flickered.

He ducked his head, twisting his grip around the bike handles. The very small part of him that wasn't built for killing or hurting. He pushed off without a word, falling into silence that lingered as they left town and kept heading east.

CHAPTER TWO

"You okay?" Laramie asked.

Gered jerked his head up, blinking to focus on her across the small electric lamp casting a glowing circle around their campsite. She sat cross-legged, bits of a travel pack in her lap.

"Yeah." But his dinner lay mostly untouched in front of him. They'd meet up with her traveler family the next day, and he hated how uneasy it made him.

"What's going on?" she prompted, tearing another piece of jerky free.

He broke off a piece of the flavorless nutrient bar, more to keep his hands busy than anything. The gentle thrum of crickets rose and fell in the patchwork woods spread over the low hills. Stars pinpricked the sky, constellations sprawling boldly through the expanse, a little brighter with the moon shaved down to a crescent.

"You sure they'll be okay with me?"

"Hey." Her gentle voice brought his head back up. "Yes." Her blue-grey eyes were earnest, but he didn't think she could really lie if she tried.

"They're my family. But you are too, now." She shrugged as if that would put everything to rest.

"Laramie …" He shook his head. "I don't know if I should …
I don't know what family is anymore."

"What about Dayo?"

Gered bit back a scoff. "I left him behind. He hates me." Or
he should after Gered had lied to him about running and then
did it anyway. Leaving him behind without a word, just like his
traveler family. "Not a good record over here."

Laramie dusted her hands off, the motion crisp in irritation.
"It's looking after each other. You did that my first day in. It's about
having someone's back. You did that with Dayo, Gioia, me … all
of your unit."

His throat tightened at the sound of Gioia's name. He'd left
her behind too. And the look in her eyes as she'd stared down at
him kneeling bloody in the dust … The bit of nutrient bar crumbled in his fingers.

"Hey." Laramie dropped down beside him and extended something. He stared at the long bar wrapped in shiny foil.
"Have some chocolate."

A small smile tugged the corner of his mouth, and he broke
off a tiny piece.

"I don't remember the last time I had chocolate," he admitted.

She took a more generous portion and popped it in her
mouth. "How have you survived without it?"

"You're right. That explains so much about me." His grin
grew a little at the shock that spread across her face before bursting into a laugh.

"I *knew* you had a sense of humor." She nudged an elbow
against his arm.

He shook his head in a slight laugh and took a small bite.
Bitter melted to sweet across his tongue.

She watched him with a grin. "It's good, right?"

Finishing the last of his piece, he allowed her to shove the bar back in his face for another helping. "No wonder you never have chocolate around."

Laramie wrinkled her nose at him and took another piece. "Can I ask you a question?"

He nodded, flicking his hand to decline more of the bar.

She picked at a loose bit of foil, carefully folding it back over the bar. "Why did you change your name?"

Gered turned his right hand up, tugging at a bit of gauze wrapped around his palm. *Marcus Antonio Solfeggietto.* The sound of his true name was almost as foreign as the idea of family.

"When the Tlengin first took me, I wouldn't tell them my name. Refused to talk, really. They had taken everything, so I didn't want to give up my name, the last part of myself. Maybe it was stupid. But they gave me this one. It doesn't mean anything." He shrugged. "Just like I have no name."

"Dust. You just made me hate them even more." Laramie shook her head.

He smoothed a thumb across the bandage. He never talked much about his past with the Tlengin—eleven years lost to surviving their hidden mobile villages and trained to be one of them.

"Why don't you use yours?" He hadn't been able to bring himself to use hers yet. *Melodie.*

"The travelers have been in Natux almost as long as the Itan. Back in Aclar, when magic was still around, names had power. And giving someone your true name was more meaningful. They still have the same tradition here, even though magic is long gone. Among the travelers, only true family uses your real name." She darted a glance at him.

18

"Laramie is taken from part of a word in Aclar—more like an idea, really. It means one who has no true home, or drifter."

"You gonna keep drifting after we get there?"

Her shoulders lifted in a quick sigh. "I don't know. I'd stop and show that picture in any town I went to, looking for other Itan …" She cast a quick glance at him. "Or family. And now I found some."

There it was again. Family. She still knew what it meant. Had someone to remind her for the last sixteen years.

"I don't really know how to be a brother anymore."

"That's okay." Laramie shrugged. "I don't really know how to be a little sister."

"Sure?" Gered raised an eyebrow. "You've got the annoying part down."

She gasped and shoved his side harder, knocking him off-balance for a second. Her laugh brought another quick smile from him.

"Figure it out together?"

He pulled his knees up to drape his arms over. "Yeah." After a moment, he asked, "Your family use your real name?"

A faint noise caught in her throat like she might want to argue his phrasing. "They do when I'm there." A pause, then she nudged his side again. "You don't have to, if you don't want to yet."

He snuck a quick glance from the corner of his eye. She'd turned to face him, the earnestness back. It radiated from every pore of her being. He couldn't remember if he'd ever been like that. He dragged a hand through his hair. It'd gotten a bit longer in the last week, and a bit of blond had started peeking out at the roots, defying the dark dye that Rosche enforced.

"What name do you want me to give them for you?"

Always to the root of the problem.

"I don't know."

She tipped her head and raised an eyebrow. It drew a faint smile and the answer from him.

"It's just … I buried everything that was Marcus and our family. It's like …" He cast about for the words. "Like I don't want to ruin the name by who I am now. I want a chance to try and earn it back." Heat tinged his cheeks at the honesty.

Laramie nodded slowly. "I get it. Gered it is for now."

A breath eased from his chest.

Her fingers twisted together in her lap. "You know, the thing about drifting is you're free to do whatever you want."

But so much in his life had been about earning. "I think it'll be awhile before I'm used to having choices again."

She blinked a few times. "Like I said, family is about being there for someone. I'll help however you need."

Pressure nagged the back of his eyes. "Thanks." *I just hope you won't regret it.*

CHAPTER THREE

Dayo rotated the beer in his hands. Around and around. The dull buzz from the alcohol couldn't kill the memory of the words crackling over the radio.

Saddle up. We've got a runner. The drifter. And. The pause still lingered in his mind. *Gered is with her.*

His next drink went down more bitter than normal. Gered's red jacket still lay crumpled on the opposite bed, road-ripped and bloodstained. Dayo lurched up and hurled the can across the room. It hit the wall with a clatter, tumbling to the ground to spill across the floor.

He screamed, droplets of beer scurrying down the wall to escape the profanity.

A gentle knock responded. He threw the door open. Gioia leaned against the frame, hands tucked in her back pockets.

"How you doing?" she asked softly.

"How do you think I'm doing?" he sneered, leaving the door open for her to come in as he stepped back.

"Dayo …"

He tossed a hand up to cut her off. She waited in silence. Dayo scrubbed his palm over his coarse hair cropped close in the military-style haircut. His hands dropped to his hips with another sigh.

"Sorry."

"I don't know if I'm supposed to be pissed or heartbroken, so…"

He turned to see Gioia's rueful smile. For a second, the fight left him at the sight of the young woman who'd survived Rosche and then dared to love Gered in secret.

And then Gered had gone and left both of them.

Dayo slumped back down on his bed atop the messy pile of his blankets. The springs creaked as Gioia sank down next to him. She laced her fingers together, quiet. His hands twitched restlessly, the snake tattoo winding twice around his left wrist in a solid, dark spiral atop his black skin, wriggling as if trying to escape.

"You think they made it?" she asked quietly.

He tapped his thumbs together. He'd gotten Gered down from the posts, barely conscious and breathing. Then watched over his shoulder as the drifter drove away with him. Still trying to sort through the anger and betrayal and relief.

"Laramie never gave up on anything. I think maybe they did."

A shaky smile flashed over her face.

"You don't care that they left together?" he asked.

Gioia drew a deep breath, staring at the wall. No, at the red jacket.

"I do. But …" She glanced sideways at him. "He told me he was going to try and run." The admission came rushed.

Anger flared quick and bright.

"I said no."

It died just as fast at Gioia's pained admission.

"Because I'm too much of a dusting coward. And I figured, even though I believed him when he said there was nothing between them, if I was too scared to even try, maybe he deserved someone who was brave enough to do it."

"You're not a coward, Gioia." No one who fought her way out of Rosche's bed and then held her own for two years in the gangs could be labeled a coward.

"I'm not?" She turned an almost-challenging frown at him. "Then why wouldn't I go?"

"Because no one ever makes it." In the three years Dayo had been there, no one ever had. And those who had tried had been brought back to be killed, or had been killed by Gered's rifle.

He should have known better. Especially after I put him back together the last time he tried.

Her shoulders slumped. "So just a smart coward, then?"

"At least he told you!" Dayo snapped, jerking back to his feet again, starting to pace to fill the restlessness winding endlessly through him.

Gioia stared at him. "He didn't …?"

Dayo tossed his arms wide. "Why would he need to? He knew what I'd say, right?"

Because he would have said no. But then he would've been out the next morning, bag packed, bike fueled, ready to ride. No questions asked.

But Gered hadn't given him the chance. Instead, he'd left Dayo behind without a word. And at that moment, it felt worse than what his traveler family had done to him three years ago.

The crackle of the handheld radio sent him stooping to sweep it up from the ground by Gered's bed. Exchanging a grim look with Gioia, he clicked the receiver.

"Dayo."

"Rosche wants to see you. Out."

Dayo turned it over in his hands. He'd been expecting the call. Word had gone out the previous morning Rosche had finally woken up. If nothing else, he could be grateful the drifter did such a number on the warlord.

Unit Four didn't have a technical leader, though they'd all been deferring to him over the last three days as Gered's former lieutenant. The units hadn't been going out, so there'd been no chance for him to really solidify his position.

I don't even know if I want it.

"You think he'll just confirm the position?" Gioia asked.

Dayo tossed the radio on the bed, grabbing his dark jacket with the small viper skull pin on the collar and shrugged it on. "Maybe. Or maybe he'll come after me and I'm not walking out of there."

Gered had scrapped them up to the rank of Four on the strength of his skill and reputation. Most outside the unit wouldn't be sad to see him go. And most didn't know him past the stony expression and quick violence he didn't hesitate to inflict.

But Dayo? Most might see him and Unit Four as easy pickings.

He holstered his pistol on his right thigh. A knife on his left, and a second blade in a sheath in his right boot.

"Want me to go with?" Gioia's question took him off guard.

She stood, hands in her back pockets again, jaw clenched tight as she waited. As much as he'd prefer someone at his back, no way was he making her walk into a meeting with Rosche.

He eased his careless smile onto his face and shrugged. "No, I'll be good."

Her posture shifted in relief, and she tipped a nod, standing back to let him pass. He stopped once in the kitchen to drain a water bottle and rinse the taste of beer from his mouth. Then out the door into the brilliant sunlight.

Keeping hands in his jacket pockets, he kept his head high as he walked from the bunker toward the towering Barracks tower. Riders walking past or lounging on the stairs leading up into bunkers watched him as he went.

Unit Four was marked. The unit leader and the trainee he'd staked had upset the order of things. And now Dayo was heading to see what the score would be.

Sweat trickled down his back under the touch of the sun. Even autumn starting two days before hadn't brought a bit of cool. It wouldn't for weeks yet this far into the desert.

Not like in the territories further east above the Rift. He clenched his fist, driving away the memories of riding in his family's caravan, stopping off in towns in the upper country to trade goods or skilled labor before moving on. Before they'd decided to cross the Rift and try and drive through Rosche's territory.

The tower blocked out the sun, casting a wide swath of shade toward him. The three steps up into the tower seemed taller than normal. He paused once inside the doors, blinking to allow his eyes to adjust to the sudden dimness of the atrium. Cool rushed around him, bringing a quick rush of goosebumps up his arms.

Two staircases wound up each side of the atrium to the second floor. Oversized flags draped from the railing, a forceable reminder to anyone who walked through that they were under Rosche. The scarlet cloth sported the same coiled serpent winding its way through his skin.

Dayo took the left staircase, stepping off into the broad hallway. To his right was the war room and radio room. He'd only been in the war room once. Anyone lower than unit leaders didn't usually get summoned. Keeping left, he headed toward Rosche's rooms.

Soft lights illuminated the plush carpet that muffled boot-steps. Several other doors branched off the hallway, closed and likely locked.

A burly rider leaned against the wall at the end of the hall. Dayo tilted his head side to side, readying himself as he approached. The rider pushed away from the wall, the patch on his right sleeve marking him Unit One. Barns seemed to collect beefy guys who glared at the world through hooded eyes.

Dayo tipped his chin up in greeting. The rider crossed his arms, staring at him for a moment before sniffing and pushing the door open.

Giving a mocking salute, Dayo sauntered past him into Rosche's room. The acidic scent of sterilizer and the beep of machines hit him, for once not settling him with the familiarity. Once he'd trained to help and heal instead of maim and kill.

A bed took up most of the room, a wardrobe to the right, and the left wall taken up by windows looking out over the compound. Dayo flicked a glance out the window, noting that it gave a clear view of over half the Barracks, adding to his theory that Rosche lurked in the upstairs floors and watched the comings and goings like a stalking jacklion.

A flicker of shadow drew his attention to his right. Moshe and Barns both stood in the corner of the room. Barns with the smile telling the world he knew more than it did, and Moshe with the level gaze that could assess the room—and a person—in seconds.

"Dayo." Rosche's smooth baritone, a little ragged from pain and meds, drew his attention to the bed.

The warlord reclined against the ornate headboard, left arm tucked in a sling. Lines ran from his right arm to the machine at the side of the bed. Dayo pitied the poor soul who'd had to lug that up the stairs from the med center on the first floor.

"Sir." He managed the proper amount of deference in the salute.

"I assume you know why you're here?" Rosche tipped his head back against the pillows.

"I've always been told I'm smart, sir." He clacked his jaw shut. *Keep sharp. There's no one to run interference anymore.*

But Rosche allowed a faint smile. "Then tell me about Gered."

Dayo let the betrayal and anger tighten around his heart. "What about him, sir?"

Rosche arched an eyebrow. "I heard you were among the first to reach the traitor and the drifter when they ran."

The brightness of the sun against the asphalt, the whine of his engine straining at its max speed, and the fury writhing in his gut as he closed in on Gered still tasted as fresh as if it had been hours instead of days ago.

"Just following orders, sir."

"And when you cut him down from the posts?" Harshness in Rosche's eyes leaked into his voice.

Uncuffed an unconscious and half-dead Gered from the posts and loaded him into the drifter's transpo truck, all technically under Moshe's command, but a small bit fighting through the fury in Dayo's heart during those hours had been glad to follow them.

Dayo inclined his head to the unit leaders against the wall. "Following orders, sir."

If Rosche was looking for someone to take down, he was giving the warlord as many options as possible.

"Hmm." Rosche grunted and pinned the two leaders with a glare indicating he already knew about the order and wasn't happy about it.

Sorry to have dumped all over your reputation there. Dayo schooled his features into nonchalance.

"And if Gered was standing in front of you right now, what would you do?" The warlord's cold eyes pinned him in place—a squirming groundsquirrel under a nighthawk's talons.

Punch him directly in the face. And then probably hug the dusting idiot. But neither of those answers were going to keep him and Unit Four safe.

"What needed to be done."

"Hmm."

The grunt grated across his eardrums.

"You'd pull the trigger?"

The way he forced a swallow betrayed him, he knew it did from the light of triumph in Rosche's eyes. If Laramie hadn't won her challenge, and Rosche had ridden through the gates instead, he would have shoved a gun in Dayo's hand, told him to shoot Gered in the head, and then given him Unit Four.

For a split second, he'd be angry enough to do it. Gered wouldn't have argued, just knelt there, ready to be dusted. And once that second had passed, Dayo wouldn't have been able to do it.

"Yes, sir."

"Hmm."

Dayo clenched his hands in his pockets against the hum.

"You've been a loyal soldier, Dayo. Reliable, useful. Something your traveler family might have failed to see."

His spine snapped straighter, and the grate of his back teeth against each other seemed painfully audible.

"I'll give you a chance. A few have been lobbying for Unit Four to be absorbed into another unit. Your numbers are down, and there's a certain … taint … about you now." Rosche plucked at the sling, still watching him through narrowed eyes, waiting for the crack to expose the weakness he searched for.

Dayo kept his chin angled up slightly, shoulders loose and careless, a daring expression in place.

"They can shift right off, sir. Unit Four's always done what needed to be done."

Rosche inclined his head. "You did clean up against those rebels and didn't hesitate to go after the runners. Barns."

Unit One's leader shoved away from the wall, scooping up a bundle from a chair. He shoved a dusky red leather jacket against Dayo's chest.

"Have fun defending that," he whispered, a smug grin in place.

"Shift off." Dayo tugged it free from the man's hold.

Barns's lip curled and he sauntered back over by Moshe.

"There will be a briefing tomorrow at eight hundred hours," Rosche said. "I look forward to seeing you there."

The phrase came loaded with another meaning. Once Dayo walked out of there with the red jacket, the challenges could begin in earnest. Rosche didn't care about him. He never had. It was about how much entertainment Dayo could give before earning his place. Or falling.

"Thank you, sir." Dayo saluted again and spun on his heel.

Back outside the door, the guard glanced from the jacket to him, an eyebrow twitching in interest.

"You wanna go right now?" Dayo spread his arms wide, the jacket dangling from his right hand.

The rider allowed a slow smile. "I don't think so. But you've got it coming, traveler."

Dayo's jaw hardened again. He flipped a traveler gesture at the man and stalked back down the hall. For some, it wouldn't even be about the jacket, it would be about him. Some stigma people had decided to raise against travelers. Like the Tlengin had decided to raise against the Itan years ago when they wiped the tribe out.

Travelers weren't meant to be alone. Even before they'd immigrated from Aclar to Natux, they'd been close-knit societies. Remnants now, crisscrossing the upper and lower countries in their caravans with colorful leather bands denoting their original tribes.

But he was. No braided leather cords around his left wrist. He'd cut it off three years ago. No family to back him up. They'd given him up without a second thought. And now, left behind again. A lone *kinin* in the midst of strangers.

He stepped out into the sunlight, the heat chasing away the chill of the room and Rosche's stare. A figure leaning against the wall with hands in back pockets made him pause.

Not alone. Not completely, anyway.

Gioia fell in beside him, the sunlight making the hundreds of freckles spilling across her coppery-brown skin a little darker.

"That went better than you thought?" She tipped her elbow to the jacket.

"Yeah. Maybe." His jaw already ached from keeping it clenched.

"I've got your back."

"You sure? It's gonna be a rough few days." His fingers dug into the leather. *Is it dusting worth it?*

But he wouldn't do well under someone else's command. Gioia wouldn't either.

"What's that word you say? *Kamé?*" She hesitated over the Aclar word.

He flashed a smile. At face value it meant friend. But it could mean brother or sister.

"You sure you want to keep claiming me as a friend?" he asked.

"You're right, you are really annoying." She smiled before sobering just as quickly. "Where do you think I'm going to be standing?"

He let out a short breath. "Okay then, *kamé.*" He lifted his fist. She knocked the back of her fist twice against his.

"Go round up Four."

She saluted with a grin and jogged back to the bunker.

CHAPTER FOUR

Unit Four had assembled in the rec room when he slowly made his way up into the bunker. Unit Five, their sister unit, wasn't around. Dayo stared at the riders as they watched him expectantly.

Seven riders were all that were left. Seven riders with identical military haircuts and color, and the same viper tattoo winding around their left wrist. They'd lost one to the rebels in Conrow, another in Springer. And then Gered. They'd all listened to Dayo as lieutenant before. Now to see if they'd accept him as leader.

"Okay, before I put this on, any objections?" He held up the jacket.

Heads shook around the room from the riders perched on chairs and couches. But a few hands tapped together, a few knees bobbed.

"I'm gonna do my best. But there's seven of us. Some units are gunning for us to be absorbed into another unit."

A scoff broke from Sani, a lithe man with the hooded eyes and bronzed skin of the lower country tribes. "And who thinks they're taking us?"

"My guess is Zelig," Dec piped in. Barely older than a kid, his lighter skin was constantly burning and peeling and freckling under the sun. He looked even paler against the dark dye in his hair, turning it the same shade as Rosche's.

Snorts of derision ran through the riders. Dayo allowed his own agreement. The Unit Fourteen leader was notoriously short on brains and had decided to have some grudge against Gered and Unit Four for years. He'd also gotten half his unit killed during the ambush down in Springer.

"We stay as Four," Gioia said from her position at the back of the room. A few riders glanced at her and nodded agreement.

Dayo bunched the jacket between his hands. "Okay. Stay in pairs until we prove ourselves again. I'll check the trainees for someone to stake. I'd rather bring in fresh blood than recruit from a unit."

Another flurry of nods passed.

"Dayo." Sani stood. He swept a hand around. "Gered screwed all of us, too. We'll stand behind you."

But there wasn't much anger in their faces. They'd had a good position under Gered. He didn't collect the kind of men who enjoyed hurting people. Not like some other units. It seemed that, just like Dayo, they were a little glad he'd made it out with the drifter, and a little sad they couldn't have done the same.

"Okay then." He tossed his dark jacket aside and pulled on the red jacket. It fit well, a little snug where his well-broken-in coat settled looser. *Guess I'll get used to it.*

Gioia gave him a sharp nod of approval. He smiled, hoping the careless mask was solidly in place. The real fight started as soon as he stepped back outside.

Decision made, the riders disbanded back to whatever they'd been doing before. Dayo headed back to his room, punching in the code to unlock the door. He dumped his old coat on the bed and sank down beside it.

Restlessness stole back in, an undercurrent of adrenaline already flaring in anticipation. The rule of the Barracks—anyone could be challenged. The pecking order could be upset. Positions were only held by those strong enough to keep hold of them.

He dug into the pocket of his old jacket, pulling out the small container of cigarettes. Flipping open the lid, he pulled out a slim tube. His hand paused automatically while reaching for the lighter.

He never smoked in the room. Not while Gered was there. *Screw him.*

But he pushed to his feet and headed outside. His boots thudded down the steps and he slammed his back against the sun-warmed wall of the bottom floor garage. A curse escaped as he reached for the lighter in his breast pocket. Not there. Still inside.

Measured footsteps snapped his attention to Unit Five's leader coming down the stairs. Dayo let his hands fall to his sides. Connor and he had never gotten along. It looked like his first challenge might be sooner than he'd anticipated.

"Relax." Connor waved his hand, coming to stand beside Dayo.

He didn't relax, even as Connor melted back against the brick wall. The unit leader's sardonic smile flitted over his face.

"I'm not here to challenge, Dayo." He reached into his pocket and proffered a lighter.

Dayo took it hesitantly, quickly lighting up and passing it back to Connor. He exhaled a plume of smoke.

"What are you here for, then?"

Connor dug in his own pocket, produced a cigarette, and lit his. "Let's get this out here. I don't like you. Never have."

Dayo took another drag, holding it in a moment before

breathing out. "Rest assured, it's mutual."

The lazy smile flickered again. "But me and Gered? We respected each other. He ran a tight unit."

Dayo tipped a bit of ash away.

"In-house fighting's not going to do either of us any good." Connor tucked the cigarette between his lips. "Besides, you're going to be busy enough."

"So what? We square, then?"

Connor held a breath, then let smoke stream out between his lips. "Yeah, we're square." He tossed the cigarette down and ground it out under his heel.

He paused before leaving. "Pick someone you trust to have your back as your second. You're gonna need it."

Dayo flicked ash again, studying the glowing end of the cigarette before looking at Connor. "Thought you didn't like me."

Connor huffed a laugh, rolling his eyes. "I don't, but I respected Gered. You held his back, and then got screwed over. He likes to see people fail." He jerked his head back toward the tower. Something else flickered in his cold, green eyes. "And screw him."

He turned and headed back inside. Dayo leaned against the wall, taking a contemplative drag of his cigarette. Unit Five tended to keep to themselves, all a little not quite right around the edges. And that included Connor and his second, Corinne—the only other woman in the units. Between her knives and sharpened nails, she acted ready to take a bite out of someone. In more ways than one.

The smoke calmed a bit of the storm inside. Like Connor suggested, he needed to name a second. And he knew exactly who he was going to pick.

CHAPTER FIVE

Almost there. Laramie leaned into the rushing wind as she and Gered drove down the highway.

The last stop had been an hour ago. Now the late afternoon sun sent their shadows scurrying ahead of them. A blue sign announced the upcoming turnoff. She lifted her hand from the handle and waved once.

Gered raised fingers from his clutch in acknowledgement. She darted another glance at him. The grey dustscarf rippled and tugged around his neck, trying to hide parts of his chin and face. The sunglasses obscured his eyes, the only gateway for emotion he seemed to allow most days.

At the med center a few days ago, it seemed like they'd made some progress. He'd talked a little more, smiled. Had even laughed a few times—a deep laugh that stirred memories of another man with blue-and-grey eyes. He had the same angle to his cheekbones as their father, something Laramie mostly remembered from the picture, but Gered's held a stern edge.

But over the last two days, he'd gone back to the expressionless unit leader mask he barely let slip even around Gioia and Dayo.

Sure they'll be okay with me? His question over the campfire the night before came back to prod at her heart. He wouldn't be an imposition, the family would welcome him, she sternly reminded herself.

She downshifted, slowing and leaning into the turn. The smaller highway rose and fell over the hills before them, stretching out like a black-and-yellow striped snake. Hints of orange and yellow tinged the trees marching across the hills.

Gered matched her slower pace. A few white-tailed deer grazed along the highway, backing a few steps away from the blacktop as they rumbled by before returning to graze around the clustered cacti proudly residing in any open meadow.

Laramie glanced at him again in her side mirror. He tilted his head enough to be looking around them, taking in the scenery.

Or scanning for threats. She shoved away the guilt of watching him out the window of the chocolate shop for a few minutes. Just to check and see what he'd do on his own. See if she really should trust her gut about him and the decision to bring him home.

She lifted her face to the wind, taking in the sweet smell of the hill country and the fainter scent that marked the Rift. Most people couldn't smell it. But those with the bits of color still in their eyes, still with a link to the magic that had once run through the earth, could.

Bitter-sweet, like a campfire about to burn out. *Wind must be strong across the Rift today.* Usually she had to be right up on the chasm to smell it.

They topped another rise and she saw home. A smile broke across her face at the sight of the twenty long caravan trailers in a loose double circle, parked a quarter mile off the road in a wide, open clearing.

Their wheels ground and spat rocks on their slow way down

the loose gravel track from the highway out to the camp.

A tall figure watched their approach from the wider space between two caravans. Her smile grew as the man stepped back and waved his arm.

"Melodie!" the traveler shouted as she rumbled up. His warm smile of welcome faded a little at the sight of Gered on her heels.

She pulled to a halt right outside the caravan border. Technically, they'd have to welcome Gered in. It was a bit more of a risk than she cared to admit, bringing him there without at least telling Ade first.

"Melodie!" The woman in question rushed toward her. A thin red scarf held back enthusiastic curls poufing around her head. The summer sun had given her black skin a tinge of gold.

Laramie killed her engine and hurled herself into the arms of the mother she remembered the most. Ade hugged her back just as tightly.

"Where have you been this time?" she asked in the traveler tongue.

"Oh, lots of places." Laramie squeezed her tight again, basking for a moment in the feel of being home—warmth, safety, love, and kindness all wrapped up in one place—and not stuck in a warlord's camp.

Ade stood back, holding her at arm's length. Dark eyes with tiny specks of gold studied her. "I was expecting you a few days ago."

Laramie propped her sunglasses up on the top of her head. "I got held up a bit." She turned to gesture at Gered, who sat on his bike, hands still on the grips, jaw set like he might be considering running. "Too busy finding my brother."

"Your …" Ade's jaw dropped.

Laramie beckoned to Gered. He cast one look at the traveler guard who still watched him carefully, then killed his engine and stood with the same slowness she'd had weeks ago when getting ready to confront Rosche for the first time.

He eased forward, tentatively pulling his sunglasses off and turning them between his hands.

Laramie switched back to the common tongue. "Gered, this is Ade, my ..." *Mother* stuck in her throat. "She raised me."

Ade squeezed her forearm, a small smile of understanding passed on.

"Ade, this is Gered, recently rediscovered brother."

They studied each other, Gered infinitely more wary. Ade seeing, as always, an unfair amount. She extended a hand.

"Nice to meet you, Gered."

He hesitantly accepted it. "Ma'am." His voice barely qualified as more than a whisper.

Laramie didn't have time to think on it as a shout filled up the space between caravans.

"Lodie!"

"Kayin!" she shrieked, sprinting forward to hurl herself into her boyfriend's arms.

He hefted her up off the ground, holding tight before setting her down and claiming a kiss. Tears stung for a moment as her heart flipped, all the missing from the lonely nights on the road and the fear of never seeing him again all trying to burst out at once. Tossing her arms around his neck, she kissed him back, forgetting it all with the press of their lips together.

"You're back." He rested his forehead against hers.

"Yeah." A smile bubbled again as she kissed him once more. "I am liking this." She rubbed her palms over the scruff highlighting his broad jawline.

His grin took up his entire face, crinkling around his honest eyes. "Good. I'd been trying to talk myself into shaving since I figured you'd be back soon anyway."

She laughed, sliding her arms back around him. "No, keep it."

"You bring me anything?" he teased.

"Only my gorgeous self."

"I guess I'll settle for that."

He danced back a step as she poked him in the stomach.

"There is actually one thing."

Kayin's gaze flitted past her and hardened as he caught sight of Gered.

"It's not what you think," she cut him off. "Come meet my brother."

He stared at her in confusion as she grabbed his hand and tugged him over. Gered still stood a few steps away from Ade, rubbing the smooth edge of the sunglasses' frame with his thumb, sharp eyes taking in every nook and cranny, every traveler now coming out to meet them.

Most called greetings to her as she passed. She waved back, returning the welcome home with thanks in Aclar. It rolled off her tongue with a bit more ease than her first language—something she still felt guilty about.

"Melodie!" a deep baritone called.

Kayin released her hand to allow her to step into Temi's warm hug. Bits of grey frosted his temples, but the laugh lines creasing his dark face kept him young.

"Baba." She leaned into his chest. She'd figure out how to introduce him to Gered as her father later. Right now, she'd focus on the hug and the way he rested a hand on the back of her head, rocking slightly side to side as he held her.

"We missed you." His words rumbled in his chest.

"I missed you, too."

Temi pulled back and held her at arm's length, much like his wife. He pursed his lips in a frown. "What's this I see about you bringing a boy home?"

A scoff from Kayin sent Laramie rolling her eyes. Temi cracked a smile, his deep brown-and-gold eyes glinting with mischief.

"Will you come meet my brother?" she asked.

Temi studied her, flicking a glance to Gered.

"I'd be honored," he finally said.

Laramie reclaimed Kayin's hand, squeezing it to reassure him of her words again. But nervousness speared her gut at the sight of Gered watching them. He eyed Kayin and Temi like a wolf sizing up possible competition.

He briefly met her gaze before returning to scanning, assessing. She flashed what she hoped was a calm, reassuring smile as she introduced them in the common tongue.

Gered flicked his fingers in and out of a fist after releasing Kayin's hand, shoulders still tensed. Kayin frowned, and Laramie tugged sharply on his hand.

He still hadn't said anything besides a "sir" to Temi in the same voice, lacking his normal, even strength.

Is this too much for him?

Nervousness gave way to realization plummeting down to her toes. More travelers stood together in groups, watching him as the newcomer, the outsider. Some still hadn't really accepted her, even after sixteen years, so what might they think of him? And what had happened the last two times he'd been brought to some place new and strange?

Her palm turned a little clammy in Kayin's hold, and she gently freed her fingers. Gered's attention locked on to her as she took several slow steps forward to stand by his shoulder, back turned to the family so they couldn't see her talk.

"You okay?" she asked in Itan.

His head turned sharply to her, a faint throb along his jaw betraying him. But he jerked his head.

"Monifa is the matriarch. She'll be here in a second to meet you and give you the blessing to stay." *I hope.* "Ade and Temi will be fine with you staying with us."

"Will they?" He also slipped back to Itan, eyes sharp as he studied the couple in question.

Laramie rested a hand on his arm, feeling the moment he flinched then tensed. "Yeah. They put up with me." She softened it with a grin.

A tremulous quirk appeared at the corner of his mouth, not really reaching further, but she decided to take it as a win.

"Melodie."

She turned to Monifa. The matriarch stood between her and the rest of the family. Long twists fell to her waist with small colorful threads woven around each one. Like the rest of the travelers, she wore trousers, calf-high boots, and a looser top woven with bright colors and geometric shapes, each pattern telling a different story about the family, about the craftsman, about the layers of the world.

Laramie stepped forward, resting her hands on Monifa's shoulders, and the matriarch did the same.

"Welcome home." Monifa's husky voice held the calm which had led the family through many storms.

"Thank you." Laramie smiled. "It's good to be back."

42

"And you bring someone new this time." Monifa looked past her to Gered.

"My blood brother."

The matriarch's eyebrow raised.

Laramie allowed another smile. "It was a surprise to me as well. It hasn't been more than a week since we figured it out." She took a short breath. "We found each other in ... tense circumstances."

Again, Monifa's brow arched.

"We needed each other to survive. He's ..." She searched for the word to describe what she'd just seen in Gered's eyes. "Adrift. Lost. I don't know ... I just know that he needs something, and I think that could be me, could be us, for now."

The matriarch studied Gered again, gold glinting brighter in her eyes. Her hands shifted a little on Laramie's shoulders.

"What happened to him as a child?"

Laramie swallowed hard. "The Tlengin took him." Her voice hushed. "They took him because he has more blue in his eyes than they'd ever seen. And they tried to make him into one of them."

"And did they?"

Laramie focused on the ground between their boots. Hers dust-stained, a bit of red dirt from the west still clinging to the seams—brighter, more tenacious, bolder than the tamer browns of the hill country.

Memories of Gered fighting, pulling the trigger without apparent hesitation crowded into her mind. But she focused instead on the way he'd sat in Unit Four's garage the night of the fight in Springer. The way she'd woken up to the sound of him screaming. The raw acceptance in his face when they'd been caught running the first time. The way bright-eyed Axel had wanted to be chosen for Unit Four because Gered had helped him out when he'd first arrived. The way Dayo slung an arm around his shoulders and they laughed. The way he softened just a little around Gioia.

"No. They didn't."

"I'll speak with him." Monifa withdrew her hands. Laramie half-turned and beckoned Gered forward.

He eased toward them, wary, tense.

Fragile.

About to snap.

"I'm Monifa. I speak for the family." The calm didn't leave her voice as she changed to common.

"Gered." His fingers twisted the sunglasses around and around.

"Your birth name?"

He darted a glance to Laramie.

"It's the name he's chosen to go by for now," she supplied.

Monifa nodded slowly. "This is a surprise for us. Our Melodie finding a blood relative."

He flinched a little at her true name. But he met Monifa's steady gaze.

"It was a surprise to me as well. I thought my entire family dead."

"She said you were raised by Tlengin."

Gered swallowed hard. "I was."

"Rumors say they were mostly wiped out several years ago." She tilted her head.

"They were."

"And where have you been since?"

Laramie's heart beat a frantic rhythm. Ade, Temi, Kayin—

they all leaned a little closer to hear.

"Serving under the warlord Rosche to the west."

Monifa darted a sharp glance at Laramie, who winced a little in apology. She'd wanted to find a better way to explain it all.

"And what did you do for him?"

Gered swallowed again, the lines of his face hardening even as something like acceptance filled his eyes.

"Killed. Enforced. Whatever he ordered."

Kayin stiffened beside her parents, and she sent him a pleading glance. But even Ade and Temi regarded Gered more warily, as if they wanted to pull her away from him.

"Did you have a choice?"

The question seemed to catch him off guard.

"Does it matter when it's still your finger pulling the trigger?" His gaze faltered and his fingers trembled their hold on the glasses.

The tightness around Monifa's mouth vanished. "I think it does," she said softly. "What made you decide to leave with Melodie?"

His boots shifted on the gravel, a bit of red tinging his cheeks as he cast a quick, almost shy glance at her.

"She wasn't afraid to take a stand. And it gave me the courage to try again."

"Again? You'd tried to leave before?"

He nodded, a distant look falling over him.

"What happened?"

A short breath jerked through his chest. Laramie shifted forward, bouncing her weight through her toes as if ready to throw herself between Gered and the question and the way he flinched around knives and the scars etched into his skin. Not all of which were from the Tlengin.

"An effective warning and deterrent until Laramie came

along," he finally ground out.

Monifa laced her arms across her chest, studying both of them.

"Melodie, you will stand for him?"

Laramie nodded immediately. "I will."

"Ade? Temi?" The matriarch twisted to look at them.

The couple came forward to stand with them. Gered leaned away, shoulder nearest drawing up in protection—the entire movement so subtle Laramie would have missed it if she hadn't been watching him.

Laramie clamped her mouth shut to stop the pleading words from tumbling out. They'd heard everything, and it was their decision to make.

Ade and Temi exchanged the look she one day hoped to have with Kayin—the one that held a wealth of words and understanding passing unspoken.

"We know Melodie. If she trusts him enough to bring him here, then we'll welcome him into our caravan," Ade said.

Gratitude welled up in Laramie and spilled through her beaming grin. Ade gave a soft smile in return. Temi nodded firmly. They'd stand with her.

"Very well. Welcome to the caravans, Gered. May Jaan bring you guidance and peace during your stay here."

Kayin still frowned where he stood, but Ade and Temi added their own blessing on Gered's stay. He hadn't moved, expression not changing with the news.

Monifa touched Laramie's arm, drawing her attention. "I know you will spend tonight with your family. But I do want to hear the whole story tomorrow." She inclined a raised brow at Gered.

"Yes, ma'am," Laramie dutifully promised. "And tell Esi she'll get the whole story, too." She leaned around Monifa to wave at the young woman her age who bounced from foot to foot, waiting for the conversation to be done.

Monifa's smile brightened her features. "She will have no patience."

Esi tossed her hands into air, frowning at Laramie in annoyance. Laramie grinned.

"I need to make sure things are settled first."

The matriarch nodded in understanding. "I'll let her know."

As she departed, Laramie turned back to confront the yawning divide between Gered and her traveler family, the few feet of space seeming more than ten miles.

For a moment, they all just stared at each other. Then Ade smiled brightly.

"Bring your things, both of you, and we'll get settled."

CHAPTER SIX

"Laramie." Gered reached out as the others left. "You sure about this?" He flicked a hand from his chest to the caravan circles. "Yes."

"I just ... don't want to dust anything up for you."

"You won't, Gered. You won't." She gently touched his arm. He glanced almost desperately at her.

"I ... I need to know what they might want from me."

Oh dust. Jaan, what do I say?

Slowly, carefully, she rested her other hand on his. He leaned away from both points of contact.

"Nothing. Absolutely nothing, other than to just be a guest here."

A bitter smile flashed. "How the hell do I do that?"

A half-chuckle broke from her. "Well, bring your bike. Come have dinner. There's a spare cot for you. You don't even have to talk."

"Don't tell me that," he said wryly.

Another smile eased from her. "Come on." She tsked. "You know I can do enough talking for both of us."

His muscles relaxed under her hands, and something a bit closer to a real smile quirked his mouth. But still he held back.

"You staked for me at the Barracks. I staked for you here. I know there's some fundamental differences between here and the Barracks, but I believe you'll do just fine."

He opened his mouth as if to argue, then clamped it shut. "All right, drifter. Show me where to go."

She kicked her motorcycle stand up, grabbed the handlebars, and began pushing it forward. He caught up with her, still searching out the corners of the camp. Inside the double circle, benches and tables were set around a large firepit. Colorful lights strung from caravan to caravan across the open area. The scent of smaller cookfires filled with sweet mesquite wood and traveler spices permeated the air, drawing a grumble from her stomach and a longing for non-travel pack food.

"One of the many benefits of the camp is that it does not smell like feet or like a skunk was left to rot by the bathrooms."

The almost-smile appeared again.

"And no food that's dried, pre-packaged, or made from half-cooked rice. We believe in salt and spices here."

"You always cook outside?" Gered asked.

"In summer. It keeps the caravans cooler." And there was just something inherently better about a meal cooked over open flames.

Two young girls ran by, waving and shouting a welcome. She grinned and called after them.

"There usually this many kids around?" he asked.

"Yeah. Not used to it?" she returned, half-afraid of the answer.

He lifted a shoulder. "There were kids in the Tlengin camps. But not as … happy as this."

"They're good kids. But"—she leaned a little closer—"they can get a little annoying. It's okay to glare at them occasionally."

He flattened his lips together in light irritation, but she only chuckled.

Laramie pushed her bike around an uneven patch of dirt left from a small cook pit. "Here we are."

Ade and Temi's caravan shared the same build as the others—fifty feet long and twenty wide with a door in the back. Four windows inset the left side of the trailer, and three smaller panes in a half-moon shape in the back door. A small porch extended off the end of the trailer, allowing for a few extra feet of space to stand, with four steps down to the ground.

Another motorcycle stood outside the caravan. The one Ade had taught her how to ride on.

Laramie kicked the stand down and took a moment to take in the bright yellow paint, the darker color of the transpo truck built under the front of the caravan to haul it along the road.

Home.

She undid the saddlebags and slung them over her shoulder.

Gered again moved slowly, undoing his much smaller bag. It contained all he'd dared pack to try and keep suspicion down the morning they'd run. Unit Four had kept it on his bike when they'd loaded it on the transpo truck. He pulled the long rifle from the sling on the front of the bike between the handlebars.

He tucked it over his shoulder, bending a little to absorb the weight into himself. His hand paused over the handgun strapped to his left thigh, fingers flicking quickly in and out of a fist.

Laramie offered a quick smile like she hadn't noticed the tic, the need to check weapons before heading into someplace new, someplace he already felt on edge.

She headed up the steps first and pushed in through the door. Any other homecoming, she'd dump her things by the door, plop down at the table with a full plate of Ade's cooking, and regale them with stories of her travels.

This time she stood aside to let Gered ease in with her. This time, she tried to take it in like a newcomer. But she barely remembered a time when the cozy caravan with the woven curtains brushing the long, low couch under the windows, the battered wood floors, the wall covered in paintings and half-finished projects, hadn't been home.

A small noise came from Gered. Another sudden grin flashed. She'd forgotten.

His eyes narrowed as he scanned the interior. The couch in the common area, the small kitchen and counters at the far end of the trailer, the bits of wall partitioning off the small rooms.

"It's bigger." It came out cautiously, uncertain if his eyes might not be tricking him with the placement of furniture.

"Aclar magic. Everything's bigger than you think it is." At least twice, if not more, as big as the exterior made it seem.

His grip shifted on the rifle strap at his shoulder as if to resettle himself. "How does it work?"

"I have no idea," she said cheerfully. "Sixteen years here, and they've never told me."

"That's not true!" Ade emerged from one of the rooms, carrying an extra blanket. "You've just never had the patience to sit down and try and puzzle it out."

Laramie tilted her head back. "That doesn't sound like me."

Ade flapped the blanket at her. "I take it you must like each other for Gered to have made it this far with you."

Gered shifted between his feet. Laramie clapped a hand to her chest with a gasp.

"I am a treasure!"

A muffled sound came from him again, and she caught the raise of his eyebrow. She gently nudged her fist against his shoulder, barely rocking him.

"Go get washed up!" Ade nodded her head at the rooms.

"You can dump your stuff in my room for now to keep it out of the way." She led the way to the nearest door. Inside, a low bed bolted to the floor butted out from the wall. A small workbench and hanging light sat to its left. Some shelves hung on the shared wall to the rest of the caravan. A woven blanket with geometric antelope leaping in front of triangular hills—payment from a grateful Ibenni tribesman further south on the family's route—hung over the wall between their rooms.

A puff of dust rose from her packs as she tossed them on the bed. She winced in apology. Gered glanced around, carefully setting his rifle on the floor by the workbench. The bits and pieces of projects were safely tucked away, but scraps of drawings were pasted over the walls and spilled out of notebooks stacked in precarious piles.

His pack went neatly beside his rifle. He turned his attention to unwrapping his dustscarf as if not wanting to be caught staring at the bit of life she'd comfortably carved out for herself.

Laramie hung up her scarf on the peg beside the door, tossing her jacket up beside it.

Gered carefully pulled off his gloves, gently flexing his hands against the gauze.

"How they feeling?" Laramie asked.

He never said anything, but his fingers always seemed a little stiff after a day's riding.

"All right."

"You want me to change them before we eat?"

The gloves went in a perfect stack atop the pack. He unzipped his jacket partway, then tucked his hands in his pockets, lining his shoulders up with a short breath.

"No, it'll be fine to wait until later."

"Okay. Washroom's over here." She led the way back out and along the wall of rooms to a smaller cubby inset between her parents' room and the front end of the caravan. It held enough space for a sink, a toilet, and a shower.

"Go ahead." She stepped back and ushered him in. The door clicked softly behind him. Laramie backed across the caravan floor to lean against the kitchen counter. Ade paused from mixing sweetbread.

"I have a weird favor to ask," Laramie whispered. "He's not really comfortable with calling me by my name yet. So, do you mind keeping it Laramie for now?"

Ade nodded. "Of course. I'll let people know."

Laramie flashed a grateful smile.

"Now get me the tin." Ade pointed at the cabinet behind her.

"Barely home and already being put to work." Laramie shook her head, crouching to fish the muffin tin from the cabinet. Taking a cloth and the canned fat, she smeared a thin layer around the cups before setting it on the counter beside Ade.

"Did you get enough to eat out on the road?"

Laramie bit back a laugh. "Memi, I eat just fine."

"Travel packs are not 'fine!'" Ade scowled, scooping batter into the tins.

"It has all the essential nutrients."

"Nutrients!" Ade scoffed. "I'll have to retrain you to what food is. Gered too, most likely, if you insisted on feeding him travel packs."

"Just wait until you hear what we ate at the Barracks." Laramie grimaced just thinking about the variety of ways chicken and rice could be unimaginatively lumped together.

"No starting without me!" Temi called from the main door. He stepped in, knocking his boots against the frame and letting Kayin follow. "Hope you don't mind one more for dinner, Ade."

"Of course not!" Ade beamed a smile at Kayin. It had been tradition for the last three years for Kayin to sit at their table the night she came home, her hand tucked in his under the table as she recounted her travels.

Laramie sidled around the counter and into Kayin's arms again.

"Hey," she mumbled into his chest.

"Hey," he whispered into her hair.

"Missed you."

"No cuddling of boyfriends before dinner. I need to keep my appetite up," Temi called.

Laramie laughed and pulled away. The light click of the washroom door alerted her to Gered quicker than the guarded look that stole over Kayin's eyes. She fought irritation.

We're talking later. I'm not dealing with this.

Keeping her voice light, she backed away. "I'm gonna wash up. Temi, don't scare them off."

She shut the door behind her, leaning against it a moment, breathing a sigh of relief as the murmur of conversation picked up and she caught Gered's even tone making short replies.

This is going to be interesting. Pushing away from the door, she ducked hands under the faucet. Another scoop of water slicked over the back of her neck and her face as she bent low over the sink.

Drying off, she stared at herself in the mirror. Blue-grey eyes stared a bit reproachfully back over the hint of cheekbones in her slim face. Her lips thrummed together with a sigh.

"Bring your long-lost brother home for dinner and hope your boyfriend doesn't get petty. And try and convince your family that he's really not a psychotic killer." She braced her hands on the sink. "He's not, right? This was a good idea?"

Her reflection raised an eyebrow.

"Yeah," she groaned and rubbed her eyes. "This story is going to go over great with everyone."

Warlords, escapes, shootouts, near-death challenges on her part. At least the bruising on her left temple and cheek from getting pistol whipped in an alley had faded. So had the bruising around her neck from where Zelig had tried to choke a confession from her on the garage floor.

"Maybe not mention those parts."

This is gonna go great. Shaking her head one more time, she sent a prayer to Jaan, summoned a smile, and stepped back out.

Kayin and Temi had pulled the table away from the wall and set the chairs stored about the caravan around it. Laramie took the bowl containing the last summer peaches and green melon and set it on the table.

She fell into the familiar dance of pulling cups and plates out while her mother finished dinner. A stack of thin wraps toasted in the small oven as the muffins finished cooking. A bowl of shredded goat meat, onions, and roasted potatoes graced the center of the table.

"Sauce, dear," Ade said.

Laramie spun back to the cooler and pulled out the last piece—a glass bowl of light green sauce to flavor the meat. She dabbed her little finger in to sample behind Ade's back. A burst of cucumber and dill mixed with yogurt made from goat's milk coated her tongue.

"Ade, I've missed your cooking so much."

"But not me, I hear." Ade poked her side as she placed the plate of sweet muffins on the table.

Kayin caught the look she shot him, and he grudgingly sat down beside Ade on one side of the table. Laramie ushered Gered to take the seat beside her and opposite them.

Temi led the prayer, keeping it in common for Gered's benefit, though it likely had been years since he'd heard a meal blessing.

"We don't stand on ceremony, Gered." Ade smiled gently once the prayer finished and before hands started reaching for food.

He gave a slight nod, but Laramie passed things his way before serving herself. He seemed to have taken her at her word and barely strung together a few words, and only when asked something directly.

"Catch me up on all the juicy gossip," Laramie demanded, liberally drizzling sauce over her wrap.

Taking the hint, her family and Kayin recounted the latest news among the caravans, including the newest development in the long-standing feud between Bose and Oni who still kept their caravans side by side in the double circle despite years of arguments.

"I was hoping they were finally going to be married when I got back this time."

Ade laughed. "Not when his goats ate her herb garden again."

"Are we eating one of his goats?"

Temi chuckled. "Oni would make sure they'd be eaten at a gathering, not shared over a table."

Laramie took her second muffin, nudging the bowl closer to Gered, noting that he did take another.

"Kayin, how's Lanre?"

"He's been working on something he really wants to show you." Kayin shook his head. His younger brother was a self-proclaimed inventor, and she readily allowed him to conscript her into his experiments.

"How big an explosion should I be ready for this time?"

Kayin rolled his eyes. "He almost took out a window with his last test."

Impressive, since the windows were made from reinforced plastin, able to resist bullets.

"All right," Temi said, pushing away his empty plate. "Enough time for talk of explosions later. There is a more interesting story to hear!"

Laramie shrugged. "Not really."

"Off to bed without dessert!" Temi declared.

"Okay, okay!" She laughed, folding her napkin and nudging her empty plate aside. "It started when the postal clerk in the nowhere town of Talbott told me he'd heard of some Itan heading west to the Christan Mountains."

Night had fallen, the dishes cleared, dessert served and long finished by the time she brought the story to its end in the med center in Arrow. And that was even with skipping some—most— of the more dangerous details.

"Well." Temi slouched back in his chair as silence fell. Ade sat tall, hands clasped on the table, watching both of them. Kayin still glared a little at Gered, who'd contributed small bits, mostly when she'd directly asked him to.

"Sounds like we should be thanking you for helping our Laramie."

Gered flicked a glance up from where he rubbed at the gauze

on his hands. "She makes me sound better than it was."

Kayin's eyes narrowed further. Ade and Temi exchanged a look of unspoken words and agreement.

"Still, it sounds like rough business you were both involved in. And it took some courage to stand like you did."

Gered's gaze faltered. His throat bobbed, but he didn't say anything.

"I'm glad you're home safe." Ade reached over and squeezed Laramie's hand. "And I'm glad you're here with us, Gered."

She must have seen the same thing Laramie did because she smiled.

"I'm sure you both must be tired after riding all day. Why don't we call it an early night?"

"Sounds perfect," Laramie agreed. Gered shifted slightly with a twitch of relief in his face before he closed it off again in his stern mask.

She wished her family could have seen him smile at least once, but it might take a while before he felt comfortable enough.

"Gered, we'll find the cot tomorrow. Is the couch okay for tonight?" Ade asked.

Gered pulled back a little in his seat before nodding cautiously.

"Kayin." Laramie crooked her head to the door. "Be right back," she promised Gered.

She followed Kayin outside, taking the steps down to the ground in silence to join him.

"Your brother not coming out?" Kayin tipped his head back, a faint tension in his stance.

"Don't start that." Laramie shook her head.

"What?"

She smacked him in the chest. "You know what. He's not a

threat. And he's not replacing you."

He shrugged a shoulder.

"And even if he weren't related to me, no one will ever replace you, you know that, right?"

"Sure?" He shifted again, standing a little taller. "The road seems to do a pretty good job most of the year."

"Don't ..." Laramie shook her head again, jaw setting in frustration. "We've talked this through before. You've been fine with it. Can we not argue about it tonight? I just got back." She reached out, and he let her rest her hand in his.

But he stared down at their fingers, now entwined. "Maybe it's different this time. You always have some crazy story, but warlords and challenges and killing people? And he's wrapped up in it all too?"

"He helped me survive it all." She pushed at his hand, making him meet her eyes. "We both owe each other."

His lips pursed. "Maybe."

Ire flashed, quick and hot. "Are you more upset because I keep drifting or because my attention might be split for a while this time around?"

Kayin shifted between his feet, quick anger flashing across his face.

"Maybe a little of both," he finally admitted. "But the bigger part of me is wondering when this is going to be enough for you?"

She drew back a little. "It is enough. I wouldn't change anything about this place! What—"

"Really? Then why do you keep leaving? Only staying for a few months out of the year? What are you looking for that you don't have here?" Unfamiliar hurt coated his voice and leaked through his gold-speckled eyes.

"Kay … I …" Words choked and stumbled their way from her mouth. "I'm looking for family."

"Then what are we?" He tossed a hand around at the caravans.

"Yes, this is family. Ade and Temi are my parents. I love you! But …" She cast around for the words to express the yearning driving her to the open road again and again. "What would you do if the Tlengin had wiped out the travelers? And you were brought up by Itan, only having second-hand stories of your culture and people?"

"And you think he'll have the answers?" Kayin jerked his head at the caravan. "He wasn't much older than you."

"He remembers them!" she burst out. He drew back a little in surprise.

"He remembers our parents." This time the words came hushed. A nagging pressure surfaced behind her eyes. "I don't remember them. I hardly remember anything about that first part of my life, okay? I … I have family here. And I wouldn't give it up, but I had a life before this, and I just want to remember it."

His hand squeezed hers gently. "Okay. I'm sorry."

She drew a shaky breath. "And another part of it is … I grew up here, am part of the family." She lifted her left wrist wrapped in the traveler bands. "But I'm different than you."

Laramie tugged their hands wrapped together, tanned skin against black. "I won't ever truly be one of you. And part of me wants to claim that little bit of me that is different. That is still Itan."

Despite her best efforts, a tear freed itself from her eye and trickled down her cheek. She brushed it away and scrubbed at her nose. It only prompted another tear.

"That's all I've been looking for. Someone to help me remember."

Kayin's featherlight touch wiped the tear away. "Okay." He pulled her into his arms, and she leaned against his chest. "I'm sorry."

"Me, too," she murmured. "I should have told you, but I think I only really realized what I wanted this last time."

He gently rubbed her back.

"Can you give him a chance? Please?" She pulled back enough to tilt her head up to him.

Kayin's lips pursed at the corners.

"I know what he seems like. I do. I had the same thoughts before I got to know him a little better. I still don't really know him that well," she admitted. "But I know that he was raised by the Tlengin and they did awful things ..." Her voice caught. "And the Barracks was hell. He left people behind. And all this ... it's so different than anything he's used to."

"Okay." Kayin shifted to catch her hands again, squeezing gently, calming the rapid flow of her words.

"You don't have to keep trying to convince me. He'll have to do that himself." He paused. "I don't trust him, Lodie. There's something jagged about him, and I'm afraid it might hurt you."

"Hey, I can take care of myself." She squeezed back.

"I know. But you're not out on the open road by yourself anymore. Let me help."

"Okay. Just—"

"I'll give him a chance," he interrupted gently, a reluctant smile appearing. "Just don't expect me to be very happy about it."

Laramie pushed up on her toes to give him a kiss. It lingered between them, turning into several more.

She rested her forehead against his. "You should probably go before Baba comes out and pretends to chase you away."

He laughed, stealing another kiss. "See you tomorrow?"

"Tomorrow," she promised.

Kayin pulled away, tucking hands into his trouser pockets as he walked away. She rubbed her arms, watching the easy swing of his shoulders in the speckled moonlight and colorful lights strung between the caravans.

Woodsmoke filled the air, gentle murmurs of conversation hovering as a backdrop for the brighter chirrups of crickets out in the hills. A coyote howled in the distance, and a dog barked a challenge back.

Laramie tilted her head back to take in the expanse of stars. Luc, the winged bull, swept through the southern sky, on the rise with autumn. It trailed Marcaan, the waning winged lion who ranged the northern sky. Jaan and Maatu's constellations hadn't risen yet.

She found the brightest star in the eastern sky, the Giver. The lord of all. She usually addressed her prayers to Jaan, one of his winged messengers, sometimes Maatu, the messenger preferred by the Itan.

But the moment felt like a more somber prayer was needed. *Help Gered, please? We got out, but I'm worried about making him feel trapped here. I just ... want to have a brother again.*

But when she slipped back inside, the lights were already dimmed, and he was rolled in a blanket on the couch, back set to the room. She paused at the door to her bedroom, watching him a moment. He didn't move, no sign to show he was awake or asleep.

Ade tiptoed over to press a kiss against her forehead. Laramie leaned into her touch.

"Thanks for welcoming him here," she whispered.

"Will he be all right?" Ade flicked a glance over her shoulder.

A sigh caught in Laramie's chest. "You think you have enough room in your heart for another broken Solfeggietto?"

Ade patted her arm. "Of course. We'll be careful with him."

Laramie gave a soft smile, bidding her mother goodnight. She leaned against her door a moment longer, catching the gentle rise and fall of his chest.

"Good night," she whispered.

CHAPTER SEVEN

Gered stared at the faint bit of sunlight starting to creep through the curtains. Silence reigned in the caravan, broken by the faint chime of the time counter marking seven hundred hours.

He'd been awake for at least one already, staring at the light blue fabric of the couch a few inches from his nose. He'd barely slept all night, hyperaware of new surroundings. Even with Laramie's reassurances, the welcoming smiles, and the best meal he'd had in years.

The butt of his handgun pressed against his stomach as he shifted slightly. Pushing it away, he slowly sat up and folded the blanket back. He'd only used the one, even though Ade had given him a whole stack and an extra pillow as if she'd been afraid the couch wouldn't be comfortable enough.

It was odd not waking up to Dayo's snores across the room. Smelling something other than the slightly sour scent of the bunker. He slumped back into the couch, picking at the bandages. Another day of not seeing Gioia. Not being able to apologize to Dayo.

It's been long enough. He's probably been named unit leader. And the rest of the Barracks would try and use it to upset the order. He leaned down, making sure his rifle was still tucked up next to the couch where he'd placed it after pulling it and his pack from Laramie's room.

It had taken her stepping outside for the dam to break and desperation to be alone for a minute to sweep in. And then hearing her and Ade's quick whispered conversation in the traveler language hadn't helped the paranoid corner of his brain.

But nothing had happened.

Yet, his mind taunted.

His weapons hadn't been confiscated. No one had barged into his face, spoiling for a fight. Except maybe for Kayin.

Gered rubbed his eyes and dragged a hand through his dyed hair. Another bit of evidence that Laramie had a firmly established life in the caravans, and he had absolutely no place.

Shoving away the blankets, he grabbed clothes from his pack. Ade had left out a towel and soap with the reassurance to use the washroom whenever he needed. Might as well take advantage before anyone was up and could tell him different.

Inside the safe confines of the washroom, he set about peeling the bandages off. Hissing a breath between his teeth, he freed his skin from the tape's tenacious hold. A bit of scab came off his side with the dry gauze.

Should have done this last night.

After a quick shower, he placed new bandages on his right thigh which had taken the brunt of the damage from the road. Carefully pulling on clean trousers over the bandages, he assessed his side.

A wide swath of healing skin tore through the spotted jackal tattoo which leapt from his back up across his side to spill onto his chest, blood dripping from its fangs. It gave him an odd sort of satisfaction every time he saw the Tlengin tattoo artist's work ruined.

Gathering up the old clothes, he cautiously stepped back out again. His bare feet whispered across the wood floor as he returned to the couch. He set bandages and supplies on the table, gingerly pulling out a chair to sit.

A door clicked and he froze. Ade flashed him a soft smile and came to stand on the other side of the table. A bright green scarf wrapped around her head, hiding the curls.

"Morning," she said.

His tongue stuck to the roof of his mouth, hesitation curling his fingers into fists. He settled for a nod.

"Need help with anything?" She rested her arms on the back of the chair.

The urge to blurt "no" almost won over common sense. But he couldn't effectively bandage his wrists with just one hand.

"My wrists. Please," he finally managed.

She offered the smile again and took the seat at the corner, close enough to reach but not enough to crowd him. Pulling the bandages and ointment over, she rested a hand palm up on the table. Another moment more and he eased his arm forward.

"You two weren't lying last night. This is a bit of a mess," she said.

New skin peeked out from under the peeling flakes where the sun had scorched and blistered. The cuffs had dug deep grooves into his wrists, and the few days on the road hadn't really helped them heal. He'd just been so desperate to get out of the med center and on the road, putting distance between them and Rosche. If he was even still alive.

He's psychotic. He'd stay alive just to keep making the world a miserable place.

Gered stared at the snake tattoo winding twice around his

left wrist, the mouth opening wide on the back of his hand at the base of his thumb. Now it looked like the snake's head had been severed from the body.

She finished with his left hand and reached for his right.

"That looks Itan." She nodded down at his arm.

His third tattoo, and the only one he liked, covered his right forearm. Two lines ran from his elbow to just above his wrist, letters curling and looping in the Itan script.

"It is."

"You mind me asking what it says?"

He softly said it in Itan first, the gentle lilt soothing some of the panic hovering just out of sight, then translated it into common.

"How shall I fear that from which I'm protected by Heaven's wings?"

"Beautiful."

Gered lifted his hand from her touch, brushing fingers over the new bandage covering his wrist and palm. He took a short breath.

"It was a way to try and remember my family."

"And what about this one?" Ade pointed at his side.

He drew back a little. He should have bandaged it in the bathroom, should have put a shirt on. But at least the look in her eyes was something he knew—weighing, assessing, trying to figure him.

She took another sheet of bandage and touched his arm. He turned slightly and lifted his arm, letting her closer though his frayed nerves screamed at him not to.

"Tlengin status symbol," he spat.

He stayed tense, waiting for more questions, more probing into his life, his … skill set.

"I can find something to get the dye out of your hair, if you want."

Gered stared at her until she raised her head to meet his eyes. Her cheeks creased with her smile.

"Unless you want to stay dark, then we can get some dye to match."

He mutely shook his head. He hadn't seen his true hair color in years—the same dusky blond as Laramie's. Itan.

What would it be like to see it again?

"All right, then. We'll be headed out today to our next stop. I can get something in town."

Ade finished with the dressings, and Gered eased a clean shirt on, a bit of relief stealing over him as it hid the scars and bandages from view.

"Laramie probably won't be up for a while. Girl always loves to sleep in her first day back." Ade shook her head. "But I'm going to make breakfast anyway. Anything in particular you want?"

Gered shook his head, trying not to stare in complete incomprehension at her. Why would it matter what he wanted?

"Okay, bacon and flatcakes it is." She pushed to her feet.

Temi stepped out of their room, receiving a kiss from Ade as she walked by into the small kitchen. Gered stared at the new bandages on his hands. He remembered his parents doing the same thing. Restlessness pushed up against his chest, fighting and clawing for release.

He needed air.

Pushing his chair back from the table with a sharp scrape, he grabbed his boots and headed outside. The caravan was on the outer circle, closer to the wooded hills. A quick glance around ensured he was alone, and he headed across the six yards to the tree line.

A few birds chirped, fluttering wings and preparing for their day. A quick rustle alerted him to a startled deer taking off through the trees, white tail flashing. He tugged shirtsleeves down to his wrists, but no matter how many times he repeated the action, they never covered the snake tattoo or the bandages.

He turned to study the camp. A few flashes across the gaps between caravans showed signs of activity beginning to stir.

What am I doing here? The thought came back to haunt him again. It was painfully evident that he didn't belong in a place like this. And he'd reached that conclusion long before dinner.

He flexed his fingers and wrists against the tightness of the bandages. Anywhere else, he'd know already where he stood, what was expected of him. Would have already had to demonstrate his skills with a gun or his fists.

But not here.

Just be a guest.

His hand paused as it dragged through his hair. Ade had offered to strip the dye if he wanted. Who did that?

A sigh cut from him, startling a nearby groundsquirrel with its force. The place freaked him out, but a small part of him had begun to stand its ground and want to stay. He automatically flicked a glance to his right, disappointment stinging when Dayo wasn't there with a sarcastic comment about his interpersonal skills.

The sweet scent of burning mesquite wood began to permeate the air, marking more people up and about. He drew a half-step farther into the woods. Back at the Barracks, he'd just go hide in the garage and work to keep his mind and hands busy.

Already, his hands itched to pick up a tool and work. Create. Repair.

It was against everything Severi and Rosche had wanted him to do. To use his hands for killing or shooting or hurting.

The crunch of footsteps sent tension ricocheting through his muscles. He pivoted to see Temi approaching, hands in his pockets.

The traveler offered a smile, staying several steps away. "Morning!"

Gered swallowed, trying to find his voice which had disappeared the night before.

"Breakfast is ready, if you want to head back in."

Dust, why couldn't he speak or move?

Temi shifted a little, tilting his head to fix him with a searching gaze. "You doing all right, Gered?"

Not really.

He managed a nod.

Temi pursed his lips in a thoughtful look. "This is all a bit different than you're used to?" He jerked a thumb over his shoulder.

Nodding seemed all Gered was capable of, so he offered it again.

"You talk to Laramie about it?"

Laramie. They'd been using her drifter name. She'd probably asked them to make him feel more comfortable. It was something she'd do. And for her sake, maybe he could try.

"Yeah," the word whispered from him. "She seems to think I'll do okay here." His voice gained a little confidence.

"That's our Laramie." A smile lit Temi's face. "What about you?"

Gered slid hands into his trouser pockets, wishing for the thicker armor of his jacket. "I think she wants to believe the best of me."

"She's usually a pretty good judge of character."

70

She'd certainly gotten along with Dayo and Gioia immediately. Had thought nothing of barging her way through his defenses. Somewhat to his relief.

"She doesn't know me as well as she thinks she does."

Not even Dayo and Gioia truly knew him. The darkest bits of him the Tlengin had forged in fire. Or maybe they'd been there all along, and Severi had only helped to bring them to the surface.

"Anything we should know about you, then?" Temi asked, the thoughtful look back.

Gered drew in a short breath, studying the play of light through the forest off to Temi's left. They seemed like good people and needed to know just what he was capable of. Maybe end this whole charade sooner.

"There's a lot she left out last night. I am a mechanic. But I also ran a unit at the Barracks. I can shoot someone at point-blank range or at seven hundred yards, easy. Twelve hundred if the wind's right. I don't miss. I was the best fighter, uncontested, in the Barracks, besides Rosche. If you need something shot, maimed, or killed, I'm your man." A humorless scoff escaped. "But I don't think you do."

Temi shook his head, but his bit of a smile hadn't dimmed. "Can't say that we do. But …"

Gered's heart stalled at the pause.

"We could always use another mechanic around here. Laramie's by far the best we have, but sounds like you might be better."

Heat pricked his cheeks. He rolled his shoulders in a shrug.

"And sometimes there's trouble on the roads. It's not such a bad thing to be able to fight and protect."

He dared himself to look at Temi. The man appeared serious. Any words he might have had in reply locked back up in his chest.

Temi shrugged. "It might take some getting used to around here, but Ade and I are willing to help you get your feet under you. And I know Laramie is as well. All you have to do is ask."

And if I don't know how to do that?

"Now, come on for breakfast. Don't want it to get cold." Temi waved him on, turning and heading back to the caravan without a look back.

It took an extra second for Gered to force his feet forward. He trailed Temi, still watching and waiting for any change in the friendly demeanor. But everyone had seemed genuine. The small bit of him grew bolder, pushing with more confidence the desire to maybe stay and figure out how to belong. Maybe figure out how to be a brother again.

CHAPTER EIGHT

"Well, well, looks like Four got a new leader. You think you can stick it with real fighters?"

Dayo glared at Unit Seven's leader. Annen smirked back, hands loose by his sides, comfortable with his meathead lieutenant next to him.

"Why don't you go find a real fighter and we'll see." Dayo sidestepped to move around, but Annen blocked his path again. Irritation with an annoying bit of nervous fear spiked through his stomach.

First test.

And out in the middle of the compound right in front of the tower, there were plenty of people to see.

"Got your back," Gioia's soft voice floated on his left.

With the brief murmur, Annen's attention shifted to her.

"And so the whore speaks!" he sneered. "You 'ask' Dayo to give you that pin?" He bucked his hips a little.

Dayo held his ground with an effort. He couldn't fight Gioia's battles any more than she could step in to help him with his. It was every man for himself in the Barracks, and if he couldn't stand on his own feet, he wasn't going to be able to stand at all.

But he shifted enough to keep her in the corner of his eye.

Gioia squared her shoulders, bringing her chin up in mimic of Annen's confident position. But the slight tremble at the base of her jaw gave her away to someone who knew her.

Damn you, Gered. You knew what would happen if she got left here.

Because no one messed with Four when Gered, or the threat of him, was around.

You too, drifter.

But just as suddenly, Gioia sidled closer to Annen. The unit leader smirked down at her. She batted her eyelashes.

"You really want to know why he gave it to me?" She dropped her voice a husky octave.

Annen dared reach out to brush her hair.

"You gonna show me?"

Gioia's smile turned sharp.

Get him, Gee.

A smirk flashed across Dayo's face before he could stop it. Doubt creased Annen's face milliseconds too late.

Gioia thrust her hand up into his throat. He stumbled back. She grabbed his arm, smashing her forearm down across his elbow with a pop. His face went slack in surprise and pain. Pivoting under his arm, she rammed her elbow into his stomach next, spun again, and delivered the final blow with a kick to his groin.

He crumpled. Gioia tucked her hands into back pockets and stepped away with a contemptuous spit.

The lieutenant's shock turned to a glare. He pushed forward an angry step toward Gioia, halting as her handgun pointed at his forehead.

"Remind me of the rules again, Dayo." Her voice stayed even. Taut.

Dayo leveled a tight smile at Annen as he began to lever himself up, cradling his arm.

"I'm thinking it's other riders are off-limits," he said.

"I could have you strung up for attacking a unit leader," Annen rasped, glaring at both of them.

"Maybe I'll let everyone know how easy it was to take you down. Maybe Seven isn't as strong as you think." Gioia shrugged.

"Maybe Four should be more careful," Annen sneered back, but a quick flick of his eyes to the side warned Dayo in time.

He whipped out his handgun and pulled the trigger, embedding a bullet in the ground between another Unit Seven rider's feet.

The discharge echoed across the entire compound, reverberating in the back corners as if surprised to be heard in a place like that.

"Trouble, boss?" Sani sauntered up, backed by Dec. Both had a hand dangling near their guns, watching the confrontation with sharp eyes.

Annen jerked his head, and his rider backed off. "Need your entire gang to fight your battles for you, Dayo?" he sneered.

Dayo's chest expanded in a short breath. He and Gioia had discussed what would happen as soon as he stepped out of the bunker with the red jacket, and her with the viper skull pin on her collar. She had his back, and he had hers and the rest of the unit's. No going back.

"No, and you can let every other unit know that I'm ready for them whenever they feel they have the stones enough to try."

Annen and his riders backed off with scowls and a promise to do just that.

Dayo holstered his handgun.

"You okay?" he asked Gioia as she took a few extra seconds to holster hers.

"Yeah." But her voice hadn't lost the near-frightening evenness. She took a deep breath, the motion shaking through her shoulders. She turned a slight smile to Dayo. "You practice that line in the mirror this morning?"

A grin swerved across his face. "A few times, yeah."

She gave a short chuckle, the sound returning her more to herself.

"How was the delivery? Honest opinion."

"Eight out of ten." She gave two thumbs up.

"Not ten out of ten? Harsh." He shook his head.

A more genuine smile lurked around her lips. "Only because I'm now five minutes late for breakfast."

Dayo shoved his hands in jacket pockets, spinning the lighter in the right pocket between his fingers. "I expect a different answer once we get some food, then."

She rolled her eyes. Sani and Dec stepped up to join them.

"All good?" Dayo asked.

They nodded.

"Been a bit of jawing, but nothing serious yet," Sani said. "Probably carrying info back to unit leaders who are interested in challenging."

Dayo turned his gaze up at the tower. Who was going to carry tales back to Rosche? Barns and Moshe had barely been off the upper floors. Movement into the tower drew his attention down to a flash of red and an ugly sneer.

Zelig. Of course. He'd had it out for Four. And now Dayo seemed like the easier option to take down.

Dayo tilted his head side to side and strode forward into the tower with the confidence of a man who had nothing to fear. As much as he still held on to—and nurtured—his anger at Gered, the dusting idiot's words when Dayo first came to the saints-forsaken Barracks still rang true.

Stand tall and don't be afraid to pull the trigger. Dust the rules. You show weakness, you might as well lay down and die right now.

He strode up into the tower, pausing only to take Gioia's "good luck" before he jogged up the stairs, tugging at his new jacket as he went.

The war room was filling with red jackets, men clustering in groups, waiting for the meeting to begin. Dayo slipped in, leaning against the back wall and watching. Not everyone was in yet, and there were still five minutes to go.

Annen limped in, shooting a glare as he caught sight of Dayo, who gave a mocking wave. Annen derided Dayo's mother and heritage in an impressive stream of words before moving away to join Zelig.

Dayo sniffed and returned hands to his pockets to keep spinning the lighter. Glances around the room darted his direction, and he returned them evenly, chin lifted slightly, shoulders squared, the way he would if he'd been backing up Gered in the same situation.

Connor lounged over, tucking a boot up against the wall. "Annen's nothing."

"Think I don't know that?" Dayo locked eyes with Unit Fifteen's leader, who gave a slight nod and returned to his conversation. Pearce had gotten his red jacket only weeks before when Rosche had executed the former commander.

Connor shrugged. "Heard some rumblings. Yanis might go for it."

"I don't know what's more unsettling. The idea that Yanis thinks he could take me, or that you care enough to tell me."

Connor gave his careless smirk and shrug. "I don't want new bunker mates, Dayo. Take care of business."

Dayo gave a mock salute. "Yes, sir."

Connor gave a scoffing huff and sauntered off. Moshe slipped into the room and headed straight for him.

"Making friends, I see," the Unit Two leader said.

"Still hanging out in shadows like a freak, I see." Dayo switched to flicking the lighter top open and closed in his pocket.

Moshe quirked an eyebrow. "Forgot how mouthy you are."

"This is a scintillating conversation, Moshe. What do you want?" Dayo cracked his neck.

Moshe had always been square with Four. He didn't feel much of a threat from the other unit leader. Other than Moshe might have been behind the guns supplied to rebels in Conrow and Springer that had taken out two of their unit.

Moshe's shoulders lifted. "Just checking in. Hate to see you waste all Gered's work."

"Yeah, well, maybe the asshole should have thought of that before he tried to run. Know anything about that, Moshe?" Dayo swung to face him.

Rumor was Gered had reached out to Moshe on the radio before making the strike for the border. But Moshe had said it was only a check-in and he'd thought nothing of it. But he had also lobbied for the drifter's challenge to be upheld and let her drive off with Gered.

"Nothing in particular. But might be checking in with you later after this meeting. Rosche has some announcements," Moshe said.

Great. Dayo snapped the lighter shut.

"Attention!" Barns's voice cracked through the room. A sharp rustle marked every unit leader straightening up and drawing back into an even line around the room.

Dayo raised an eyebrow but followed Moshe to join the others. Barns pulled back out of the doorway and reemerged pushing Rosche in a wheelchair.

The warlord looked like death warmed over. His shirt, usually stretched tight over a bulky chest and arms, hung looser on him. The dark leather jacket draped around his shoulders didn't disguise the sling holding his left arm up or the hunch to his shoulders.

Dayo's medic training almost had him shaking his head at whoever had dug out the wheelchair and allowed the warlord to get up. Though he was probably looking right at the man who'd given the order.

Barns wheeled him around to the head of the long wooden table. Rosche's silhouette against the wide, open windows framing the Christan mountains remained less than impressive.

"Listen up," Rosche's deep baritone rasped. It still sent a wave of alertness through the gathered unit leaders. "I want patrols out. Rumors are circling about me. Quash anything that might seem a threat."

He leaned back in the wheelchair, drawing the jacket farther over the sling.

"As for this, once I'm back on my feet, we're hunting down the drifter and the traitor. They'll be made an example of, along with anyone who helped them on their way out."

Moshe stood, hand hooked in his belt, unconcerned with the narrowed look Barns sent him.

Interesting. Maybe Dayo wasn't the only one with the same thought about the Unit Two leader.

Rosche listed off the units to go back out on patrol, and Unit Four wasn't among them.

"Dayo." The warlord's rasp brought him back to the council room.

"Sir." He managed a respectful salute.

"Heard you and Annen crossed paths just now."

Annen's coppery skin turned a shade darker. Dayo allowed a smirk.

"Nothing my lieutenant didn't handle, sir."

"Oh? And who is that?" Rosche eyed him, tapping a hand against the jacket lapel.

Bastard. You already know. And looked as satisfied as a hunting jacklion.

"Gioia, sir." Dayo clenched his fist around the lighter, letting the edges dig into his palm. He swept a quick look around the room. "We didn't have the best shot and fighter in the lower country as our leader for nothing."

Rosche's look turned poisonous. Dayo held his stare until a nudge at his boot urged him to drop it before Rosche decided he didn't need to keep living anymore.

Dayo flicked a glance back up after a quick, submissive duck of his head. Rosche stayed watchful and intent on him, then relaxed just as suddenly.

"I'm eager to see how she does. She always … performed well. Maybe someone else should test her … just to make sure she's up to the task."

Dayo's back teeth ground together, and Moshe's boot bumped his again, though the unit leader barely shifted.

He bit back a multitude of responses, trying to remind himself to keep the target on his own back and not on the rest of the unit. Even though Rosche had all but declared open season on Gioia.

"I'm sure she will, sir."

Rosche gave a small smile, a slithering viper sneaking through. "Moshe will be heading up the search for the drifter and the traitor. Dayo, you'll assist."

His heart banged so hard against his sternum the mountains might have heard it. "Sir."

"That's all. Head out as soon as bikes are fueled," Rosche ordered.

Dayo hung back a second, standing firm among the press of shoulders going out of their way to bump him on the way out.

"Yes?" Rosche settled back in the chair, eyeing him as he strode forward.

"We're down two riders from the fights in Conrow and Springer, sir. I wanted to stake some of the trainees early to help spread our numbers."

Rosche rubbed his chin. There was no slyness, only the consideration of a commanding officer. "Any thoughts on who you might want?"

Dayo dug out the names of two younger kids in the trainees. He'd gone the night before to catch the end of the training session. "Yaz and Chris."

Rosche frowned. "They're young."

Dayo nodded. They were, but he didn't like the look of the other three—they had violence in their veins and a not-so-subtle eagerness to earn a snake tattoo.

"Fewer bad habits, according to Harlan. I need them up to

Four's standards, and they seem like the better fit."

"Taking charge. Good to see that, Dayo."

The lighter jammed his palm. "Thank you, sir."

"You want to take them on a run?"

"I think that'd be best, sir. I'd like to test them before I officially stake for them." Though he'd probably stake them anyway, even if they did suck. He hated to watch what happened when a trainee didn't make it into the units.

"Okay, then. Let Harlan know I support this. I want a report on them when you get back."

"Sir." Dayo snapped a salute. If interactions with Rosche stayed like that, he could maybe get through them.

"Ride safe, Dayo."

Dayo nodded and strode from the room before his face could reveal his disdain for the sentiment. *Like he dusting cares?*

At the bottom of the stairs, he turned to pass under the trailing banners and headed into the mess hall. Pausing only to grab a nutrient bar and water bottle instead of a food tray from the line, he headed to Four's table.

They sat, a sad sight of six riders clustered together, eating with none of the same easiness they would have two weeks ago.

"Rosche is sending out patrols again. We're staying in for now. But fuel up for some training."

Nods passed around, and they hurriedly shoved the remainders of breakfast down. Gioia drained her cup.

"We get the trainees?" she asked.

"Yeah, I'm gonna grab them from Harlan for the run."

"I'll get your bike fueled." She stepped over the bench.

"Thanks." His fingers beat a rhythm on the water bottle. He chugged half of it before he realized he wanted the dryer taste of beer instead of water. Turning his back on the mess hall, he strode outside. It had been twenty hours since he'd had a drink. He usually took a flask out on patrol to tide him over until they got back to the bunker.

But he couldn't this time. He had to stay sharp.

A pang struck his stomach along with the stronger desire for beer or something with a little more kick. He bit into the nutrient bar with an almost savage intensity. Just one more thing to beat.

CHAPTER NINE

"Dayo, wait up!"

The call sent the muscles in his back tensing. But he slowed enough to let Moshe catch up with him.

"What?" Dayo growled.

"We're going to be partners for a bit. You gonna keep the attitude?" A slight smirk accompanied Moshe's brow raise.

"Moshe, the list of people I actually like around here is very short, and you're not on it." Dayo clapped him on the shoulder with a look of feigned sympathy before he continued to the trainees' bunker.

But Moshe allowed a chuckle. "How did he put up with you?"

The water bottle crunched in Dayo's grip. Gered had a sense of humor no one got to see outside of him and Gioia. And it had a fatalistic slant that paired well with Dayo's stream of sarcasm.

"He didn't ask stupid questions all the time like everyone seems to these days."

"Okay, I hear you. Try not to make a scene, then, when I ask you the next question." Moshe stuck his hands in his pockets.

Dayo aggressively twisted the cap off the water bottle, slamming back a drink. He knew what the next question was going to be.

"You know I'm supposed to find them."

"I don't know where they are, if that's what you want to know," he snapped.

Moshe spread his hands peaceably. "Look, all we know is that the drifter took off northeast. After the border, it's all fair game. The lower country's a big place. But ... she did have a traveler band."

Another spike of anger and betrayal hit Dayo's heart. He pivoted to Moshe and jerked his left hand up. "You see a band here?" he snarled.

Moshe regarded him through calm eyes. "No, but I know that one traveler might know something about another traveler."

Dayo curled his fingers in a fist. True, all the traveler families kept in some sort of contact. They all ran different routes through the upper and lower country. Every few years, there'd be a large gathering of multiple families. He might have even crossed paths with Laramie's family before. But he would have remembered seeing a pale Itan girl among the black-skinned Aclar. It would have been talked about around fires or behind the closed doors of caravans.

"I don't know who her family is," he finally said.

If he tried hard enough, he could probably remember the families who ran the eastern side of the territories. Remember whose bands were red, brown, and blue. Probably lower country. His family had routed through the upper country until the fateful decision to strike down below the Rift. He had no idea where they even ran now.

And I don't care.

"Not even to point me in the right direction?"

Dayo scoffed. "What makes you think I'd even want to help you?"

Moshe gave a humorless smile. "It might be worth it in the end."

"Yeah, to watch his high-and-mighty dickness kill my friend?" Because as much as he really hated Gered's stoic guts, there was no way, when it came down to it, he was anything but a friend. And it really pissed Dayo off.

Moshe's smile turned grim. "Let's keep walking." He inclined his head a fraction.

Dayo flicked a glance to follow the motion. They stood in full view of the open windows on Rosche's floor.

He slowly turned and walked in the opposite direction, waiting for Moshe's next words. When they passed around a bunker, Moshe halted.

"Let's just say I have a vested interest in finding Gered, and it's not necessarily for Rosche," he said.

Dayo stared at the man. Moshe maintained the same, unconcerned posture, but the tenseness in his eyes belied it.

"Yeah? This have anything to do with guns down in Conrow?" Dayo dropped his voice.

Moshe allowed an impressed frown. "He said you knew about it."

"Gered?" Dayo pulled back a little.

Moshe inclined his head. "We had a talk, the two of us. We laid out information known by both parties and agreed on silence in exchange for a favor."

Dayo's fingers tapped the water bottle in a frantic staccato. "He radioed you the day they ran."

Moshe shrugged a shoulder.

"Dust." The word hissed between Dayo's teeth. "So what is it you need him for?"

"Let's just say I might be interested in a regime change. No one anticipated the drifter's challenge or the fallout, but it might give me a better opportunity than guns in podunk towns."

"You want to take over the Barracks?" Dayo arched an eyebrow.

"Dust no, kid." Moshe shook his head with a roll of his eyes. "But some people are interested in opening the lower country back up."

People. Like the governor-general.

"Who are you, really?" Dayo asked.

Moshe allowed a humorless smile. "Someone who's been waiting a long time for an opportunity like this, and I'm not about to let a traveler with a massive chip on his shoulder dust it up for me."

Dayo worked his jaw, but the tension refused to leave, burrowing further into the joint to linger. Take the risk?

Gered had, and it hadn't really paid off for him. Though Moshe had made sure Laramie got Gered into a truck and pointed at the border.

"Look, I still don't know what family she's from. There's plenty of caravans running the lower country. She could have headed home or somewhere else. They could have split or stuck together." His throat choked on the words. If Gered had even survived long enough to make it to the border.

"Best guess?"

"Head east, see what you can dig up."

"Thanks, I hadn't already planned that," Moshe said dryly. He rubbed a thumb along his jaw. "I'm headed out soon to the radio tower to put the word out with some contacts I've got outside."

"Rosche know that?"

"He does." A sly smirk flashed across Moshe's face. "I was,

however, vague on the details. Once I've got something, we'll head out."

Dayo shook his head. "You picked a hell of a tune to dance to."

Moshe stuck his hands back in his pockets. "That I did. And I'd appreciate it if you didn't whistle it around."

Dayo took the warning. "All right, Moshe. I'll play along. But Four's already neck-deep in this dust, so you do anything more to threaten us, I will take you down."

Moshe nodded. "I hear you, Dayo. Gered and I stayed square. No reason that can't continue with you." He began backing away. "I'll be in touch."

He vanished around the corner of the building, leaving Dayo feeling lost among the sand grains skittering over the packed ground.

He rubbed his face before hooking his hand behind his neck. If Moshe wasn't lying, there might be a bit of freedom in the future. But after three years of the same walls, the same routes, enforcing Rosche's rules, and playing the game of survival, it seemed like too much to even hope for.

CHAPTER TEN

"Gered, you up to helping me for a bit?" Temi pushed away from the table, moving to put his plate in the kitchen sink.

Gered closed his hand in and out of a fist. "With what, sir?"

"Checking the transpo truck. She's been kicking out some more exhaust recently. We'll be heading out this afternoon and I want to make sure we can make it to the next town all right." Temi rinsed and wiped his hands.

Gered darted a glance at Laramie's closed door. He could, but … "Wouldn't Laramie do that?"

Temi flashed his wide smile again. Between him and Ade, Gered hadn't seen so many happy expressions in years.

"Oh, she won't be awake for a while yet. And then Monifa asked to meet with her this morning. Figured it might give you something to do as well."

Gered nodded and eased out from his chair, taking his plate to the sink. Ade had heaped it full of bacon and flatcakes, then ushered him to the table to eat with Temi. Now she took his empty plate with a smile and added it to the stack to be washed later.

"Thanks," he managed.

"Of course!" Her face came alight with her smile, so much that it almost hurt to look at. He slid away and followed Temi from the caravan.

"Rummaged up some gloves to keep those bandages clean." Temi handed him a pair. They rounded the front of the caravan, Gered eying the side again and trying to reconcile the innocuous exterior with the large and cozy interior.

"I can keep her running in a pinch, but Laramie's always had a better head for it. Probably the Itan in her. She's been working engines all around camp since she was eight or nine." Temi propped the hood open.

"Had many problems with the engine before?" Gered asked, leaning over the edge to peer into the workings.

"It's been taking an extra time or two to turn over in the mornings. Been crossing my fingers Laramie'd be back soon enough to fix it." Temi crossed his arms and stared at the engine.

"Keys?" Gered asked cautiously.

Temi dropped them into his hand, and Gered circled around to the driver's door and stepped up into the truck. Sure enough, the engine rumbled and coughed when he turned the keys in the ignition. He tried again and got another annoyed rumble. Once more, and a catch. The engine thrummed to life, vibrating through the floorboards before settling into a steady hum.

Acrid exhaust followed soon after. He wrinkled his nose and shut the engine off.

"Well?" Temi glanced at him as he returned.

"How's it been driving?"

"Fair. We're lagging a bit, though, I can tell."

"Could be the fuel injectors. Shouldn't take much to check and clean them." Gered shrugged. Easy job. He'd been doing it since he was eight or nine.

"Perfect!" Temi grinned. "Tools are around here." He went

around to the west side of the caravan, undid a latch Gered had missed the first time, and folded down a section of the wall. Within was a full outfit of tools and parts.

Gered shook his head. If he had to guess, this was right by the kitchen, but there was no way a tool kit this size wasn't taking up room under the cabinets.

Temi tapped the side of his nose. "It's all about how you stack and fold things into place."

A faint smile quirked Gered's mouth. "This is going to take some getting used to."

"Ah, but you'll find it's really handy." Temi clapped him on the shoulder.

The friendly gesture caught him a bit off guard. He covered by starting to pull out what he'd need.

"Can I help?" Temi pulled a grease rag out.

Gered shook his head. "It won't take long."

"All right. We'll be packing out right after lunch, so I'll be around getting everything else ready to go. Let me know if you need anything."

Temi headed back into the caravan. Gered shook his head again. So trusting. But the engine called to him, and he dove into the work, tucking his sleeves back to avoid grease and carefully sliding the gloves over the bandages to keep them fresh.

More and more voices broke through the silence hovering over the camp. The clatter and hustle of a camp being packed up underlay conversation. One voice rose in song and another answered.

Gered paused to listen for a moment. A deep baritone joined in, and then more and more until the whole camp sang the same song as they went about their individual tasks, some hands tapping on any available surface in a rhythmic beat to keep the time. The traveler language gained a depth and richness in song. It dipped and fell, circling back around to a refrain.

His hands hovered above the workings. Did he dare?

Listening again to the song, he waited for the refrain. Once more through, then he gingerly began working again, humming lightly under his breath with the tune.

The tips of his fingers tingled, his vision sharpened a little, and he swore he caught an answering hum from the machine. His hands worked a little quicker.

He hadn't dared in years. What had changed?

A laugh cut across the song, the hum died in his chest, and the world returned to normal.

"Morning!" Laramie ducked around the hood, flatcake wrapped around bacon in her hand.

"Hey." Gered flicked his fingers as if to get rid of the last little bits of magic trying to escape.

"What is it this time?" She leaned on the edge, tossing her braid back over her shoulder.

"Fuel injectors."

"I swear, this thing is one step away from breaking down completely, but Temi refuses to build a new one. Or to let me do it." She shoved more flatcake in her mouth.

"Why?" Gered laid his tool aside. Something else caught his eye—some wires out of place.

Not out of place, extra bits wired throughout the workings.

"He pretends it's because it's been in his family for over a gen-eration, but really, the idea just stresses him out, and it's gonna be a big job."

Gered only half-listened to her description of taking the

caravan off the transpo truck as he followed the path of the wires. More and more bits and pieces stuck out. A small smile cracked his face. Bits and pieces of the mechanic beside him with each repair she'd done, following the song of the Itan inside.

He tipped a glance to her when he realized she'd lapsed into silence. She watched with a grin.

"What do you think of this one?" She hooked a finger under the engine mod.

He studied it a minute. Another variation of an engine booster. "You've got a fascination with speed, don't you?"

An impish smile took over. "You know what we should do?"

"Why do I get the feeling this'll be a bad idea?"

"Hear me out. You have a gang bike." She hooked a thumb at herself. "I have an engine booster that I can refill with curated lightning."

He started to shake his head, but she pressed on with a growing grin.

"A mod to your bike will be cake. And then we find a stretch of road and see what happens."

A smile snuck through before he could stop it. "You know it can already top one-thirty, right?"

"But imagine." She spread her hands. "One-sixty."

"You're a little insane, you know that?"

Laramie tossed her head back with a laugh. "Just think about it."

He threw her the keys. "Start it up."

She wrinkled her nose at him but jogged around to lean into the truck and jam the keys into the ignition. It started right up.

A bit of satisfaction thrummed through his chest along with the sound of the engine. Laramie cut it off and came back around to help him lower the hood and pack up the tools.

"How you doing?" she asked in Itan.

Gered scrubbed a bit of grease from the gloves. He felt a little more settled after the work. "This is going to take some getting used to."

She pushed up on tiptoes to latch the door as he held it closed. Dusting her hands off, she faced him, head tilted a bit.

"I'm here if you need anything, you know that, right?"

His hand twitched as he stopped himself from putting hands in jacket pockets that weren't there. "*Sa.*"

"Hey." She rocked back and forth on her feet. "I'm sorry I didn't tell you about Kayin."

He shrugged. "It's okay."

"It's not, really." She shook her head. "It's not that I didn't want to overwhelm you with everything, or *not* tell you—"

"Laramie," he interrupted. "It's okay. I'm not ..." He searched for the words, trying to figure out what he felt. "Not upset that you have a family here. I'm glad you do. And I don't mind that you think of them as your parents."

She seemed to collapse into herself as relief shone on her face. "You don't?"

He shook his head. In truth, he fought a pang of jealousy that she'd been able to find parents again.

"I didn't know how to ask," she admitted shyly.

He lifted a shoulder, rubbing a thumb along the smoothness of the tape holding down the bandage on his hand.

"Temi said something about heading out today?" He turned the conversation with an effort.

She acknowledged it with a little smile. "Yeah, it's one of the next stops before the official winter campgrounds. Still a couple hundred miles to go." She rocked again. "I'll be riding with Monifa today. She wants to hear the ... our story."

"You know she's gonna ask about me, right?" He gave a humorless smile.

"I'll highlight your redeeming qualities." She nudged his shoulder with a fist.

"Hey, make sure you talk about how I have no dusting idea how to be normal," he managed in a light tone.

"Oh, good. We are related, then."

He shook his head, a smile worming its way out at her pleased grin.

"Kayin's going to ride my bike. Figured you'd want to ride yours and maybe get away from all the fuss for a bit."

"That easy to tell?" Gered quirked an eyebrow.

Laramie chuckled. "You've been stuck with only me for company for almost two weeks. I know you want some peace and quiet."

"You are pretty annoying, drifter."

She clapped a hand over her heart, seeing straight through his easy words. "I feel closer to you already."

Gered rolled his eyes. Laramie beckoned him on with a toss of her head.

"I usually help Temi load up. You can help, if you want."

He lifted a shoulder. Not like he had anything else to do.

"And ..." She paused again, rubbing the back of her neck. "Heads up that Kayin is being a touch overprotective and might take it upon himself to stick to your side on the ride. Try not to take it personally?"

"You know where I've been living the past few years, right?"

She snorted a laugh.

"I think I can handle it," he reassured her.

"Thanks." The smile she beamed at him bolstered his confidence a little to make the turn around the caravan and offer to help Temi as if he did it every day.

CHAPTER ELEVEN

This might be worse than the Barracks.

Gered glared at the rider in his left side mirror from the privacy of the helmet Kayin had tossed at him. Gered had purposefully not turned on the radio embedded in the helmet, ignoring Kayin's glares and the way the traveler had shadowed his every step since Laramie had left them alone with a final pointed look in Kayin's direction and an encouraging glance in his.

The fact that Kayin hugged his left side mirror irritated him more than anything. It had been Gioia's post for the last two years. And seeing Kayin's bulk on Laramie's drifter bike instead of the unit rider who'd wormed her way under his skin was another stake through his heart.

He restlessly twisted the throttle, the engine revving. The road rushing away in front of him begged to be raced down. The wind rustling over the hills whispered to be leaned into, to let it whip away the restlessness.

But the caravans lumbered slowly on. And Kayin stayed tight on his left.

Laramie was somewhere in the line of caravans. She'd disappeared into one with another woman about her age full of bright laughter and tumbling curls. Not having her around made his skin itch with the feeling of being watched by unfriendly eyes—the same ones who'd leaned close to each other and whispered behind hands as he'd wheeled his bike to Ade and Temi's caravan.

The ones like Kayin who saw the violence still staining him.

He flicked his wrist on the throttle again, weaving side to side to take the urgency out of the acceleration and keep his bike meandering alongside the line.

Ade and Temi hadn't said anything when he'd taken his pack and rifle out with him to place on the bike. Ade had just smiled and offered to store them safely in the caravan for the trip. But he'd shook his head, his tongue again forgetting how to form words.

Kayin had just given a little scoff and shake of his head when he'd seen the rifle. Gered glanced in his mirror again. Still there.

The speedometer hovered around a sedate sixty miles an hour. Laughable after the speeds he'd ridden almost his entire life.

He looked forward again as the wind tugged on his dustscarf, begging him to leave the snails behind. Technically, he didn't know where they were headed, but the road only ran in one direction across the hills.

And he'd bet his rifle the shadow behind him would follow and be able to guide him back should he get lost.

Dust it.

He wove farther to the left side of the road, giving himself plenty of room to pass, and gunned the engine.

The front wheel lifted for a moment before settling back and catching the pavement to hurtle him forward.

He leaned into the wind, letting it rush over him as he pushed eighty, ninety, one hundred, one-ten.

What was he supposed to do there?

One-twenty.

What was he supposed to do with all the pent-up energy and anger?

One-thirty.

He screamed into his helmet.

Topping another rise, he didn't stop, kept pushing and pushing, leaving the snaking line of caravans so far behind they didn't even glint in the rearview.

He had everything he needed. He could keep going. Leave it behind. Let Laramie get back to her normal life. Find somewhere he'd fit, or maybe just someplace to lay low for a while and figure out how to live.

Except …

Except the smiles flashed again in his mind. The genuine kindness shown by Ade and Temi. The hopefulness in Laramie's eyes as she bounced on her feet, watching him with the look that said he might be worth something more than bullets and fists.

Gered eased off the throttle, slowing as he crested two more hills. A large rise loomed ahead, and he rumbled to a halt at its top, dropping his feet down on the asphalt and tugging the helmet off.

The light breeze brushed some of the heat from his face. He tilted his head back toward the achingly blue sky and drew a deep breath.

"I believe you'll do just fine."

Of course he got stuck with the eternal optimist for a sister.

How shall I fear that from which I'm protected by Heaven's wings?

He huffed a sigh. It didn't seem likely that Messengers of the Giver lived years in hell and then got sent someplace so different it might as well be a little piece of heaven.

Gered dragged a gloved hand through his hair. Ade had offered to strip the dye. Might as well hang around and let her do it, right?

Resting his helmet in front of him, he crossed his arms to lean on it and waited for his shadow. It took several minutes—time he spent staring out over the green forested hills broken at the horizon line by a wide, barren something—before Kayin appeared on the rise.

Taking one more deep breath and touching the rifle for a bit of reassurance, he prepared himself. Kayin rumbled to a stop in front of him, bike turned sideways to block the road forward. Ripping off his helmet, he glared at Gered.

"What were you thinking?"

Gered tensed at the anger in his voice. "Thinking things were moving a little slow for me."

"So you just decided to drive off, no radio, and no indication of where you were going?" Kayin tossed his arm wide.

"Road only goes one direction, doesn't it?" Gered bit back.

Kayin's lips twisted in a scowl. "You running off?"

Gered rolled his eyes. "Yeah, I'm running and decided to stop here for ten minutes waiting for your slow ass to catch up."

Gold glinted a little brighter in Kayin's eyes as they narrowed. Gered stared back, unperturbed.

"So what's she see in you, then?" Kayin's lip curled in a sneer.

"You tell me." Gered leaned his weight forward more on the helmet.

Kayin scoffed. "Look, if you hurt her, I'm coming for you."

Gered stiffened, in irritation more than in response to the threat. "She can take care of herself."

"I know she can," Kayin snapped. "But that doesn't mean I can't still have her back. And I don't trust you."

"Feeling's mutual," Gered retorted. At least he had a frame

of reference for Kayin's attitude. It was the look and swagger everyone in the Barracks maintained. Don't trust anyone and you'll survive to the next day.

Until another annoying traveler had declared them friends and had refused to leave his side. Gered angrily banished the thought of Dayo. His lieutenant would be at his side snarking away at Kayin if Gered hadn't left him behind.

Lieutenant. Gered shifted his gaze down to the shimmering deep blue paint of the helmet under his hands. Why not just call Dayo what he was? A friend.

He adjusted his seat on the bike and picked up the helmet. "We heading back, or you got something more to say to me?"

Internally he flinched at the contention in his voice. He'd told Laramie he'd try, and he was pretty sure this wasn't what she'd meant.

Kayin huffed and turned his helmet in his hands, prepping to pull it back on. "Turn your radio on. *Laramie* freaked a little when you bolted and she couldn't reach you. And I'm not helping you when she gets ready to kick your ass when we get back." His smug features disappeared behind the dark visor.

The corners of Gered's eyes tightened with his humorless smile. He flipped the switch inside the helmet before pulling it on. Kayin turned Laramie's bike around and took off down the hill, not glancing back to make sure he followed. Gered waited another ten seconds before following.

Kayin rumbled along at a thankful eighty miles an hour, still on the upper end of slow. The temptation to leave him behind again flashed hot, just to see what he'd do. Just as fast, Gered shook his head at himself. He didn't need to keep riling up Laramie's boyfriend. Especially if she'd already be upset when they got back.

She wouldn't be above threatening to kick his ass. In a straight brawl she couldn't. That wasn't what scared him. Because Laramie wouldn't come at him head-on. She'd come at an angle, relentless and tireless until she'd worn him down.

Sooner than he wanted, the caravan came into view. They hadn't stopped, still lumbering along with dogged persistence. Kayin lifted his hand and waved at the lead.

"Gered!"

He winced at the intensity of Laramie's voice bursting into his helmet.

"Hey," he replied.

"You okay?" A bit of panic underlay the question, and he imagined her leaning forward in the seat, peering out at him from the windshield of the caravan.

"Yeah." He paused, not sure he knew how to put things into words. Not sure if anyone else was listening on the channel. "Things were just moving slower than I'm used to." And ... saints help him, he wanted to reassure her somehow and keep the smile on her face. "Wanted to see if that booster on the bike would be a good idea."

A bit of static accompanied her wild laugh. "You know it is!"

It nudged a smile from him. "You're still crazy," he said, switching to Itan.

A snort broke over the radio. "You'll change your tune when we try it."

"I doubt that."

She laughed. "There's a town coming up where we'll camp a few days. Come meet Esi when we stop."

He drove slowly past the line of caravans until he had enough room at the tail end to turn around and follow. "Okay."

His hesitance seemed painfully clear, even to him.

"Just for a bit, if you want."

"Okay." The hesitation shoved its way back in. He just couldn't figure out a way to extend a bit of himself to people after hoarding every particle of himself to protect it.

"Hey, you gonna keep your radio on?" Her concern still lingered.

"Yeah, don't worry, drifter."

A humor-filled huff sparked in the helmet. "Okay."

The radio fell silent, and the tension inside him eased more with the quiet. Until Kayin appeared around the end of the caravans and came up on his right side this time. And didn't shift until the hills opened up around a town, and the caravans circled up in an open field just outside the city limits.

CHAPTER TWELVE

Gered hung back, watching the process of the transpo trucks and long trailers falling into some preordained pattern and forming the same double ring. Once engines began to cut off, he found the cheery yellow caravan and parked at its side.

Temi leaned out the window of the transpo truck to wave at him. Gered lifted a tentative hand in response. He killed the engine and pulled the helmet off, the muscles between his shoulder blades tightening again now that his feet were back on the ground.

Kayin pulled in beside him. He killed the engine and pocketed the keys.

"Keep the helmet, if you want," he practically spat, and walked off.

Gered followed his path, the tension sneaking into his chest, entertaining the idea of chucking the helmet after him.

"He'll come around." Temi's voice drew Gered's attention back. The traveler had hands on his hips, a bit amused as he stared past Gered to where Kayin now leaned close for a kiss from Laramie before pressing the keys back into her hand.

Gered turned his attention down to the helmet. The sight only made him think of Gioia. And everything he couldn't ever have with her.

"Sure about that?" he asked, pushing up from his bike. "Maybe he's the only intelligent one around here."

"Give me some credit here." Temi smiled. "If you're up for it, I could use some help getting set up."

Gered nodded, hanging the helmet off the handlebars and tapping his rifle once as he stood. Another tap to the handgun on his left thigh. His right hand met air. The bone-handled pistol was still buried in his bag, waiting on him to find a new holster. Until then, he'd feel lopsided without the balanced weight on both legs.

No one had said anything about him keeping the gun out. Though there didn't seem to be many others armed with anything other than knives.

Temi walked him through setting out the step on the back, unfairly stacked and packed up in an impossible manner against the end. Another traveler knack. Then up to the front to hook up some tubes to the pipes sticking up from the ground.

"Our family has been running the same route for years. And before us, there was another family. This town's been playing host to travelers for generations, so it's been set up for our caravans almost since the beginning," Temi explained.

"What about the last camp?" Gered asked.

"We've got our own secret spots staked out along the way. Can't spend all our time outside towns where folks might get too nosy or too greedy for traveler items." A small frown twisted Temi's mouth, smoothing out some of the laugh lines.

Gered dusted off his hands. "That happen often?"

"There's a few places we have an arrangement to stop by for some trades when we come through, but we don't stay more than a day." Temi placed hands on his knees and pushed up to standing. "Been a few spots of trouble here and there over the years, but nothing we haven't been able to handle."

"And this place?" Gered inclined his head to the houses two hundred yards away where people had begun to gather to watch.

"Nothing to worry about here. We'll stay for about three days and then keep heading on." Temi opened the passenger side of the truck and pulled out a heavy box, handing it to Gered.

He shifted it in his arms to avoid the sharp edges digging into his chest.

"What do you do here?"

"Fix things, trade things, sell things." Temi leaned into the truck again and hauled out a crate filled with paper-wrapped objects. "Your people, the Itan, are architects, mechanics, builders. But Aclar are craftsmen."

He balanced the crate against his chest and tugged back a bit of the paper to reveal a carved red wolf, forepaws braced against the ground as it threw back its head to howl at an invisible moon. Its mouth pulled back at the corners, throat shifting with the force of its lonely call as a night breeze ruffled the fur on its shoulders.

Gered blinked and it settled back to a piece of wood. It had been so long since he'd seen so many bits of magic. There hadn't been many at the Barracks. And among the Tlengin, it focused on hiding their mobile villages and into their warlike tendencies.

The Tlengin tribes had always been warriors, even before the Rift had torn through their tribal lands, throwing them into disarray and away from the practice of the high God and his Messengers to follow a nameless being they insisted dwelt deep in the chasm.

They didn't bother to create much anymore besides blood and destruction.

"I noticed you had a red wolf on your bike," Temi said.

Gered shifted between his feet. "Yeah, it was the sigil I picked for my unit."

It was a steady, solitary creature, nothing like the spotted jackal—the warrior trickster the Tlengin claimed served the chasm god.

"Good choice. They're amazing creatures." Temi knocked the door closed with his knee and headed to the caravan entrance.

"Gered!" Laramie waved across the campground. The young woman he assumed to be Esi stood next to her.

"If you'll set that inside the door, Gered." Temi stepped up to the back door. "I don't want to risk the wrath of the Laramie by holding you up."

Gered tilted a glance up at Temi.

A sudden twitch shook Gered's lips. "Even if it's like facing down a bobcat kit?" Sharp teeth and ready to pounce, but too fluffy.

Temi laughed, a sound that tipped his head back and flashed his bright smile. "Don't let her hear you call her that."

Gered followed him up the stairs and set the box where he indicated. Temi patted him lightly on the shoulder as he straightened.

"Thank you."

He didn't have any normal response, so he settled for sticking his hands back in his jacket pockets and nodding. Laramie had lost patience in the few seconds it took him to step inside and back out, and she and Esi were heading over to the caravan.

"Couldn't have waited?" Gered arched an eyebrow.

She wrinkled her nose and swept her hand to the young woman. "Gered, this is Esi."

Esi regarded him for a moment from brown eyes turned dark

amber by the sun's light. She inclined her head back, a small frown in place. Tiny braids held in place by bright threads wove into her curls. Squared earrings ran around the rims of her ears.

"You definitely look like each other," she said.

"It's my smile, isn't it?" Gered didn't change his even expression. Esi's frank assessment had done more to put him at ease than anything else.

Laramie tossed her head back with a laugh.

Esi allowed a grin. "And sarcastic too, I see."

"Family trait, I think." Laramie darted a quick look as if to make sure he was okay with the term.

He lifted a shoulder. It didn't seem impossible at the moment. "Maybe I've just spent too long around you, drifter."

Laramie tilted her head. "Doubtful. You ran with someone who could give me a run for my money."

The easy mood threatened to crumble before he forced it back together. Dayo was irreverent on a good day. And the first one to make him laugh in a long time. He could remember that, at least.

"Esi's coming over for dinner. She makes the most amazing cakes."

"Have a preference, Gered?" Esi asked, propping a hand on a hip with a light jingle of slender gold bracelets against her traveler band.

He just lifted a shoulder. Admit he didn't know the last time he'd had cake? Her eyes narrowed thoughtfully, lips parting to say something before Laramie jumped in, thumping a hand against her chest dramatically.

"Esi, the Barracks was a lawless place that didn't even acknowledge the existence of chocolate. And if I showed the cook the word dessert, he'd probably think I'd misspelled desert. If he could even read."

Gered shook his head, fighting another small smile and roll of his eyes. Laramie gave the triumphant little grin that helped ground him.

"That place definitely sounds like a hell-hole," Esi said.

"I honestly probably couldn't name a kind of cake," he dared to admit.

"Do you like chocolate?" she pressed.

"After it was shoved in my face?" He looked pointedly to Laramie.

"Whatever. You liked it." She tossed her braid over her shoulder.

A crack of a smile snuck through. He took a small breath. "To be honest, discussions about cake are something I never thought I'd have, so do whatever you want."

Esi drew her brows together as if trying to decide whether or not to be offended.

"Next stop in Carbenth, all three of us are going to the sweet shop, and Esi and I will educate you on the ways of dessert. This is a devastating hole in your life," Laramie said.

"She's very down-to-earth, in case you hadn't noticed." Esi swayed to the side under Laramie's gentle shove to her shoulder.

"All right, sounds like the great cake experiment shall begin." Laramie rubbed her hands together. "She will find a cake you like, and this will benefit me greatly because there is not a cake I don't like."

"This doesn't surprise me." Gered let her tap his shoulder in mock-offense.

"Esi!"

The call turned the women's heads to see Monifa waving her daughter back over.

"Okay, surprise cake tonight." Esi snapped her fingers at him and jogged off.

"Come on," Laramie chuckled. "Now that we've threatened you with cake, let's help Temi and Ade finish setting up. Townspeople will start heading over in about an hour and start trading or dealing. We might even pick up a few mechanic jobs if you want to keep busy."

The thought brought a wave of relief.

"Yeah, wouldn't mind that." He tucked his hands farther into his pockets. Anything to keep busy and avoid standing around feeling even more like an outsider.

Laramie laughed softly. "I've been picking up my own jobs for years, even before I started drifting. I don't really fit in when they start doing business. I tried to help Ade and Temi on a project once, and let's just say it ended in disaster." She shook her head with a wry smile. "So I stick to engines, and they are free to make some exquisite craftsmanship."

She grabbed the railing and swung around it to take the steps two at a time. "Oh, and I think Ade has something ready for you by now."

He came to a halt at the foot of the stairs.

"Nothing bad, I promise!" She frantically waved a hand. "Come on."

He tentatively followed her into the caravan.

"There you two are!" Ade smiled down from her perch on a chair. "Almost done with this."

Gered watched in confusion as she attached long curtains to the ceiling, humming low under her breath all the while.

"There!" She stepped down and propped hands on her hips to survey it. "Figured you might want some more privacy than the couch or the cot stuck in the middle of the room." She beckoned him forward.

The curtains took up a small square along the wall where the workbench had been shoved down to make more space. A small opening had been left just beside the outer wall of Laramie's room and her door. Ade pulled it back to reveal a cot and a small bench against the wall. In true traveler fashion, it was bigger on the inside than the outer borders suggested. A string of small lights looped twice across the ceiling.

"It's all we had on hand. But we could help you turn it into something more if you want to later." Ade tucked the curtain back farther.

Hooks on the wall above the cot were visible now, perfect for hanging a rifle. The blankets and pillows from the night before had found their way onto the cot in neat piles alongside several thinner stacks that looked like clean shirts and trousers. All, thankfully, in more subdued colors than the bright patterns the travelers seemed to favor.

Gered stared in silence. They'd done it for him. And it seemed too much. Laramie watched him with a knowing tilt of her head. He had to clear his throat and force himself to meet Ade's eyes to say a hushed, "Thank you."

Ade reached out and tapped his forearm, and he didn't flinch.

"You're welcome." She seemed to have a little something in her eye as she clapped her hands together briskly. "Now, let's get ready for business."

CHAPTER THIRTEEN

"What do you think?" Dayo nudged his sunglasses up against the brightness of the afternoon sun pummeling the desert.

Gioia tipped a drink of water, keeping one hand tucked in her back pocket as she studied the trainees tentatively hovering at the edge of the unit.

"I've seen better, and I've seen worse."

Dayo snorted. "You got that right."

Though he really couldn't blame the kids. He'd yanked them from training that morning and brought them on a run with a marked unit whose leader may or may not survive the next few days. They could be staked into Four or be absorbed into another unit if it all went to hell.

He'd be anxious, too.

"But," she said, capping the bottle again and reaching over her bike to tuck it into the saddlebag, "I don't really want any of the other trainees."

He nodded, tossing back another gulp of water. The bottle crunched in his hands with unintentional force as he lowered it and capped it. Rolling his neck, he breathed through the gut-punching desire for a stronger drink.

"You good?" Gioia slid hands into her back pockets again.

"Yeah." But it came out a bit forced and strangled.

"We gonna grab a beer when we get back?" She cocked her head, eyebrow arching above the glasses lens.

Dayo huffed a laugh. "No."

Her lips turned down into an impressed frown as she nodded. "You noticed?"

The eyebrow appeared again. "Dayo, you've been walking around with a water bottle instead of a beer can for at least a day. Yeah, I noticed."

He twisted the bottle in his hands. "It really sucks, in case you were wondering."

She chuckled, freeing a hand to tap her glasses back up her freckled nose before returning to her stance. "I'm glad you're doing it, though."

"Trying to be responsible is the worst." He took another drink as if that would sate the thirst nagging the back of his throat.

"Can't skate by on good looks and charm anymore?" she teased.

"So you admit I'm charming."

"You have your moments. When you're not smoking."

He laughed and flicked his hand in and out of a fist. "One thing at a time, Gee."

Gioia leaned over to press her elbow into his arm. "Let me know if you need help."

"Yeah. Don't be afraid to punch me if I look like I'm falling off this precarious little wagon I'm on." He was already teetering dangerously, and walking back into the bunker stocked full of beer in a few hours wasn't going to help.

"I already feel like doing that most days." Her expression turned serious. "I will."

"Thanks." He rubbed a hand over the newly shaved side of his head. "So, we keeping them or not?"

"They ride decent. We know how they do at the range or hand-to-hand?"

"We could find out right now. You wanna go beat up some kids?" He pointed at the trainees, leaning forward as if ready to go.

She snorted a laugh. "I can take them to the range when we get back."

"Sure?"

Best-kept secret in Four was that Gioia was one of the top shots behind Gered. And that was because he'd taken a trembling, skittish young woman out to the range for hours until she could empty a mag into the bullseye or point an empty gun at him and pull the trigger without hesitation.

"Yeah. Already started attracting attention to myself. Might as well let everyone know." Her throat bobbed and her boots shifted in the red dirt.

The pool of anger always in motion in the pit of his stomach roiled a little faster.

"We'll get through this, Gee."

Her jaw hardened, sharpening her into something narrow and fierce. "Yeah."

Dayo forced his feet to move, striding back to the trainees. They snapped to attention, one fumbling through a salute. Yaz, he thought. They both looked the same. Lower country boys with coppery-brown skin and dark hair already cut in the military style Rosche enforced.

"Not bad so far," he said. "We'll go through some more maneuvers on our way back in."

They both nodded, lips pressed tight together.

Dayo propped hands on his hips. "Anything to say?"

The second trainee hesitated, running a hand under his bottom lip, searching for scruff that wasn't there.

"Just ... sir ... Dayo ..."

Dayo rolled his eyes, circling a hand to keep the stammered words coming.

"We all know what went down ... and not that we wouldn't want to be in Four!" the kid rushed to qualify. "It's just ..."

"Are you gonna have a unit in a few days?" Dayo finished.

"Yeah." The kid withdrew, shoulders bracing as if nerving himself up for a physical strike. Maybe Harlan or someone else would have, but not Dayo.

"Dust, kid, who knows? But ..." He crossed his arms over his chest, making sure his voice rose enough so the entire unit could hear. "You knew Gered, right?"

They both nodded, fearful admiration on their faces.

"Sure, he scrapped the unit up to Four, but he didn't keep dead weight around either. We're not the flashiest unit, but we are one of the most efficient. And we still have standards around here. Gioia and Tamar" —he hooked a thumb at the shorter olive-skinned man with a perpetual squint—"two of the best shots in the garrison. And Sani almost beat Gered once on the mats."

Eyes widened at that. Gered had an unbeaten record in the ring, Barns just below him with his only losses being to Gered himself.

"Benj"—the wiry rider always fidgeting with something until he got on a bike—"can outride anything. Dec and Ray? They don't carry those knives for show."

The kids swept new eyes over the unit. Like most others in the Barracks, they'd probably assumed the riders rode Gered's wake and reaped the benefits. But Gered had made sure each and every one could keep up in the ring and on a bike.

"Feel up to it?"

Slowly, they nodded.

"Okay, get back on your bikes and let's head back in. You'll go to the range when we get there."

Crisper salutes were given, and they hurried to start up bikes with the others. Dayo headed to his, settling down on the seat as Gioia swung her leg over her bike.

"I'm feeling inspired already." She smirked before pulling her helmet on.

He dug in his pocket like he was looking for something, then slowly lifted his hand, middle finger raised. Her shoulders shook in laughter muffled by the helmet. She snapped the visor shut and revved her engine.

Dayo donned his helmet and started up the engine. Silence met his ears before he realized he still automatically waited for the even "check in" from Gered.

Hands tightening around the handlebars, he looked around to see featureless helmets staring back at him.

"Check in," he said, hoping the tightness in his voice wouldn't carry over the radio static.

Six names came back, the same call order as before, the two trainees sounding off at the end. He took one last look at the peaceful desert, hills covered in low cactus and mesquite trees, a few groundsquirrels making frantic dashes between burrows to avoid the possibility of aerial predators. And all blessedly free of Rosche and the pressures of new leadership.

He assigned the trainees to two different riders on the way back as guides during the different formations. They rode into the

Barracks in a double line, moving slowly across the packed dirt and strangled grass patches to bunker four—the squat two-storied building that had been home for the past three years.

Engines cut off on the cement block just outside the doors. Gioia nodded past him and he turned to see a red-jacketed rider approaching flanked by a rider with a viper pin on his collar.

The joints in his hands cried out against the tightness of his fists before he released the grips and stood, pulling his helmet off to better face off with the unit leader.

Yanis, Unit Twelve's stocky leader, watched Dayo with a smirk.

"Fights tonight, Dayo." He leaned over and spat out a stream of brown.

Dayo shrugged his shoulders, keeping his head tipped back slightly in carelessness.

Yanis shifted the chew in his bottom lip with his tongue. "See you in the ring."

Without waiting for Dayo to respond, he turned and swaggered away. His lieutenant exchanged a nod with Gioia. Formal challenge, so they'd make sure it got seen through. And if Dayo flaked, Gioia would be in the ring in his place.

All right. Here we go.

CHAPTER FOURTEEN

Dayo stared down at the bloody water sluicing from his skin to crash onto the tile floor of the shower. Bracing his hands against the wall, he let it wash away the fights, soaking through the clothes he hadn't bothered to take off before stepping in.

Five fights. Five victories.

He spat out another gob of blood, wincing as he probed a split on the inside of his cheek with his tongue.

Yanis had gone down after ten minutes.

Then Annen had sent his lieutenant into the ring with a knife. The cuts stung under the hot water, but they weren't deep enough to be concerning. He could bandage them later.

Unit Six had gone down scrapping. Might have cracked his ribs on the right side.

Unit Seventeen hadn't lasted long. Good thing, too, because he'd been exhausted before the rider dropped into the ring.

Unit Nine tried to bait him into drawing out the fight, wearing himself out even more. But he had a few tricks in the traveler fighting style along with three years of having sparred with Gered on the mats.

It was a long way from pretty and might have even gone against him when he thought the fight finished and the rider pulled a knife.

Dayo straightened with a wince and pulled the soaked shirt overhead, balling it in his hands to push against the still-bleeding cut along the left side of his ribs.

The water started to run cleaner, pooling around his bare feet, ebbing away and flowing back with bits of swirling scarlet.

And it wasn't over. Zelig hadn't challenged, and he'd seen plenty of looks as he limped his way from the arena. Some had waited to size him up. He didn't typically go head-to-head, preferring to sit back and drink until the world went hazy in a fog he'd been comfortable existing in.

The heat began to dissipate, and the small jets of water began to hit colder against his skin.

Three more days until they could leave for patrol.

Three more days of challenges.

He slammed a hand against the tile and immediately regretted it as pain lanced through his bruised and swelling knuckles. He switched off the shower and stumbled his way out, reaching for a towel.

After struggling into dry clothes and shoving his feet back into boots, he limped his way back up to his room. The damp clothes went over the chair to dry, and he placed bandages with shaking hands. He cursed softly and reached for the cigarettes and lighter still in his jacket.

The riders straightened in the common room when he emerged.

"Hey, boss, how you doing?" Sani leaned forward.

Dayo jerked his gaze from the beer can clutched in the rider's hand. "I'm good. Just gonna be outside." He held up the lighter.

Nods passed, and they eased back into the couches and chairs.

Except for Gioia, who angled her head in a silent question from where she sat on the back of the nearest couch. He reached out to give her shoulder a tap with a fist.

"I'm good, *kamé.*"

She didn't say anything, just let him past and out the door.

Dayo braced a hand against the wall and eased down to sit on the second step. The lighter clicked, and a comforting reddish glow appeared on the end of the cigarette. Taking an inhale, he tipped his head back and exhaled with a sigh. Smoke obscured his view of the night sky for a moment before the light desert breeze whisked it away.

Jaan's Wake draped across the sky in a streak of light surrounded by ripples of lighter ethereal clouds and stars. His people looked to Jaan, who took his form as the Giver's Messenger as a winged eagle, for a patron.

A medal was buried somewhere in his things alongside a knife-torn braided leather band. He'd never really been religious, and it definitely left a bitter taste in his mouth to pray to the patron of the family who'd left him to scrap for survival without a second's hesitation.

But a loneliness he'd kept at bay for three years with a haze of alcohol and smoke swept back in. It prodded at every aching bit of his body. He took another pull at the cigarette and dragged a hand across his head.

He glanced back up at the sky. Maatu's constellation, a winged warrior, had begun to rise above the bunker to the west.

Consider looking after the last two Itan in this stupid country? He shook his head, taking another pull and tapping away ash. *Probably not how I'm supposed to pray, but I don't know what to do anymore. Don't think Jaan's probably happy with me right now.*

He wasn't exactly happy with himself, and it mostly had to do with the fact he didn't have a beer in his hand. And maybe a little at how much he missed having the person he'd dared to consider family not beside him in silent commiseration.

And I wouldn't mind an extra dose of courage to make it through the next few days.

The door softly clicked behind him and light footsteps descended the stairs. Gioia settled beside him and extended a water bottle.

He tucked the cigarette in the corner of his mouth and unscrewed the lid. Tipping a glance back up at the winged warrior in the stars, he allowed himself a snort of humor. Gioia was courage, if nothing else.

All right. I hear you.

He flicked more ash and took a long drink of water.

"How you doing?" Gioia leaned elbows forward on her knees.

Dayo took a deep breath. "Not bad, all things considered. A little beat to hell, but what am I gonna do?"

"Keep winning so I keep making money off you."

He half-turned to regard her with mouth open in mock surprise. "You ... were betting on me?" He pressed a hand to his chest. "I'm horrified. Horrified, I tell you."

She chuckled.

"Completely lawless." He shook his head.

"You want your share or not?"

"Obviously." Dayo ground the cigarette under his boot and pulled another from the pack. His hands shook so hard he almost dropped it.

"Here." Gioia took the lighter and lit it for him.

"Thanks," he mumbled around the cylinder, rubbing his head

again as if it would drive away the low-level headache plaguing him since the day before.

"You look like hell, Dayo."

"Thank, Gee. Appreciate it."

She raised her eyebrow at him. Dust. It was almost as scary as Gered's same expression could be.

He huffed smoke. "I've got another couple days of this if I want to get over the initial symptoms. Free advice, Gee. Don't get addicted to anything."

Her hands rubbed together a moment, and she drew a breath before replying.

"I smoked my share of joints after I got out of the tower. Unit Ten usually had some stronger stuff around, too. Tried them so I could sleep at night ... and forget. Didn't really help until Gered staked me and moved me here to the bunker." Gioia's voice came quiet as she continued to rub her hands together.

"Stopped after a few months of being in Four, but it still sucked. Helped having my grandmother's disappointed face pop up in my mind every time I went to light up." A small smile appeared.

"Thinking of my family would just make me want to do it more."

"Hey." She leaned her shoulder into his. "Family's what you make."

"Yeah? Seems like part of that family still left me behind." He took another pull at the cigarette.

The comforting pressure of her shoulder didn't let up. He should probably tell her Rosche had ordered Four to help hunt down Gered and Laramie, but he could barely stomach it himself. He didn't want to make her share the feeling just yet.

"Sorry, don't mean to dump my abandonment issues all over you." He managed a smile.

"You're still stuck with me though, *kamé.*" This time her elbow prodded his side.

"Ouch," he complained, but a bit of warmth flickered through the ache. "And we've got to work on your pronunciation."

"That's how it's gonna be?" She drew back, eyes narrowed a bit in fake anger.

He lifted a shoulder.

She grinned. "Okay, then. Teach me some more while you're at it."

"Really?" He ground out the second cigarette and stopped his shaking hands from reaching for a third by clenching them together.

"Why not?"

"All right. Curse words first, obviously."

Gioia snickered. "Obviously."

She stayed with him out on the steps as the light over the garage flicked on and off in response to small desert mice scampering about. The stars moved overhead, and the moon sank lower in the sky until his hands stopped shaking so much that he finally felt still enough to try and push through several restless hours of sleep.

CHAPTER FIFTEEN

Gered stared down at the darkened water rushing from his hair to splash against the steel sink. He braced his hands on the counter on either side of the sink, propping himself up as Ade worked the soap through his hair and rinsed and rinsed.

A stray trickle tried to invade his right eye, and he blinked to clear it. Water crashed over his head for several long minutes until it began to run clean.

"Almost there," Ade reassured. "It's looking good."

His lower back had started to cramp at the forced positioning, but it was worth it to see the effect. Finally, she shut the sink off and tapped his arm. He pulled the towel draped over his shoulders and ran it over his hair and face.

Ade looked critically at the finished product, reaching up to tug some bits of his hair. He braced, but she barely brushed him. Her gaze dropped to his eyes and a smile bloomed across her face, bringing brightness to the gold in her irises.

"There. Go see."

She took the towel from his anxious hands, and he slowly made his way to the bathroom, taking an extra few seconds to work up the nerve to look at himself in the mirror.

His next breath lodged in his chest at the near-stranger looking back. Dusky blond hair sagged a little under the residual dampness, a few bits of black still lingering here and there, but another part of the Barracks had been washed away.

It made the drops of blue in his eyes stand out sharper against the grey. And now, the resemblance he shared with Laramie finally showed a little better. The same cheekbones edging under their eyes, the same slant to their noses. But he didn't share the laugh lines creasing around her eyes and mouth when her easy smile appeared.

"Did it work?" Laramie's cheerful voice announced her return along with the clack of the door.

Gered pushed away from the sink and dared himself to leave the bathroom to show her. Laramie came up short, her irrepressible grin taking over her face as she took it in.

"There you are," she said.

He allowed a smile. "It's going to take some getting used to."

"It looks good." She blinked a few times, suspiciously fast. "Saints, sorry!" She rubbed her eyes. "You just ... um ... really look like the picture."

She fanned a hand in front of her face, and Ade crossed over to rub her arms and pull her into a hug. Gered swallowed hard, staring down at his hands.

Looked like the picture she'd let him keep in his jacket pocket. Looked like their parents.

It stirred up an odd mix of pride and fear. Fear that the gold-tinted memories of his parents wouldn't be welcoming to him if he walked through the door the way he was now.

"Hey." Laramie's voice jerked his head up. She stood in front of him, tears under control but still lurking in her watery eyes. "Didn't mean to get emotional there."

He lifted a shoulder, not sure what to say.

"I picked up a job for tomorrow. Another transpo truck repair, if you want to come help me out," she said.

"Yeah, I could do that." Gered's fingers curled up against his palm. He wanted to, so why was he so anxious?

"Great." She gave him more space, stepping around the corner into the kitchen. "I'm definitely eating more cake. You want some?" She pulled a plate down.

Ade shook her head, a fond smile in place as she watched her adopted daughter.

"No, I'm good. Think I'm gonna turn in." He tipped a thumb at the small room they'd cobbled together for him.

"See you tomorrow." Laramie's smile never faltered.

"Good night, Gered," Ade said.

He jerked his head in acknowledgement and retreated though the curtain. Sinking down to the cot, he leaned forward on his knees, running a hand through his still-damp hair. Inside the room, there was finally blessed quiet, a chance to process.

Reaching over to his jacket, he pulled out the photo. The back side with names written in curling script stared up at him. His name. Laramie's true name. Their parents' names. He'd said he wanted to earn his name back, but since coming to the caravan, he hadn't known what to do. He felt shattered into pieces with no way of knowing how to start putting himself together.

He flipped the photo over and four innocent and happy faces smiled back. A young couple wrapped their arms around a young boy of seven whose birthday had only been a few days before. A girl of five who'd charged after him without a care in the world, laughing at any mischief they found their way into. Blond hair, grey eyes spotted with blue. And the simple belief that life would be happy and content in a clapboard house with roses under each window.

The picture shook so much he had to use both hands to steady it. The memories of life as it had been sixteen years ago were tucked so far back inside his mind that it hurt to try and bring them out. Some stubbornly refused. And he knew Laramie wanted to hear some of them. He wanted to try and remember for her, for himself, but it was like he'd wrapped them in barbed wire to protect them from the Tlengin, and any attempt to move them stabbed at him.

He sniffed away the sting in his eyes. His mother and father's expressions were filled with love, something he barely remembered. They'd taught him to be kind, that much he did remember, and sometimes the lessons stayed with him even through the Tlengin camps and the Barracks.

The bandages on his hands scraped a little rougher over his eyes, the sting retreating a little. He sniffed again and carefully tucked the picture away.

The soft murmur of Ade and Laramie's voices in the rolling Aclar tongue, accompanied by the light *tink* of forks against plates, came from the kitchen. She could switch between languages as easily as he could, but he didn't care to use his third language the way she did.

Kicking off his boots, he reached over to the wall and flipped the lights off before rolling into bed. They'd given him some loose pants and a shirt to sleep in, but he couldn't bring himself to wear them yet. It was safer to sleep ready for anything.

He curled on his side around one handgun, the other pressed against his back. A faint sliver of light snuck through the curtain, and he stared at it until the lights switched off and the caravan quieted to the soft creaks of night, and for several hours after that until he finally fell asleep.

～

Gered wrenched awake with a hoarse scream. He scrabbled against the blanket wrapped around his waist, sobbing a breath when it finally came free and he found his gun.

His panicked brain finally comprehended the darkness around him, the softness of the quilt, the smell of savory spices— the caravan. Not Severi's trailer.

Gut twisting hard, he lurched to his feet and stumbled to the washroom, fumbling for the light.

"Gered?" Laramie's sleepy voice sounded from outside the door.

He braced hands against the wall beside the toilet, trying to calm his breathing and convince his body not to eject the last bits of dinner.

Another door clicked and a low voice murmured, Laramie responding in reassurance. Then a gentle knock.

"Gered, you okay?"

His tongue stuck to the roof of his mouth.

"You need anything?"

His head hung low between his arms. It had been too much to hope that the nightmares wouldn't have followed him to the caravan. There hadn't been a bad one since the night after the slaughter in Springer. When he'd murdered innocent people in cold blood.

Grabbing the sink, he pulled himself over and splashed water across his face. Laramie had gone silent on the other side. Letting the droplets trickle down his face, he slid to the floor, pulling knees up to his chest and draping arms over them.

He sat until his back muscles began to cramp around the door frame and a chill teased at his bare feet.

Any other time and Dayo would have been there, waking him up, making sure he wasn't going to stroke out. Then making himself stay awake until he knew Gered was finally falling back asleep. Gered smashed a fist into his thigh. If Rosche had survived, it was going to be hell on Unit Four.

Rosche would mark him as a traitor and make sure everyone knew it.

And Dayo would be trying to weather most of it to protect the unit. And Gioia. She and Dayo would look after each other. It was some small consolation. He could only be grateful that no one else knew about … whatever it was between them and make things worse for Gioia.

He pulled himself to his feet, avoiding the mirror as he turned to push out of the bathroom, and came up short.

Laramie sat on the ground just outside the door, head tipped back against the wall, dozing lightly. Her eyes flew open and she scrambled to her feet.

"Hey."

"What … what are you doing?" He stared at her.

She tucked arms over her stomach, bare toes curling against the cool floor. "Wanted to make sure you were all right."

Her long hair tumbled loose over her shoulders, the sight triggering a memory of their mother, hair tickling his cheek as she pressed kisses to his forehead and tucked him into bed.

Gered turned away sharply. "I'm fine. See you in the morning."

She said something, lost as he pushed around the curtain and lay back down. It took several long minutes before the caravan plunged back into darkness and Laramie's door clicked shut, but he heard a low "good night" in Itan whispered at his door before it did.

He turned over, his back to the opening, shoving arms tight across his stomach. According to the time counter, only a few more hours until dawn. He dragged the blanket up around his shoulders and settled in to wait.

CHAPTER SIXTEEN

Dayo worked his bruised jaw against the stiffness and tapped his sunglasses up on his nose. He leaned against the bunker wall, cigarette dangling from his fingers, watching Unit Ten's leader stride toward him.

The door clacked at the top of the steps and Sani sauntered down the stairs, hands tucked in his trouser pockets, head tilted back slightly in watchful carelessness. Dayo tipped a small nod.

Gioia was out at the range with the trainees.

Dayo tucked the cigarette in the corner of his mouth and pushed away from the wall.

"Your turn, Ashton?" he called.

Unit Ten's leader scowled. "Might as well, Dayo. Never liked you, and it seems like a good enough time to try and move up."

"The feeling's entirely freaking mutual, my friend." Dayo tossed the cigarette down and ground it out. "We doing this now, or what?"

Ashton leaned back in surprise. "I ..."

He didn't get any further as Dayo threw his sunglasses at Sani and charged.

Ashton threw up his hands to block the first punch. Dayo brought hands up by his head to block the returning blows, then pivoted and caught Ashton's wrist in his right hand as it flew past. He slammed his elbow into the rider's chest, knocking the breath from him, then yanked Ashton forward by the wrist and kicked his feet out from under him.

Ashton hit hard and rolled to find Dayo leveling his gun.

"We done here?" Dayo cocked the hammer.

Don't hesitate to pull the trigger.

Ashton slowly raised his hands in surrender. Dayo stepped away, gun still held low in both hands, watching as the rider pushed up to his feet.

But something felt off. He'd surprised Ashton, but he'd seen the rider fight in the ring before. No way he should have gone down that easy.

"Something in this challenge for you, Ashton?" he asked.

The rider spread his arms a little wider, still in a slightly defensive position with the gun out.

"Maybe there was, maybe there wasn't."

Dayo huffed annoyance and raised the gun to bear at the rider.

"Okay!" Ashton said more forcefully, hands opening wide in a stopping motion. "Zelig's planning something. Probably a challenge. He paid for some more people to get in line ahead of him. I got no real beef with you, Dayo."

"Idiot." Dayo uncocked the pistol and slammed the safety on to holster it. "Tell him if he wants Four so bad, grow some stones and challenge me himself."

Ashton allowed a thin smile and began backing away. "I don't care that much, but he's gonna move soon."

Dayo shooed him off, and the rider turned and walked away. Sani offered him the sunglasses back and Dayo slid them on.

"You knew he was coming?"

Sani shrugged. "You were waiting for him, too."

Dayo worked his stiff hands in and out of fists. "He was looking fishy at breakfast."

"You doing okay, boss?" Sani slid hands back into his pockets.

"Everyone seems suddenly so aware of my health," Dayo groused, dipping a hand back in his pocket for another cigarette.

Sani leaned his head back to study the brilliant blue sky spread wide over the desert without a cloud in sight.

"Had a cousin once who decided to stop drinking."

"For the love of—" Dayo scowled. "Gioia been talking?"

"Boss, you've been drinking since day one here."

"Suddenly everyone's a freaking expert on me."

Sani huffed a laugh. "Like I was saying, my family has a tea that will help smooth some things for you."

Dayo left the cigs and pulled out the lighter, flicking it open and shut. "Your family?"

Sani's smile flickered. "Ackana tribe. We never really came out of the mountains even before the Rifts. We still hold to many of the old ways, know of different remedies for many different ailments."

Rosche controlled the lands along the mountains but had never really struck up into the heights. No patrols ran up into the Christans as far as he knew. Dayo swung around to study him more. Sani had never talked about it, but it made sense. Guard your past and what you might be worth. No silver in Sani's dark eyes.

"So why you here?"

Sani's angular features settled into something harsher. "Give a man what he wants, and he doesn't look too much closer, does he?"

"Dust."

"Indeed."

The lighter clicked in his hand. "So what's in this tea?"

Sani inclined his head. "Mountain berries, dewdrops from cactus flowers, a bit of evermore bark."

"Sounds very mystical."

A short laugh broke from Sani. "It won't take away the want, but it'll negate some of the symptoms. Help you focus better."

"Wouldn't happen to have any on you, would you?" Dayo worked the lighter around and around in his fingers. The cigarettes helped drive away some of the desire for alcohol, but he couldn't rely on them completely. And they couldn't sate the constant thirst in the back of his throat.

"I can get some in town."

"Really? They have magic Ackana tea in town?" Dayo arched an eyebrow. He'd heard rumors of the Ackana's healing ability, still hanging on in some ways with the silver drops in their eyes. It was every medic's dream to convince a tribesman to let them study.

A shrug rippled through Sani's shoulders. Dayo studied him a moment longer. He wished someone from his family cared enough to leave someone behind to check on him. But he hadn't exactly volunteered to join up with the vipers.

"Okay, then you officially have a few hours to go into town."

Sani freed a hand for a crisp salute. Dayo waved him off. The rider strode off in his rolling gait, hands still in pockets, careless and daring anyone to try and take him.

Dayo reached for another cig, then stopped himself, flexing his hand. Bruising spread across his knuckles in dark splotches. A sigh trapped itself in his chest. He stuck hands back in his jacket pockets and headed toward the west gate to check in with Gioia and the trainees.

His feet slowed as he reached the middle of the open compound between the command tower and the other bunkers. Nothing stirred. A few riders leaned against walls at the top of the stairs of their bunkers.

Pulling hands out of his pockets, he reached down to click the safety off his gun and loosen the knife on his other thigh. No sign of his unit anywhere. He hissed between his teeth. Benj had taken Dec out to the track, still determined to make the kid stop grinding his clutch. Tamar had gone with Gioia. That left Ray somewhere. And him alone.

Breaking your own damn rule. Good job, Dayo.

Figures stepped out and formed a loose line blocking his path forward. Scuffing drew a short glance over his shoulder to a few more riders circling behind. Ridgeback hog patches on left sleeves marked Zelig's unit. And pronghorns marked Unit Seventeen.

Ten total.

Dayo darted a glance around. No other units stirred to help either Zelig or him. A few more riders stepped out onto stairs to watch.

Zelig swaggered forward. "Got time for me, *kamé?*" He accented the traveler word in all the wrong places.

"Clearly you've got some confidence issues, Zelig." Dayo flicked a hand around at the riders. "Seventeen already went down last night."

"No rule about challenging again." Zelig shrugged. A sneer curled his lip. "And no rule about how to challenge either."

"Yeah?" Dayo's hands twitched by his sides as some riders slid forward. "Still salty about being taken down by a girl?"

Rage contorted Zelig's face. "I think I'm gonna do you slow and then leave you to imagine what I'm gonna to do to the rest of the unit. Maybe even Gered when we catch up with him."

Dayo shrugged. Still no sign of his own unit. Motion behind the waiting line caught his eyes. Barns sauntered past, met his gaze, gave a smug little smile, and kept walking. Dread slammed into Dayo's stomach.

Barns usually refereed things around the Barracks, but he wasn't getting any help from Rosche's second. Moshe had ridden out the day before with a few of his riders to the long-range radio towers at the edge of the territory to better contact his "friends." Three and Five were out on patrol. Any help he might be getting was gone.

And they stood right under one of the large banks of windows on the tower's side.

It really galled him to be considered entertainment for Rosche.

"You gonna talk about it all day or actually try something?"

Zelig jerked his chin up in a signal.

Dust! Dayo sprinted to meet the first two riders who rushed him. He grabbed one's swinging arm and ducked under it, slashing with his knife. The man crumpled over a stomach wound. Dayo pivoted around and stabbed into the second's shoulder.

Another rider charged his left side. Dayo spun, yanking the man's arm and smashing the hilt of the knife down on the elbow joint with a sickening pop.

He released the rider and went into a crouch, his back toward the nearest bunker, knife ready as Zelig and the other seven riders circled up again. Zelig stepped carelessly over the fallen riders struggling to pull themselves away.

"Not bad, *kamé,*" he sneered. "But Gered-boy's not here anymore to run interference."

A pang struck Dayo's stomach so hard he flinched. The tremble shook his hands. *Not now.* He swallowed against a dry throat.

"Not looking so good there, Dayo." Zelig crept forward, pulling his own knife.

A rider rushed his left side, slamming into him as the tremors kept him pinned in place. Screaming hoarsely against his frustration and anger, Dayo forced his limbs back to action.

He jammed his knife into the rider's thigh and delivered a punch to the man's face that rocked shockwaves through his already aching hand.

Scrambling to his feet, he took a kick to the chest that threw him back to the ground. The boot kicked the knife from his hand. Throwing both arms up, he caught the foot as it came toward him again and twisted.

Swinging his legs up, he kicked at the stunned rider's back and sent him falling. Dirt and gravel clawed at his palms, puffing up to try and choke him as he shoved against the ground again to try and gain his feet.

Another foot came at his chest. Wrenching around, he threw himself to his back. The heavy boot swept over his jacket to slam awkwardly onto the ground. He punched into the back of the knee, rolling into the strike and further knocking the rider off-balance as he came out from under the unstable leg.

This time he lurched to his feet to take Zelig full against his chest as the unit leader tackled him. The impact of the ground knocked the air from his lungs, and he lay powerless as the rider's fist crashed against his face once, twice, three times.

Coppery wetness flooded his mouth, shocking him back to the present. Zelig hauled back for another strike. Focus snapped in and Dayo swung his arm up, swatting his hand against Zelig's wrist to throw the punch away from his face.

Off-balance, Zelig slammed a hand against the ground. Dayo kicked his legs up, wrapping them around Zelig and wrenching to the side to roll them both over and take the upper position.

He drew back to deliver his own punch when something impacted hard into his back. It threw him forward to land face-first in the dirt, mouth open in shock. A reverberating crack found his ears.

Did I just get shot?

A strangled gasp came from him. His hands brushed the dust. Zelig shoved at him, knocking him off.

Dayo tried to pull himself forward until a boot pressed into his back, grinding him into the ground.

"He's wearing a vest!" Zelig shouted in frustration.

The click of a gun being cocked echoed loudly in his stunned ears.

"Beat this one, then."

"You first!" a new voice snarled.

Gioia.

"Put it up, Zelig."

Dayo managed to lift his head to see Gioia standing in front of him, handgun raised, a frighteningly intense look in her eyes.

Flanking her was Tamar, gun pointed at some other threat, and the two trainees, pistols out but unsure what to do.

He took a short breath, easing his hands underneath him. A quick glance to his left showed Zelig's boots beside his shoulder.

"This is a challenge, Gioia. No need to get involved."

"Yeah? Where in the rules does it say someone else can shoot a fighter in the back to help some coward's ass out in a fight?" She didn't move her gun.

Zelig didn't shift either. "You sure that's what you saw?"

"You think I'm stupid? He's got a bullet hole in his back, Zelig. And I saw you about to get your ass handed to you."

"It's all within the rules, sweetheart."

Dayo pushed his hands into the dirt.

"Okay then, since we're playing by the rules, I think I'll stick around to make sure this fight stays fair. Dayo?"

He allowed a grin.

"Kick his ass."

Dayo twisted onto his side, whipping his legs up and around to take Zelig to the ground. He lurched forward, knocking the gun from the rider's hand and delivering a satisfying punch to his face.

Zelig redirected his next strike and pushed back. They scrapped to their feet, circling one another. Blood dripped from Dayo's nose and mouth, and throbbing stung his back in an expanding circle.

He feinted forward and Zelig danced back, evading.

"How'd you ever get to unit leader, Zelig?" Dayo sneered. "Starting to think you don't have a pair on you."

Zelig scowled, a bit of tension taking over his movements as Unit Four shoved back at the riders he'd brought, ensuring the makeshift ring stayed clear of anyone else.

"Still, gotta hand it to you. Pulling this off in broad daylight?" Dayo spread his hands a little. "You pay everyone off?"

"Wasn't hard," Zelig panted. "Between you and Gered, Four doesn't have many friends."

"Aw, you might hurt my feelings if I cared at all." Dayo spat some blood out.

Zelig sidestepped away from his probing strike. They circled again. Frustration began to rise again, urging him to give into an attack.

He blinked and it was Gered in front of him, the faint smirk on his face when he knew he'd sufficiently worn down Dayo's patience.

Growling annoyance at himself, he allowed another circle around. But Zelig didn't have a trace of smugness about him. He kept arms up by his face, shifting away from Dayo with an almost comical focus.

He might actually be scared.

Dayo punched again and Zelig evaded.

Dust it.

He charged, forcing Zelig to engage, shoving in close and following him step for step, keeping him in the fight. Zelig stayed on the defensive. The ring opened up as Dayo shoved him back, riders stepping back to give them more space and to readjust the borders.

Finally came the crack of desperation he'd been waiting for. Zelig threw a wild strike. He redirected it and threw his entire weight into a punch in Zelig's stomach. The rider staggered back, wheezing. Dayo grabbed his arm, yanking it up and sweeping a leg behind Zelig's, sending him onto his back.

Dayo pulled his gun and cocked it. Zelig froze, staring up the barrel at him.

"All right, we all good here?" Barns's deep voice drawled.

Dayo risked a glance up to see the unit leader standing a few feet away, arms crossed over his chest. A few Unit One riders had gathered around, shouldering through the ring and shoving riders apart.

"Glad to see you finally show up, Barns," Dayo scowled.

Barns narrowed his eyes over a faint sneer. "Let him up. Rosche wants to talk to you both."

Dayo stepped away with another contemptuous spit at Zelig. The rider carefully gained his feet and edged away. A comforting presence came up on Dayo's left side. Gioia stood there, gun still dangling in her left hand.

Ray had joined the others at some point. "Sorry I'm late," he said as he flicked his gun at a nearby Unit Seventeen rider.

"How'd you all get here?" Dayo asked Gioia.

"He came running out to the range and told me." She lifted her chin at a young rider hovering just off to the side. The kid who'd hung around Laramie and who had been staked into Unit Two after Springer, just waiting on his snake tattoo.

Dayo gave him a short nod. A brief look of relief spread over the kid's face and he returned the gesture.

A door creaked open on the western edge of the tower, and Barns's lieutenant accompanied Rosche out. The warlord made his way over slowly, arm still bound up in a sling.

The medic took over and Dayo shook his head, watching the way the warlord favored a leg, the halting stride length, and way the knee threatened to buckle despite the bulky brace hidden under the trousers.

Rosche came to a halt, a faint sheen of sweat gleaming on his forehead in the sunlight.

"I'm impressed, Dayo. Didn't know you had the skill."

"Sir." He settled on a reply, trying desperately to rein in his instinctive reply. Now that the adrenaline was fading, the tremors were starting to come back.

"Caught the whole thing."

Of course you did.

Rosche turned to Zelig, a bit of disgust edging his eyes. "I expected more from you. Ten riders couldn't keep one down. And a shot in the back?" The warlord shook his head. "That's dishonor of the highest degree." He cocked his head, an unnerving look taking over his eyes.

Dayo swallowed. Gered had told a story once of seeing that look in the warlord's eyes. They'd been several beers deep and it had sort of stumbled from him. The warlord ran a harsh rule which kept him powerful and fed and everyone outside the Barracks miserable and hungry. But no one disrespected his rule or his twisted sort of honor code. Some remnant from his days as a soldier in the Cricean War before seeing his entire unit slaughtered in front of him.

"Get on your knees." His quiet voice still carried over the compound.

Zelig's browned face paled. "Sir, you told me I could—"

"And you should have had the stones to do it. But you failed."

Dayo shook his head. Of course Rosche would have sanctioned the attack. Zelig stared at him in disbelief, like he'd really somehow expected Rosche to still be on his side.

"You're weak, Zelig." Rosche leaned over him. "And there's no room for weakness here."

But he didn't draw the gun holstered on his thigh.

"Dayo." He beckoned.

Dread anchored him to the ground until Ray prodded him in the back. Barns's smirk never faltered, expectance in his look. He was ready for Dayo to fail the next task.

"Zelig attacked you, tried to take you out with a cowardly shot. But you fought back against ten men and defeated him in the end. I want you to do it." Rosche looked at him like a proud father telling his son to collect some reward.

A tremor rocked his hands, running up his arms into his chest. He shrugged a shoulder to try and hide it.

It'd be different if he'd pulled the trigger during the fight. But now, kneeling on the cold ground, it was nothing short of execution. And he didn't know if he could do it.

Unit Four watched him. Gioia gave the slightest of nods. Don't do it and be branded a coward, same as Zelig. Get shot by someone willing to pull the trigger. Leave the Unit to the mercy of the Barracks.

Dust. He really hated how he wanted to keep proving himself.

"Gered wouldn't—"

Dayo raised the gun and pulled the trigger. Zelig collapsed, dead, shot through the head.

"Well." Rosche's voice turned impressed.

Dayo stared at Zelig, his hand slowly lowering to his side, stomach churning.

"I think you've earned your place as Four's leader, Dayo."

He didn't even care that Rosche had called off any more challenges.

"I expect to see you keep performing like this. I hate to see talent wasted." The warning was perfectly clear.

"Yes, sir." Dayo impressed himself with how even his voice came.

Rosche turned and began to limp his slow way back to the tower. Dayo forced his feet to move, striding away from the blood and dust back to the bunker.

It wasn't until the cool air and dimness of the common room hit him like a shock wave did he come to a halt, drawing a shaky breath and coming back to himself. He sniffed and flicked the safety back on, holstering it after two tries.

Another forced breath helped quell some of the nausea. He'd killed before, but always in a fight. He'd shot someone like that just once. In Conrow, when the last two rebels were on their knees and he couldn't let Gered kill them by himself.

He'd thrown up later behind one of the buildings, Gered leaning against the wall beside him, saying nothing, only offering a hand to grip until he forced himself back together.

The door slammed open behind him like another bullet, sending a flinch through him. He turned to see Gioia storming toward him, the rest of Four filing in behind.

"Dusting hells, Dayo!" She grabbed his jacket lapel and jerked him into a hug.

It took a moment to get over the shock before he hugged her back. "I'm okay."

She pushed away, shoving a hand against his chest. "I thought they'd actually killed you, you idiot! What were you doing by yourself?"

He shrugged. "Sani had to grab something."

Gioia scowled, already preparing to go after Sani once he showed his face again. "Thank the saints you were wearing a vest."

"Withdrawals make you paranoid." As did constantly watching for some sort of challenge or knife around corners.

She shook her head, a faint smile forming. "Sure it does. Well, your face looks slightly better than normal. Dec, you and Yaz go get some ice."

The trainee saluted and headed out with the rider.

"We officially staking them now, or what?" Dayo asked, moving over to the couch and unzipping his jacket.

"They're not bad," Tamar said, helping him shrug out of the jacket.

Dayo undid the strap of the vest, wincing as the motion pulled at the bands of pain wrapping his ribs.

Gioia stuck her thumb through the bullet hole in the jacket. "I can patch this for you."

"Thanks."

He tried to pull his shirt off, but gave up after another flash of pain like someone driving a stake through his back.

Tamar tugged his shirt up.

"What's it look like?" Dayo asked.

"Uh ... bad?"

Dayo rolled his eyes. "Besides that."

Chris, the other trainee, pushed forward, jaw clenched nervously. Something prodded around the area. Dayo hissed a breath.

"Doesn't feel broken," he said.

"Deep breath," Chris said, pressing his hand over his back.

Dayo turned an impressed frown and complied.

"Don't feel a crack." The trainee pulled away. "But it's already swelling and bruising bad."

"All right. How long am I keeping ice on?" Dayo eased his shirt back down.

"On and off for twenty minutes at a time for up to two hours."

Dayo waved him around, taking the damp cloth from Gioia and starting to dab at the blood still oozing from his face.

"Where'd you learn?" he asked.

Chris shifted between his feet, gathering up the courage. "My uncle runs the med center in Teague. I helped him out for a few years before I decided coming here was going to be better for my family."

Teague. It was a town on their route. The kid probably had come up to the Barracks to help keep his family safe in case anything happened. And it was better money in the gangs than anything else he could do in the territory.

"All right, looks like we're staking you and the other kid. I won't mind someone else around to help patch up these idiots."

Chris wavered a small smile.

"There's an empty room, so you and Yaz will bunk up here and run with us for a few weeks before it's official and you're in."

Chris bobbed a nod. "Yes, sir."

That's going to get old.

"I'll let Harlan know later. Make sure to bring your bikes over too."

Gioia helped him to his feet as Dec and Yaz came back with some small bags of ice. He waved them to follow and headed to his room. He eased onto the cot, not bothering with his boots or holster.

"You okay?" Gioia asked as he softly cursed his way down to his side, pressing a hand against his ribs.

The silence before he mustered a "yeah" told the truth of it.

"I think I'm gonna pass out for a bit. You're in charge, Gee."

Cold pressed up against his back. He reached up for the other pack and nestled it against the spot on his ribs which had taken a new beating.

"Can I leave the door open so I can make our new medic check on you?" she asked, tapping a fist against his shoulder.

"Sure." His eyes flickered closed. "Hey, thanks for the backup."

Her fist tapped his shoulder again. "No problem. You did good, Dayo."

A small smile spread before the last dregs of adrenaline whisked away and let him plunge into sleep.

CHAPTER SEVENTEEN

Gered scowled down at the truck workings, his fingers slipping in the grease.

No wonder this dusting thing isn't working. He ducked out from under the hood and grabbed the rag, trying to clean the gloves off. His frustration deepened. The bulk of the worn leather wasn't letting him feel what he needed. But ... the bandages.

Dust it. Ripping off the gloves, he tossed them aside. The bandages around his hands went next, but he hovered over the ones still wrapped around his wrists.

He turned back to the engine, a slight rise of satisfaction as his bare fingers met metal and engine. It didn't take long for grease and dirt to coat the remaining bandages in a sheen of filth. But he was past caring.

The restlessness churning away inside had only heightened as they'd finished in the last town, drove another hundred and fifty miles, and set up at another. Everyone had a purpose and a job. He was riding Laramie's wake, taking jobs with her or waiting for someone to tell him what to do.

Ames was a bit bigger than the last stop, and people had started noticing over the last few days that there were two skilled mechanics in the group. He and Laramie had separated to finish jobs more quickly in the two days still left camped outside the town limits.

He tossed a wrench down and picked up a smaller screwdriver. As he did, a quick flash of something darted back under the truck. He squatted and peeked under, but nothing was there except dust and concrete-rending weeds.

Shaking his head, he returned to work. He'd been catching glimpses of something out of the corner of his eye tracing his steps around the caravan for the last two days, but he hadn't been quick enough to catch it. Whatever it was, it was small and didn't want to be seen.

It didn't make him nervous, more annoyed at whatever it was. His more immediate concerns were bigger and human shaped.

A large dog wandered over, paws scuffing the ground, and sniffed at the discarded bandages. It sniffed a little harder and more intently around the edge of the truck, maybe trying to figure out his mysterious stalker.

It gave up and came back around to him, nudging his knee with a nose. He glanced down at it and met its liquid gaze.

"What?" he asked.

It stared back, shifting on hind paws, reaching out to dab his knee again with its nose. Sunlight glittered off a tag at its neck.

"Don't you have a human to go annoy?"

A small whine accompanied a hop on forepaws. He turned away to keep working. A huff broke from the dog, and it propped its front paws up on the truck, peering over the edge to sniff at the workings.

"You mind?" He frowned down at it.

It grumbled a small bark at him as if, no, it really didn't mind. Rolling his eyes, he ruffled its brown-and-black spotted ears with a greasy hand. Its mouth parted wider in a toothy pant.

"Ah, there she is!"

Gered turned to face the speaker. The dog pushed off and trotted away, tail waving, to circle around two men, both in the black clothes and white collars of priests. Gered gave a nod to the Aclar priest who traveled in his own small caravan with the family. He dug out the name from the flurried tour Laramie had given him. Father Amadi.

There'd been a service two days before, and Laramie had hesitantly asked if he wanted to go. He hadn't, heading outside the ring into the hills, just far enough away that he could still watch some of it.

The second priest was scratching the dog's ears.

"She yours?" Gered found his voice, stooping to sweep up the rag to wipe his hands clean.

"Sort of a partnership, really." He smiled up at Gered, open and friendly. "She seems to have a knack for finding people who need to talk."

Tightness shifted in Gered's shoulders, bringing him more firmly against truck. Talk. It's all Laramie and the family did. He hadn't minded at first, but after days of seeing the way caution dimmed the smiles of those outside of the yellow caravan, he was convinced they were waiting for him to bring trouble. Or maybe he was waiting for himself to snap or for the façade to wear off, and then they would put a gun in his hand and send him to hurt someone.

The Aclar priest studied Gered, a tilt to his head.

"This is Gered, a young man who's been traveling with us for a few days now."

Gered started. He didn't remember being introduced directly to the man. *Laramie.*

The irritation swelled and he hated that some of it was directed at her.

"Father Notah." The other priest held out his hand.

Gered's fingers twitched, another thread unraveling across his frayed edges. He held up his greasy hands instead with a look he hoped was something like an apology.

The priest smiled and withdrew.

"We were going to find Laramie." Again, there was that bit of hesitation whenever someone in the camp used her drifter name instead of her true name. "Father Notah has been having some issues with his generator." Amadi studied him for a short pause. "Would you be able to help?"

Gered's gaze fell to his hands where they worried at the rag. The snake head, jaw wide as it reached for his thumb, was now visible. It seemed to be laughing at him. He savagely smeared a bit of grease over it.

"Yeah."

"I don't want to take you from whatever you're doing now." Notah spread out a hand.

Gered shook his head, reaching down to flip the tool case lid closed. "No. I'm going to need another part for this one." He turned to lower the hood. "I'll just need to tell them."

They waited for him to circle around to the screen door and knock. An elderly woman answered the door and came out onto the porch, her wide face filled with kind wrinkles and haloed by wispy white hair.

He forced himself to talk, reminding himself that her white hair was from age, not from race. Her face fell as he informed her about needing the part. Hands clutching together, she cast a look at the truck as if deciding if she really needed it.

Fingers still winding around the cloth, he came to a decision. "It won't cost extra. But I'll have to come back later to finish up. Tomorrow, maybe, if that's okay?"

A smile broke over her face like the sun over the mountains. "Yes, that'll be just fine." She reached out a work-worn hand and patted his forearm.

He eased his arm out from under her touch and backed away. He had plenty of money stashed away in his pack—wages from Rosche and whatever Dayo split with him from fights. There was nothing worth spending money on in the territory. And it gave him a little bit of vindictive satisfaction to imagine using that money on something like buying spare parts for a repair job.

Turning, he went to retrieve the tool kit and followed the two priests who eyed him with speculation before leading the way.

Gered spun once to take in the street signs at the corner, tracing a mental path in his head as they crossed several more streets, heading ever toward a spire rising above the peaked roofs. The town held a few thousand people, but the wide streets were laid out in a grid pattern, unlike the towns in the western half of the territory which circled around the courthouse and usually abandoned churches.

A flash of green jerked his attention across the street. A large sign denoted the army office. His gut tightened at the sight, and he turned his attention away from the officer strolling down the street opposite.

His free hand curled into a fist at his side, and he touched the holstered gun there in reassurance. Though an officer might take the weapon as a threat. Another scowl creased his face. He needed to keep a low profile.

The questions the army officer had asked in the Arrow med

center had unsettled him. The man had fished for information on Rosche's territory, how they'd gotten out, gang numbers.

All the while, the thought of Moshe had lurked in the back of his mind. Moshe and his army-issued rifle. The insinuation that he had some contacts on the outside of the territory who might have been behind supplying the guns to the rebel towns and were searching for a way to bring Rosche down.

Moshe, who'd be sent to track them down if Rosche survived.

Because no one ran. No one.

Another shudder rippled down his back. They couldn't be found. If they were, it wouldn't just be Moshe. It would be Rosche and an entire gang of riders out to exact revenge and destroy anything they wanted.

And Gered bet his rifle that Unit Four would be dragged along with them.

Another reason he couldn't get comfortable in the caravans. He should leave. Put distance between Laramie and the comforting family she'd found but he couldn't have. Because he was a killer and blood had stained his hands long before he'd set foot in the Barracks.

"Here we are." Notah's voice jerked his attention up.

The whitewashed church rose in front of them, sides spotted with bursts of color depicting saints and winged Messengers. Notah headed around the eastern corner to the small house connected to the side of the church by a gated garden.

Gered heard the generator before he saw it. A rumbling, coughing sound chugged from the corner of the house where a cloistered walkway ran from a smaller doorway on the church's side to the house.

He squatted beside the generator and popped the covering

off. The faint smell of burned wires met him. Resting his hand on the outside of the box, he released a small breath. A sad hum returned through the metal. He hadn't yet dared to ask Laramie if she did the same thing—letting the bits of magic still clinging to her speak to engines and metal.

He hadn't told anyone in years, afraid to give up another part of himself to be used.

"Looks like you have more than a problem." He shifted to look up at the priest.

Notah rubbed the back of his neck. "That's what I was afraid of. It's been like that for a few days. Lights have been flickering on and off, but thankfully it's been cooling down so we don't need the fans as much."

Gered carefully sifted through the workings, pulling out some coils and pushing aside wires. He could probably salvage it, but …

"This is old."

Newer generators had been upgraded and modified to avoid some of the burnout problems.

"Yes, money for repairs usually goes to the church first. This close to the Rift, the windstorms can get fierce."

The Rift, still wreaking havoc even three hundred years later. Weather changed abruptly around it, not as quickly as stories say it used to, when, after the chasms had torn across the land, the seasons came and went with sharp frequency, sometimes two winters in a year, sometimes no summers, until the land had remembered how to cycle.

"I think I can get it up and running, but it might take a bit," he warned.

The dog flopped down beside him, softly panting as she

stared at him.

Notah chuckled. "We'll be around if you need anything." He paused a moment. "Any idea how much this might cost?"

Gered studied the generator, fingers already twitching to dive in. He stilled the annoying voice asking what Laramie would do. The sneering reply was that it didn't matter, he could do whatever he wanted, and the priests wouldn't know any different.

He pushed his sleeves up higher around his elbows and forced a look up.

"I'm new at this, but are you supposed to charge a priest?"

He allowed a faint smile at Notah and Amadi's laughs.

"How about lunch and then whatever else you think is fair?" Notah asked.

Gered inclined his head and eased onto the ground, the better to start working after he flipped the generator off. The priests went inside, leaving the door open into a tiled kitchen so he could still hear the murmur of their conversation.

Under the covered walk and surrounded by leafy bushes and flowers, the air was cooler and brushed kinder against his skin. It was something he'd missed during the five years in the western desert. It cooled in the winter near the Christan mountains, but the summers blazed hot and unforgiving, hardly any rain to temper the dust and heat.

He opened the tool kit, lent by Temi and filled with everything he might need for the jobs he'd taken from the list, and pulled out some wire cutters. The dog eased onto her side, adjusting more comfortably to nap while he worked. A faint rustle in the bushes off to his left drew his glance, and a tiny, dark shape melded into the shadows.

After a moment, he turned back around and started to work.

An oddly familiar pattern ridged under his fingertips as he tugged at an old coil. He didn't have time to brace before a memory hit.

A blond-haired man, bits of blue in his eyes, crouching by a generator.

"Look, Marcus. See how it fits in?" He pointed to a ridged coil.

A nod from a young boy more serious than the little sister waving a wrench around like a weapon behind him.

"Now push and tighten there." Gentle, calloused fingers pointed to the fittings, helping guide his smaller, unscarred hands when they slipped.

He huffed frustration. His father only smiled.

"It's all right. Try humming a little."

"What's that gonna do?" He remembered the skepticism.

"Try it and see." His father winked.

So he did. Hummed a bit of the hymn his mother was singing around the back of the house. And his fingers came alive, the humming resonating in his chest and guiding his hands more surely than they'd ever moved.

Gered blinked hard and the generator snapped back into focus. He slammed a hand against the siding, angry at the memory for coming without his permission. The dog lifted her head and cast a startled look at him.

The stinging in the heel of his hand from the contact mocked him back. Ignoring it, he grabbed new wire from the kit and started splicing.

The dog relaxed again, tail thumping twice against the shaded concrete. He kept working but didn't dare reach for the song inside.

Half an hour later, footsteps brought his attention away.

Amadi set a plate and glass of water atop the generator.

"Ready for a break?" he asked.

Gered scooted back and cleaned his hands off as well as he could, then decided he didn't really care. He only hesitated when Notah joined them with more plates and the priests settled on a bench a few steps away.

He slowly took the plate filled with fried apple wedges and a towering sandwich of thick bread slices packed with meat and cheese. A murmured blessing paused his hands again, and he waited until the prayer was done to take an apple.

"How's it looking?" Notah asked, settling back with his own meal.

"Not as bad as I initially thought," Gered admitted. "Give me another half hour or so."

"That's a relief. Amadi said you're Laramie's brother?"

He forced a nod. He still didn't know how to be that.

"How are you liking traveling with the caravans?"

Gered darted a glance. Amadi had asked the question, but open curiosity shone in both their faces.

"It's different than anything I'm used to." He settled for a safe response. He didn't think saying he felt on edge, dreaded most interactions, felt the weight of Kayin and Monifa's stares the most as if they were waiting for him to prove Laramie wrong, would be the best answers.

"Laramie said you seemed to be settling in."

A bit of bread crust crumbled in his fingers and he flicked it away. Of course she would say so. But for all her talk, she was missing the fact that he very clearly did not belong. But he couldn't bring himself to tell her that.

"Trying to," he lied.

The dog rolled onto her stomach, adjusting so she could more effectively stare at Gered. Or at the food in his hands.

"I'm glad to see another Itan survived like she did." Notah's cheery voice sent his stomach clenching around the bite he'd just swallowed.

Laramie hadn't survived. She'd lived. He'd been the one surviving.

"How'd you two find each other?"

"We met up in gang territory out west." He didn't feel like saying much else.

Notah raised an eyebrow, and Gered braced for the look of suspicion. But the priest nodded, though a more speculative glance was sent at his bandaged wrists.

"Must have been hard to get out."

Gered forced another bite of the sandwich. The day they'd made their run had turned into a blurred mess of heat and blood and pain. And he didn't care to try and remember more.

"I wouldn't have made it without her." It was safe to admit that. She'd been determined to escape from the moment Unit Four had stopped her on the highway and he'd warned her about Rosche. Then she'd gone and burrowed under his defenses, driving him to decide to run with her even before they'd discovered they were family.

"Well, like I said, Lani there is good at finding people who need to talk. If you feel a need to, I'm here, or Amadi makes a good listener."

Gered flicked a glance at them before setting his half-eaten lunch back on the generator. He needed to keep his hands busier than they were.

"You might not like what I'd have to say."

Amadi dusted his hands free of crumbs and fed a slice of meat to the dog who'd given up on Gered's lunch and had wandered over to them.

"You wouldn't be the first to walk through those doors with some hair-raising stories." He nodded to the church behind Gered. "And you probably won't be the last. But it won't get you turned away."

Gered unscrewed the bindings on a coil to carefully lift it out and wipe it off. With more room inside, he turned to cleaning the carburetor.

"Yeah? I seem to recall some lectures on punishments for things like killing and stealing."

He didn't have to look up to see the glance the priests exchanged.

"Generally frowned upon," Notah allowed. "But it's up to you to decide what to do with those things that may or may not have happened."

"What if I decide it's too heavy a debt to try and pay?" His hands faltered a little as they worked. It didn't take much to see the blood covering his hands under the layer of grease and healing skin.

"That's the beauty of it," Amadi said. "You don't have to do it on your own. We all come into this world with a debt. Most leave it drowning. But this …" He pointed again to the church. "All this is the currency we're given to help us pay."

Gered focused on the carburetor. It sounded nicer than the Tlengin way.

The raider religion was years of tradition, living too close to the Rift and diving into the depths to commune with the god they claimed lived down there. All working together, it produced tribes of warriors who weren't entirely stable anymore. There were a few families who'd left while he'd been part of the mobile camps. But Severi had kept him too close to try the same.

He didn't believe in a god that was likely the result of gases and drugs and fermented drinks produced in and around the Rift, or in tradition that spoke too clearly to the warlike impulses in the tribe.

But he wasn't sure he believed in a benevolent god either. One whose Messengers coursed the skies looking after the continents.

How shall I fear that from which I'm protected by Heaven's wings?

The dark letters on his tanned skin had declared it for years, even if he was the only one who knew what it said. At one point he might have believed in mythic beings and saints. Before his world had been ripped apart and burned in front of him.

"Guess it helps if you believe in that sort of thing," he said.

"Belief is generally encouraged," Notah said, taking Amadi's plate and standing. "But it's your choice in the end."

Choice. One day he might get used to having those.

The priest headed into the kitchen. Amadi settled back on the bench, hands tucked across his stomach, staring out across the gardens as Gered kept working. Once finished, he reassembled the interior. A flip of the switch and the generator started up with a contented hum. He took the plate from the top and finished off the sandwich.

Amadi had dozed off, the dog at his feet. Gered pushed up to take the plate to the open kitchen.

Notah turned from the sink where he washed up with a smile, beckoning him in with a soapy hand. Gered edged forward and set it on the counter.

"What's the estimate?" Notah asked, drying his hands off.

Gered eased back. "I think lunch covered it."

The conversation had stirred the uneasy jumble inside him, and he needed to find someplace quiet to think on it.

Notah nodded, then indicated Gered should wait as he disappeared deeper into the house. Gered shifted between his feet, darting a glance at the open door, wondering if he could just slip away. But the priest returned and extended something to him.

Gered took it, thumb smoothing over the small medal with a raised relief of Matteo, a winged warrior holding a sword in one hand and a scroll in the other.

"If you want it. Matthew is sacred to the Itan. Most around here look to Marc as their patron, so I have a few spares." Notah crossed his arms, tucking hands against his sides.

Another blurred memory threatened. A small statue of the same winged warrior on the mantle, a candle lit beside it as his mother guided them through prayers.

"Don't feel you have to be religious to keep it," the priest reassured.

Part of him wanted to hand it back, but he slid it into his pocket instead.

"Thanks." He hesitated. "Maybe I'll figure something with that debt someday."

Notah nodded, his face breaking into a smile. "Glad to hear it. If you come this way again, you can always stop in. Or, like I said, Amadi's a good listener."

Gered tucked a nod. He didn't have anything left in him, so he left the kitchen, scooped up the kit, and left the garden with a small glance back over his shoulder at the church.

CHAPTER EIGHTEEN

"Gered!"

He twisted to see Laramie jogging toward him, trailed by Kayin. The restlessness came back as she halted by his side.

"How's it going?" she asked.

"I need a new part for the job over on Foxglove." He shifted his hand in his pocket, fingers toying with the medal.

Her brows creased together as she turned to look the direction he'd come from and the opposite direction where the woman's truck was.

"Amadi and the other priest here asked me if I could help out before I went for the part," he explained.

The confusion cleared her face in a burst of brightness. "Got it worked out?"

"Yeah." His fingers still worried the chain and raised etching. "I need new spark plugs."

"Motor supply store is this way." She indicated the sidewalk ahead of them.

Kayin caught up and took her hand. She flashed a smile up at him that surged restlessness through Gered. He missed the comfort of Dayo on his right and Gioia on his left.

Dust, he just missed Gioia. Her steadying presence, the way

her touch against his hand—the only contact they dared within the suffocating bounds of the Barracks—could resettle him on the ground. But more than that, he regretted how she'd refused to come when he, and then Laramie, had asked. Hated that she was still trapped in the Barracks.

"Which way?" he growled more fiercely than he intended.

Laramie studied him a moment, then started down the sidewalk. She and Kayin stuck close together, leaning into each other's shoulders every few steps as they glanced in the wide store windows.

Gered stalked along in silence, ignoring their light laughs. Laramie's long sleeves were rolled up like his, bits of dirt and grease staining her hands and forearms, and a small wrench was tucked into her calf-high boot. Kayin carried her tool kit.

He shouldn't care that Laramie had been working and her boyfriend had been along to keep her company. He preferred working with silence around.

"Here it is." Laramie pulled to a halt, but her smiled faded and a paleness crept over her face before she mustered a brighter expression.

"What?" Kayin asked, instantly alert to the change.

But Gered had seen.

White hair, bronzed skin, and a smirk coming at them in the form of a man not much younger than him. Three other young men sauntered along with him, one with some streaks of white in his otherwise dark hair.

Gered settled to stillness. The young man was Tlengin. Natux legend whispered that Tlengin had lost their hair coloring along with the magic displayed in their eyes when they'd turned to the god they decreed lived in chasms. But it was probably a side effect of living next to the Rift, where anything could go sideways.

He thought he'd left them behind in Rosche's territory. Dead. But some had left the migrant villages and spread out to find their own path.

Laramie swallowed hard and turned toward the motor supply. "I'll go in with you," her voice strained.

Kayin tucked an arm around her shoulders, head bent low to whisper something in her ear. She nodded. Gered eased his hand out of a fist and stepped inside with one last look at the young man.

It didn't take long to get what he needed. Laramie poked around a few shelves with Kayin. Gered kept one eye on her, glad to see when some color came back and she sent a real smile to Kayin.

They joined him at the door as he started that direction, the parts wrapped up in a paper bag.

"Okay?" Gered asked in Itan.

"*Sa.*" She nodded, the smile straining again. "You?"

His jaw set. There was a bit of accusation in the look Kayin gave him, like Gered might have brought the Tlengin kid there or want to go talk to him. But Laramie leaned toward him as if she could see the panic the sight of white hair had set off in him too.

He pushed out the door, ignoring the young men leaning against the motor supply shop wall. Turning down the sidewalk away from them, he checked to make sure Laramie and Kayin followed.

"Didn't know any Itan were left!" a voice called. "Thought they'd all been killed."

Gered halted. Laramie pushed past him.

"Keep walking," she muttered.

"Still a bunch of cowards?" The young man shouted a rough word in Tlengin, sending Gered's hands into fists.

"Gered!" Laramie hissed at him, turning to see why he'd stopped.

The storm inside roared higher. He thrust the bag at her and whipped around to see the man and his gang coming up behind him.

The words rushed and tumbled out, harsh over the edges and long over some vowels. "And you think you're brave enough to do something here?" He leaned closer to the young man. "*Klata.*"

The man's eyes went wide at the sound of Tlengin snapping between them, then narrowed at the insult.

"How do you know Tlengin?" he scowled.

"Because I ran with the jackals." Gered twitched a hand beside his gun, wishing for the weight of the holster on his right as well.

"You?" The man sneered. "You're a dirty Itan."

"Yeah? But somehow I have the mark, and I don't think you do."

Bits of red took over the silver in the man's eyes, the Tlengin fight surging.

Part of him wanted to step away, telling himself the man was young, probably hadn't been raised long with the tribes, and just wanted to claim a heritage some family member told him about.

The other part longed for a fight.

But one of the man's friends grabbed his arm and pulled him away. With a last sneer, the Tlengin retreated, the red dying in his eyes but the threat lingering.

Gered eased hands out of fists, trying to pull an even breath past the bands of tension wrapping and squeezing his chest.

A faint sound behind him sent him whirling. Laramie stared at him, eyes wide and face pale, a tremble in her jaw.

She staggered back a step.

Oh, dust. He hadn't even thought about what hearing Tlengin would do to her.

He half reached out, not sure what he was going to do or say, but Kayin was there first. He wrapped an arm around Laramie, gently turning her and nudging her into a walk. Kayin sent another glare over his shoulder at Gered as they walked away.

It sent a pang through him to see Laramie's usually confident shoulders hunched and her arms crossed tight around her stomach.

He forced himself to follow them back out to the traveler camp, just to make sure she was okay. But they didn't make it that far. Laramie stopped suddenly, nudging Kayin aside. She turned to him, arms still pressed against herself.

"Laramie, I ..." He what?

She mustered a shaky smile. "Just didn't expect to hear it, that's all."

He took another step forward, hand halfway between them. "You're okay?"

She nodded, but her jaw clenched. "Yeah. You?"

Not really, but he tipped his chin.

Rubbing her upper arms, she took a breath. "I've still got one more job. You want to help me finish up before dinner?"

Kayin glanced between them, arms crossed over his chest. A "no" hovered on the tip of Gered's tongue, but he nodded again. Dust, he really wanted to make sure she'd be okay.

She convinced Kayin to keep heading back with the bag and her kit. He left with a searching look at her face and a gentle kiss on her upturned forehead.

Turning back to Gered, she rubbed her arms one more time with the same forced smile. "Let's go."

He really wished he'd said no when they arrived at the back of the army office. Feet dragging, he followed her to the truck painted with the town name of Ames and the Natux flag—a green square across the side of the truck, two concentric circles of stars over the block letters "Always Rise."

The snake tattoo on his wrist burned, and he felt like the officer coming out to meet them stared too long at him. The gun at his side. The bandages.

But Laramie adjusted herself to stand in front and run point. Her confident air came back as she joked with the officer and reviewed the problems with the truck. When the officer left and she turned, the tightness resettled around her mouth.

"Sorry, I wasn't thinking about this being the last job," she murmured in Itan.

"It's okay," he replied in kind, opening the hood of the truck.

They worked side by side in silence.

"You think they'll notice that tattoo?" she whispered.

He checked the oil levels. "I don't know. But I know someone's going to be coming after me. After us."

She leaned her hands on the edge of the truck, head bowed between her shoulders, drawing a shaky breath.

"I kind of hoped that we'd be able to just leave."

He shoved the dipstick back in. "If he's dead, Barns would take over. And would still send someone after us. And if he's alive ..."

"Dust." The word hissed between her teeth.

Gered savagely cleaned stray beads of oil from his hands with a cloth. "No one runs, Laramie. No one."

She pushed away as he snapped the hood shut and tossed the

rag aside. He didn't need to run any more checks. It was fixed.

He scooped up the tools and left without a glance back, leaving her to settle with the officer.

The restlessness, quelled for a time by working at her side, rushed back. She didn't catch up with him until he was in the caravan cleaning up. He stepped out of the washroom, finding Ade standing with her as they spoke quickly in Aclar.

Pivoting, he went to his room, pulling off his dirty shirt and replacing it with one of the shirts gifted by the couple. The jackal tattoo sneered at him from his ribs and chest. The Tlengin words had come so easily, and he hated how quickly he fell back into it. A language once more familiar to him than common and Itan.

The door clicked and Kayin's deeper voice joined a conversation. Gered sank onto the cot and leaned forward, lacing hands behind his neck.

What was wrong with him? He hadn't felt this strung out even at the Barracks. It was like he was losing every bit of self-control he'd ever had.

Finally, Ade called him for dinner and he joined them and Kayin at the table. Kayin didn't have any other expression than a glare for him, and Laramie kept a cheery stream of conversation going with frequent glances at him where he stabbed his food in silence, knee bobbing frantically under the table.

He shoved back from the table and headed for the door, needing air, needing silence, needing … he didn't know what, and it pissed him off.

"Gered?"

He pivoted to see everyone staring at him. Laramie was half out of her chair as if to follow him.

"Just leave me alone for two dusting seconds!" he snapped

and hated himself immediately. But he slammed the door, heading away from the caravan to hide somewhere.

A call sounded behind him and he ignored it. Alarm pricked between his shoulder blades before a hand clamped on his shoulder and whipped him around. He came swinging, and his fist connected with Kayin's jaw.

The traveler went down. Gered backed away, new horror filling him. Laramie stumbled to a halt, eyes wide.

Gered opened his mouth, but nothing came out. Kayin lurched back to his feet, wild anger in his eyes. He swung at Gered.

Instinct kicked in, and Gered slid out of the way, grabbing his arm, twisting and throwing him to the ground.

He snatched his hands away as soon as Kayin impacted again. He stumbled back and fled, hands in his pockets and shoulders hunched, not responding to Laramie's call after him.

He'd finally done it. Snapped and hurt someone she loved.

CHAPTER NINETEEN

Laramie stared after Gered's retreating figure, heart breaking a little at the collapse in his shoulders. He ignored her call.

Just leave me alone for two dusting seconds!

Had she pushed too hard?

Kayin gained his feet, and she reached out to grab his shoulder. He glared at her, sweeping droplets of blood from his mouth and tried to push on.

She jammed hands into his chest and kept him in place. "Let him go."

"You saw what he did!" Kayin jabbed his finger over her shoulder.

"I know!" The shout scraped raw from her throat, competing against the stupid tears forming.

Her fingers folded into his shirt, and she leaned against him. "I know. Please, just …"

Kayin sighed. "I told you. Jagged edges."

Laramie bowed her head. "I know." Taking a deep breath, she straightened. "You okay?"

The side of his mouth and cheek were already swelling, and more blood beaded. He rotated the shoulder Gered had used to throw him.

"I'm fine," he reluctantly admitted. "But this isn't." He jerked his chin after Gered.

She twisted to look, but he'd disappeared into the trees covering the hills around. "Let's get you some ice."

Kayin followed her back into the caravan. Ade and Temi waited with concern in their eyes. They'd probably seen the whole thing through the open windows. Ade wordlessly wrapped some ice in a towel for Kayin.

Laramie sank back into her chair, but the remains of dinner on the plate looked completely unappetizing.

What had she missed?

Besides the way he'd woken up screaming the last three nights. But each time she'd gone to check on him, he'd growled that he was fine, and she'd left him alone. Each morning, the dark circles under his eyes had grown, and his words came shorter and shorter.

And then, if seeing white hair hadn't been enough to stir nightmarish memories, he'd snapped at the man in Tlengin. Like somehow, she'd stupidly thought he wouldn't know it.

"Lodie?" Ade reached across the table to rest a hand on her arm.

Laramie stared at it for a long moment, then rotated her hand up so her mother could squeeze her hand gently.

"I don't know. He hit Kayin, but I think Kay caught him by surprise."

Kayin reluctantly admitted the same around the ice pressed to his jaw.

And Gered had looked at her in horror when he realized what he'd done.

"He hasn't been sleeping well," Ade said.

Laramie shook her head, the tears building again. It might be worse than the night after the massacre in Springer when she'd heard his anguished screams in the middle of the night. But at least then, she'd known that Dayo would be there with him. Now? They barely had a few months of knowing each other, near three weeks of riding and living together with a tentative relationship growing.

And it seemed he didn't want her anywhere near him.

"Do we need to tell Monifa?" Temi asked quietly.

Her shoulders shuddered with a breath. Disputes went immediately to the matriarch. It's how the family stayed functioning.

But she looked to Kayin when she asked, "Could we give him one more chance?"

He lowered the ice, ready to argue, but she pressed on.

"Please. I know where he came from. I had to fight to survive there too, and he was there for five *years*. And I know here, and it's so different. And he told me today he's worried someone will be coming after us from the Barracks."

Ade's hand pressed tighter around hers.

"So please, one more chance?"

Kayin sighed, sagging forward to lean on the table. His gold-flecked eyes softened as he met her pleading look.

"One more chance," he promised, taking her other hand.

Temi came around and rested a hand on her shoulder. A tear escaped finally as her family gathered around. Except she desperately wanted Gered there too, wanted him to know the same comfort of a family around to support.

"We'll do whatever we can to help him," her father promised.

"Thank you," she managed through a tight throat, looking at them with a grateful smile blurred with tears.

But he didn't come back. Even when she waited up on the couch long after she'd normally go to bed. She lay in bed for another hour, but no sound.

Muffled cries woke her sometime in the darkness of early morning. She forced her feet to carry her out the door and knock on the wall beside the curtain opening.

No reply came. She twitched the curtain aside to catch sight of him in the dim light lying on his side, back to the door, blanket wrapped tightly around him.

His name died on her lips. Maybe she needed to stop pushing. She retreated back to bed and eventually fell asleep.

⸺

She woke, groggy and exhausted, rubbing gritty eyes. Pulling on a sweatshirt she'd stolen from Kayin years ago to fight against the slight chill creeping through the caravan, she went to her door.

No sound but Ade making breakfast. Pulling her long hair free of the sweatshirt, she began to card her fingers through it and gather it into a loose braid.

Ade turned from the stove as she stepped out. Laramie's heart sank at the look her mother gave.

"I'm sorry, Lodie."

"What …"

"He left."

Laramie stumbled back, bare feet scraping the wood-covered floor. "No …"

He wasn't supposed to leave. Not without saying anything.

"Temi heard the bike. It's gone."

A bit of betrayal stung through the panic. She whipped around, forgotten half-braid fluttering around her shoulders as she tossed the curtain open.

Relief slammed her so hard she dropped to a crouch to catch her breath. His rifle hung on the pegs, and one of his bone-handled pistols, the one he still didn't have a new holster for, rested in plain sight on the neat pile of clothes on the bench.

"Lodie?" Ade came up behind her. Laramie pushed back to her feet.

"He wouldn't leave his guns behind." She knew that with absolute certainty.

"Sure?"

Laramie nodded, and a bit of relief shone in Ade's face.

"I was worried for him."

Laramie rubbed at her eyes. She wasn't sure if he'd left the gun there like that for her, letting her know he'd be coming back, but she was grateful.

"Me too."

"Just be careful when he comes back," Ade said.

Laramie tucked her arms across her chest, sinking into the sweatshirt. She'd been able to stride through life with confidence for many years thanks to the woman beside her, but now she felt dangerously close to slipping back into something not entirely safe.

"I will."

But he didn't come back all day. She rushed through the last two jobs and headed back to the caravan to wait for the rest of the day. She'd started to lose some of the certainty until the low rumble of his bike filled the air.

She held back, peeking through the window as he parked the

bike and pulled the helmet off revealing sweat-dampened hair and features sharp with exhaustion. He loosened his dustscarf and jacket but didn't take them off. He stood, hand slipping into his pocket to fiddle with something.

Jaw set, he scooped up the tool kit left abandoned by the side of the caravan the day before and walked off. She pressed closer to the wall to get a better angle through the window and follow his path toward town.

Rocking back on her heels, she rubbed at her chin. *Be careful. Give him more space,* she reminded herself, though she wanted to run after him and make sure he was all right.

But an hour later, he still wasn't back. She stepped outside the caravan. The bag with the spark plugs was gone. It wasn't an hour job to head into town, replace them, and then head back.

Unease threatened. *Am I overreacting if I go find him?*

She scrubbed her arms against a chill as she remembered the anger in the Tlengin's eyes.

He can take care of himself.

And yet …

She glanced again at the town, straining to see if a figure in a dark blue jacket might be coming back with long, sloping strides.

Frowning, she turned into the circle of caravans and went in search of Kayin. He would complain later, but he'd help.

"Lodie!" Esi jogged up beside her. "What happened to Kayin's face?"

Laramie tucked her hands in jacket pockets. "I'll tell you later."

Esi kept walking with her. "What's wrong?"

"Gered's been gone all day. He went into town and hasn't come back. I'm getting worried. Am I being paranoid?" She spun to face Esi.

Esi raised an eyebrow. "Maybe? You seen those muscles? Who's gonna mess with him?"

"Ew!" Laramie shoved her shoulder. "You been checking out my brother?"

Esi laughed. "Don't worry. Broody is not my type. So, where we going?"

Laramie wrapped an arm around her in a hug as they kept walking. "Thanks."

Kayin stood outside his family's blue caravan starting up a cookfire. He looked up, smile dying a little at her focus.

"Gered's somewhere in town, and I'm a little worried. Will you help me look for him?"

Kayin's mouth opened, ready to refuse. She tilted her head, lips pressing together, and he collapsed.

"Fine!"

"Thank you, my dearest love." She fluttered her lashes.

He pursed lips in mild annoyance, grabbed his jacket from the nearby stool, and slung it over his shoulders.

"Where am I looking?"

She couldn't remember what job he was on or what he'd needed parts for. The panic jittering through her muscles chased it from her mind the harder she tried to remember.

"Um ... take the east side? I'll go middle. Esi, will you comb west?"

"Sure." Esi tapped her arm. "Meet back in an hour?"

Laramie and Kayin nodded and they headed out toward town. They split, and Laramie revisited all the spots she remembered taking jobs, but no sign of him. Only folks heading home in the fading light or gathering on porches over dinner.

Panic had started to rise a little higher no matter how much she tried to talk herself out of it. She tracked down Esi to help finish her search. Still nothing.

Together they turned back to the caravans, the hour almost up. Her hand toyed with the medal of Jaan around her neck, hoping and praying that she could feel like a fool when she walked in because Gered would be back and fine.

Esi stuck with her and caught her arm to steady her at the sight of Kayin helping Gered stagger up the steps into the caravan.

CHAPTER TWENTY

Gered finished fitting the spark plugs in and leaned on the truck. Head hanging low, he blew out a sigh. He'd driven off to spend the day traipsing through the hills or just sitting and staring at the forest.

When he'd returned, he remembered he still had a job to finish, one that helped him keep putting off figuring out how to apologize. But his traitor feet had taken him by the church first to slip inside and sit for a few moments.

The quiet inside was different than that in the hills. He stayed a few minutes, fingers turning the medal over and over. Matteo's statue stood between stained glass windows on the east wall, watching him with stern features.

He pushed to his feet and returned to the house on Foxglove, knocked on the door to alert the owner to his return, shucked the jacket and dustscarf on a pile of discarded scraps of lumber, and finished up with the repairs.

But almost an hour later, he still didn't know what to do, what to say to Laramie. To Kayin, who probably hated him even more.

Shoving away from the truck, he let the hood *thunk* shut and bent to begin picking up the tools. But a scuffing sent a stillness through him.

"There you are," a voice sneered.

He slowly turned to see the Tlengin swaggering up, backed by the same three men from the day before.

"Anything in particular you want?" Gered asked, keeping the words in common. He didn't want to slip back into the harsh raider tongue again.

"You seem to think some Itan can run with the jackals." The man pulled a knife and Gered swallowed hard. "Maybe I want to test that."

Another knife gleamed in the hand of one of the cronies. Gered spread his hands wide, sliding away from the truck to put his back more against the wall of the house.

Four men. At least two knives. Not terrible odds.

"You should walk away," he warned.

The Tlengin scoffed a laugh at his comrades. "You should beg like the rest of the Itan."

One of the men flashed a gap-toothed grin and shuffled forward.

The small urge not to completely destroy them rapidly vanished.

The Tlengin rushed him, knife swinging. Gered sidestepped, driving his elbow into the man's back as he passed, and pushed forward to sweep the half-Tlengin's strike up and jab two punches in his stomach. A twist to the man's arm produced a crunch doused by the man's scream. Gered released him and he crumpled with a groan.

Gap-tooth rushed his side. Gered spun, arms up tight by his face, batting away two punches. A third came too wide, and he took advantage of the opening, getting in close for three quick jabs at the man's face, sending him down bloody.

A kick at his knee from the fourth man caught him off-balance, and he stumbled away to catch a slice across his ribs.

Electric panic ripped across his skin at the feel of the knife cutting into him. A faint cry broke from his lips, but his body was already moving to deal with the new threat.

An overhead thrust came down and he caught the wrist, twisting and driving his knee up into the man's stomach at the same time. Wrenching the knife free, he tossed it away.

Another spin to catch the Tlengin's attack, dodging and sliding away from knife strikes.

He could end it permanently with four quick gunshots. But he didn't want to pull the trigger again. Not after the last time he'd pulled the trigger in Springer. No more death.

Attacks came more open and reckless as he kept avoiding, and, like his friend, the Tlengin opened himself up for a counterattack.

Chop to the wrist to send the knife clattering to the ground, elbow to the gut, kick to the legs to sweep him to his back.

He turned to the next scuff and shout, and something solid impacted the left side of his head. Stunned, he fell to hands and knees, feebly trying to blink and clear his blurred vision. Ringing warbled in his ear, and his limbs gave out underneath him.

A sobbing gasp broke and he scraped his knees forward, levering himself back up onto his hands. Gap-tooth tossed away a blood-smeared plank of wood taken from the pile beside the house. The Tlengin gained his feet, jeering something down at him.

The blur didn't change no matter how he blinked or shook his head. A boot drove into his gut, flinging him off-balance to smash his back into the front of the truck.

His hand slapped against the warmed concrete, desperately trying to push back up. Laughs broke around him, a knife scraped against the ground.

A boot pressed onto his hand, grinding against the bones. A sharp cry tore from him.

Get up! Severi's voice sneered at him.

Blood soaked his shirt from the cut, sending a new shudder down his back.

A shrill voice threatened to call the officers.

"Hey!" a deep shout echoed.

Get. Up.

He tried again, making it farther as boots scuffed away from him.

One knee forward. The sounds of punches and grunts brought his head up. A new figure, dark Aclar skin, wove between two men still standing.

Dayo?

Gered heaved himself up to lean against the truck, throbbing hand cradled against his chest. The Aclar landed a kick that sent the Tlengin slamming into the wall to collapse to the ground.

Gap-tooth appeared in Gered's vision. He swung and Gered ducked, the world spinning nauseatingly with the motion. Gritting his teeth, he lunged forward, driving his knee up into the man's stomach. Gap-tooth folded and Gered spun him around, yanking him up with arms wrapped tight over his neck.

They fell to the ground under the man's struggles, Gered hanging on until he felt the moment consciousness fled, then shoved the man away. He rolled, but the Tlengin was down, and the fourth member beat a hasty retreat.

Head hanging a moment, he mustered the strength to try and push up again. But pain stabbed through the cut, and he clapped his hand over it, something like a whimper locking in his throat.

"Gered?" A hand touched his shoulder.

It stung to recognize Kayin's voice instead of the ridiculous thought it had actually been Dayo.

"Let's get you to a med clinic." An arm circled his back, and another under his right arm helped bring him to his feet.

Gered swayed.

"Oh, dust. This looks bad." Kayin's face, absent a glare for once, studied the side of his head.

"No med center," Gered mumbled, leaning heavier on Kayin's support. He didn't need to have any other record in this town. He was already on record at the med center in Arrow. He didn't need to give Moshe or whoever would be after them any more breadcrumbs.

"But—"

"No!" But he still couldn't see straight, and he hunched over against the pain in his stomach and chest.

"Fine," Kayin huffed. He started walking, slinging Gered's arm over his shoulders and keeping his other arm around him.

The blur in his eyes started to recede, along with the ringing in his ear, but he could feel the steady dribble of blood down his cheek. However, when he saw Kayin heading for a dark blue caravan, he started to doubt his recovery.

"I'm not taking you back to Laramie looking like this. She's panicked enough as it is," Kayin growled when Gered tried to pull to a stop.

"'M sorry," Gered mumbled. Somehow this was easier than facing off with Kayin.

His boot caught on the top stair, and Kayin grunted to take his weight and shove the door open.

Gered shut his eyes against the bright interior light, letting

Kayin guide him over to sit on something soft. It smelled like leather and … something burning?

"What happened to him?" a young voice asked. "And *you*?"

"Lanre, stop trying to burn the caravan down again and get me some water and cloths." Kayin sounded exasperated.

"Open your eyes," he ordered next.

Gered forced them open, finding himself slumped on a long couch facing a wall covered in leather work and a table filled with scraps of metal. A tendril of smoke rose from the table.

"Here." A younger, lankier version of Kayin appeared and handed cloths to him. "This the guy that punched you?" He stared down at Gered with interest.

"Shut up. Go get Baba and a sweatshirt."

Kayin doused a cloth with water and pushed it against the side of Gered's head. "Hold this."

Gered did as commanded, trying to reconcile the fact that Kayin was helping him.

"Yeah, I'm having trouble believing it, too." Kayin rolled his eyes and tugged Gered's hand away from his chest. "This might need stitches."

He started to lift Gered's shirt. Reflexive panic hit, and he grabbed Kayin's wrist in an iron grip, a few breaths jerking from him.

"Easy." A strange softness crept into the traveler's voice.

Gered dropped his hand like it burned. "I'm sorry."

Kayin hesitated. "No, it's … Guess I should stop startling you."

Gered turned his attention from the roundabout apology and tugged his shirt up, taking Kayin's help to maneuver it over his head and dump it in a bloody mess on the ground. Kayin sat next to him and pressed another cloth against the cut.

"Woah!" Lanre was back, standing in the door and staring at Gered. Another man pushed him aside and came over to them.

"I want to know what happened." The man's deep voice rolled through the caravan.

"This is Gered. A couple townies jumped him while he was finishing up a job," Kayin said.

"Let me see."

Gered stiffened again as the man reached toward him. He was bigger and more built than Temi, a thick beard covering a jaw Kayin had clearly inherited.

"I'm Lekan. I've got some medic experience." He spread his hands non-threateningly.

It made Gered wish more for Dayo, who'd be patching him up and complaining about the work it took to keep him in one piece.

"Can I see?"

Gered lowered the cloth from his temple.

"Oh, gross."

"We could do without the commentary, Lanre," Lekan said wryly.

"Sweatshirt," Kayin reminded him.

Gered held still as Lekan dabbed at and cleaned the side of his head. Lanre vanished and appeared again, bringing a med kit.

The cut did need stiches. Ten across his ribs, right above another scar of the same length. Kayin winced for him as Lekan closed it up.

Gered leaned his head back against the top of the couch, staring at the ceiling and focusing on the beam overhead to distract from the pulling sensation through his skin. And from the looks

Kayin and Lekan darted to the scars and tattoos all over his torso.

Lekan taped a bandage over it and helped him pull on a plain grey sweatshirt. Gered pressed a hand against the throbbing in his stomach where he'd been kicked. There'd be bruising later, he knew from experience.

Lekan hesitated, looking down at him. "You look like you've had a hell of a time."

Gered met the man's gaze. Only a hint of gold showed in his irises. "Something like that."

Lekan crossed hefty arms over his chest. "You doing okay, kid?" The question had a soft edge to it, encompassing more than the wounds he'd just patched up.

Gered dragged his oddly stinging gaze away from Lekan and stared at the ceiling. Jaw clenched, he slowly shook his head no.

"I'm no good for this place."

"Hey." Kayin sounded like he tried to protest.

"Everyone but her knows it," Gered snapped, jerking a look at Kayin.

The traveler didn't protest, looking down at his hands laced across his knees.

"Why don't you go get some rest and some ice on your head," Lekan said. "Things might look different in the morning."

Gered's fist tightened. That was if they wanted him back in the caravan.

"Hey." Kayin shifted again. "Those four guys were pretty beat already by the time I got there. If you want something more pro-ductive than hitting my face, we've got punching bags upstairs."

"Of *course* there's an upstairs," Gered muttered as he shifted forward to sit up.

A chuckle broke from the travelers.

"Come on. Lodie's worried." Kayin helped him up.

Gered tried to stand on his own, but he listed a little, a new headache drilling into his skull. Kayin was there again, arm tucked around him.

They made their slow way down the stairs and across the camp to the yellow caravan. He managed to stand on his own for Kayin to push open the door.

He limped in with Kayin's steadying hold still on his arm.

"Gered!" Ade rushed over, no anger in her eyes, only bright concern as she rested a hand on his shoulder.

He almost let himself reach out to her.

"Marcus!" Laramie barged in, panic smeared over her face. "What happened? Are you okay?"

Ade stepped aside to let Laramie shove in close. Gered let her pull him into the hug he realized he'd wanted for days. He folded his arms around her as Kayin kept a steadying hand on his back.

"I'm sorry," he mumbled into her shoulder.

Her head shifted against him. "I'm just glad you came back."

His heart twisted. She'd really been concerned. She hugged him a little tighter, then released.

A wince creased her face as she studied his. "Come lay down."

"He needs some ice for his head." Kayin helped usher him to the couch.

"Too bad we don't have some beer around," Laramie said.

A smile broke for a second and Laramie grinned back. She punched the pillow Ade set down a few times before Gered eased down.

"Baba said he didn't think it was a serious concussion, but probably wake him up once or twice just to make sure," Kayin said.

Seconds later, Gered remembered his boots and tried to sit up, but Laramie waved him back down and tugged them off. Ade appeared with a bundled towel and pressed it to the side of his head.

"Thank you." He got his arm up to keep it against his temple.

She smiled and tugged the quilt from the back of the couch down over him. Gered closed his eyes, content to let Kayin explain what he knew.

He hovered on the edge of sleep when a weight depressed the edge of the couch. Cracking open an eye, he found Laramie sitting there.

"Sure you're okay?" She leaned over him.

"Yeah."

"Guess we'll match now."

His glance flicked to the tiny scar on her left temple. "Thought I was smart enough to not get jumped in back alleys."

A smile swerved across her face. "We might be related after all."

A sound jolted from him and he realized it was a laugh. She reached over and adjusted the ice against his head.

"Get some rest." She pressed his shoulder and made to get up.

"Hey, Dee?" His eyes were closing already, but he wanted to make sure he said it again. "I'm sorry."

She squeezed his hand. "See you tomorrow, *kamé*."

———

He pushed back to wakefulness sometime later to find the caravan quiet, the lights out except for one dimmed in the kitchen. Soft footsteps came over as he shifted, and Ade appeared at his side.

"How are you?" she asked.

He blinked a few times. The world stayed steady, and even the headache seemed less than he remembered. But exhaustion wrapping closer than the quilt over him limited him to a mumbled, "Okay."

"I'm going to get some more ice." She disappeared again.

He managed to shift more onto his side, back to the couch. The cushions dipped and cold pressed against his temple.

Freeing his hand seemed like too much effort, though he tried. A gentle touch to his shoulder stilled the movement.

"Can I hold it on?" Ade asked. "It won't be long."

"Please?"

Sleep dragged him back under, but not before a gentle touch brushed his forehead and bits of his hair.

It made him feel warmer and safer than he'd felt in a long, long time.

CHAPTER TWENTY-ONE

The sizzling smells of breakfast helped coax Gered awake. He blinked slowly, the familiar walls of the caravan coming into focus. Another blink and he remembered why he lay on the couch, cocooned in a quilt.

Fighting back a grunt of pain, he managed to ease himself up to sitting. A low-level headache lurked behind his eyes. He gingerly prodded at his left temple, feeling a row of butterfly bandages among a crust of blood and swollen tissue.

"Morning!" Ade kept her voice low.

He offered a slight smile as he levered himself up, keeping a hand pressed to his stomach as he limped to the washroom.

He studied himself in the mirror. *Lovely.*

Bruising spread around his eye and down his cheek. Pulling up the grey sweatshirt, he found the bandage, still clean and taped evenly over his ribs. Bruising had appeared on his stomach, blotching across his side.

It was going to slow him down for a few days. He pushed away from the sink and stepped out.

"Oh! Gered." Ade half-turned from the counter. "Lekan stopped by and left that for you. Might help with any headache." She pointed to a bottle on the counter.

But Gered froze, focused on the knife in her outstretched hand. New pain speared through the fresh cut on his side.

Part of his mind argued that she didn't mean anything. But the larger part took over and screamed at the danger from the shining blade. A blink and the melon juice coating the knife turned to blood. His blood.

Alarm flashed through him, mind racing to shore up the barriers under the panic. The small part recognizing a non-threat was lost in the roaring mess.

A sound caught in his throat. He couldn't move.

"Gered?" She twisted, knife still in hand.

He stumbled away, hand stretched out between them, until his back hit the wall.

"What ...?" She shifted toward him.

He tried to do something, anything, other than freeze in terror. So his legs gave out beneath him and he slid to the floor.

This was how it would happen. Not from failing a task, but from causing too much trouble.

No! He tried to focus, but all his body wanted to do was curl up like a scared ten-year-old. The knife wound throbbed harder and harder, joined by phantom pain from every other scar on his body.

Voices shouted. He heard his name, but he only tucked closer in on himself.

Then hands cradled his face and brought him up to see Laramie there.

"Hey," she said gently. "It's okay. You're okay."

The lilt of Itan broke through his panic and he latched on to it. "I'm sorry ..."

"Just breathe. No one's going to do anything." She rested her forehead against his. "You're safe here."

He gripped her forearm with a trembling hand.

Safe.

Another sound broke from him and he relaxed a fraction. Enough for her to pull him into a hug. His hands fisted into the back of her shirt.

Gradually the tremors wracking through him stilled, enough to begin loosening the iron grip he held her in. But the soothing motion of her hand over his shoulder didn't stop. A shuddery breath eased from him.

He shifted, and she pulled back to look him in the eye.

"What do you need?"

But heat rushed to his face as he fully came back to himself and realized he was sitting on the caravan floor, holding on to her for dear life.

All because Ade had innocently held a knife and he'd freaked out.

"Nothing. I'm … I'm sorry." He shook his head, trying to stand and having to accept her help. He couldn't bear to lift his head and see the look on Ade and Temi's faces where they stood in the kitchen.

Laramie kept an arm under his as he went to his room.

"I'm fine," he choked out and ducked through the curtain. Inside the safety of the room, he stared down at his shaking hands. He'd started breaking apart, and there was nothing he could do to stop it.

—

Laramie pushed her door closed and sank to the ground, pressing her hands against her mouth to smother the wracking sobs finally able to break free. Squeezing her eyes shut, she tried to control the way her body heaved.

She thought seeing him bloody and road-torn in the Barracks had been awful.

Had felt punched in the gut seeing him stagger into the caravan the night before.

But the look of utter terror and panic on his face as he curled against the wall had been a bullet through her heart.

Ade had dropped the knife like a poisonous snake when Laramie had snapped in her own blind panic. But more than that, she didn't know what she was supposed to do. He'd shown two different extremes in as many days.

She rested her head back against the door. *Jaan, how do I help him?*

Pulling the sleeves of her sweatshirt over her palms, she scrubbed the soft material over her face, wiping away traces of tears. Mustering herself, she dressed and stepped back out. Ade looked up from where she leaned on the counter, Temi gently rubbing her back.

"Is he …?" Laramie whispered.

"He went outside. Said he needed some air." Ade sniffed and rubbed her eyes. "I'm so sorry, Lodie."

Laramie crossed over and hugged her. "You didn't know."

She'd seen him around knives before and, while there'd been stirrings, there'd never been anything that extreme.

The lump rose again in her throat and she sniffed, burying her face against Ade's shoulder.

"Hey, now." Ade switched to comforting just as fast. Laramie pulled away, crossing and uncrossing her arms.

"I just don't know what to do, Memi." Laramie pressed her

hands to her cheeks. "I want so many things … and he's my brother … but the past few days …" Her shoulders fell.

Ade beckoned her back into an embrace. Wrapping her arms around Ade, she leaned against the woman who'd held her on so many sleepless nights. Ade didn't say anything, waiting as she knew how to do.

Laramie sighed. "You were always there for me, helping me through it. And I know it didn't happen overnight for me, but …"

"I didn't know what to do either, Lodie." Ade rubbed her shoulder. "All I knew is that I had a scared five-year-old who'd just lost her family and community in a terrible way. A little girl who wouldn't speak to me for so long. But I remember your first smile." Ade's voice wavered and her arms tightened. Laramie squeezed gently back.

"Oh, it was beautiful. But we still had a long way to go after that. Talking, healing, breathing."

"But he's not a kid."

"I think in some ways he might still be. I don't think he ever got to stop being scared. Not like you did." Ade pulled back, placing hands on Laramie's shoulders. "I was here for you. But ever think you might need to be that person for him?"

Laramie scuffed her boot against the floor, wrinkling her nose to try and drive away the sting. She'd tried, but he seemed to only keep her at arm's length. "What if I don't know how? What if he doesn't want me to?"

Ade pressed a hand against her cheek. "You'll figure it out. How many different things did we try?"

Laramie allowed a nod.

"And he looks for you everywhere. I don't think he feels comfortable until he can see you. You're the familiar thing. The safe thing. He trusted you enough to come this far with you, didn't he?"

She held a breath, easing it out and squaring her shoulders. "Okay."

"I know what he said the other day, but you should go check on him," Ade said. "And tell him sorry from me."

Laramie leaned her forehead against Ade's another moment. "I will."

She stepped outside, but as expected, no sign of Gered. Rubbing her arms against the chill, she halted at the foot of the stairs.

"Where'd you go?" she whispered to herself. He seemed to spend a lot of time in the garage at the Barracks. And he'd gone off by himself the day before.

Somewhere quiet.

But that could be anywhere in the mist-covered trees outside the camp. She rubbed her forehead, trying to decide where to start.

A faint *mrow* drew her eyes down. A tiny black paw emerged from under the caravan, followed by a dark nose and long whiskers. The cat looked up with wide gold eyes. It meowed again and set off, keeping its brown-and-black ringed body low in the tall grass, prowling around the next caravan and slinking straight out toward the trees.

She paused a second, then decided following a cat was more of a lead than anything else. They usually didn't come from the nooks and crannies under the caravans until dark, so there must be a good reason this one was out in the dawn hours.

And sure enough, a few feet into the tree line, she found Gered sitting on a stump, leaning forward on his knees, hands laced behind his neck. He'd changed from the sweatshirt back into a plain long-sleeved shirt, his calf-high boots neatly laced over trousers.

"Hey." She moved toward him.

He jerked up, surprise fading into caution she tried not to let sting her as she settled on the fallen tree beside him. The camp was still visible from the seat, elevated on the hill to look down into the caravan circles.

She rubbed hands over her thighs, not sure what she wanted to say or how to begin. "You okay?"

He nodded, still tense. Waiting for her to take advantage.

"I wanted to talk to you." Laramie rubbed her thumb over the end of her braid.

Gered watched a moment, then nodded warily.

She offered a slight smile, and he relaxed enough to lean elbows back down on his thighs, hands loosely clasped.

"The past few days got me thinking …" She rubbed her palms over her thighs, trying to scrub the nervousness away.

He stared at his hands, understanding breaking through.

"Wait," she said as his chest expanded to say something. "It's not … not what you think, probably."

He pressed his lips together but didn't look at her.

Oh, dust. She stilled her hands, tucking them in her lap instead to pick at a hangnail.

"I haven't really talked about this with anyone. Everyone here knows some of it. But after … everything, when the travelers found me, I didn't talk for months. I was petrified. They found me huddled in a kitchen cabinet, hungry, exhausted. I'd peed myself at some point. They didn't let me see anything when they carried me out. I didn't ask for mom or dad. Or you. I think, somehow, I knew already that all of you were gone."

Gered rubbed his hands together slowly, still staring at the dewy grass.

"Everyone but Ade and Temi kind of gave up on me after a few weeks. Thought I would never talk. But Ade kept smiling, coming in when they heard me crying at night, trying to figure out what food I liked best. Little things. Ade told me just now, she … she remembers the first time I smiled again." Laramie rubbed her nose, blinking away the sting.

"But it was almost like I'd forgotten who or what I was. I still didn't talk for a while after that. I jumped at everything. Wouldn't leave the trailer without holding on to her hand. I'm sure she got annoyed real quick with that." She smiled.

"But she never let me see it. I remember one of the raider trucks backfired. I remember hearing it every few minutes. Bang." She snapped her fingers.

"For a long time after that, I'd just kind of shut down if I heard a car backfire. Freaked Ade out the first time it happened. I ran and found the smallest, darkest place I could to hide. She couldn't find me for almost half an hour. Sometimes it would hit so hard that I'd just drop to the ground like my legs were cut out from under me, and I'd curl up into the smallest ball I could. A year of that, until Ade figured out how to teach me to breathe through it, focus somewhere else. Sometimes even now, years later, if I hear it unexpectedly, it'll trigger the same reaction. Not as strong anymore, but I have to remind myself how to breathe."

Gered's jaw tightened and his fingers flexed and unflexed. She wondered if he knew what car it was that backfired. Swallowing hard, she kept going.

"It took a while before I didn't freak out seeing someone with white hair, even if they were just a friendly old person on the street. I thought all people with hair like that were raiders. Took a long time before the nightmares only happened once a month or so, then even less than that. Though sometimes they'll come back if I hear a bad motor or catch a whiff of something burning. I'm just saying, it's going to take time."

His shoulders sagged, and he laced his hands behind his neck again as he stared out at the forest. "You were a kid and had someone here." His voice came a little rougher and uneven. "I didn't. And everything Severi did to me … it dusted me up pretty badly." He moved his hand, dragging it over his face. "Maybe I'm too broken."

"Hey, I don't think that." She leaned closer.

"But you've wondered it." He angled his head, fixing her with a knowing eye.

Her posture collapsed under the weight of it and her silent admission.

"It's okay." He picked at his fingers. "I know it. I know I'm too … messy for things here. I can't even look at a dusting knife." He shrugged.

But something pricked her memory. "What about before?"

"What?"

"My knives. When Four picked me up. You took my knives and kept hold of them until you gave them back. I was there almost the whole time. You didn't look like you did in the kitchen." She pivoted, tucking one leg up, the rough bark catching at her boot laces.

"Then maybe I've finally snapped." He drew one shoulder up almost like a barrier between him and her new position. "I wish I wasn't falling apart here. I don't want to break all over this place."

"I don't think so. What changed?" As she asked it, she looked over the loose circle of caravans. The lights strung between each trailer, open fire pits with breakfast being cooked. Kids starting to stir and run around laughing. Couples able to sit together without fear.

"It's this." He jerked a hand out. "It's so … different. It dusting scares me." He ducked his head again. "Everything in the last sixteen years has been waiting on orders, having a gun put in my hand and told who to hurt. Or just waiting for someone to try and take me down because they decided I'm finally the threat. I don't know how to do this. To be normal." The vehemence faded to wistfulness as he looked over the lights again.

"Maybe you could learn to be."

He scoffed. "I can't. Look at me, Laramie! I'm a killer wound too tight and ready to snap."

The words twisted her heart. "I don't think you are."

A scornful laugh broke, and he jerked his hand in almost a shooing motion as he made to stand up.

"I don't think you are," Laramie repeated with more conviction.

He paused, looking over his shoulder, desperation lurking in his eyes.

"I only saw you forced to kill. Or kill in self-defense. You didn't like it. You hated it."

He eased back a little on the stump, eyes locked on hers.

"You always tried to do things different than the Tlengin or Rosche, didn't you?"

Slowly, he nodded.

"And it seems to me that ruthless killers don't go around helping newbies try and protect themselves in saints-forsaken places."

Silence fell between them and she prayed he could maybe

believe a little of what she'd said. A bit of motion returned as his palms scraped each other again.

"But you have to admit that I'm not right."

"It's okay to admit that," she said simply. "I wasn't for a long time. But Ade helped me pull my pieces together." She hesitated a moment more. "Look, I started drifting because I wanted to find Itan. Even though I have a family here, I wanted to see if any of my people were still out there. And I found more than I'd ever hoped for that night you told me your name. I know I latch on to a thing and push and push until I get some result. And if that's too much for you, tell me. Please. I think you know how I get," she said wryly.

For the first time, a bit of humor flickered around his mouth. She took it as a win.

"Ade was that person for me. I'd be that person for you, if you want. If a machine's broken down, you don't give up on it, right? You get some new parts and put it back together. Sure, it might look a little different or run a little differently than before, but that's okay."

He curled the fingers of his right hand to his palm and back out.

"What do you say?"

"What if you can't find a new part to fit?" he asked softly.

This time she dared reach out and nudge his shoulder with a fist. "We're Itan, right? We figure out how to build one."

A reluctant smile appeared. He let his head hang a moment, then turned to meet her gaze again.

"You think you might be able to teach me how to breathe?"

"Yeah. Yeah, I do."

CHAPTER TWENTY-TWO

Dayo rolled over with a groan and stared at the bunker ceiling. *I'm alive.*

"How you feeling?"

He lifted his head to see Gioia leaning on the frame of the open door, hands tucked in back pockets. Rubbing a hand over his face, he considered.

"Really dusting awful."

Her light laugh brought a faint smile to his face. Boots scuffed as she came to stand beside him.

"Two days, Dayo. You pulled through. Want some food?"

His stomach growled in response.

A snort of laughter broke from her at his sheepish look up.

"Go shower. You smell awful, too." She spun on her heels and left.

Dayo rubbed his eyes again and came slowly up to sitting. Two days. His body had taken advantage of the exhaustion following the fight in the courtyard and decided to officially wage a vengeful war on him for quitting alcohol.

He'd barely been able to get out of bed, wracked with shivers one second and heat the next. Sweating and almost vomiting up the water Chris and Gioia forced him to drink. The bitter taste of Sani's tea lingered in the back of his mouth. He'd left the darkened room only for necessities and to choke down whatever they brought back from the mess hall.

No one had said anything outright, but he'd caught mumbled conversations outside his door and calming answers from Gioia.

Good thing Rosche called off the challenges.

Fumbling for clean clothes in the crooked dresser, he stumbled his way to the showers to wash off two days of misery.

When he finished, he made it back to the room, having to rest a moment to combat a rush of lightheadedness before reaching for his boots.

He felt wrung out and tired. But the constant craving had died to only a faint murmur for the moment—maybe he had the tea to thank for that. And for that matter, his cracked ribs didn't ache as much as they should, and the bruising all over his body was less pronounced than it should be for the punches he'd taken in the last five days.

Though maybe he'd just been exaggerating how bad it all had been right after murdering a guy. His hands squeezed tight as he closed his eyes, willing away the hyper-focused memory of killing Zelig.

Sani stuck his head in. "Food's here."

Dayo took an extra moment to get to his feet again, tucking his sleeves up around his forearms. The snake tattoo grinned up at him from his left wrist, laughing at him for having survived.

Walking into the hallway, he came to an abrupt halt. It smelled way too good to be Barrack's food. His feet moved a little faster.

Gioia stood behind the kitchen bar that separated the tiny area from the rest of the common room. A tall pot steamed on the stove and she stirred a few times, raising her head to glare at the riders loitering around.

"What is this?" Dayo limped forward.

A faint bit of red touched her cheeks as she kept stirring. "Something I made."

"You …?" He rocked back on his heels to regard her.

"Yeah, you should have seen her marching into the kitchen and requisitioning everything from the cooks." Dec dared to lean closer to watch the bubbling soup. "They didn't know what to do."

Gioia tapped the spoon on the side of the pot and pointed it at him. "Get bowls."

Dec clamped his mouth shut and slid past her into the kitchen to rummage through the cabinets.

"You invaded the kitchen?" Dayo leaned back against the counter, tucking his arms over the ache starting up in his ribs. Maybe he was just overthinking his recovery.

Her lips twisted a little. "I couldn't let you eat mess hall food again."

Dayo grinned. "Can I be sick more often?"

She rolled her eyes and started spooning soup into bowls as Dec handed them over.

"I didn't even know the stove worked."

It had been hidden under cases of beer for as long as Dayo had been in the bunker. But now the kitchen was conspicuously absent of cans and cases, the countertops clear for the first time maybe ever.

"It took a bit of fiddling," Gioia admitted.

Dayo took the bowl and spoon, his stomach grumbling again. Dec silently handed him a bottle of water as well, a bit of hesitation in his glance.

Ignoring it for the moment, Dayo went to sink down onto one of the couches. He dug his spoon into the soup, the bite halfway to his mouth when the crackle of the radio sounded in the kitchen.

He froze. Gioia's shoulders tensed and she reached behind her and lifted the hand-held radio. Dayo pushed up and extended his hand for it.

He flipped the button. "Dayo."

"Rosche wants to see you in the war room. Bring Sani. Out."

Silence coated the room. Dayo set the radio down with exacting slowness. It wasn't surprising Rosche already knew. Not if Gioia had been in the kitchens demanding supplies to cook. That was never done.

But Sani? Rosche never called for a rank-and-file rider. Dayo had barely gone with Gered to the war room as his lieutenant.

Gioia tucked her hands in back pockets and stared at him.

Dayo rubbed his chin and gestured to Sani. "Let's go."

The rider placed his bowl on the counter and stepped up with him, confusion playing in the crease between his eyes. Dayo met Gioia's look again and gave a small nod.

He had someone watching his back this time. He'd be fine. Hopefully.

"Wait." Her voice stopped him. She disappeared into the hallway and reemerged with his jacket. He caught it as she tossed it, huffing frustration at himself as he shrugged into the red leather.

Already forgetting he was unit leader and would be expected to present that front to Rosche.

Sani tailed him as he pushed out of the bunker. A welcome coolness hit his face as he descended the steps in the dusky twilight. Floodlights popped on across the compound, and sentry lights flickered on the walls, illuminating the figures pacing the walkways with rifles in hand.

"Any idea what this is, boss?" Sani asked behind him.

"No idea." Dayo shoved hands in his jacket pockets and walked a little faster. The square shape of the lighter nudged into his palm.

"You don't have anything you need to tell me before we get up there, do you?" he asked.

Sani shook his head. "No idea."

The lighter's sharp edge jabbed deeper. *Dust.*

Dayo pushed through a wave of lightheadedness as he jogged up the stairs to the landing. He really wished he'd gotten to eat. Though depending on what awaited them after the meeting with Rosche, maybe he'd end up grateful for an empty stomach.

Light spilled into the darkened corridor to his right. Thin lines of light crept under the door of the comm room as he passed. Another minion always monitoring the unit's comms while they were out. The way they'd caught Gered and the drifter leaving weeks ago.

Dayo pushed back the memory and stepped up to the open door of the war room. The chair at the head of the polished oaken table had been removed to make room for Rosche's wheelchair. He sat, turned to the open bank of windows, staring out at the shadowed silhouette of the mountains thrust against the darkening sky. Thin strokes of yellow and orange attempted to hold back the darkness from overtaking the fading pale light sinking lower and lower behind the valleys and peaks.

For a moment, the warlord's profile reminded Dayo of the way his family's patriarch used to watch the sunsets. The jab of the lighter brought him back into the present.

"Sir." He added a crisp salute. Might as well start off on a good foot.

Rosche spun the wheelchair and rolled the few feet up to the table. He gestured to the seats on his left. The calculating look was back. Dayo strode forward, determined not to show any hesitation.

Sani eased into the chair beside him, giving Rosche a sharp nod and "sir."

Rosche leaned back in the chair, his free hand loosely draped over his sling. "Heard you were sick, Dayo."

Dayo snuck his hand back into the jacket pocket to spin the lighter. "Nothing I couldn't shake, sir."

Rosche lifted his chin, a faint look of amusement and compassion mixed together in his sharp green eyes.

"Quitting alcohol is no mean thing."

A swallow nearly stuck in Dayo's throat.

The warlord nodded, the friendly commander back. "I know the signs. Saw them in you before that fight. Why'd you decide to stop?"

He couldn't stop the shift that ran through his body. "Figured I needed a clear head to do the best for Four." Admitting that to Rosche hadn't been high on his list of things to do.

Rosche tapped his thumbs together. Behind him, the light faded to pinpricks of starlight in the velvet sky.

"I can respect that. How are you feeling?"

"Better, sir." His leg began to bounce under the table, unsure how to redirect from unsettling small talk about his health to the real reason Rosche had summoned them.

"Sani, how is your family?" Rosche's attention shifted so fast it nearly gave Dayo whiplash.

"Just fine, sir," Sani's even voice replied, showing no sign of surprise.

"It seems you had a few errands in town while Dayo here was recovering." Rosche tilted his head, the viper-like calculating back.

"Just getting some things for Chris. Apparently the kid is something of a medic." Sani shrugged a shoulder.

"Yes, I suppose your bunker medic was down." Rosche allowed it with a glance at Dayo.

The lighter stabbed into his palm again. He wouldn't have made Chris that useful yet, but Sani had bigger secrets to keep.

"You couldn't have gotten them from the med center here?"

Sani shrugged. "I'm not medically inclined. I just went for errands."

Rosche rubbed the hard edge of his jaw. "Indeed. Well, you look … much better, Dayo."

Unease coiled through Dayo, pulling at his gut and reaching to wrap around his heart. "Anything we can do for you, sir?" he dared ask.

It wasn't what Gered would have done. The idiot would have sat there and stared at Rosche with a solid impersonation of the mountain's face and waited to be told.

A sliver of a smile teased Rosche's face. "You're direct. I like that about you, Dayo."

An incline of his head was all he managed, retorts lost somewhere in the confusion inside.

The warlord turned his attention down, picking at his thumbnail. "Moshe got word back from a contact this morning. Thinks he's picked up a lead on Gered."

Two stalled heartbeats later, Dayo forced a dry, "Did he?"

The knowing glint surfaced again. "You care about him still? After he left you behind?"

Like your family. The rest hung in the silence like heavy rain-clouds ready to unleash torrents on the unwary.

A light click of the lighter's top sounded in his pocket. "We were friends, sir." As close as could be in the Barracks. "Then he screwed us all over." His voice gained strength and coldness at the end. Maybe even enough to convince Rosche.

"So he did." Rosche leaned forward, a wince creasing around his eyes he could barely hide. "But if Moshe has turned up something already, that means I don't have enough time."

The unease built until it felt like the air right before a thunderstorm on the plateaus of the upper country.

"Once it is confirmed, we will ride." The light built in Rosche's eyes, and Dayo physically drew back from it. "But time is something I do not have." He cast a disgusted hand down at himself.

"I need Sani for an errand of my own."

Dayo managed a glance to his right. Sani's bronzed skin had turned several shades lighter. His gaze flickered from Rosche's down to the table, as if he already knew not to deny anything the warlord said or might say.

"Sir?" Dayo pressed.

Rosche didn't take his piercing gaze from Sani. "This stays between me and Sani for now. You'll be looped in if needed. Perhaps I'll need your medical advice later."

Sani wasn't offering anything, and Dayo had no idea what to do next. He settled on the obvious.

"We're supposed to leave for patrol tomorrow, sir."

"You will be leaving with Moshe first thing tomorrow, Dayo,

to hunt the traitor down and bring me a report."

It felt like nothing was supporting him. He was flailing in midair, trying to find something to latch on to. "Sir ..."

"Gioia can take lead. She can handle it, can't she?" A smirk curled Rosche's upper lip, and Dayo's hand twitched to lash out.

"Yes, sir."

"Good." Rosche's hand jerked in dismissal. "Sani, report to me tomorrow morning to get the details on the brief."

No choice left. Dayo pushed back from the table, the legs of the chair grinding against the flooring. Sani followed silently back down the stairs and to the courtyard.

"What the hell was that?" Dayo hissed as they crossed the open dirt between the tower and bunker four.

"Rosche isn't an idiot. He knows the old stories about the Ackana, just like everyone else from here."

Dayo paused mid-step. "What, he thinks you have something to cure him?"

Sani shrugged. "I don't know what he wants. He might not even know what he wants, but that's never stopped him."

"So what are you bringing back from this errand?"

"Whatever he dusting wants," Sani nearly spat. "I've got people around here, Dayo, and he knows it."

And Rosche wouldn't hesitate to use whatever or whoever against him. A light popped on in the upper floors of the tower. Dayo kept walking like nothing happened.

"Just be careful, Sani."

A bitter smile formed on Sani's face. "You too, boss. He's got you going after Gered. And no matter what you think, Rosche has hold over all of us. There are things I'm not willing to sacrifice. Just make sure you make the choice that's best for you. That's all we can do around here."

Dayo clenched the lighter in his fist as Sani outpaced him, jogging up the steps into the bunker first. What was he willing to sacrifice?

CHAPTER TWENTY-THREE

Gioia was on her feet as soon as they walked back through the door, concern written plain over her narrow features. Sani didn't say anything, just refilled his bowl and went to sit on the couch.

Hunger pressed its sharp way back to his stomach, but Dayo faced off with the unit. It took a moment to force the words.

"We're supposed to leave on patrol tomorrow, but there's a slight change of plan. Rosche wants Sani to run an errand down south. And I'm … headed out with Moshe tomorrow. We'll be gone a few days. Gioia, you'll run point on the patrol."

Confusion stirred, and Gioia looked at him with eyes wide in panic. Her mouth opened, but Dayo cut her off.

"Any concerns with that?"

The unit shook their heads. Gioia stared at him, now attempting to bore a hole through his skull with her gaze.

"Where are you going with Moshe?" A dangerous tightness laced her words.

Dayo forced himself to meet her gaze. "Moshe thinks he picked up a lead on Gered. We're going to check it out."

She took it with frightening calm, her face blank. The rest of the riders paused, looking to one another and then to Dayo. He forced his feet to move instead, topping off his bowl and jerking his head to Gioia.

"We need to brief so you're ready to go first thing tomorrow." He headed to his room, the softer tread of her boots following.

Taking a seat on his bed, he waited. Gioia gently closed the door, hands and forehead pressed against the surface a moment before whirling on him.

He waved her to a seat with his spoon, mouth full of still-steaming soup. They hadn't been gone long enough for it to truly cool.

But she came to stand in front of him, arms crossed over her chest. Feet braced wide and chin clenched, she looked ready for a fight.

Dayo half-heartedly pushed a chunk of chicken around the bowl. "I don't know what I'm supposed to do here, Gee."

The fight evaporated from her, and she sank to the bed beside him.

"Where's Sani going?"

Appetite dulled for a moment, he kept shifting the spoon around. "I don't know. Rosche is keeping it under wraps. But it's probably something to get him back on his feet."

"To go after Gered and Laramie himself?" she finished in a whisper.

He nodded.

"Dust."

"Yeah." He forced a bite.

Her hand clenched a moment in the longer hair atop her head. Slowly she released and leaned down to rest elbows on her thighs.

"What about you and Moshe?"

"Guess I'm gonna be the first person to leave the territory with his permission." The chicken turned to ash in his mouth.

Gioia didn't react. The joke sucked anyway.

"Dust, I don't know." He shook his head, fingers on the verge of trembling again, but this time not from a need for alcohol. "It's probably just some sick test from Rosche to see if I'll follow orders, hunt down my best friend, and report on him so I can take all of Unit Four out on the manhunt to go kill him."

Gioia's fist nudged his forearm, managing to slow his rapid breaths. They sat in silence for a long minute. Warmth leeched from the bowl to Dayo's hands, but he couldn't bring himself to eat anything.

"Just tell me this shifting place isn't going to get us." He mustered a poor smile.

"Hasn't kept us down yet, yeah?"

"It's making a damn good effort these days." Dayo dragged the spoon through the soup again.

"Hey, don't give up on me, *kamé*." She knocked a fist against his. "Tell me what to do on patrol."

He lifted a spoonful, trying to enjoy some of the flavor. "You'll meet with the mayor in each town, get the reports and any updates from them, and then leave."

"That's it?" She arched an eyebrow. "It always seems like we sit outside the offices for a lot longer than that."

"Gered would go over specifics with them if he needed to." He tapped the side of the bowl with a finger. "When you talk to Mayor Daffy, let him know that I'll keep the same arrangement. Ask him about the numbers and if anything ... needs to be adjusted."

Gioia slowly straightened. "What's that supposed to mean?" Her eyes narrowed. "Was Gered skimming?"

"No!" Dayo protested. "The oil fields there are drying up. He's been fixing the numbers a little every time to keep Rosche from docking supplies too much to the town."

Gioia blinked rapidly a few times. "Of course he was."

Dayo cleared his throat. Daffy had been ready to accept his fate when it started to get obvious, but Gered had looked at the numbers, at the mayor, outside the window to the dust-eaten town with pumpjacks and rigs filling the fields, and told him to bump up the rig reports in a few places.

"They've got those four new wells they're hoping to help increase production. Make sure you get the reports on those."

She nodded. "Anything else?"

"Barrington down in Ector City is a jerk." He flashed a short grin. "Uncomfortably long eye contact usually shuts him up."

It got a light laugh from her. But she lapsed into silence, still staring at her hands. Dayo kept eating and waiting.

"What are we gonna do?" Her words came hushed.

The spoon dragged through the thick broth, disturbing floating bits of spices. "About Gered?"

A miserable nod moved her head and shoulders.

"Rosche has already confirmed we're part of the crew going after him."

"Dust." She shook her head, bracing against extended arms, but every bit of her body held defeat.

He gave a bitter smile. "At least you won't be the one expected to kill him."

Gioia's head hung between her arms. Finally, she sighed and straightened a little. "Maybe he'll have something figured out."

Dayo mustered a poor excuse of a smile. In this case, it was better to have no hope than any at all. Even with whatever game

Moshe was playing, it still involved Gered. It still involved Rosche going after him. And most likely ended with Gered and the drifter dead. Because no one ran. Ever.

But Gioia looked at him with desperation in her eyes. Like she wanted to believe but knew it was a fool's errand just like he did.

"Maybe he will," he said.

She gave a small smile and blinked away the dampness in her eyes. "Be careful out there."

"I will. Ride safe, *kamé*." He knocked a fist against her knee.

She sniffed and stood. "Will do. Maybe the control will finally go to my head and I'll challenge you when you get back."

He finally grinned. "I'll give you the jacket right now. I'm perfectly happy going back to being lieutenant."

"Oh, who said you were gonna keep the job?"

"Jerk."

"*Nemin*," she responded, perfectly at ease with the traveler insult.

He handed his empty bowl back to her as she extended a hand for it. But he didn't release it just yet.

"Hey, whatever happens, whatever we both feel, we have to make the choice that's gonna carry us through. You know that, right?"

The fight came back to her jaw and shoulders. "I know. But maybe I'll make the choice I've wanted to for the last year. And I don't think I'm going to have any regrets if I do."

A tight smile creased his lips as he released the bowl into her hand. If it came down to it, he hoped there wouldn't be any regrets. Dust. He *really* hoped there wouldn't be.

CHAPTER TWENTY-FOUR

Dayo stood outside the garage and watched Gioia lead Unit Four out of the Barracks. The trainees tagged along behind. He dug out a cigarette, but it wasn't what he wanted.

Sani was already gone, and Dayo felt too much back to normal already. It made him worried for whatever Sani might be bringing back.

"Dayo?" Moshe strode up. "You ready?"

He tucked away the cigarette and the lighter and nodded.

"Okay. I've got to fuel up, then I'll be ready to go," Moshe said and turned back to Unit Two's bunker.

Dayo tucked his sunglasses on, trying not to look up at the command tower where Rosche was guaranteed to be watching. Swinging a leg over his bike, he started it up and pulled on his helmet.

Moshe waved him forward and he slowly drove to join him. The unit leader gave him the comms frequency they'd be using and Dayo switched over.

He kept silent after the initial check-in and for the next few hours' ride east. When they stopped at a refueling station off the side of a lonely stretch of road, Moshe broke the quiet.

"No snarky commentary? I'm surprised." He punched in the

code to release the locks from around the gas pumps.

Dayo rubbed sweat from his forehead with a gloved hand and glared at Moshe, turning his attention instead to filling up his tank.

Moshe leaned against his bike as he waited for the pump to finish. "Well?"

Shaking his head, Dayo finally turned to the other man. "What do you want me to say, Moshe? I'm so happy to be part of this little scouting expedition to go hunt down one of the few people I care about?"

Moshe crossed his arms. The sling on the front of his bike held an army-issued rifle that reminded Dayo too much of Gered again.

"I'd have thought you would have asked about the plan by now."

"Well, if you're so bound and determined to lord it over me that you have a plan and I'm along for the ride, spill the dusting beans already," Dayo snapped. The pump clicked and he jerked it from the bike and grabbed the extra fuel can.

A dry snort of humor came from Moshe. "All right, I can see where you're coming from."

"Can you, Moshe?" Dayo glared up at him.

"Calm down for a second." Moshe rolled his eyes. "They got a hit in some town named Ames. I've got some friends keeping tabs on where they went from there. My plan is to touch base with Gered and the drifter and see what we can set up."

"You think they're going to go for that?" Dayo lifted a cynical eyebrow. "If Gered gets a whiff you're coming, you know you won't get within twelve-hundred yards of him."

"Let me worry about that." Moshe began filling up his extra

fuel can. "I just need to know if you'll back me on this."

"What do you mean?" Dayo jammed the dispenser back into the pump and the latch clicked into place, blocking anyone but the gangs from using it.

"I mean, you've been even more sporadic lately. Can you follow orders and keep this under wraps?"

The warning was plain in Moshe's voice. As he looked up, the mask slipped and Dayo was looking at someone just as dangerous as Rosche and Gered could be.

He nodded mutely. "As long as it ends with Rosche dead or dealt with, then yeah."

Moshe returned the dispenser and made sure the locks fastened again. "I mean it, Dayo. No one outside of me and you can know about this."

He automatically opened his mouth to protest, but Moshe held up a hand.

"How do you think Rosche knows everything that goes on in the Barracks? How do you think he knew Gered and the drifter were planning on running?" Moshe tilted his head and Dayo had no answer.

"Someone told Rosche that Gered and the drifter were talking Itan and informed on them. Could have been Unit Five. Could have been someone from Four. You can't trust anyone, Dayo."

"It wouldn't have been Four." Dayo shook his head.

Moshe gave him a glance that held slight pity. "Loyalty is all well and good, but it might not mean sparks when faced with Rosche. He's the real power in this place." He swept a hand around at the empty desert and dusty road.

"Yeah, then what makes you so sure you can take him down?"

Moshe swung a leg over his bike and started it up. His smile became grim as he picked up his helmet. "Let me worry about that, Dayo. I've got the plan, and I need you to back me up to make sure we can pull this off."

Dayo swallowed hard and turned his helmet over in his hands before pulling it on and snapping the visor shut. The road stretched out before them.

Once he thought he knew what loyalty was. But back then he'd been a young medic training to keep providing for the family despite having no magic remnant in his blood. And then a warlord had given the family the option—death, or sacrifice one of their number to him for safe passage, and Dayo's name had been called without a second's pause. But once in the Barracks, he'd decided to befriend a stony-faced and desperately lonely gang rider. Who'd then turned around and left him too.

Maybe he didn't know what loyalty was. But there was an annoying bit of him that was certain he was going to do whatever it took to protect Gered and the drifter from Rosche.

And he hated himself a little for it.

"You coming?" Moshe's voice cut through the comms.

"Yeah. Let's go." Dayo pushed off and followed Moshe back onto the road and toward the unknown.

CHAPTER TWENTY-FIVE

Gered pushed the blankets away and swung his legs over the edge of the cot, rubbing his throat aching from screaming.

Again.

Quiet still lingered over the caravan as he shoved feet into boots, not bothering to do up the laces for once, and stepped around the curtain. He didn't need light to make his way to the door, softly sliding the latch open and slipping out.

Cool night air hit his face in a rush, and he stepped down to the ground. Tilting his head back, he took in the vast expanse of the sky above. The clean scent of rain still lingered, though the clouds had been chased away before sunset. The rusty buzz of crickets rose and fell in the forested hills around the camp.

The family had left Ames the day after the attack, Monifa thinking it prudent to move on even though the officers had been on Gered's side in the ordeal. With the witnesses and Kayin's testimony, added to the fact that the four instigators were outsiders who'd been stirring up trouble for a few weeks in town, nothing had happened to him.

Except that he'd been forced to talk to the officers, and they'd gotten a closer look at the snake tattoo. He'd watched one of the men stare at it for an uncomfortable five seconds.

The elderly woman whose truck he'd been working on had been right behind the officers, bringing his jacket and dustscarf back, along with a paper bag of cookies and a few awkward minutes of fretting over him while Laramie tried not to grin.

They'd taken their leave, and the travelers had packed up and driven fifty more miles. And now, two days later, they were officially settled into the winter campgrounds, one mile from a new town.

Another chill breeze rushed in to tug his shirt, and a light shiver ran across his arms. He shoved hands into trouser pockets as if that would stave it off instead of going back in for his jacket, or even the sweatshirt Kayin had said he could keep.

A huff escaped him as he realized the greater source of his reluctance to head inside. He was waiting for Laramie.

Even when he'd snapped at her or ignored her, she'd still tiptoed out to ask if he was okay. Maybe he'd been too fast tonight, even if it was the first time he'd gone outside after a nightmare.

Or maybe she'd just gotten tired of checking on him, even after everything she'd promised.

He turned his attention back to the sky and the comforting blink of stars gathered in clusters. And breathed. In and out, filling his chest and holding the air to press into the farthest corners of his lungs. Pulling in calm and exhaling the last anxiety jittering in his muscles from the dreams.

A piney scent tugged at memories of long ago. The towering giants had been a rare sight in Tlengin territory, and he'd never really made it up into the Christan Mountains to see the wilder, rugged cousins of the stately trees around him.

The light *click* of the door sent him turning. A small smile found his face at the sight of Laramie standing under the dim porch light, two steaming mugs in hand and a blanket tossed over her shoulder.

Jerking her head in an indication to join her, she sat on the top step. The wood creaked as he eased down beside her. She set the mugs between her boots, carelessly shoved on over her loose sleep pants, and handed the blanket over. He wrapped it around his shoulders. A thick hooded jacket he was fairly sure had been stolen from Kayin kept her warm. Locks of dusky blonde hair spilled into the hood and snuck down over her shoulders.

"I didn't wake you up, did I?" he asked.

"No, I was already awake. I don't know which is worse, dream Zelig or actual Zelig." She touched her throat. The bruises had long faded, but he mentally kicked himself for forgetting them.

"He's a nightmare either way."

A laugh snorted from her. "You're not wrong." She handed him a mug. "Hot chocolate."

"Again with your chocolate obsession?" He quirked an eyebrow.

"Shut up." She leaned comfortably against his arm across the spare two inches between them.

Laramie watched over the rim of her mug as he took a tentative sip. Warmth slid down his throat, bringing with it a creamy, chocolaty taste that lingered pleasantly.

"You don't have to admit it's amazing because I'm obviously right." Her smart-ass smirk shone full force.

"I might give you this one. Might." He took another sip.

She chuckled and took a drink. Turning the mug between her hands, she stared out into the darkness for a long moment.

"It's … it's something I remember from before." Her thumb traced over the rim of the mug. "At least, that's what I tell myself.

So many of my memories came after Ade and Temi took me in. Sometimes it's hard to remember what was the house and what was the caravan."

He drank again and let himself remember. "We'd drink it by the fire after dinner on cold nights. Sometimes Dad would build a small fire in the backyard, and we'd go out to look at the stars."

A sniff came from her. "And heat sugar puffs over the fire on sticks, right?" She sent an almost shy look at him.

"Yeah." He half-smiled at the detail. "You'd get so mad when yours got burned."

She closed her eyes as if that would help her remember. He stared down at his drink, the warmth comfortably leeching into his hands cupped around it.

"But Mom would say she liked them that way and would trade you for hers."

"You and … Dad once tried to see how many you could stuff in your mouths," she said with more confidence.

An unexpected laugh broke from him. "Yeah. And we both felt sick after."

She smiled into her drink. "You should do that more often."

"What?"

"Laugh."

He rubbed a thumb over the divots in the ceramic surface. It was like, with the attack and the way he'd completely shut down the next morning at the sight of the knife, something had finally broken loose and dislodged a few other pieces as well.

Something that helped him breathe a little better. Working up the courage to talk to Father Amadi for a short time the day before had helped grind more of the edges off.

"I think I'm going to try to."

She leaned into his arm again. "Good."

As she yawned, he noticed the dark circles beginning to edge under her eyes.

"Hey," he began gently. "I know I'm not the best at stuff like this, but if you need to talk about anything that happened at the Barracks, I'll listen."

She propped her chin in hand as she angled her head to better regard him. "Thanks. Might have to take you up on that if Rosche decides to invade again."

"Again?" He shifted toward her.

"Yeah." She sighed and tipped another drink. "I hadn't really had one since you were in the med center, but hearing he might be on the hunt brought back some unpleasant memories of the race."

Gered stared down at his mug. And she probably hadn't said anything because she was the kind of person to worry about him instead.

"I probably should have just killed him, shouldn't I?" The words strangled from her, rushing to squeeze at his chest.

He would have. Without a second's hesitation.

"Mercy isn't weakness." Even if the opposite had been cut into him for years.

"What about justice? Don't tell me he wouldn't deserve a bullet in his head?"

"No." He paused before speaking again. "The Tlengin have a saying—more of a belief, really—that everyone has a bullet with their name on it. And one day it'll fly and there's nothing you can do to stop it. Living among them and in the Barracks, it's not hard to believe. This is the first place in a long time where I don't think that."

A faint smile touched her face, encouraging him to keep going.

"But for someone like Rosche, that's true. So maybe that bullet just wasn't in your gun. But it's out there, waiting for him."

"And he won't be able to outrun it when it comes?" A bit of fierceness came into her voice.

He shook his head.

"Part of me hopes I'm there to see it."

He hoped the opposite. Because he didn't want her to have to cross paths with the warlord ever again.

But he understood the sentiment.

"Hey, how do you think they're doing?" Laramie tucked hands further into her jacket sleeves and cradled the mug.

Gioia. Dayo.

An unexpected ache surfaced to prod at his chest. "I don't know," he admitted. And it killed him.

"Dayo probably got made unit leader." And he'd hate every minute of it. Not only that, but some in the Barracks would see it as an opportunity to challenge. Men like Zelig who hated the fact that Gered seemed to never do much and still kept the position of Four.

"And Gioia?" she gently prodded.

He stared down at the faint tendrils of warmth wicking from the surface of the hot chocolate.

"She can look after herself." He'd made sure of it.

"I think a lot about how I should have tried harder to get her to come," Laramie admitted.

Gered shook his head. "You were only there for a few weeks. It's different when you've been there for years. And she had a harder time of it than you when she was brought in. It's a hard thing to overcome."

"You did."

"Because I was dusting desperate." A bit of vehemence came with it. Maybe neither of them were desperate enough to make it with him.

"But she and Dayo … they'll be okay, right?" she pressed.

"They know how to survive." It took an extra moment for him to say it. And he didn't have the heart to tell her that when someone inevitably came after them, Unit Four would be along for the ride. To make sure that this time, he stayed down.

"Is there anything we could do?"

He jerked his head up in surprise. She stared out into the darkness, gnawing at her bottom lip pensively.

"What? You want to go back?"

"Not really." She gave him a wry smile. "I guess it's been easy for me to slide back into life here and try and forget some of what happened. But after everything the last few days …" She rubbed her nose. "I guess it's a little like survivor's guilt. And I can't stand the thought of anyone with a shred of decency still being stuck there. Especially Gioia. I know how you feel about her."

The snake tattoo shifted as he flicked his hand in and out of a fist. It was laughing again.

"I don't even know how I feel," he admitted. "What the hell do I know about love?" The pang struck again as he said the word.

After he'd found her, blank-eyed in a back alley trapped with two other riders, safety still on her gun, he'd claimed a transfer for her into his unit. Demanding it under pretext of needing another rider. The unit leader she'd been assigned to as a trainee had blustered and sneered, but Gered stared at him until it happened.

He'd taken Gioia back to Four's bunker and gotten her a door that actually locked. Shoved a gun in her hand over and over until she didn't hesitate on the trigger. He taught her how to harness the cold lurking in every person and use it to defend herself. It had led to some uncomfortable questions from Rosche when he heard. But Gered had been able to answer just fine back then because he hadn't cared. Yet.

He didn't notice at first, intent on his own survival. A few months after she'd officially made it into Four, he happened to look up and she was there, new determination in her eyes. He started looking more often. She dogged his steps until finally she blurted that she felt a little safer around him. Him and Dayo.

He'd stared in shock. No one ever felt safe around him.

Dayo let her edge her way in until they were a group of three instead of two. And then he started to feel more secure with her intensity on his left edge.

And the day she made him laugh—really laugh—for the first time in a long time, was the day something changed between them.

But he had no idea about love. If that's what it even was, or if seeing her was just a way to keep his sanity somewhat in check.

"It's a choice," Laramie said. "A choice to show up every day for that person. To have their back no matter what. Sure, you'll disagree sometimes. Kayin hates that I drift." She set her empty mug down and tucked her hands into her lap. "But he still waits for me."

"He wouldn't go with you?"

"He offers every time. But the family needs him here. He and his dad, they look after the safety of the caravans. And Lanre gets really anxious if one of them is gone for a long time. He's been that way ever since they lost their mom when he was a kid."

"What happened?"

"She had a blood sickness when she was young. It came back a few years after Lanre was born. They actually left the family for a bit to stay at a town with a good med center to see if that would help." Laramie leaned elbows down on her knees.

"Between that and Lekan going off to fight in the Cricean war for a few years, it kind of did a number on him. And I care about all of them, so I can't take Kay away like that. But it doesn't stop me missing him every second I'm gone."

The callouses on his hands caught on each other as he rubbed his palms together. "I don't know. It's ... I don't feel settled until I can see her on my left."

His heart stammered at revealing that bit of himself, even though Laramie wouldn't use it against him.

"And I've gotten really good at not caring about things or people. Maybe she got me to start changing that. But it's hard to think that I'd be good for anyone. I think I have too many jagged edges."

Laramie shifted to lean against the caravan wall, facing him. "The best people help us round off those jagged edges into something better. And she and Dayo seem to think the opposite of you."

"Dayo's an idiot." He lifted a shoulder.

Her chuckle filled the space between them. "What about Gioia? She that person for you?"

"Maybe she could be. But the chances of me finding out are slim now. Anyway, she made her choice and let me go."

A snort came from Laramie. "I don't think it's that easy for her. There's no way she just forgets about you."

But his last memory of her was the way she'd looked down at him as he knelt in the dust, bloody and road-battered, after they'd been run down on the highway. It had been anger, sorrow, and acceptance that he'd die, and she'd move on and keep surviving.

"Hey." Laramie leaned forward and bumped his arm with her elbow. "Trust me. I'm an excellent judge of character."

Her grin brought a small one from him.

"I like her a lot. And if you want to take a chance for her someday, I'll be right there with you," she promised.

"Thanks." But he didn't feel like he could risk her. She'd started to feel dangerously like a sister.

A tug at his laces jerked his attention down. A tiny black paw reached through the step slats and caught them again.

"What the …?" He shifted his foot.

Laramie laughed lightly. "Looks like you're about to meet a rift cat." She leaned down and drummed her fingers on the step.

A small furry body hauled itself through the opening and onto the step. It crouched and looked up at them with golden eyes, its whiskers and mouth set in a frown. Laramie scratched its head and it responded with a throaty purr, incongruously deep for its small body.

It butted its head against his boot. He cautiously reached down and let it sniff his fingers before it rubbed against them.

"You what's been stalking me the last few days?" he asked.

Thrumming harder, it settled up against his boot.

"They're good judges of character, too." Laramie watched with a smile.

"Where did it come from?" Gered rubbed down the black-and-tan rings on its back.

"They live up under the caravans. Usually only come out at night to hunt. They're why we never have rodents around."

Gered withdrew and the cat followed, slinking up another

step to sit with black tail curled around forepaws and stare at him until he resumed petting.

"I've never heard of them."

Its attention wavered as Laramie wiggled her fingers. It stretched closer to her, the grumpiness never leaving its face.

"They're from Aclar. When the travelers first came over, they hitched a ride somehow. And they've never left the caravans to spread. Temi says it's because they have a little bit of magic too, and they help the travelers keep it around."

A rustling drew the cat's focus, crouching and watching the darkness intently. Its hindquarters twitched as it sank lower, then it sprang down the four steps and vanished into the night to chase whatever had caught its attention.

Laramie picked up her mug, shifting and preparing to stand. He let her move first before standing on the second step to give her room to go into the caravan.

She paused, hand on the door. "We're pretty close to … to home."

Home. The word settled heavy in his chest. Where they'd both been born and seen some of life before it got ripped away.

"I've been back a few times. I wasn't sure if you wanted to go back at all, but I'll go with you if you want."

He slid the blanket away from his shoulders, carefully folding it over his arm. It might mean confronting more memories. But maybe he should.

"How far is it?" The question bubbled out before he'd made the decision.

"A few hours' ride. There's a bridge pretty close we can take across the Rift."

The edge of the blanket rolled between his fingers. "I'd like to."

"Okay, just tell me when you want to." She offered a smile and started to push the door open.

"Tomorrow?" It burst from him.

She paused in surprise. But he was afraid he'd lose his nerve if they didn't move.

"We can leave first thing," she said. "We can fuel up in town and head out from there."

He nodded. Just as quick, his reluctance shifted to a windstorm of anxiety and eagerness to see it again. It felt like some of his cracks had started to fill in over the last few days. Hopefully he could hold on and not break apart again.

CHAPTER TWENTY-SIX

Laramie settled her dustscarf around her neck and slipped out her bedroom door, knife and gun belt in hand. Ade half-turned from the counter, eyebrow raising at the sight of her already up and dressed in the early dawn hours.

She tip-toed into the kitchen, setting the belts down and grabbing a cup of water.

Ade leaned on the counter and waited. Laramie darted a glance at the curtain. She hadn't heard anything from Gered yet.

"He doing okay?" Ade asked in Aclar.

It wasn't hard to hear every time Gered woke up. Laramie offered a smile.

"Yeah. We talked for a bit outside last night. I think he's doing better."

Ade straightened with a pleased nod. "Going somewhere?" She turned the look at the belts.

"We're going to go ... home." The glass wobbled against the counter as she set it down. Ade's warm hand covered hers.

Laramie squared up her shoulders. "I told him we were close, and he asked to go."

"You sure you'll be all right?" Ade's gold-flecked eyes watched her.

She pressed her lips together and nodded. For Gered, she would be.

"I'm gonna go let Kay know and maybe grab an extra mag from them."

Ade released her hand with another pat. "I'll pack some lunch for you."

"We have travel packs."

Ade's lips pursed in outrage. "Those are not a meal, Lodie."

Laramie strapped the knives to her thighs with a grin. After days without wearing them, feeling comfortable and safe within the camp, it was time to become more of Laramie the drifter and don the confidence which helped her navigate the outside world.

The holster settled against the back of her belt. "If he's out before I'm back, let him know?"

Ade nodded and shooed her out of the kitchen. Outside, Laramie shoved hands in the pockets of her olive-green jacket and strode across the campground to the blue caravan. Her boots disturbed the frosted dew crusting the grass, and wisps of mist twisted away.

A light was already on in the caravan. Probably Lanre fiddling with something. She jogged up the steps and knocked gently on the door.

It cracked open and Lanre's face peeked out. His features softened to a grin as he opened the door farther.

"Kay awake?" she asked.

"Just a second." He disappeared from view.

Laramie stayed on the porch, turning to survey the camp. Mist hung about the caravans and sat heavy in the surrounding trees like trapped clouds. She hated the way it muffled sound and obscured her vision. It reminded her too much of smoke.

"Lodie?" Kayin's sleepy voice sent her turning on her heels.

He leaned in the doorway rubbing sleepy eyes. A short-sleeved sleep shirt showed his muscles admirably. He stepped out onto the porch with her, shivering a little, his bare feet curling against the porch.

"Sorry to wake you up this early."

He crossed arms over his chest against the chill. "Going somewhere?" More alertness came into his eyes as he looked her up and down.

"Gered and I were talking last night. We're going to visit home today."

Kayin instantly reached out to touch her arm. "You want me to go with?"

She freed a hand from her pocket to rest over his. "No. This'll be his first time back." And it was probably going to be as intensely personal for him as it had been for her.

Even the second time she'd gone back as a lanky seventeen-year-old, she'd spent hours curled up beside Kayin on the couch in silence the evening she'd returned.

He nodded in understanding and rubbed her arm. "He going to be okay?"

She tilted her head in surprise. Something had changed between the two men the night Kayin had helped Gered back to the caravans. She wasn't sure what had passed between them, but she'd seen Gered talking with Lekan for a while the day before. And she was pretty sure he'd spent some time over at Father Amadi's place too.

"I think so. We're going to try and be back tonight."

"Let me know if you want me to come over."

"Consider this your open invitation as soon as you hear the

bikes back."

He pulled her into a hug. She looped her arms around him, leaning into his chest and soaking in his warmth. Resting his cheek atop her head, he held her until she felt ready to let go.

"You have an extra mag or two handy?" she asked.

"You say such sweet things sometimes."

She rolled her eyes and shoved his chest. He retreated with a grin.

Laramie leaned against the railing as she waited. Movement across camp drew her attention to Gered stepping out of the caravan, jacket and dustscarf neatly in place and rifle tucked over his shoulder.

She gave a light whistle, drawing his eyes to her before he turned the corner to the bikes. At her wave, he started across the camp to join her.

Kayin stepped out as Gered halted at the base of the stairs. He glanced to Gered as he handed Laramie two full mags for her handgun.

"You have any spare bullets for that rifle?" he asked.

Gered nodded. "I packed out another full mag from the Barracks."

"What about your pistols?"

Gered's hand fell to the empty space on his right leg. "Wouldn't turn down another mag or two."

Kayin frowned thoughtfully and vanished inside. Laramie slid the mags in the extra pockets on her trouser legs.

It didn't take long for Kayin to return, two mags and a thigh holster in hand.

"Looks like you could use this, too." He handed it all to Gered.

Gered set his rifle gently against the caravan and strapped on the holster, taking his second bone-handled pistol from the back of his belt and sliding it in. His shoulders settled into something more confident, and the unflappable unit leader from the Barracks reappeared.

"Thanks." He gave a slight nod to Kayin.

"It's freaking me out a little how well you two are getting along." Laramie watched as Kayin gave the same small gesture in return.

Gered rolled his eyes, the movement dampened in the bruising still around his left eye.

Kayin pulled her in for a kiss. When he pulled her away, he rested his forehead against hers. "Ride safe."

"Always, *ayanfe*." She kissed him again.

Gered fell in beside her as she tracked back to the caravan.

"Ade's threatening to send us with half the kitchen. You want to check the bikes, and I'll get the food?" Laramie asked.

He nodded and they split at the stairs.

Temi had joined Ade in the kitchen, helping store wraps in waxy paper and containers with a cold pack.

Ade took down another container and filled it with some fried *shuku* balls.

"Don't think I haven't noticed he has a bit of a sweet tooth," she muttered.

"Memi, you know we'll be back tonight, right?"

Temi smiled as Ade packed them away. He looped an arm around Laramie's shoulders and tucked her against his side. She leaned into him, watching as Ade stacked and restacked the containers.

Finally, Ade settled hands on the counter. "It's hard on you to go back. And what if it's just as hard on him?"

"We'll be here for both of them," Temi reminded her.

Warmth bloomed in Laramie's heart at the open concern for Gered. The couple who'd become her parents had truly not hesitated to bring him into their hearts as well.

The door clicked open, and Gered's even tread halted inside the door. Ade clapped her hands together.

"Gered, don't let Laramie eat all the *shuku*."

A low laugh surprised Laramie, and she turned to see the slight smile on Gered's face.

"Yes, ma'am."

Ade radiated joy at the simple response. She tapped hands on the counter as if resisting the urge to go give him a hug. Laramie slid out from Temi's hold and picked up the containers, making a show of handing the one with the dessert to Gered along with his meal.

Temi reached out to Gered, and he shifted the boxes in his arms to clasp the proffered hand.

"You both ride safe."

"Yes, sir." Gered nodded.

Laramie hugged Temi again, taking some last strength from him to take on the road for what lay ahead.

Ade joined them, reaching out to rest a hand on Gered's arm. "Be careful." She rocked forward then back onto her heels. "I won't hug you, but I'll still worry about you until you get back. Both of you."

Gered's gaze fell to the floor then back up to Ade. Shyly, he opened his arms a little wider in invitation.

New smile lines appeared around Ade's eyes as she gently folded him into a hug. Laramie hugged the containers to her chest, her own smile unstoppable at the sight.

Ade pulled away, daring to rest a hand against Gered's un-bruised cheek. "I know it might be a hard day for you, but we'll be waiting for you to come back."

He searched her face, his grey-and-blue eyes cautiously searching for any deception. Finding none, he softened slightly.

"Thank you."

She moved her hand to tap his shoulder. "And I mean it about those *shuku* balls."

"Yes, ma'am."

Laramie leaned into her embrace next. "Take care of your-selves," Ade whispered.

"We will, Memi." Laramie stepped to the door. "Let's go before she remembers something else to send with us."

Ade shooed her away, and Laramie ducked out the door with a smirk.

They packed up in silence. Laramie swung a leg over the seat and settled onto her bike, feeling a bit more of the drifter coming back. The engine started up with a rumble, and the itch to roam the road tickled her feet. Pulling on a helmet, she waited for Gered to don his before checking the comms.

He tapped the stock of his rifle slung in the holster on the front of the bike and nodded. She pushed her bike backward, moving away from the caravan and toward the dirt track that led into the campsite before accelerating.

Gered fell in on her right side as they eased onto the highway leading into town. A short stop at the gas station to fill tanks and the spare fuel cans, and they were on their way.

Fifty miles down the highway, a small junction split off, head-ing directly north. Laramie slowed enough to lean into the turn.

An hour's fast riding later, the Rift came into view.

A vast scar across the land, it stretched for hundreds of miles in either direction. Two miles across at its widest, the ragged edges plunged straight down for hundreds upon hundreds of feet where not even the sharpest eyes could pierce the lurking dimness.

At her side, Gered began to slow. She did the same and they pulled off the road, rumbling across the hillocks and patchy dirt up to the edge. He took his helmet off, resting it in his lap as he stared out over the Rift. Laramie did the same, brushing away some bits of hair fallen from her braid out of her face.

"Been a while since I've seen it," he said.

"I never know how to feel when I see it." It was a mix of sadness and horror at the tear in the land. A soft song, just out of reach, lamenting the exodus of magic and the way the world had changed, never able to go back to what it was.

"I know what you mean." He stared pensively, shifting a little to track the specks of white wheeling over the chasm and diving down to feed off whatever lurked inside. "But those ..." He pointed farther west.

The river bridge.

She smiled. When the Rift had opened, the three great rivers flowing from north to south had been disrupted, pouring their rage into the canyon and leaving the lower country desperately void of water.

Then the Itan had come at the pleading of Natux. They dammed the rivers upstream and built the wide bridges, sinking supports into the bottom and sides of the Rift and spanning the width with a system of bridges and turbines to funnel the water back to the lower country and self-generate power to keep a bit of magic still thrumming through them.

The same wistfulness in his face filled her as they watched the never-ending spray misting above the sides as the river churned across, settling once again in its bed on the southern side to make its eventual way down to the sea.

"Can you hear it?" he asked abruptly.

She cocked her head. The roar of the river echoed over the Rift as if angry to have to use the bridge to cross it even after three hundred years.

But that didn't seem to be what he meant. So she listened again.

And caught it.

The hum underlying the roar. A resonance from the bridge mirrored in her very bones, urging a bit of herself to reach out, to run her hand along the surface and discover the long-lost secrets of the metal.

It was the same way she'd discovered how to open the lightning harnessers years ago and repair some of the workings. The first person in likely a hundred years to do so.

"The song of the Itan," she murmured.

An almost smile hovered on his lips. "Try humming."

She smiled, humming a few bars of an Itan lullaby she remembered Ade singing to her. The thrumming in her blood intensified, tingling in her fingers, making them flex with the urge to build, to create with the magic straining within her.

It was another thing she remembered from life before. Much like the traveler camp, the house and the town were always full of songs. With magic bled out, they didn't hold as much power as they did in the old days, but the practice wasn't completely lost.

A breeze ruffled up over the Rift's edge, bringing with it the bittersweet smell of burned-up campfire. But Gered wrinkled his nose and turned away.

"Don't like it?" she asked over the radio as they pulled helmets back on.

He shook his head. "It's not so bad here, but further west, where the Tlengin used to run camps, it smells like ... like whatever or whoever they threw over the edge was burning up in invisible fire."

Whoever. Her stomach drew into a tight ball. He'd told her once she didn't want to know what happened to any other Itan the Tlengin took on the raids.

He backed away without another word and rode back onto the road and to the second bridge. The Itan had built the river bridges and then built more where the canyon walls narrowed slightly for passage across the Rift.

Two wide lanes divided the bridge, its hum not as loud as the river bridge. But the metal and stone components had a shimmer to them that spoke of magic and lost skills. She hugged closer to the center line, something about the chest-high walls still not enough to reassure her of safety over the deepest parts of the Rift.

A guard house stood on the northern end. Two green-uniformed men stepped out, waving them down.

Rumbling to a stop, Laramie flipped her visor open.

"Where you headed?" one leaned close and shouted over their engines.

"Up to Lanton for some business." Technically, they'd probably stop there on the way back around to eat. She couldn't bring herself to say the name of her birthplace just yet, or try and explain it to the guards.

"Papers?" He extended a hand.

She cursed internally. She hadn't thought of that, and she had no idea if Gered had any.

But she pulled out her papers from inside her jacket. It listed her drifter name and true name, registering her home as the town just down the road from the winter campgrounds.

The second guard stepped over to Gered, tapping the side of his head.

Gered flipped open his visor, other hand tightening on the handlebar as the guard shifted the rifle over his shoulder.

"Papers?"

Laramie glanced over, but Gered reached into the saddlebag and pulled out a wallet. He handed over a creased paper.

The guard flicked a glance at him over the paper.

"Mind taking off your helmet? Both of you." He lifted the papers. "Just to check."

Gered was slower to comply, and he didn't take his sunglasses off, expression set in something unreadable.

"This is a few years out of date." The guard waved the paper.

Laramie's heart stammered. But Gered didn't shift.

"Been out of the territory a few years, sir. Haven't had a chance to update them yet."

The guard nodded and handed it back over. "Where you been?"

"Nowhere worth telling." Gered tucked the paper away.

The man regarded him a moment, but Gered's face revealed nothing as he rested hands back on the grips.

"Make sure you get those updated in Lanton while you're there."

"Sir." Gered inclined his head.

As soon as her helmet was back on, Laramie dared ease a sigh of relief. The guards stepped aside and waved them on.

Clear of the bridge, she tapped the radio.

"Sorry, I completely forgot about the checkpoint."

"It's okay." But he shifted to glance back over his shoulder at the guard post vanishing behind them.

"Wasn't expecting you to have papers, either."

A huff came over the radio. "Forged to help me get into towns easier to scout for the Tlengin if they needed."

She winced, glad he couldn't see the reaction. The highway angled north and west, splitting off another road that they took. The Itan settlements had gathered close to the bridges for the inhabitants to keep maintaining the bridges even as the magic faded over time.

Forty-five minutes slower ride and the broken silhouette came into view, exposed in the open green plains spreading away from the river.

By unspoken agreement, they both slowed, creeping along until the stone sign set at the roadside by the Aclar sixteen years ago came into view, letters etched in common on its surface.

In memory of the Itan killed here in Sarzano.

They'd made it. Home.

CHAPTER TWENTY-SEVEN

Heart thudding, Gered pulled his helmet off.

Sarzano. Home.

Half-collapsed buildings sagged twenty yards away, grass and weeds pushed up through the silent streets. Scorch marks still stained the stone and weathered wood. Rusted trucks and a few collapsed motorcycles were visible, the earth trying to take over them as well.

A row of tall pines ran along the main road into town, branches spreading at will, draping long arms over the road toward the houses and buildings on the other side as if trying to reach and pull them into a mournful embrace.

He killed the engine, the sound desecrating the somber quiet. Laramie did the same, her helmet coming off to reveal a jaw set as if facing off with an enemy. Hooking the helmet over the handlebars, he slid keys into his pocket and started forward, feet moving under some hidden force.

The scuff of boots announced Laramie following. He ducked under the pines, the scent grounding him to the earth as memories of blood and screams, fear, and destruction tried to assault him.

But other memories pushed in.

A yard, overtaken by waist-high grass and bobbing sunflowers where he'd played with another kid. There might be scraps of metal wind-up cars hidden in the mess.

The schoolhouse, front blackened and leaves and dust piled in the yawning doorway, where he'd learned to read and write Itan and remember enough years later to write out the verse for his arm.

His feet traced a path until he came to a halt in front of a house in a row of three. Paint chipped and peeled from clapboard siding. Like the other houses, grass had overtaken the yard and had tried to hide the stone pathway from view. Riots of yellow roses clambered on the trellises, taking the place of the windows that might still exist somewhere on the other side.

The roof had collapsed, the door—burned and hacked—had been finished off by rot from the rain which blessed the upper country more frequently.

Staring at it, an odd detachment came over him. Like he knew it had once been a place for belonging, but there was no way it could hold anything ever again.

Laramie stood beside him, arms crossed tight over her chest, a lost look on her face. She didn't know how to belong there any more than the house or the town knew how to hold people again.

He reached out and touched her arm before his feet pulled him forward again. Stepping carefully around the grasping grass and weeds, up the one stone step, pausing to touch the weather-worn door frame, and then into the house.

Dampness trickled down his cheek as he stood in the small entry. To the left, the dining room gave way into the kitchen. A faded square above the kitchen door marked the place the verse inscribed on his arm had once hung.

A short hall filled with broken frames and collapsed ceiling extended before him. Any photographs or pictures had long been taken by the elements. A few more steps to the living room where a couch slumped under the weight of a fallen support beam and the long-abandoned nest of some creature.

The bedrooms were on the other side, but the ceiling sagged in the center and it didn't seem safe to move forward.

Instead, he turned back to the dining room. Smashed bits of painted dishware had sunk into the carpet attempting to protect the wood floor.

He paused in the doorway once to brush fingers over the notches in the frame which charted their growth and the growth of their father as a small child. He found the last notch his mother had nicked in the wood as he'd proudly watched—grown more than an inch in the six months since she'd last measured.

Another tear pushed itself forward, bringing with it the ghosts of memories, bloody from pushing themselves past the barbed wire protecting them. But once free, they eased a sigh of relief, moving about with gentle reassurance.

A faint gasp escaped.

Laramie—*Melodie*—sitting on the counter, licking a stirring spoon as their mother put a birthday cake in the oven.

Dinners eaten at the smaller, cozier kitchen table, now in shambles on the floor.

Scraps of projects laying across the table and counter, both their mother and father bent over them together, laughing as they compared notes, bringing their children up into their laps to show them how the pieces fit together. How to listen to the song humming faintly in their blood.

Races through the house, trying to escape bed, only to devolve into a pillow fight in the living room while he and Laramie dog-piled on top of their father.

Songs and forehead kisses. Hugs and kindness.

It felt too much all at once. He looked to Laramie to anchor himself again. She stood a few paces away, arms still crossed tightly over her chest, staring at a cabinet under the rusted sink.

He touched her arm, drawing her eyes to him instead, then picked his way through the kitchen, through a small mud room, and shoving out a stuck back door to the yard.

No better than the front of the house, the grass there fought with raucous sprays of flowers from the beds his mother had kept alongside the garden. Broad leaves and twisting vines shifted in a small breeze to show plump melons and squash growing unchecked. The leaves of the oak tree in the corner whispered in surprise that something alive had come back.

He sank down onto the back step, leaning elbows down on his knees. His hands clasped around the back of his neck. A gentle tap against the front of his shirt marked the shift of the Matteo medal he'd slipped on two nights ago.

In so many ways he felt like the house—broken and lost to self and purpose. A few more rogue tears escaped and fell to splatter against the stone between his boots.

Laramie eased down beside him, and her arm rested across his shoulders. He leaned into her a moment. Unlacing his hands, he scraped them over his face with a ragged breath.

She withdrew to tuck her arms against her stomach, leaning into them as she stared out over the yard.

"I don't know how I feel about this place anymore," she said, voice hushed. "There's the feeling of love and happiness still in the back of my mind, but my biggest memory is hiding in that cabinet. It just makes me feel … raw inside to come back."

He rested his chin against his clasped hands.

"I came back when I was thirteen. I thought I was old enough, brave enough, to handle it. Temi had to help me walk out. Then I came again, by myself, when I was seventeen. It didn't make it easier. But that's when I decided to start drifting. To see if maybe there were some Itan left somewhere who could help me remember something."

A slight smile tugged her lips as she finally looked at him.

"Just tell me when you want to remember something," he said. "I got good at hoarding the memories away, trying to keep them separate from the Tlengin. Sometimes for years. But I think I want to start bringing them back out."

She nodded but kept staring out at the ragged brick fence still standing against the vines and weighty tree branches.

"How did it happen?" It jerked from her. "How did they…?"

He drew in a breath, rubbing his palms together as he stared at the tiny white flower proudly growing from a crack beside the toe of his right boot.

"I don't know who killed Dad. He was already dead when I saw him again. I think he'd been trying to protect some others."

The medal bumped his chest as he shifted again. The warrior Messenger was the patron of the Itan for a reason. Architects, builders, and fighters.

"Severi was the one who killed Mom," he said softly, his voice sounding more like the seven-year-old who'd lived it than the man of twenty-three who now remembered. "Over there." He pointed to the corner of the yard under the spreading branches.

"He pinned me down and had started to cut up my stomach when he stopped to look at my eyes. Then he picked me up and threw me in the back of a truck." A truck that had backfired every few minutes.

Gered scooped up a bit of grass, shredding it into pieces.

"Tell me he's dead," Laramie whispered savagely.

"He is." Gered tossed the bits away. "I killed him."

"You did?" Laramie shifted a little to look at him with wide eyes.

"Yeah." Gered kept his gaze at the ivy-covered back wall. "When the Tlengin tried to move on Rosche's territory, there were a few survivors. Severi was one. He talked himself—and me—up. But Rosche had already seen how valuable I could be after I took out half a unit with my rifle before they'd even pinpointed my position. He gave Severi a unit leader position, and Severi made sure I stayed with him."

Another grass blade twisted in his fingers. "He ran it like a Tlengin camp—every man for himself. He built up a reputation, bolstered it with me. But I was already making a name for myself. A lot of riders only saw an eighteen-year-old kid they thought might be easy pickings. Or to get revenge for someone they knew who I'd killed."

A breath eased from him. They'd quickly found out how wrong they were.

"About a year in, Severi started getting careless. He was making deals, trying to build up more power for himself in the Barracks."

"Bet Rosche didn't take kindly to that," Laramie said wryly.

Gered scoffed a dry laugh. "Yeah, he figured out Severi was skimming pretty quick. But when he got Severi on his knees, he didn't pull the trigger. He told me to do it."

He paused, the gentle haze settling over the overgrown yard so different from those few moments.

"I didn't hesitate. Severi even started trying to talk me out of it. Like I might feel something for him. I pulled the trigger. Right through the head. Clean. Like he'd taught me."

Another breath.

"And then Rosche looked at me like I was supposed to be grateful to him. Like he'd just *saved* me or something." Gered shook his head.

"Dust." Laramie shifted back, staring out across the yard, her jaw tense as she shook her head.

"Didn't stop him from using a knife on me the second time I tried to run. Severi had told him how to 'control' me not long after we got inducted in."

"Saints," Laramie whispered. "How did you end up fairly well adjusted?"

He laughed—a broken sound. His boots crunched the ground as he bent to tug another grass blade free.

"I wasn't for a long time. The crazy thing was, I almost missed Severi because he was all I had known. Then it was just me surviving for another year, working my way up through the ranks. Rosche started looking at me for unit leader. We were the unit that stopped a traveler caravan and picked up a new recruit. I tried to make my second run shortly after that. Got brought back and got my ultimatum from Rosche—one more chance and he wouldn't be as 'merciful.'"

"And then?"

"Dragged myself back to the room I was sharing with the new kid. He turned on the lights and wouldn't let me rest until he got me patched up."

A smile began to form on Laramie's face.

"A day later, he tracked me down behind a bunker after two

riders tried to take another piece out of me. Sat down next to me and said he wasn't going to let his hard work go to waste. He'd watch my back if I watched his."

"Yeah?"

Now a bit of a smile tugged Gered's face. "Said it was because I wasn't a complete dick."

Laramie snorted laughter. "Sounds like Dayo."

Gered rubbed the base of his left index finger. "I just kind of let him stick around. I had no idea what having a friend was like."

Laramie leaned in closer, a grin still tugging at her lips. "I can imagine Dayo just declaring you to be friends."

"He didn't give me much say," Gered acknowledged. "But we all know I'm not great at talking, so …"

"I do enough talking for the family." She leaned into his shoulder.

He nudged her back. "But he got me used to trusting someone again. Then came Gioia." He paused over her name. Talking about her last night had only deepened the ache. Placing it gently aside, he looked to Laramie. "And then you."

She stared back, face unreadable for a moment. Then she blinked and nudged his arm. "Don't make me cry again today."

He sat taller and looped an arm around her shoulders.

"You're getting better at these." She rested against his side.

He half-smiled. After avoiding contact as much as he could for years, he was finding hugs strangely addicting. They sat in silence for a few more minutes, staring out over the tangled vegetation, a vibrant mess of golds and fading greens as the cooler weather urged it to make way for winter.

"There's one more place you should see." She pulled away and pushed to her feet, extending a hand down to him.

Accepting her help to stand, he swept one last look around the yard and the peace that came with the quiet. They stepped back through the door, taking a moment to set it shut again.

Gered looked back at the house as they exited into the street. It would never be the same. But it was as if the house and the yard had taken time to mourn and had now given itself over to the transformation.

Laramie led the way back to the bikes, then drove around the outskirts of town before halting in front of a vast grassy mound.

She killed the motor and Gered followed again, hesitation marking his footsteps. He knew what this was.

Another stone had been set into the earth, this one with smaller words etched in rows. He scanned the line until he found the name.

Solfeggietto.

"Temi and Ade told me the first time we came that they had no way of knowing who belonged to who in some cases. Everyone's buried here." Laramie swept an arm over the place. "They went through and found papers, if they could, to at least put last names on the stone."

Gered crouched and brushed fingers over the names. The town had housed over four hundred Itan—men, women, and children had lived in the houses, played in the streets, gone out to check and repair the bridges on a schedule that hadn't changed in three hundred years.

And now, most of them lay under the earth because a Tlengin holy man, high on Rift gases, declared that the Itan, who'd lived along the Rift in peace for hundreds of years after building and maintaining the river bridges, must be destroyed for daring to try and tame the chasms.

The rest were in unmarked graves somewhere in the western hills or in the Rift.

His vision blurred and he bowed his head. Somewhere before him were their parents.

"This was one of the last places they hit on that run," he said. "The war had taken too many soldiers, and with Tlengin magic hiding them, they couldn't be found or stopped in time."

Laramie knelt beside him. "Every few years, traveler families will meet up. That year was one. The family had decided to risk it. They thought the Tlengin weren't going to come this far east. But they saw the smoke and radioed another family to come help. It was too late by then. But they found me, put out what they could, and let the dead rest in peace."

Gered scraped a hand over his face, rubbing at his eyes.

"Do … do you think any survived?" Laramie touched the stone to balance.

He gave a small shake of his head. "Not that they took. And I was dragged on a few other runs to know. Not unless they'd gotten out before the raids came."

He was only saved from being killed or hurled over the edge of the Rift by a howling warrior driven wild by the chasm drinks and the frenetic preaching of the crazed holy man, because Severi had found a use for the magic still lingering in his blood.

A tear dropped from her cheek to land on the stone. "Monifa reached out to the families who run the upper country to let us know if they ever find any. Three years, and we've never gotten word."

"Doesn't mean they're not out there," Gered said. "There's places travelers don't go, right?"

Laramie used the edge of her dustscarf to dry her eyes. "Maybe."

He pushed to his feet and extended a hand down to her. Smiling, she let him pull her up.

"Ready to go?" he asked.

Tucking hands in her jacket pockets, she took one last look over the hills. "Yeah."

He did the same, holding a silent *goodbye* around his heart before backing away and settling onto the motorcycle.

By unspoken agreement, they decided to cross back over the river bridge, leaving the upper country and its memories behind before stopping again to eat.

But guards waited on the bridge as they rumbled up—five men strung across its width in a loose line. Unease stirred in Gered's gut, and he freed his hand from the brake to tap the pistol on his left thigh.

A soldier wearing the silver bars of a captain on his chest held up a hand. Easing to a stop, Gered stayed tense, hands ready to move for a gun. The man with the rifle carried it in his hands now instead of easily over his shoulder as he had several hours before.

The captain tapped the side of his head, and Laramie exchanged a glance with Gered before they removed their helmets.

"Help you, sir?" Laramie kept her voice bright and cheerful, though her left hand brushed closer to her knife.

"You two mind getting off the bikes? Just got some routine questions for you." The captain's features stayed smiling except for the tenseness around his eyes. Ready for trouble.

Another glance shared and they stood from the bikes, Gered dismounting to stand closer to Laramie. Another two soldiers sidled out of the guardhouse to come up behind them.

Fingers twitching, Gered let his hands fall to his sides. He didn't want to pull the guns, but he would if he had to.

"What's this for?" Laramie dropped the friendliness, sharpness in her tone now.

He brushed a hand alongside his right thigh, clicking off the safety as he did.

"Just a friendly chat, I promise," a familiar voice said.

Gered whirled, gun drawn and leveled at the newcomer, red jacket unzipped and hands in his pockets.

Moshe.

CHAPTER TWENTY-EIGHT

A sharp intake of breath came from Laramie. Gered tightened his hold on the pistol. Moshe stared at him, unconcerned, as the rustle of guns being raised all around sent lightning bolts of danger through him.

"Easy, now." The captain raised a hand in caution, but his other still held a gun. Gered flicked a glance his way then focused back on Moshe.

Laramie stood to his left, hands out from her sides, but he could practically feel the alarm radiating off her.

"What is this, Moshe?" he growled.

Moshe crept a step forward. "Remember that chat you and I had at the range?"

Gered kept his breath steady. "Yeah."

Moshe took his hands from his pockets, spreading them wide as Gered lifted his gun a little higher in warning. Gered didn't relax at the emptiness.

"These are my friends. And I need to talk Barracks business with you."

Gered didn't answer. Moshe scoffed.

"Look around you, Gered. Even you aren't getting out of this." He darted a glance to Laramie. "You really want to involve her in this?"

It sent his heart thudding an extra beat.

"Gered." Laramie's quiet voice snuck in through the tension. It was a caution and a reminder that she'd have his back.

But he couldn't risk her. He didn't recognize any of the men, which meant they weren't Barracks. Maybe they really were Army. Dust. He lowered his gun and spread his hands.

"Good choice," Moshe said grimly.

The soldiers swarmed in, disarming them both and shoving them away from the bikes. Laramie's jaw clenched tight, and she gave him a look. Panic and some fear shone bright in her eyes. But he didn't have the voice to say it'd be all right.

A soldier came up behind her and swept a cloth bag over her head. She jolted in alarm and Gered lunged forward. Hand to the man's throat in a quick strike, follow up to his sternum to knock him backward. He twisted to see Laramie yanking the bag off her head.

Shouts and the sound of guns cocking sent him spinning protectively in front of her. Two pistols and a rifle aimed right at his chest.

"Don't be stupid," Moshe warned.

Stupid. He'd told Laramie once that stupid didn't survive. But that had been back when he thought he didn't have anything to lose.

"Gered." Laramie's whisper cut through again.

He eased out of his stance, muscles tense as soldiers grabbed his arms and yanked them behind his back. The cold of cuffs cut into his wrists, chafing against the raw new scars there. Laramie twisted as she was similarly restrained.

Fight roared again inside him at the sight of her pale face

disappearing under the cloth. Then darkness swept over his head, and he took a breath to stop the alarm from overtaking him. Hands shoved him forward until a voice told him to step up. A touch on his head sent him hunching forward, and he stumbled up into a transpo truck.

"Gered?" Laramie's voice came muffled to his right.

"I'm here," he reassured. He picked up a faint increase in her breathing pattern. "It's okay."

A sharp jab in his upper arm sent him cursing in surprise. Laramie's exclamation of surprise and the sense of her struggling beside him faded away as he sagged to the side. Reassurance died on his tongue as the drug took effect and he slumped into unconsciousness.

―

Gered's fingers twitched. Cotton filled his mouth, and his neck ached from hanging at an odd angle. He let awareness creep back in, keeping his eyes slitted, a dim light showing he sat in a chair, legs sprawled out before him.

Something was keeping him upright, and the ache in his wrists throbbed a little louder. Cuffed behind him to the chair. He kept still.

Where are you? Severi's voice grated in his mind.

Cement floors, dank smell, dim lights. A bunker of some sort. His jacket and dustscarf were missing, allowing a faint chill to attack his arms. Maybe underground. Who knew how far from the river bridge?

How many in the room?

A faint rustle behind him marked at least one. A sniff and

louder breathing pattern to his right marked a second.

Where was Laramie?

Focus! Severi's memory snapped, and a shiver traced its way uninvited down his back. The word would be accompanied by the feel of a knife against his skin.

You missed one.

He tuned into the room again. A third sound from somewhere in front of him sent his focus honing forward. The click and flick of a lighter opening and closing. He froze.

Dayo?

"How you feeling, Gered?"

No, not Dayo. Moshe.

Moshe, who knew he was awake. Gered shifted, straightening in the chair and bringing his head up. He'd been right. Three men in the room, the other two surprised to see him move. They didn't wear army green, clad instead in black trousers and dark grey jackets.

Moshe slouched in a chair across a table a few feet from Gered. His right hand played with the lighter as he watched Gered.

"I have a headache." He matched Moshe's stare. The ache pulsed just behind his eyes. Dust, he hated being drugged.

Moshe slid the lighter away and leaned both arms on the table. "Sorry. I told them you were dangerous, and they might have taken it to an extreme."

But no one moved to uncuff him.

The restraints held firm as he tugged against them. He shrugged his shoulders, moving against the chair in an obvious attempt to get comfortable. And to shift his hands closer to the back of his belt.

"What do you want?" His fingers swept along the belt until

they found the belt loop. And the small piece of metal folded over the worn leather.

"To talk."

"So talk." The metal slid into his palm.

Moshe arched an eyebrow. "The *attitude* you and your unit have."

Gered refused to let it needle him. Didn't want to think about Dayo and Gioia. Not when he was already trying to focus on Moshe in front of him and not panic about where Laramie was.

"Freedom looks good on you. Is it the drifter?" Moshe wiggled his eyebrow suggestively.

One, two tries before he got the metal into the cuff lock.

"Start. Talking."

Moshe held out his hands defensively. "All right, we'll skip the pleasantries." But he turned serious just as fast. "Rosche is still alive."

Even though he'd expected it, the news still hit like a punch in the gut.

"And you know what he's planning."

Gered focused a moment on the lock, more to try and control the rush of fear and crippling acceptance.

"When?" he asked.

Moshe leaned back, arms over his chest now. "Soon."

The lock hesitated a moment before he hummed to it under the pretense of clearing his throat. "So, what's this, then? You bringing me in?"

"Not exactly. I was hoping maybe we could make a deal."

"Yeah? The last deal we made didn't work out too great on my end." A soft click and release of pressure around his left wrist sent his fingers curling in relief.

"I don't know." Moshe lifted a hand from his bicep and gestured around. "This look like the Barracks?"

Gered leaned back in the chair and it creaked warningly. "This looks like another choice made for me."

Moshe regarded Gered. "Dust, kid. Forgot that your life sucks."

Despite himself, a small smile tugged at Gered's mouth. That was one way to put it. Swapping hands, he unlocked the other cuff but left it loosely done around his wrist while he replaced the metal pick in its place.

"So you're giving me a friendly heads-up that Rosche is coming for me?" he asked.

"You and the drifter. And not so much a warning as a request."

Gered moved, tossing the cuffs on the table. "Yeah?"

Moshe's lips pursed together. The soldiers started forward, one pulling a gun. Gered lunged up, twisting around the barrel and jamming an elbow into the man's throat before catching the gun as it fell.

Pointing it at the other soldier, he snapped, "Touch me again and I'll break your dusting arm."

The man lowered his arms and the syringe he held. Moshe hadn't moved.

"Done?" he asked in a weary tone.

"Tell your boys to back off." Gered kept the gun raised.

Moshe rolled his eyes and nodded to the man and the soldier slowly gaining his feet. Gered holstered the gun and eased back onto the chair.

Leaning forward on the table, Moshe laced the cuffs together before tossing them at one of the soldiers.

"Look. Rosche trusts me because I've done what I have to in

order to stay in his good graces and earn his trust. It also helps that I have a convincingly dirty record from life on the outside."

Gered crossed his arms. "If you're still in cozy with the army, why haven't they just marched in and taken the territory back?"

"And start an all-out turf war?"

"Like guns in Springer was any dusting better?" he hissed in anger.

"That's what will happen if the army marches in. Except it's more innocents caught in the crossfire. What do you think Rosche would do to the farms and the livestock and the dusting oil fields if someone marched in? He'd destroy everything."

"So the governor-general is more worried about resources than people suffering?"

Moshe tossed his arms again. "Welcome to politics, kid."

"Dust." Gered shook his head.

"I didn't think the guns would work." Moshe's voice came quiet. "I didn't want to be in Springer any more than you did."

Gered bit back his angry reply, not wanting to relive those horrifying moments between Rosche telling him to murder two people in cold blood and the rebound of the gunshot through his hand.

"The way we do this is to draw Rosche out. Draw out some of the units. Take him and any contenders down, and then it's easy stuff for the army to get back in."

Gered rubbed at his jaw, shaking his head before Moshe even finished. "How are you going to do that?"

Moshe just looked at him.

"Dust," Gered whispered.

"You made it out, Gered. The drifter challenged him and won. Left him beaten. He's pissed. And he's coming after you and her. I want to make sure that it works out favorably for all parties. Except Rosche," he amended.

His hands curled into fists, and he leaned forward on his knees to try and stop some of the wriggling anxiety. Head right back toward Rosche? Maybe there was a way to keep Laramie out of it.

"What about Laramie?"

"She'll have to come to sell it. I don't want to risk him sending another unit after her. My bet is he'd go after you first. He gave you two more chances than anyone else got, and you still made it out."

And the beating he'd take, and the threat of knives would be the absolute least of it if he was caught.

"Your choice, Gered."

A scoffing laugh broke from him. "It's not a *dusting* choice, Moshe."

He glanced up to see a bit of pity in the unit leader's eyes.

"I know." Moshe sighed. "But this is the best chance we have. This is what I've been waiting for ever since I got myself in almost four years ago. I have to go back to the Barracks, and I've got to tell him something. He already knows I picked up your trail."

The soldiers in Ames.

"Look, I tell him I spotted you, he doesn't need to know where exactly. We'll pick the spot to take him down. Somewhere out of the way of more people. Don't need him getting any ideas about taking more land."

Still, Gered hesitated.

"Look, Gered. I've got as much or more riding on this as you. If he gets a whiff of what I'm doing, I'm done for, and kiss the chance of taking him down goodbye. Maybe he stays content in the territory for a few more years, then maybe he decides to start expanding. Not so hard. Conscript more kids into the gangs, teach 'em to shoot, and bam. You have an army."

"I know …" Gered rubbed his hands together, an itch in his fingertips calling for a tool so he could think better while he worked. "What about Four?"

"What?"

"You take him down. What happens to Four?" He met Moshe stare for stare. The gangs wouldn't get any special treatment from the army, other than a darker jail cell. But he wasn't letting his unit—*it's not my unit anymore*—suffer for it.

"I think something could be arranged. You help on this, you can ask for anything you want from the governor-general himself and he'll give it to you on a dusting silver platter."

Maybe there was a chance he could get Dayo and Gioia out. He just couldn't make the decision completely by himself.

"Where's Laramie?"

Moshe pushed to his feet and jerked his head for Gered to follow. The soldiers closed in behind him, still keeping a cautious distance. One eyed the gun in Gered's holster, but he didn't make any move to return it.

A short walk down a corridor with bright lights trying to make up for the ceiling pressing down atop him before Moshe halted by another door. He opened it and stepped aside.

Dust!

Gered lunged forward into the room where Laramie sat cuffed to a chair, bag still over her head. He ripped the bag off, and her wide eyes met his. A desperate sob broke from her before her body dissolved fully into the shudders she'd kept at bay in her twitching feet.

"It's okay, it's okay," he murmured in Itan, pressing a hand to her cheek.

Lips pressed together, she nodded and squeezed her eyes shut a moment.

"Gered."

He turned to catch the keys Moshe tossed him and unlocked her cuffs. She lurched forward, folding her arms underneath her chest as she leaned atop them.

Gered cautiously knelt beside her, placing a gentle hand on her shoulder as a few more shudders wracked through her body and she stilled.

"You good?" He nudged her gently. She slowly straightened, dragging a hand down her face and nodding.

The instant she looked past him to see Moshe still standing there, her jaw tightened and the defiant drifter came back. He near smiled in relief to see it.

"Drifter," Moshe drawled as if he hadn't witnessed a near breakdown.

Laramie's gaze snapped to Gered, full of questions.

He gave a small nod. "The three of us need to talk."

CHAPTER TWENTY-NINE

"You sure you can trust him?" Laramie said softly in Itan.

Gered paused, matching her intense stare. "We might not have a choice."

Laramie stood, one hand drifting down to her right thigh where an empty scabbard sat. "Let's do it, then."

Moshe pushed away from the door. "This way." He jerked his head back to the hallway. Laramie ghosted to Gered's right, and he felt a little more settled to have her in his periphery as they followed the unit leader.

But the cement gave way beneath his feet as they entered a different room. Another red-jacketed figure stood there, arms crossed and scowling.

Gered's heart caught in his chest like a faulty engine. Laramie pushed past him through the door, trying to see what had made him stop.

"Dust." The word hissed between her teeth.

"Dayo?" The name came hesitant from Gered, the anger leaking from Dayo sending him frantically trying to shore up any sort of defenses.

Moshe stood to the side, watching the two of them in sudden standoff. Then Dayo lurched forward, striding toward him with a vengeance. Gered flung his arm out to stop Laramie as she shifted. And he let Dayo slam a hand into his chest and propel them both out into the hallway.

For a second, silence lingered between them, and for the first time in his life, Gered broke first.

"Dayo?"

"You left me!" Dayo punched his shoulder, anger swirling about him like a dust storm.

Gered staggered back a step under the force. "I ..."

Dayo kept coming, punching the same spot again. "You *left me*. Without even asking!"

A little of his anger transferred to Gered. "Because I didn't want to see you die!" He leaned across the gap between them.

"That's my dusting choice, isn't it?" Dayo sneered.

"I couldn't watch you die!" He needed Dayo to understand that.

Dayo's fists closed in Gered's shirt, and he shoved him into the wall. "Like I wanted to see what Rosche did to you? You left me, Gered! Just like them!" Dayo's voice cracked.

Dust. That close, thin control Dayo had been holding became painfully clear. Holding it since Gered watched Dayo's own father choose him without a moment's hesitation to pay the tribute to Rosche.

He reached out to tentatively curl a hand against Dayo's shoulder. "I'm sorry. I'm—"

"Shut up!" Dayo said roughly and hauled him into a hug.

It took a second for Gered's brain to catch up, and then he returned it just as tightly.

"I really want to stay pissed at you right now," Dayo mumbled into his shoulder.

Something almost like a smile tugged Gered's mouth. "You can if you want."

Dayo moved, pulling away but still keeping hold of Gered's left shoulder. "It's a lot of work, staying angry at your stupid face."

Gered took a good look at him—the new red jacket, the fading bruising on his face, the something he was trying to shove down behind the careless recklessness again. He'd known since waking up in the med center in Arrow what he'd done to Dayo by running. And he needed his friend to know it.

"I should have told you," he said. "I should have asked, and I'm sorry, I just ..." He faltered, but Dayo waited with surprising patience, a new clarity in his eyes.

"I'm not good at this." Gered gestured between them. "You're the first friend I've had in a long time and I ..." He shrugged. "I guess I thought I might not be worth it."

"Not ...?" Dayo stared at him. "You dusting *idiot*!"

"I know." He smiled ruefully. "I'm working on it."

Dayo shook his head and jostled Gered's shoulder. "And getting into fights without me, looks like."

"You're one to talk."

"You were my impulse control. And since you're gone ..." Dayo shrugged, the almost smirk back, but still not quite hiding the something underneath.

"You okay, Dayo?"

The traveler paused so long that Gered almost asked again. Then he met Gered's glance and slowly shook his head.

"I'm so tired of scrapping. I kept us at Four ..." His hand lifted half-heartedly between them. "I killed Zelig ..."

Gered froze, hearing the story in those three words.

"And he's going to make us come after you, Gered. I can't..."

"Hey!" Gered grabbed his shoulders, his nudge shaking Dayo's glazed stare back to him. "Hey," he said more gently. "You'll make it through."

"Maybe." Dayo's face twisted in a smile. "I quit drinking, so everything just sucks more clearly now."

"You did?" Disbelief edged Gered's brows higher.

"Yeah. Got six losers to take care of now instead of just one."

Gered flicked a glance past Dayo. The hallway was empty, and the door had been shut at some point, giving them some privacy from Moshe.

Swallowing hard, he pushed the question out barely above a whisper. "How is she?"

Some of the edge came back to Dayo. "She's holding her own." It didn't really bring any sort of relief. "This is breaking her heart."

Eyes stinging, he looked down at the ground.

"What do you want me to tell her? That you thought of her at least once after running off with the drifter?" The snap of anger was back, but as Gered glanced up, he saw it wasn't directed entirely at him.

"It's not like that," he said, but the rest froze on his tongue. He didn't know what might be heard, and he didn't want to give away what Laramie really was to him. "It's not. She's a friend."

Dayo studied him a long moment. "Okay." He stepped back. "Moshe's got some sort of master plan, and I'm ready to stick it to Rosche."

Gered nodded, drawing up the walls again at the mention of the warlord's name. He'd need them anyway to get through whatever was coming. Dayo pushed open the door and they stepped back in.

Moshe lounged in a chair against the table on the far side of the room. Laramie stood by the door, arms crossed and glaring at Moshe as if standing sentry for them.

She glanced at both of them, silently asking the question. Gered nodded and she relaxed a fraction.

"Drifter." Dayo's voice still carried a hint of a growl.

"Dayo," she returned, not backing down. He softened slightly, offering her a faint nod.

The snap of a lighter flicking open and closed jerked his attention back to Moshe. "You two finished kissing and making up?" he drawled.

"Shift off, Moshe." Dayo strode across the room and dropped into another chair. "Let's get this started."

Moshe pointed to the other chairs around the table. Gered slowly eased into one, Laramie yanking back the one next to him and sitting in it, her arms not losing the aggressive posturing. The unit leader allowed a faint smirk in her direction. One other chair stood empty.

The door creaked open again, and heavier footsteps entered. A man in green army fatigues seated himself, completing the sharp divide across the table. Moshe and Dayo on one end, him and Laramie on the other, and the officer right in the middle.

"This is Captain Ramses." Moshe pointed at the soldier. "He's going to help us plan this out."

"And what is *this*, exactly?" Laramie's voice hadn't lost any of its sharpness.

"We'll get there, drifter."

Laramie stiffened again, and it almost coaxed a smile from Gered. Always ready for a fight. Another thing he liked about her.

"Okay." Moshe leaned forward on the table, tossing the lighter from hand to hand. "I've got the scrapings of an idea here. We want to draw Rosche out. He's already spoiling to come after you two, so there's the incentive for him to leave the territory."

"So just take him down once he's out," Laramie said.

"Guarantee he's leaving Barnes in charge, and Barns'll be more than happy to pick up right where Rosche left off. Or someone else gets it in their head to take over, and we're dealing with a war between the army and the gangs."

"Which we want to avoid, since the territory gets caught in the crossfire," the rumbling voice of the officer broke in.

Laramie darted a glance to Gered. "And that's a lot of people."

He nodded. He'd gotten good about not caring over the years, but it was still towns and people and livelihoods standing to be destroyed.

"So he comes after us." He mustered his voice. "What then?"

Moshe's gaze fell to Laramie for a second. "This is where it might get dicey." He paused until Gered almost snapped at him to keep talking. Dayo hadn't moved, just watched with sharp eyes.

"Rosche knows you're a traveler, drifter. So it stands to reason you might have headed back to your family."

Laramie dipped the barest of nods. Dayo's throat bobbed and his hands fisted on the table. But he was too far away for Gered to silently tap his arm.

"I got this far because I've got contacts who happen to be army buddies of mine keeping an eye on the main roads. And they fed me a report of an Itan getting into it in a town not far from here."

Gered silently cursed the soldiers down in Ames again.

"People around there said you were with some travelers. These are just facts." Moshe spread his hands. "But I also know that the travelers have set up at their winter camp." He glanced to the officer, and Laramie turned a frigid look to the man.

Ramses just shrugged. "The travelers have been setting up there for years. Common knowledge around here."

"Your point?" She scowled at Moshe.

"If your traveler family agrees, we get them to move to a point we've chosen, far enough out that communication with the Barracks isn't going to be easy. Away from towns, but where some army backup is ready. Then I bring Rosche and the units he picks right to your door."

But Laramie was already shaking her head, even as Gered's stomach knotted in trepidation.

"No. No way am I bringing my family into this."

Moshe lifted a hand and continued like he hadn't been interrupted. "The family doesn't even have to get involved. All he has to do is see you two, make his move, and then the army can step in."

Gered willed some moisture back to his mouth in order to speak again. "So you take him down out here. Maybe. That doesn't solve your problem back at the Barracks."

"If it all goes right, I'll be riding back in with my unit. And I've got a plan for Barns." The lighter closed with a snap. "Then I'm in charge and I facilitate a far less bloody takeover of the territory."

Gered curled fingers in and out of a fist. It had merit, but it also had more holes than a Tlengin target round.

"If we get Rosche taken care of, what's your plan for us?" The question scraped from him. It didn't take a genius to see that the military might want him after seeing what he could do with the rifle strapped to his bike. And he couldn't ride back to the Barracks and into what might become a war.

He forced himself to meet Moshe's look, finding that strange look of almost compassion—something that still looked so foreign on anyone wearing a red jacket.

"You take care of Rosche and you walk free. As far as I'm concerned, you got out of the units, so you're free of any other business."

Ramses inclined his head in agreement.

"And Unit Four?" He couldn't quite meet Dayo's intense stare. "We all know they're part of the units coming after me."

Moshe and Ramses shared a glance. "Like I said earlier, you work with us on this, and whatever you ask for, you get."

This time Gered held Dayo's stare. "They get out once Rosche is taken care of. All of them. And they get to go free."

Dayo's lips twisted in a pained sort of smile.

"Deal," Ramses said.

"Okay." Moshe swept his hands over the table, squaring them up side by side. "Drifter, what's it gonna be?"

Laramie's chin jutted as she shook her head.

"I don't like it either," Gered said softly in Itan.

"It's too risky. I don't like bringing the family into it," she said, switching as well.

A faint quirk of irritation formed around Moshe's eyes. But Dayo just watched with interest as they kept talking.

"Can they look after themselves?" He hated how cold and practical it sounded coming from his mouth.

"Lekan runs everything to protect the family. There could be enough fighters around." Her fingers dug into her upper arm.

"What if we could draw him away?"

She swiveled to face him. "Could we? Would he go for that?" Her grey-and-blue eyes swept around the room. "What if you found some spot and just … took him out?" Her shoulders drew up and she stumbled over the words.

Maybe his gun held the bullet for Rosche. He could do it. Pull the trigger and end Rosche. It might be so simple.

"We don't know who else he'd bring with him. What if they keep going to attack the caravans or overrun Two and Four?" He jerked his chin at Dayo and Moshe.

"Care to share?" Moshe asked.

"Hey, you kidnapped us to this stupid bunker." Laramie whirled on him, switching to common. "Wait your turn."

A grin spread over Dayo's face, and a strangled laugh filled Gered's chest. Moshe held up his hands in a mocking surrender.

"Dust, I don't like this," she whispered in Itan.

"I don't either. But he's coming, and maybe this way we can control the outcome somehow."

Maybe there was a way for the people he loved to come out the other side alive. Maybe he made it through without paying Rosche's price.

"Okay." She jerked a nod. "I'll stand with you on this."

He flashed a small smile, grateful she was the sister fate had kept alive for him.

Laramie turned back to the table with a hint of deference to Ramses. "I am not making the decision for the family. I'd rather keep them clear of that psycho and this insane plan. But … where are you thinking we lay the bait?"

Ramses pulled a folded map from the pocket of his jacket and unfolded it on the table. The lower country spread out underneath the line of the Rift at the top of the page. To the west was another sharp line and the word *Rosche* scrawled in on a largely blank area.

He hadn't seen a map from the other side of the territory boundary in a long time.

For the next hour, locations, secondary locations, plans, and counter plans were thrown around. Gered, for the most part, stayed silent, staring at the map. He'd finally started to hope that he could step away from it all, despite the nagging knowledge in the back of his mind that Rosche would be coming.

Hoped that he wouldn't ever have a gun put in his hand again and told who to hurt.

But here he was again, prepping to do the only thing he was good for. Killing.

I don't want to.

"*Kame?*" Dayo's voice jerked him from his thoughts to see the traveler standing beside him.

His heart started to pound, panic welling up. He could already feel the blood on his hands again. See the looks of satisfaction at a good kill on Moshe and Ramses's faces. They wouldn't let him go. He was too valuable. He'd be dragged along to keep killing.

Dayo's hand dropped on his shoulder, squeezing tight and anchoring him back to the world and the musty smell of the bunker.

"We're all walking out of this, *sa?*" The Itan came slow and rough from Dayo.

A breath shuddered through him. Laramie had locked in on him again. Her resolve never wavered.

"*Sa.*" He nodded.

Ramses helped him stay barely afloat. "Okay, looks like we've got most of a plan. But we'll need the travelers' cooperation for some of it. Why don't you two head out and pass all this along."

The officer shoved back from the table. "I'll get you a radio to send word back to me. Then I'll loop Moshe in, and we'll finalize plans."

"We'll need word by tomorrow morning," Moshe warned. "Then we'll head back to the Barracks and start it all rolling. It'll still be a few weeks before Rosche is up and moving, so that'll give us some time."

Words vanishing again, Gered just nodded. Laramie took her weapons and the handset Ramses brought back. Gered's jacket and dustscarf were returned, along with his pistols.

Dayo stuck his hands in jacket pockets. "See you soon, *kamé*." He glanced to Laramie, hesitating only a second before saying something in the traveler language.

She swept a glance from Gered back over to Dayo and made a reply.

"Let's roll." Moshe strode to the door, but Gered paused, leaning toward Dayo. The traveler came to stand in front of him.

"Tell her …" What? Tell her what? Gered swallowed hard. Dayo's features softened.

"I'll let her know you're okay," he said.

Gered nodded, hands shaking inside his own jacket pockets. If it worked, he might get a chance to tell her himself.

"Take care of each other," he said.

"Always." Dayo's chin lifted, the carelessness coming back. And for once, Gered hated seeing it.

"Let's go." Moshe urged him on.

Ramses waited in the hallway with two other soldiers. They both held bags.

"Standard procedure," he said apologetically as the canvas swept over Gered's head.

"Not like I wanted to come back to your stupid secret lair," Laramie muttered through the cloth. A smile tugged at the edge of his mouth.

This time, the cuffs were kindly left off, and a gentler hand on his arm guided him down the hallway, up a flight of steps, and into the sudden warmth of the outdoors. A voice warned him to watch his head and step, and he pulled himself up into a transpo truck again.

Fifteen minutes driving and the bags were taken off. They were back at the river bridge. Soldiers let them out, and their bikes were unloaded from the back of the truck.

"I need an answer by nine hundred hours tomorrow at the latest," Ramses reminded Laramie. She waved the radio in acknowledgement before tucking it into her saddlebag.

A quick check of their motorcycles, and they shared their silent readiness. The soldiers moved out of the way as they pulled helmets on and started up the engines.

The few hours' ride back to the caravans passed in silence. Gered didn't know if he had the words to show how he felt. Or afraid that if he tried, it would only end in a burst of anger or violence.

But the sight of the caravans in the dimming evening light steadied his heart in a way he hadn't known was possible. Laramie led the way back through camp to park beside the cheery yellow caravan. They unloaded bags in silence. He slung his rifle over his shoulder, realizing that they hadn't stopped to eat the food Ade had packed.

Laramie took the lead up the steps and pushed in through the door. Ade swiveled at the workbench, and Temi looked up from the kitchen where he was elbows-deep in soap suds and dishes.

"You're back!" Ade beamed and another piece of him settled.

But Ade and Temi's smiles dimmed and faded at the sight of their faces.

"What happened?" Temi strode toward them, toweling off his hands.

"Can you get Monifa and Lekan over here?" Laramie's voice trembled for the first time since he'd raced to her side in the dim bunker. "We need to talk."

CHAPTER THIRTY

"What happened? Are you two all right?" Ade rushed to them. Laramie's chin trembled and she dropped her bags, lurching into Ade's arms. The traveler woman looked over Laramie's head to Gered, who just tightened his grip on the rifle strap. How to even start?

"Gered?" Temi's touch on his shoulder brought Gered turning almost desperately to the man.

It hit him in a rush. Seeing his first home, Moshe, Dayo, the plan to take out Rosche. Risking the people who meant the most to Laramie in the entire world. Those who were starting to mean something to him … It was enough to send him rocking on his feet.

"I … we…" His own voice was shaking. Dust, what was happening to him?

Temi pulled him forward into a hug. He thudded against the traveler, slowly unlatching his hand from the strap and fisting it into Temi's shirt.

"It's okay." Temi let him stay, somehow folding his arms around Gered's rifle and bag still tucked under one arm.

A gentle touch on his shoulder brought his head up to see Ade's concern. Laramie was scrubbing at her face and red-rimmed eyes. Gered didn't realize he'd moved, but somehow Temi had surrendered him to Ade's hold.

It threatened to undo him. He didn't even want to try and put up the shields which had gotten him through countless debriefs before. Like her husband, Ade let him stay until he felt strong enough to step away. Her face blurred in front of him before a hard blink cleared his vision.

Laramie leaned against Temi.

"Something happened," Ade stated. "More than just going to Sarzano."

He nodded, but still couldn't find his voice. Laramie sniffed again and stooped to pick up her bags.

"Something big happened. And we need to talk with Monifa and Lekan," she said again.

"I'll go get them." Temi squeezed her shoulder.

"Go put your things away and clean up." Ade waved them away from the door.

Wordlessly, they obeyed. Gered stepped behind the curtain of his small room and carefully racked his rifle. He stared at it on the wall, wondering how long it would be until he slung it over his shoulder and tried to outrun fate again.

Three times he'd tried to run. Succeeded once, and only because of Laramie. Rosche was coming, and if he thought Gered cared about anything, he'd use it to try and get to him.

"Gered?"

He glanced over his shoulder where Laramie leaned in the doorway.

"I didn't really ask before. You okay?"

In the few months since he'd known her, she'd already seen him at a low point several times. But this was something different.

"Hey!" Her gentle voice brought him back to focus on her, now at his side. "What's going on?"

He shook his head slightly. How she could go from her own spiral to caring about him so fast...

"I don't want to kill again. I don't..." His hands were shaking. "What if I'm never really going to be out?"

Calloused hands closed over his, squeezing tight.

"You're stuck with me, yeah?" Laramie didn't waver. "So that means I'm at your side the second someone tries to make you do something you don't want to. I didn't haul us out of the Barracks to see you get drawn back into someone's war or campaign, okay? We got out, and we're gonna stay out. *Sa?*"

"Lodie?" Kayin's voice accompanied the clack of the door.

Laramie's eyes flicked toward the sound but then returned to Gered, her hands not loosening their grip until he nodded.

"*Sa.*" Then he nudged her away. "Go on, drifter."

She probably wanted her boyfriend more than someone tenuously holding on to their sanity. Laramie quirked a quick smile and squeezed again.

"We're going to get her out. We'll get them both out."

She stepped back around the curtain, leaving Gered staring after her. Slowly, he scraped a hand across his face, willing his traitor emotions back into submission. It took another minute before he could bring himself to leave the small sanctuary and head back out to face the travelers.

Monifa and Lekan were already there, standing with Ade and Temi who were shrugging and looking to where Laramie sat on the couch in Kayin's protective hold. As soon as Gered's boots scuffed the wooden floor, all eyes turned to him.

Swallowing hard, he kept coming. But there was no anger

in their faces. Even Kayin looked concerned for him. Laramie pushed herself up a little taller, but not too far from Kayin so his arm stayed around her shoulder.

She patted the cushion next to her, and Gered slowly went to sit on the edge of the couch. The others pulled up chairs in a half-circle around them.

"What's going on, Lodie?" Monifa asked.

Laramie's hands scraped together, and the churning started up again in Gered's stomach. Should he just offer to leave? Try and draw Rosche out himself?

"You all know some version of what happened when I was gone." Her voice trembled a little and she glanced to Gered for support. But he didn't know what to give.

"There's a rule there that no one runs. We were the first to manage it. Gered even tried twice before and didn't make it ..." Her throat bobbed and Gered stared at his hands. "To get out, I challenged Rosche to a race and managed to push him off the side of a cliff."

It sounded so simple, but she'd told him every detail of the harrowing race when he was still recovering in the Arrow med center.

Monifa nodded, not losing any focus. Lekan crossed his arms, face unreadable.

"On our way back today, we got stopped at the river bridge. And ..."

"One of the unit commanders was there," Gered picked up as she trailed off. Laramie jerked back to focus and gave him a wavering smile.

Lekan leaned forward on his knees. "And?"

"Moshe's ex-army. I already knew that about him. And he'd

let slip to me that he was still with them and trying to figure out a way to bring Rosche down. He left a route open when we first tried." Gered drew a short breath. "I knew he'd be the one to track us down if Rosche was still alive."

"And it sounds like he is." Monifa was piecing it together.

Lekan rubbed his jaw, looking to Laramie as she curled back against Kayin.

"He is, and he's planning to come after us. Me because he gave me three chances because I'm too ~~dusted~~ valuable and I finally got out. And Laramie because she took him down. Moshe had a … a plan. To work with us and bring Rosche out and take him out."

"Take him out?" Lekan paused. "Kill him?"

Gered stared down at where his fingers curled around each other. "That's the only way to truly stop him." And it might be down to him to do it.

"They want to try and open up the territory again," Laramie put in. "And they want him outside of the border to give themselves a better chance."

"What else?" Monifa studied them shrewdly. Laramie and Gered shared a look. Hours ago in the bunker, it had seemed like the only option, but he didn't want to risk anyone.

"Rosche knew I was a traveler." Laramie held up her left wrist with the bands. "So Moshe's plan, which I don't want to do, might hinge on the family."

She slowly explained the plan, and Lekan's face grew more and more impassive. Temi and Ade drew closer together. Monifa stood and began pacing on the other side of the table.

"We'd have army help?" she asked.

Gered nodded. If Rosche took the bait, he'd bring riders to deal with the caravans.

"What about you two?" Ade asked.

"I'll stay with them."

All heads swiveled to Kayin.

"Kay—" Laramie tried, but he drew himself up taller.

"You'll need someone else to help watch your back. Both of you." Kayin glanced over her head to Gered. The look in his eyes was one he'd seen in Dayo's before, and nothing was going to stop him.

"But…"

"He has to see you two, right?" Kayin pressed. "You can't have any soldiers tagging along. Isn't that the plan?"

Laramie looked slightly betrayed as Gered nodded slowly. Lekan just watched his son silently.

"Look, I don't like watching you ride off to drift, anyway. You think I want to watch you leave to try and stay one step ahead of some insane warlord?" Kayin was facing off with Laramie now, his hand still on her shoulder.

Gered stayed silent. He wouldn't mind some more backup, but if something happened to Kayin…

Laramie looked to Lekan for backup, but he only nodded. "If that's your decision, son, I'll go with it."

It didn't make it sit right with Gered. Lekan was a soldier. Gered had been fighting since he was seven years old. Kayin and Laramie both deserved to stay far out of a life like that.

"Or I could get them to work the plan with just me," he said softly.

"Gered, no!" Laramie whirled back to him.

"Rosche would still take the bait if it was just me. He might leave some units looking for you, but he'd come after me and…"

"No," Laramie said firmly. "I'm not letting you face this alone."

She sighed and looked to her boyfriend. "And I guess Kayin's not either."

"You're family to Laramie, Gered." Monifa's voice drew his gaze to her. "And it sounds like you have settled a bit since coming here. We will stand with you, too."

The burning in his eyes surfaced again as he stared at the matriarch. Her features softened into a small smile, showing only truth there.

"Tell me the details again, Lodie, and we will make our own plan."

CHAPTER THIRTY-ONE

Dayo lay on his uncomfortable cot and stared at the rust-spotted pipes running across the ceiling. As much as he disliked the bunker back at the Barracks, this underground one filled with soldiers and Moshe's special forces buddies might be worse.

He rested hands on his stomach, shifting his lighter in one hand. Though it could be seeing Gered the day before. He almost wished he could have stayed angry at his friend for longer. Gered had known what he'd done by leaving him behind, but the look on his face and his halting apology had softened the anger significantly.

Flicking the lighter open, he summoned the flame, then closed the lid, cutting it off. Over and over.

Now they were just waiting for the call back. The yes or no from the drifter's family. He really wanted to be more angry with her too, but clearly whatever they'd been up to had been good for Gered.

Open, closed.

This was the farthest east he'd been. Farthest he'd been from the territory in three years.

If he hadn't left Gioia behind, he might make his own bid for freedom.

Open, flame, closed.

Except he didn't have a family to go back to.

They were out there somewhere, but clearly didn't have any room in their hearts for him.

Open, searing heat against his thumb, closed.

"I thought I might not be worth it."

"They get to go free."

How'd he get stuck with the biggest idiot in the lower territory?

And now he had to go back to the Barracks, pretend like he still hated Gered, and somehow give the orders to Four to join the hunt for the unit leader they all cared about but who was too stuck in his own head to see.

Open, closed.

Fingers curled around the lighter, Dayo shook his head slightly. How the hell did Gered do it? How the hell was *he* going to do it?

Part of him hoped the travelers would say no. But the stupid part of him still holding on to some sort of hope that life wasn't four walls of hell prayed it would work, that Rosche would go down, and he and Gioia would walk free.

"Dayo." Moshe stood in the doorway.

Dayo turned his head against the pitifully thin pillow.

"They're on the radio." Moshe jerked his head toward the hallway. Dayo sat up and swung his legs over the edge of the cot.

He took another moment to stand, straighten his red jacket, and slide the lighter away before following Moshe to the communications room.

Ramses was there with the radio tech. Once they entered, Ramses tapped the tech's shoulder.

"Go for comms," the tech said, adjusting some knob on a board array.

The channel clicked, and then an eternal five seconds later, Gered's even voice came over the radio.

"We're in."

———

Three days hard ride later, the squat shape of the Barracks, silhouetted against the setting sun and the mountains, came into view. Dayo's heart sank lower in his chest. Only the lurking need for a drink produced a worse feeling inside.

Moshe tipped a glance from his position to Dayo's left. "You got this, Dayo?"

Dayo's hands clenched tighter around the handlebars. Get through the report with Rosche, and let Moshe do the talking. They found Gered, tracked him back to where the travelers had made winter camp. Or would in a few weeks when Rosche gave the order to ride.

Then keep his dusting mouth shut about the whole thing until Rosche was in custody or, more hopefully, dead.

"Yeah," he growled.

Moshe's unconvinced grunt came back filled with static. "Don't be stupid."

Dayo clenched his jaw. *Don't be stupid. Stupid doesn't survive.* Gered's mantra.

Now back in the territory, with the rage-inducing threat of Rosche imminent, the anger at Gered was coming back.

He couldn't even tell Gioia.

The figure atop the wall waved in response to Moshe's signal, and the gates swung open. They rumbled across the courtyard, slim tendrils of dust chasing in their wake. A rider sagged in the posts, and for a second Gered's slumped figure flashed in his head.

He hated this dusting place.

Riders lounged around on the open porches of bunkers, taking advantage of the cooler air outdoors. Most followed their path up to the main tower, the weight of their stares slamming into his shoulders.

He killed the engine and pulled off his helmet, breathing deep of the sharp desert air. Jaan's Wake started to peek out as the sun sank into a bed of orange and gold on the other side of the mountains.

"Come on," Moshe waved his hand.

Dayo jerked his eyes away from the sky and the thought of maybe praying again. Sliding hands into pockets and finding the lighter to squeeze, he followed Moshe into the tower.

In the second it took for his eyes to adjust to the dimness, Dayo thought he imagined a figure on the stairs. But it morphed into Sani stepping down the staircase on the right side of the atrium. The rider came up short, guilt creasing his features before he ducked his head and hurried past.

Dayo stared after him, about to call out, but Moshe tugged his sleeve and jogged up the steps, turning down the hall toward the war room. A sudden, frantic need to do something more with his hands sent Dayo brushing at his dusty jacket.

"Stay still," Moshe hissed.

Dayo jammed hands back into his pockets. He was good at pretending not to care, being a little louder than needed to distract. But he was sparks at actually lying.

Moshe pushed into the war room where Rosche already waited. They both came up short. The warlord turned from the windows, standing tall and with no sign of compensation for his knee. His right arm was out of the sling and carefully tucked behind his back with his left in a parade ground position.

Any remaining moisture left Dayo's mouth. There was no way the warlord had healed that fast. Something had happened.

"How was the ride?" Rosche asked.

Moshe kept walking until he was at the head of the long table and leaned on the second chair from the top. Dayo edged behind, keeping several chairs away from both men.

"Good. Fast."

Rosche raised an eyebrow, barely hiding the flicker of discomfort as he moved his right arm. "I trust it was also productive?"

"Yes, sir. We found him." Moshe kept leaning against the chair, tone even like they were discussing the weather.

Rosche leaned forward, eagerness lighting his eyes. "Where?"

"Two days ride east. They set up with some travelers. Sounded like it might be their winter campground or something." Moshe shrugged as if he hadn't grilled Laramie on her family's travel patterns.

"Good. Good." Rosche moved his right arm with unnerving ease and brought his left up to rub his chin. "Show me."

Moshe went over to the wall and unpinned the smaller map of the lower country hidden behind bigger sheets of the territory and the routes. Placing it on the table, he took a moment to point out the spot. Despite himself, Dayo edged forward another step to make sure it was the rendezvous point and not the actual location of the family.

His heart jammed a second at the sight of Moshe's finger on the agreed-upon coordinates.

"Anyone see you?"

"No, sir. Other than a contact pointing me in the right direction."

Dayo had to hand it to Moshe and the half-truths rolling off his tongue.

"How'd he do?" Rosche's sharp glare descended on Dayo, and he froze under it.

Moshe lifted a shoulder. "Fine. Followed orders and had some tips to give on travelers."

The lighter dug painfully deep into his palm. A sickening smile spread over Rosche's face.

"I suppose you don't have too much love for either the travelers or Gered right now, do you, Dayo?"

Moshe tilted his head to look at Dayo like he really didn't care, but the threat was plain in his eyes. He would waste Dayo if he ended up being a threat to the plan.

"They all proved they didn't really care about family or bonds," Dayo said, tasting the bitterness for his family and spitting it all out.

Rosche's broad features softened into the almost paternal look which made Dayo want to gag. "Proving again that you belong here, Dayo. You've made some very important contributions recently, and I value those."

"Thank you, sir." It scraped out.

"And I know it must not be easy having to track down Gered." Rosche was coming around the table. Dayo stiffened, but the warlord placed a hand on his shoulder, squeezing compassionately.

"But he betrayed my rule, betrayed you." He accentuated with a light shake. "You are doing the right thing. And what needs to be done."

Dayo only had strength to nod, afraid to even look Rosche in the eyes and expose the hate burning hotter than the mid-summer sun.

"I have noticed your dedication, Dayo. I'm proud of you."

Moshe's lazy eyes flicked to his again, the warning reappearing.

"Thank you, sir," he said.

Rosche patted his shoulder and moved back to his place at the table, tucking his right arm up over his chest to brace as he stared at the map.

"My arm is nearly back to strength. We leave in twenty-four hours."

Moshe visibly started and Dayo froze. They'd been planning for weeks at least before leaving. Rosche could barely walk when they'd left a week ago. And now he was moving with no limp in sight. What had happened?

"Tomorrow, sir?" Moshe asked.

Rosche turned a piercing stare at him. The unit leader gave a slight shrug of deference.

"Just wasn't expecting you to be back on your feet so soon," Moshe said.

The warlord bared an almost savage smile. "Not many did. But Unit Four is making up for Gered's mistakes in several different ways."

Dayo's feet locked to the ground. Sani.

"Units Two, Three, Four, and Five will ride with me. Moshe, you will take us to the travelers, and we will deal with the traitors." The warlord's eyes swept up to Dayo, assessing for any change.

But he'd gone numb long ago and could only stare back. Whatever Rosche saw there must have pleased him again.

"We have a briefing tomorrow at eight-hundred hours and then pack to leave."

"Yes, sir," Dayo and Moshe said in unison.

Dust, he needed air. Needed out of there.

"I was pleased with Gioia's report of the route she led." The sly smile quirked the corner of Rosche's mouth, and anger smashed its way through the numbness. "It was very … informative."

Every heartbeat rammed against his ribs. He needed *out*.

"Dismissed."

He barely managed a salute and an even pace out the door and down the hall before he tore down the stairs. He was halfway to bunker four, not caring that Rosche could probably see him, was probably watching out the window, when he came to a sliding, dusty stop at the sight of the figure coming toward him.

"Dayo?" Gioia's mouth puckered in concern as he gaped at her, frantically checking her over.

"You okay?" he gasped.

"Yeah?" Her head cocked. "Hi to you, too?"

"Oh, dust." He sagged over, propping his hands on his knees.

"Dayo, you're freaking me out a little."

Tilting his head up, he dragged a hand down his face. "I'm gonna get my bike."

Gioia fell into step with him, hands tucked in her back pockets, gun and knives in place on her belt and thigh holsters. She kept watching him, waiting for some implosion he would have welcomed at the moment. Instead, he grabbed the handlebars and wheeled his bike toward the garage.

She punched in the code and hauled the door open. Once in, she clicked the light on, pushed the door down, and the lock whirred back into place.

"You gonna tell me what that was?" she asked.

"Just something Rosche said about you."

Her shoulders went rigid as she shifted into a defensive position, feet braced wide.

"You okay, Gee?" he whispered. "I didn't think about you having to report to him … I didn't …"

"Hey!" She crossed over to him, hauling him into a hug. "I'm okay. He didn't try anything."

Dayo sagged against her in relief. "Didn't realize you were such a hugger."

She pulled back and bumped his shoulder with a fist. "Well, it's been a weird few weeks."

A half-laugh broke from him. Dayo scrubbed a hand across the side of his head. "When did you get back in?"

"Three days ago."

"Was Sani back already?"

"Yeah." Gioia angled her head, eyeing Dayo sharply. "Why?"

"When you went to report to Rosche, what was he like?"

Motion jolted through her shoulders, and he hated making her think about it again. "His usual arrogant self." The words twisted and spat from her.

"No." He shook his head. "Was he walking around?"

"Yes. Why?"

"Dust." He stepped around her and headed for the stairs up into the bunker. She called after him, but her lighter bootsteps followed, so he didn't bother replying.

Some of the unit sat around on the couches, beers in hand that they guiltily put down or awkwardly tried to nudge out of sight as he came through. But Dayo wasn't looking at the beer. Instead, he honed in on Sani leaning against the door to the back common room.

The rider gave a bitter smile. "Hey, boss."

Confused silence followed Dayo's stalking steps toward Sani, not breaking as he shoved the rider away from the wall and into the smaller room.

"What did you do?"

Sani straightened his shirt as his face twisted into something pained. "What I had to do."

"Magic tea that has a little something extra in it?"

The look didn't leave Sani's face at the open accusation. "Yes, my tribe supplied the thing that got him back on his feet in a quarter of the time. But if I didn't, he'd go after the entire tribe. Right after he killed my brother in front of me."

"Brother?"

"My younger brother." The admission came pained. "I didn't want him to come, but he wouldn't stay behind years ago."

A knot formed in Dayo's stomach.

"So you'd use your tribe to cure Rosche?" He spat the name like the curse the warlord was.

Sani's features twisted up in a sneer. "One of many things I've done over the last few years to keep my family safe. Just because yours dumped you doesn't mean you get to come after me all high and mighty."

Dayo grabbed the rider's shirt and slammed him into the wall.

"Dayo." Gioia's quiet voice broke through. He released Sani and saw a flicker of remorse in the rider's eyes. But his words came back. As did Moshe's warning. He shook his head, not wanting to believe it.

"You turned Gered in?"

This time, Sani had the grace to look ashamed. But he lifted his chin up in almost defiance.

"My brother has been living out in town since I've been here. Rosche found out, and it didn't take much for my brother to become the bargaining chip. I keep an eye on Four, report anything, and he gets to live." Sani shook his head. "So yeah, I told Rosche that Gered and the drifter had been talking in Itan. He's never done that. I figured they were talking about finding a dark corner somewhere." He shrugged.

Dayo couldn't stop his gaze darting to Gioia for a second. She stood rigid, arms crossed over her chest. Somehow, over a year of practice maybe, she didn't flinch.

"So you'd turn on Gered?"

"I didn't think he was planning on running," Sani retorted. "I was here the last time he tried. I thought he'd learned his lesson."

Dayo shook his head. For all he cared, this was the bigger of Sani's sins.

Sani deflated a little. "Look, if I'd known, I would have said something. Why do you think he had Connor put the tracker on?"

It made too much sense. Loyalty was a tricky thing in the Barracks, and it seemed even Rosche didn't care to keep all his chips in one pile.

"I'm not apologizing for what I did. It's my family on the line. I care about all of you, but in the end, if you make me choose, I'm choosing them."

Bitterness nagged the back of Dayo's throat.

"Well, glad you did because you just put Rosche back on the warpath after Gered."

Because that's who Dayo would choose in the end. Gered and Gioia.

Gioia followed him back through the silence which told him everyone had heard the conversation just fine despite them being in the other room. She stepped into the bedroom after him.

"Want another hug?" She lifted an eyebrow, but the same

anger simmered in her eyes. He gave a sharp shake of his head.

Her hands slid into her back pockets. "How was it, Dayo?" A tremor snuck through the words.

A reply stuck in his throat. Moshe's warning echoed again.

"You can't trust anyone, Dayo."

But it was Gioia.

And anyone else might be listening.

"It was fine." His throat tightened, closing off the words he wanted to tell her. That he'd seen Gered. That Gered had asked about her, that he was doing fine. "Thanks to Sani, Rosche is back up to almost full strength weeks early. We're riding out in twenty-four hours. Two through Five are going."

"Dust." Gioia's brown eyes swept around the room, seeking out something in the shadows, throat bobbing before she spoke again.

"Did you see him?"

Dayo scuffed his boot against the faded carpet.

"Dust." Gioia yanked a hand free and ran it through her hair. "How was he?" She leaned close, keeping the words between them and the motes of dust floating in the pale light.

"He looked okay," Dayo finally admitted.

She dropped to a crouch, hands lacing around her neck. A few shuddering breaths ripped through her. Dayo waited for her to pull herself back together and stand.

"You gonna tell me the plan for getting out of this? There is a plan, right?"

When he didn't answer, she shook her head, jaw tensing. "I'm not an idiot, Dayo. You and Moshe are up to something."

Dust. He glanced around the room, settling on the ripped red jacket on the empty bed. "Look, I can't, okay? Just … just know that there might be a way out for us at the end of all this."

"Don't dusting promise me that, Dayo." Her eyes gleamed bright.

"Hey, I know. I know." He reached out and tapped her arm before curling his fingers into a fist. "I ... can you trust me?"

The tenseness didn't leave her, and she shook her head slightly. "Okay. I don't like it, but okay."

"We're all getting out of this, Gee."

"Sure." She smiled, but belief didn't appear anywhere close to her eyes. His gut tightened, but he kept his mouth shut. If it got them both out, Unit Four safe, and Rosche taken down, then he'd keep it to himself and ask her forgiveness later.

CHAPTER THIRTY-TWO

Laramie turned over, pulling at the blankets twisted around her body with an irritated sigh. It had been three days since the kidnapping and the river bridge, and she hadn't been sleeping well. And it had nothing to do with the fact that Gered wasn't either.

Motorcycles and dust and Rosche and Zelig appeared in her dreams to chase her round and round, the helping hands of Gered and Kayin just out of reach. And beyond them, Gioia and Dayo just glared reproachfully, blaming her for them still being stuck in the Barracks.

The reinforcing beams across the ceiling came slowly into view through the darkness. Tangling a hand in her hair, she blew another sigh. How much trouble would she get into if she snuck out and knocked on Kayin's door? They wouldn't do anything, but she just wanted his arms around her and to feel the steadiness of his heart.

A muffled cry made its way through the wall. Silence followed. Laramie propped up on an elbow and waited, biting her lip in concern.

Sure enough, it came again. Pushing the thought of Kayin aside, she kicked back the blankets and flipped on her light.

Squinting against the sudden brightness, she fumbled to her feet and snagged the sweatshirt draped over the desk chair.

By the time she opened the door, Gered had already flipped on his light and sat hunched over on the edge of his cot, blankets bundled up around him. Laramie rapped her knuckles against the wall before tucking her hands in the sweatshirt pocket, waiting as he worked through a few breaths.

Finally, he looked up and offered a faint smile. "Hi."

"Hey." She pushed away from the wall and came to sit beside him. "You're doing better at that."

"Practice makes perfect, so they say."

He'd finally started wearing the short-sleeved sleep shirt Ade had given him weeks ago. Scars traced over his muscled arms, and the road rash on his right upper arm had mostly faded into fresh scars.

The tattoos on his wrist and forearm shifted as he worked his hands in and out of fists.

"Doing okay?" she asked.

"Think I broke out of it quicker tonight."

"Hey, that's something."

"Yeah." He pushed up taller. "What about you? You seem very awake."

Laramie twitched a humorless smile. "I think you're passing your insomnia to me."

"Sorry."

"Oh, no, I fully intend to let Zelig and Rosche have it when I see them next. Completely their fault." She tried to lighten it with a smile but didn't quite succeed.

Gered looked back to his hands, rubbing them together. "Dayo killed Zelig."

"*What?*"

"He told me." Gered swallowed hard. "Zelig challenged Four and Dayo took him out."

"Oh, dust." Laramie sat back, and they stared at the wall in silence. "Was he okay?"

They hadn't really talked about Dayo, about the whole crazy few hours, since they'd been back. Just sort of kept on, prepping for some of the caravans to leave, training more with Lekan and Kayin, and making sure their bikes were ready to go.

Even though logistically Dayo and Moshe would just have made it back to the Barracks, Monifa had planned for them to head out in the next twenty-four hours to set up the new camp since they wouldn't know when Rosche would be coming.

"Not really." Gered's jaw tensed. "He's not a killer."

Like me. The unspoken words hung heavy between them.

"He say anything about Gioia?"

He shook his head. "Just that she was doing okay. Guess everyone thinks we ran off to be together."

Laramie's face twisted, and she shook her head. "They're in for a surprise later. Or did you tell him?"

Gered picked at a callous on his palm. "No." It came soft, hesitant, like she might be mad at him.

"That's fair. Less leverage someone might have in the meantime."

His eyes went a bit wide as he glanced up.

"What? It makes sense." She shrugged. Relief shone for a second before he turned back to messing with his hands.

A half-smile tugged her lips. If they were anything alike— and the time they'd spent together showed that they might be in many ways—he would want something to do with his hands right about now, the way her fingers were itching for a tool.

"You planning on going back to sleep any time soon?" she asked.

He shook his head.

"Me either. Come on." She stood and inclined her head to the door.

Gered followed with some hesitation, pausing in her doorway as she headed back in. She pulled out a box of random bits and pieces and added her tool kit to the top of it. Setting it on her bed, she plopped down and jerked her head in another invitation.

Bare feet whispered across the floor, and he eased down on the other side of the bed. She pushed the crate into the middle of the blankets.

"Spare parts, half-finished projects, or things that haven't yet worked out the way I want them to. Sometimes I pull them back out just to try again when I'm bored or need something to do with my hands."

His bare quirk of a smile appeared, brightening the blue in his eyes behind the rings of exhaustion and worry. Wordlessly, they both began to dig through the crate and set to work. Laramie tucked her feet up cross-legged on the bed, flipping open the tool kit to rest between them.

Laramie let her fingers guide her, the song lurking inside her blood drawing her to each piece. She worked until her eyelids grew heavy and she finally put down her project and curled up on her side of the bed, sleepily telling Gered he didn't have to leave. He stayed, and she watched him work until sleep pulled her in.

When she dragged her eyes back open, sunlight fell through her open door in a wide swatch from the windows in the living area. She tugged at the blanket she didn't remember pulling over herself before she'd fallen asleep.

Rolling over, she saw the empty side of the bed first. The crate was gone, the spare parts cleaned away. She pushed up on an elbow. The only thing on the bed was the almost-finished sphere she'd been working on, her tool kit, and something else atop the leather kit.

Coming all the way up to sitting, she picked up the small conical item. Turning it over in her hands, she tried to make sense of it. A small lever near the bottom of the piece turned up at her inspection. She nudged it upward and the cone whirred and clicked, opening and unfolding itself into a rose of copper wires and gears, a few bright bits of glass which had struck her fancy years ago threaded through and catching a bit of the morning sunlight.

She stared at the flower now taking up her entire palm and tears budded. He'd made a rose. The man who thought he was only good for death and destruction and hurting had made a rose.

Sniffing hard, she pressed the lever again and the rose wound up, curling up like a real one would into a bud. Humming a low tune, she turned it over in her hands again, feeling the care which had gone into the crafting, the details, and the one bit of the mechanism which had given him trouble for almost an hour.

Opening it again, she tiptoed to the door. The living area was empty, the time counter announcing it was almost time for Ade to be up and about.

Turning instead to Gered's room, she glanced in through the curtain still tucked back. He slept on his stomach, one arm dangling over the edge of the cot, the other thrown up about his head. A blanket haphazardly covered him.

She leaned against the wall, turning the rose in her hands,

hoping that one day he could see the pieces of himself she was glimpsing more and more of everyday.

Maybe Marcus wasn't buried as deep as he thought.

The little bits he'd told her and helped her remember of their life before had brought a few more things back past the terrifying darkness that swallowed most of her memories of Sarzano.

He'd been quiet back then too, but always ready to jump into any escapade. Let her crawl into his bed when she was convinced there was a monster under hers. Ready to stand up to the kid who'd seemed so huge and was intent on pulling her hair. But kind. Always kind.

It made her eyes sting again and she turned away, retreating before she could wake him up with her sniffs and attempts to corral her tears.

She wasn't sure what was worse—remembering how he used to be or seeing how much the Tlengin and Rosche had tried to take away from him.

He'd put the crate at the foot of her bed. She grabbed her sphere and slid to the floor next to it. The rose went carefully on the floor as she pulled the tool kit into her lap. A smile hovered as an idea formed at the sight of the leather case.

Kayin had made hers. Maybe she could get him to make something similar. Though she might wait on the name until he decided.

A soft knock drew her head back up before she could begin working again. Ade stood in the door.

"Morning."

"Hey." Laramie returned her mother's smile.

Ade came and sat next to her on the ground. "Up late last night?"

She knew what the box meant. It had been her idea years ago when Laramie was first discovering the song still faintly singing inside. But now it only came out when something wasn't quite right.

"Yeah. We're both a little on edge about this whole thing," Laramie admitted.

She drummed a small screwdriver against her palm. Part of the plan that she and Gered had insisted on was leaving Ade and Temi and their caravan behind. Panic had risen in Gered's eyes when the couple had tried to insist on coming. Ade had taught her how to ride, but she was no match for the gangs. And Temi couldn't even hurt a fly.

"Your baba and I haven't been sleeping well either." Ade leaned into her shoulder. "I don't like saying goodbye anyway, but this seems like it might be more final, somehow."

A shiver raced down Laramie's arms. "Don't say that."

Ade's arm wrapped around her, and Laramie leaned into the embrace.

"I'm sorry," Laramie whispered.

"For what?" Ade murmured.

"For bringing trouble like Rosche to the family. If I'd been more careful months ago, this wouldn't have happened."

Ade gave a thoughtful hum. "Maybe. But what about your brother in the other room? If you'd avoided those gangs and got through, you wouldn't have met him."

And he'd still be fighting and killing and losing more of himself every day.

"Maybe," Laramie allowed. "I just don't like this whole plan."

"We don't either. But it seems like the best there is. The problem won't go away if we hide, so facing it head-on is the only way."

"Yeah, but that sounds like work." Laramie pushed a tease into her voice.

Ade poked her in the stomach with her free hand, and Laramie squirmed.

"What are you working on?" she asked.

Laramie turned over the half-finished project. "Music box. I'll need to go talk to Oni for the music part, but I think I'm getting it."

"What song are you thinking?"

Laramie studied the gears locking together. "I was going to ask if she still knew some Itan songs. I thought maybe he might like to hear them again, too."

Ade's arm tightened around her. "I know she's kept some just for you. She'll be glad to share."

Laramie picked up Gered's project and passed it to her mother. Ade turned it over and found the lever. It spun open, and Ade's arm slipped from around Laramie's shoulder to cradle the rose in both hands.

"It's beautiful." Awe made the bits of gold in her eyes glint brighter.

Laramie twitched her stinging nose. "Gered made it."

Ade brushed a finger over the edges of the wire petals. "There's so much brightness in him."

Tipping her head to rest against Ade's shoulder, Laramie watched her turn the rose over and over in her hands, admiring the entire thing.

"I just hope that it will survive what's coming," Laramie murmured.

"I think as long as you're there, it will." The rose curled up in Ade's hands, and she handed it back to Laramie. "And since you're up, you can help me with breakfast." She patted Laramie's leg.

With a mock groan, Laramie pushed to her feet, tucking things carefully back into the crate.

Gered slept through breakfast and through the morning. Laramie took over the table, parts strewn across the worn surface as she kept working on her music box. Ade sat with her, a cloth spread neatly across one end of the table as she repaired a set of broken dishes, sanding them down and repainting designs.

A rustle brought Laramie's head up, and she grinned at a still-disoriented Gered.

"Morning!"

He blinked and turned to the washroom. Several minutes later he emerged, looking more awake.

"Feeling better?" Laramie asked.

"Sorry, didn't realize what time it was," he said.

Ade looked up at him from her chair. "You needed it."

A faint quirk disturbed his lips. "I looked that bad?"

Ade chuckled. "Close enough."

He turned into the kitchen, and it sent a bolt of warmth through Laramie to see him comfortably retrieve a cup of water. Tentatively, he brought it over and sat with them at the empty corner of the table.

"What time did you finally go to bed?" Laramie peered at the tiny screw she was spinning into place.

Gered rubbed at his eyes. "Around four hundred hours, I think." He picked up a small bit of wire and began fiddling with it. "Couldn't take your snoring anymore."

Her jaw dropped and she threw the nearest gear at him. He snagged it midair and threaded it onto the wire.

"I do *not*!"

Ade laughed. "You do, dear."

"Okay, rude! My own mother!"

A bit of regret speared, but Gered continued like he hadn't noticed. "Surprised Gioia didn't kick you out."

"Um … we're getting the true answer from her." Laramie waggled the screwdriver at him. The almost smile appeared again.

"Who's Gioia?" Ade paused in interest, holding two pieces of cup together to let the glue set.

They both hesitated and Laramie answered first, since it looked like Gered was still trying to sort it out. "Someone we're hoping to get out of the gangs when all this goes down."

Ade nodded, approval in the tight set of her jaw brought on when the gangs were mentioned.

Gered spun the gear between his fingers. "She's … important to me."

Laramie flashed a small smile.

"Then she sounds like someone I'd like to meet," Ade said.

His fingers stilled over the pieces, then he offered her a smile. The quiet was broken by Temi stomping his way in through the door.

"No one told me we were having a family meeting." He made his way over to press a kiss against the cheek Ade tipped up to him. He circled around to tap Gered's shoulder.

"Morning."

"Sir." But the word had an easiness to it. Temi flashed his wide smile, taking it as a victory after all the days of near-silence from Gered.

"Baba, I'm being slandered," Laramie said, tilting her forehead up for his kiss. "Do I snore?"

Temi stared at her a moment, then dusted his hands in a brisk manner. "Who wants lunch?"

"Rude!" Laramie drummed her fist against the table in offense.

A lower rumble joined Ade's laugh, and the blue gleamed bright in Gered's eyes with his amusement. She stuck her tongue at him, only making him chuckle again.

"But who wants food?" Temi asked.

"Are you making lunch, love of my life?" Ade batted her eyes at him.

"Anything for you, dearest." He blew her a kiss before turning to Laramie.

"You know I'm always hungry," she said.

"Gered?"

He nodded, then set the wires back down deliberately. "Do you need help?" It came a little cautiously.

But Temi only grinned. "I won't turn it down. Come on."

Laramie smiled softly as she watched them in the kitchen working side by side. He was starting to fit in small places. It was starting to feel like family.

And she wasn't going to let Rosche take it away.

CHAPTER THIRTY-THREE

"Time to go," Kayin said from his bike.

Gered swallowed hard and gripped the strap of his rifle over his shoulder. All around, the caravans were starting to move, breaking out of their circle so the chosen ten could move out with them. Ten to give the appearance of an entire family set up at the campsite the army had chosen. Not all would even be inhabited, just for show. The travelers displaced would bunk up with those staying.

Ade and Temi had opened their caravan to another couple and to Lanre.

It had only been four days since they'd spoken to Ramses and Moshe, but Lekan and Monifa had decided to head to the coordinates. Better to already be set when the call came through from Moshe. But it meant leaving the safety of the yellow caravan, a place he'd cautiously come to think of as home.

Laramie clipped her saddlebags to her drifter bike. He really hoped the lightning booster, the thing which had caused so much trouble her last few days at the Barracks, would keep her ahead of the gangs if they gave chase.

Ade and Temi came out one last time. They didn't say anything, just wrapped him in a hug one by one. Ade pressed a hand to his cheek.

"Stay safe out there, Gered. We'll be here when it's all done."

Temi's eyes held the same promise.

It sent another crack through the last walls still standing.

"Take care, son." Temi rested a hand on his shoulder. And something told Gered he really meant the last word.

"Marcus," he blurted.

The couple looked at him in surprise.

"My name ... it's Marcus Solfeggietto." He swallowed hard.

Ade reached out and squeezed his arm over the Itan tattoo. He was starting to think that maybe the travelers had a bit of Heaven's wings protecting them. Matteo's medal tapped comfortingly against his chest.

"Nice to meet you, Marcus." She smiled. "Come back home safe, hear?"

"Yes, ma'am."

Temi pressed his shoulder again and gave a wordless nod that carried all the same sentiment as Ade.

Gered turned back to his bike as they moved to make a last farewell with Laramie. He caught Kayin's look, and the traveler gave him a little nod.

Sliding the rifle into the holster on the front of his bike, Gered tapped the stock out of habit. Then the two extra mags on the belt over his chest, supplied by Lekan. Pistols in place, jacket zipped, and dustscarf on, he settled onto the seat and started up the bike.

The roar brought a strange comfort. He'd always felt secure on a bike. Even the fall and injuries he'd taken hadn't damaged the feeling.

He pulled on the helmet, making sure the radio was on.

Laramie swung a leg over her bike, and the dull rumble of her engine filled the air. Ade and Temi stepped back, arms crossed tight. Laramie tugged on a dull grey helmet and looked to him, sunglasses obscuring her eyes through the visor.

"Check in." The words came automatically from him.

"Got you here," Kayin's voice rumbled through the radio.

"Loud and clear, *kamé*," Laramie's echoed after.

Friend. Brother.

He was starting to know what those meant. He looked back to the traveler couple. They had his name, and he had a place with them.

Time to make sure it all stayed safe. The visor clicked closed and his world quieted.

"Let's go."

He led the way out to the road, stopped and rested a foot on the pavement while they waited for the caravans to finish the shuffle.

"So," Laramie's voice broke through. "Can I start calling you Marcus now?" There was a cautious tease under the question.

Gered looked down at the transpo truck moving the bright yellow home. Then to the open road winding through the trees and over hills.

"Let's get this finished first."

If it went according to plan, everything that was Gered could finally be left behind, and he could keep figuring out how to be Marcus again.

Laramie's featureless helmet looked to him, and she nodded. "You got it, drifter."

It brought a smile to his lips.

Drifter. He could work with that.

CHAPTER THIRTY-FOUR

"Time to go."

Dayo clicked the radio off and pressed it against his forehead. Time to go. He took one last look around the bunker room he'd lived in for the last three years. Gered's tattered jacket still lay on the bed opposite him.

Crossing over, he folded it neatly and pressed it back down on the blankets. "We're coming, *kamé*. Don't do anything stupid."

He tapped a hand against the heavy armored vest strapped around him, then zipped his jacket. Check his guns and knives. Extra mags stowed away. Then he took up his saddlebag. They were supposed to pack out for "as long as it took."

But he was taking anything else he might want. And buried at the bottom was a knife-torn traveler band and a small Jaan medal. If it all went well, he wasn't coming back to the saints-forsaken place. Even if it didn't and Gered was gunned down on the side of the road, Dayo had already decided he wasn't coming back. One way or another.

Stepping out into the hall, he shut the door, the action ringing with finality. His boots echoed into the common room where Units Four and Five waited. They'd been packed up and ready since the briefing that morning, just waiting on the official word.

Moshe had admitted on the tower steps after the council that he wasn't going to have time to get out to the long-range radio towers to send word ahead to Ramses and Gered. Not without alerting Rosche to the entire plan. They had no idea what they were headed into, and Gered and the drifter and their army allies had no idea they were coming.

Eyes shifted up to meet him. Gioia, leaning against the counter, jacket zipped up and shotgun strapped to her back, was barely managing not to look sick.

"Just got the word," Dayo said around a dry throat. "Head out."

No words were exchanged as the riders shifted to their feet and grabbed weapons, extra belts of ammo, and their bags. Connor paused by Dayo for a second, turning his sunglasses over in his hand.

For once, the unit leader's green eyes didn't hold any disdain. Instead, a bit of foreign sympathy lingered there before it was shuttered away.

"Remember, do what you got to do, Dayo," he said quietly, keeping the words between them. "The unit comes first."

"I'll keep that in mind." He pushed past Connor and plunged into the dimness of the garage.

Sani hauled the garage door open, and riders began wheeling bikes out. Units Two and Three began to filter out of their garages. The rumble of bikes filled the air. The units staying behind had begun to step out of their bunkers to watch.

No one made it out. No one. And Rosche was going to make sure that message was driven home. If the plan didn't work and Gered was run down, he'd be brought back to the Barracks so no one ever thought about running again.

Dayo started up his bike and yanked on his helmet. The red wolf emblem snarled up at him from his left sleeve. He'd finally patched it onto the jacket, not caring to pick something else for the unit.

"Check in."

Gioia's tight voice crackled over the radio first. Then the rest of the unit and the two trainees last. They didn't have tattoos yet, but if they rode back into the Barracks, they'd be getting them.

Rosche rode up on his motorcycle, a rifle strapped to the front of his bike and fresh red paint streaked over his black helmet. Going to war.

Dayo glanced up at the deep blue sky as if heavenly beings resided just above the wispy clouds.

Jaan, let this work. Please.

The radio crackle brought him back down to the dust and rumbling engines and guns and vengeance.

Rosche's snarl echoed in his ears. "Let's ride."

CHAPTER THIRTY-FIVE

"That's some impressive hardware."

Gered glanced across the table where Lekan cleaned his own handguns. The pieces of his rifle were spread in neat rows on a cloth. He'd cleaned it once since arriving at the caravans with Laramie. Once, in the dead of night when he couldn't sleep.

"Had it long?" Lekan asked.

Gered brushed invisible dust from the scope and set it back down. "I built it when I was sixteen." It came out guarded, but less stilted than it might have if Laramie had been there. But she'd been out with Kayin since breakfast an hour ago, and Gered felt more at ease with the former soldier and the familiar motions of cleaning weapons.

"Did a good job. What's your range?"

"Twelve hundred with perfect conditions." He swallowed hard, running a brush down the barrel.

An impressed whistle came from Lekan. "I think I knew one man in the entire platoon who could almost match that."

Gered nodded. He'd heard that before. But most didn't have the benefit of a little magic still in their blood.

Lekan checked the handgun slide, tilting it different ways before setting it down. "I know Ade and Temi are hoping you'll stick around. I could use someone to help run security. Most of the men and women who help just have training experience. That would have been me too, if I hadn't decided to go off to war."

Gered set the brush aside and dabbed some oil on a cloth and began the last sweep over before reassembly.

"Get much trouble?" he asked.

"Not usually. Until an Itan comes along and decides to get into a fight with townies." But he softened it with a smile. Gered relaxed a fraction. "You don't have to give me an answer now. And I won't be offended if it's 'no,'" Lekan reassured.

Gered darted another glance at him. The traveler hadn't batted an eye at seeing him bloody and battered on his couch. Had drawn him into a conversation on one of the days he'd come to check on Gered after the fight at Ames. And then had offered the punching bags on the inexplicable second floor of the caravan again.

An offer Gered had taken up since arriving at the new campsite two days ago.

"I'll think about it." He might never get used to having his own choice.

Lekan nodded and they fell back to work. Gered ran one last inspection and then reassembled the rifle. It and the handguns were things the Tlengin had shoved at him and forced him to learn. But with both, he'd taken them and made them his. Found ways to construct a weapon different from the Tlengin. Something his. Something even Rosche hadn't been able to make him give up.

A bang at the door sent him reaching for his pistol laying square to the cleaning cloth. Laramie pushed through, her face white as a sheet, with Captain Ramses right on her heels. The bench scraped against the floor as Gered lurched to his feet.

"They're almost here."

"*What?*" The blood drained from Gered's face.

"Something changed from what Moshe thought. Rosche left right away. Moshe couldn't get to the radio towers to send word ahead. The best he could do was a short-range signal. Ten miles at most."

Gered yanked up his pistol and started checking mags. "Nothing's ready."

"I know!" Ramses's frustration only held a fraction of the panic rising in Gered. The backup troops hadn't arrived, thinking they still had time.

A burst of profanity escaped as Gered shoved pistols into holsters and started racking bullets back into the spare rifle mags he'd intended to clean.

"Bikes fueled?" He looked to Laramie.

She nodded, lips pressed tight together.

"I was only able to get a small group of twelve out here with me," Ramses said, tossing the belt Gered reached for. He clipped the mags on and reached for his jacket, sliding it on. "We're getting others mustered up, but Moshe said they've spread their forces out."

Laramie still hadn't moved. Gered hissed frustration and tossed her two loaded handgun mags. "Get Kayin and get to the bikes!"

The rifle settled over his shoulder. Laramie lurched for the door.

"What's the plan, Gered?" Lekan reached out to stop him as he strode around the table.

"We'll lead them away. Ramses, can you and your men here help protect the caravans?" he asked.

316

The officer nodded. "What about you? We don't have anything in place out on the roads."

"Then we'll pick a direction, and you figure out how to get some dusting soldiers out after us," Gered snapped and pushed out the door.

Ten miles. The hills and winding roads would slow them down a little. Rosche was probably sending out advance scouts, spreading forces out. Didn't even know how many units with him. Two at least, between Moshe and Unit Four.

They had minutes, at most.

Outside, Laramie and Kayin had their bikes running, jackets and weapons in place.

"Get out into the hills," Gered ordered. "Pick a place you can hit the road fast. We're working on the fly here, but the plan is to lure him away from the caravans."

"Then what?" Laramie hadn't lost her tight-lipped look. She knew as well as him what Rosche was capable of.

"Then we try and stay a few steps ahead. I'll figure it out." He snagged his helmet and flipped the radio on. "Let's go. We don't have time."

Kayin looked past him as Lekan joined them.

"Gered's right," Lekan said. "Ride hard. We'll have someone after you as soon as we can."

Gered started up his bike, swinging a leg over the seat and keeping his rifle settled on his shoulder. "Let's *go!*"

It got Kayin and Laramie moving. One last look back at Lekan and Ramses and then they were driving carefully through the caravans and the sudden bursts of activity as soldiers and travelers hurried to get into some sort of defensive positions.

Out in the wooded hills, Gered pulled to a stop.

"What are you doing?" Laramie yanked open the visor of her helmet.

"Incentive." Gered stood from the bike and began moving about, finding the best vantage down the road leading up to the caravans. Assuming Rosche and the units were even using a road.

"Pick a direction," he said over his shoulder.

"Gered ..."

"Pick a direction." He hardened his voice. "We don't have time. Get out to the road. I'll follow once I've got his attention."

"Head due north," Kayin said. "You'll have to cut over about a mile, but there's a road that heads northwest that we'll aim for. Radio us once you're on the move and we'll be ready."

"Okay." He set the helmet on the ground and started the check on his rifle.

"Marcus ..." Laramie leaned closer.

He forced himself to meet her eyes, framed through the helmet. "Get going, drifter." He managed a smile.

The lines around her eyes didn't shift. She wasn't smiling back. "See you soon."

"Soon," he promised. And prayed it was going to turn out better than the last time they'd saddled up and tried to outrun the gangs.

The dull rumble of their bikes faded as they slowly picked their way through the scattered pine trees. As soon as quiet settled, the throb of gang engines started up.

Stillness swept over him, and his heart thudded painfully into a slow rhythm with every focused breath. Sinking down to one knee, he brought his rifle up to fit into the curve of his shoulder.

One minute later, the sickeningly familiar bulk of Rosche and his motorcycle came into view around the curve in the road.

Lekan and another traveler, armed conspicuously with a shotgun, stepped out to meet him.

Two units ranged in lines behind him. One had three black lines across the right side of their helmets. Connor and Unit Five. The other ... Gered's heart stalled at the sight of the dark line running down the center of red helmets. A quick look through the scope confirmed the red wolf on jackets. Dayo rode at the front, shoulders squared and hands gripping the handlebars.

Right behind him, shotgun strapped to her back and a glint of something silver on her jacket collar, was Gioia. The helmet obscured her features, but he still drank in the sight of her. At the end of the line were two unfamiliar figures, red helmets blank of any sigil. Trainees, dragged along to make sure they saw firsthand what happened to runaways.

"What can I do for you?" Lekan's even voice sent his gaze back to the front of the line where Rosche had flipped up his visor.

"Looking for someone. Two someones." Rosche's voice rang clear from the helmet. Smug. Like he already knew the answer.

Gered eased a finger toward the trigger, clicking the safety off. Two units on the road. No way was Rosche just bringing two units along. And Unit Two wasn't one of those on the road.

Dust.

"Goes by the name of Gered," Rosche was saying.

Lekan shrugged. "We don't host many outsiders here."

"What about a drifter? Pretty young thing. Made for some interesting company." Suggestion lined Rosche's voice, and Gered thanked the saints Kayin and Laramie weren't there to hear it.

Again Lekan shrugged, but the traveler beside him tightened his grip on the shotgun.

Easy. Gered settled the crosshairs at Rosche's head.

One shot. Quick. It was thirty yards, if that. He could make it in his sleep.

But Moshe was missing, and he knew Unit Two was out there. Moshe might want to bring Rosche down, but it didn't seem like the right time. And Gered didn't know where Connor's loyalties lay.

"I'll ask one more time, and then I'll lay waste to these pretty wagons." Rosche pulled a gun and raised it to bear at Lekan.

The former soldier didn't flinch.

Gered almost did.

He changed aim and pulled the trigger.

The discharge snapped across the hills, drawing all heads to his position. Rosche turned his gaze from the small hole in front of his tire up into the hills. Through his scope, Gered could look right into the warlord's eyes.

One shot.

"Good to see you too, Gered," Rosche called.

Gered slowly picked up the helmet beside his knee, still sighting the warlord as he pulled it on with one hand, keeping the rifle steady in the other.

"Ready?" he asked over the radio.

"Not really," Laramie's tight voice came back.

"Well, about to head your way." Gered raised the rifle and shot again.

It sent Rosche yanking his foot away and almost off-balance on the bike. His shouted order was lost on Gered as he surged to his feet, not making any effort to hide, and sprinted back to his bike.

Dumping the rifle into the sling on the front of the bike, he slung a leg over and revved the engine. One look back confirmed Rosche pointing up the hill at him.

Snapping his visor closed, he took off in a spray of dirt and pine needles.

CHAPTER THIRTY-SIX

"You've got a tail," Ramses's voice broke over the radio. Gered wove around the thick pines, noticing the pursuit just fine in his mirrors. "He left a unit here, but don't worry about it. Under control."

A check confirmed that Unit Four had not been left behind.

"Headed north." Gered leaned precariously left to maneuver around a tree, tires catching in the thicker dirt.

He never thought he'd miss dust.

"Got it. Keep heading north. I'll get a troop mobilized. Check in as you can, and we'll track you that way."

A crack sent Gered curling his shoulders forward. In his mirror, Rosche raised his gun again. Gered gunned the engine, swerving and skidding in a zig-zag. Rosche gave up, needing two hands to steer himself.

Dayo and Four were hanging back, taking a more cautious approach to the terrain even though their broad tires could handle it. Or maybe they were trying to give him a head start.

Blacktop gleamed through the trees ahead. He caught the flash of two riders in blue-and-grey helmets zip away. Another rev to the engine spat him out on the road, and he accelerated on the smooth surface, his bike jumping forward eagerly.

He stayed a few feet behind Laramie and Kayin, matching each turn and twist of the road. It didn't take long for pursuit to appear in his mirror again.

"They're coming," he said.

"This is uncomfortably familiar," Laramie said rigidly, humor probably supposed to be in there somewhere.

"Just got to stay ahead of them until Ramses gets into action," he replied.

"We know when that is?" Kayin interjected.

Silence fell over the radio, Gered having no answer.

A muttered Aclar oath crackled with static, and he mentally agreed with the sentiment. A sign flashed by, warning of a cutoff in a mile.

"Oh, dust!" Laramie's brake light flashed. "On the left!"

Two riders roared out from a narrow dirt track. One raised a gun.

"Turn!" Gered shouted, and they swerved and skidded onto the turnoff, leaving the riders braking and attempting to correct.

Sparks flashed on the pavement in front of Gered, sending him leaning left again, away from the shot. He chanced a glance up the hill, and the flash of another gunshot sent him flinching down over the handlebars. Two more riders roared from the trees to fall in pursuit.

Two green stripes ran down the center of the red helmets. Unit Three.

Where the hell is Moshe?

No more shots were fired, but at the next turnoff, another pair of riders blocked the forward road. They didn't move, so Laramie and Kayin led the way right down the clear highway.

Gered broadcast the location to Ramses, but there was no

answer.

"I don't like this," Laramie said.

"This road doesn't lead anywhere good," Kayin interjected.

"How do you know?"

"Because I look at maps, *ayanfe.*"

"*This* time you look at maps?"

"Where does it lead?" Gered cut in.

"Up around the crest of a hill then down to a bridge. Who wants to bet someone's waiting there for us?"

"Dust." Gered shifted gears as the road began to climb upward as Kayin predicted. "Be ready to cut cross country. Five stayed at the caravans, and I've clocked Units Four and Three following us. Moshe's still out there somewhere."

"How many did Rosche bring?" Laramie still managed to sound peeved.

"As many as he thought it would take. You should probably be flattered." Gered shifted again. A yellow sign warning "bridge ahead" flashed by. "Start slowing down, just in case."

They followed his lead as the road wound upward before preparing to dip down the far side of the hill toward the bridge. All three ground to a halt at the sight of the six riders spread across the entrance to the bridge below. Red helmets with a black-checkered pattern on the right side. Unit Two.

Rumbling sent Gered twisting on the seat. Gang riders began to slow and come to a halt, forming a barrier behind them.

Faceless helmets stared at him, and hands fell to pistols, waiting for him to move. He swallowed hard. The bulky figure of Rosche slowly wove through the bikes.

"Kayin, how good are you on a bike?" he asked, tracking Rosche's approach. He figured Laramie could make it. He could make it.

In answer, Kayin revved his engine, and he and Laramie took off down the side of the hill. Riders startled, whipping heads to follow their plunging descent. Gered waited. Waited. Rosche hadn't taken his focus off him.

He could take him out now. And then be shot by Unit Three riders, letting Laramie and Kayin be picked off at their leisure. As long as Rosche was alive and they stayed ahead of the gangs, they had a chance.

Because Rosche would want him alive.

Cursing into his helmet, he gunned the engine and jumped his bike over the edge. His tires hit and skidded in the loose dirt. Grasping brush scraped his boots and trousers. It took every ounce of focus to lean and turn around the boulders and loose rocks, finding the easiest path down.

Laramie and Kayin had made it safely and waited.

"Go!" he screamed through the radio, jamming his foot into the ground to keep himself upright as he swerved around a larger rock the crumbling hillside threw him toward.

They obeyed, lurching forward in spurts of dust. Finally he hit more level ground, and a glance in the mirrors showed some of Unit Three and Two making the same descent.

Open ground stretched in front of them, the same coarse dirt and brush scattered across it, thicker grass trying to hold the rest down in patches.

"Where's the next road?" Gered asked breathlessly.

"Should be able to cut straight ahead and get back to the thirty-three cutoff we were rerouted from," Kayin said, skirting a larger section of brush.

"Okay. Let's try and lose them in those trees."

Another wall of pine and red oak rose a hundred yards ahead.

"Gered!" A new voice cut into his radio, sending him flinching.

"Moshe?"

"Yeah!" The unit leader sounded breathless. "Finally got in touch with Ramses and he gave me your frequency. Where the hell are you, kid?"

"I could ask you the same damn question!" Gered shifted and his rear tire ground out of a softer patch of dirt.

"I know!"

"We're off-road, trying to get back to the thirty-three cutoff."

"Dust! Rosche is sending riders over there to head you off. He's not too far behind."

"We don't have a lot of dusting options here, Moshe!" Gered snarled, entering the tree line which had lost the allure of safety.

"Just keep stalling however you can. Ramses got some more men mobilized and headed to you. Rosche called us all in, so I'm headed that way with the rest of my unit."

"Hurry," Gered said grimly.

"Trying, Gered. Just hang on."

"You both hear that?" Gered asked.

"Yeah, not too encouraging," Laramie replied.

"We got incoming," Kayin interrupted.

"Go right." Gered skidded around a broad red oak, changing direction away from the incoming Unit Three riders, Laramie and Kayin following in sync.

But it placed them perpendicular to the riders coming after them.

Ahead of him, Laramie jumped her bike over a fallen tree. Kayin ducked under some low-hanging branches. Futility swept over him.

No one got out.

Gritting his teeth, he slammed on the brakes, spinning his motorcycle sideways and kicking the stand down. Yanking the rifle free, he slid off and knelt with the bike between him and the oncoming riders.

"Gered!" The rest of Laramie's frantic call was lost as he tossed the helmet down. Settling the rifle into his shoulder and nestling his cheek against the stock, he took aim.

Its roar echoed through the woods as the bullet pierced the front tire of the closest rider, flipping him over the handlebars to the ground. The rider's companion drew a pistol. Gered pulled the trigger and the rider tumbled off the back of the motorcycle. It wobbled forward before thudding to the ground.

Clearing the chamber, he changed aim. But the six riders coming from the hill had seen their companions fall. They slammed brakes and came to a halt, withdrawing into more cover.

Staying low, Gered began to back away from his bike, vanishing into the heavier cover of the trees.

The sharper crack of handguns and pings of bullets against metal confirmed his decision. Ghosting off to his left, he found a better angle and unloaded another two rounds. Splinters flew as one bullet impacted a tree, and a rider staggered back, taking the second bullet in his arm.

Changing positions again, Gered cut farther left.

"Gered!" Laramie hissed from somewhere behind him. He glanced over his shoulder to see her and Kayin crouched behind trees, guns in hand. "What are you doing?"

"What are you two doing?" he whispered furiously. "You should have kept going!"

"Not a chance." Laramie's jaw set. "What's the plan?"

Gered turned back, settling his cheek back against the gun. "Keep stalling." The recoil from his next shot rocked through his shoulder, and another rider foolish enough to leave a hint of his boot visible went down.

The empty casing fell to the ground. As he checked the scope again, his heart stalled. Rosche had arrived.

The warlord stood fearlessly in an open space between two trees. Unit Four was standing behind him, most with helmets off and guns pulled. His chest squeezed tighter at Gioia's features in his scope.

"Gered!" Rosche called.

The other riders fell back to Rosche, still clinging to any cover they could find.

"Come on out, Gered. You can't do this forever." Rosche tapped a hand against the gun on his thigh.

Gered adjusted his grip on the rifle, trying to keep his focus.

"Okay." Rosche yanked his gun free and shot Dayo in the chest.

CHAPTER THIRTY-SEVEN

Gered surged to his feet, a scream threatening to betray him as Dayo fell. In a second, Unit Four was surrounded, guns aimed at them from all around.

Gioia knelt beside Dayo's crumpled body, one hand on his shoulder, the other reaching slowly to her pistol, a look of fury turned up at Rosche.

Don't do it, he silently willed.

"I'll waste them all, Gered," Rosche called. "I know it matters to you."

Gioia began to ease her gun free when Dayo jerked, limbs thrashing a moment before he lifted his head.

A faint gasp of relief escaped. *He's wearing a vest.*

Rosche gave a thin smile. "Dayo follows orders, so I'd hate to waste that. But the next bullet goes through his head." He lifted his gun in promise.

Dayo and Gioia stilled.

"Five seconds, Gered."

Helplessness raged.

"Five."

No one got out.

"Four."

Keep stalling.

"Three."

What the hell was he going to do?

"Two."

Matteo's medal shifted against his chest. *Heaven's wings.*

Swallowing hard, he stepped out.

Rosche smirked even though Gered's rifle never wavered from the warlord's chest.

"Well, well. Where's your little drifter?"

Gered prayed Laramie would keep out of sight.

"What do you want, Rosche?" It took effort not to call him "sir."

Rosche gave him a pitying glance. "You know what I want."

A sharp laugh broke from Gered. "Not much incentive for me there."

A more genuine smirk spread over Rosche's face before his eyes narrowed. "I gave you three chances, Gered. You know my law."

Gered shifted his hold on the rifle, darting a glance again at Dayo and Gioia, threatening to give more of himself away.

Law. An idea hit. An insane idea. But it was no more than what he'd told Laramie months ago when they didn't know each other, when he was just an unfeeling unit leader and she was a strange, bright-eyed drifter.

She'd followed it and left Rosche on the side of the road.

"You gave me three chances, but here I am."

Rosche's eyes slit in anger.

"How about one more?"

The warlord cocked his head. "You challenging me, Gered?"

"I'd rather go out in a fight than from a bullet in the head."

Rosche inclined his head, a bit of respect in the tilt of his mouth. "Odds are stacked against you. Not like you to get desperate."

"What have I got to lose?" Gered willed moisture back to his mouth. "Unless your arm isn't up to it?"

A crack in Rosche's mask appeared. "I'll kill that bitch next," he sneered.

"Yeah? She did a good job of leaving you on the side of the road. Maybe I'm liking my chances after all."

"You plan just to piss him off?" Kayin muttered from somewhere behind him.

"It'll work," Laramie reassured.

Gered hoped she was right because the unsettling light was coming into Rosche's eyes. And he needed the more rational warlord to accept.

Dayo was shifting again.

Stay down.

But Dayo looked over his shoulder, and Gered could see the wide-eyed panic directed at him before Dayo managed to tamp it down.

"One more fight, Rosche."

The warlord stirred and he focused in on Gered again. "Suppose I can grant a dead man one last wish."

He holstered his gun, but Gered didn't shift his rifle. Rosche pointed out toward the open field outside the trees.

"Shall we take this somewhere else?"

Gered nodded tightly. Rosche gave orders and the riders began to move, keeping Unit Four under guard. Gioia helped Dayo to his feet, one hand under his arm as he hunched over, arm pressed across his chest. She still wasn't looking at Gered, though he would have given anything for her to.

Laramie and Kayin joined him as they picked their careful way toward the tree line. He kept his rifle up, one eye on the units and Rosche keeping even with him.

Once in the open, Gered made sure Laramie and Kayin stayed behind him. Rosche looked at Kayin in interest.

"I wondered who your friend was." He shifted his attention to Kayin. "Sorry your family won't be around. Or maybe you'll see them in whatever afterlife you believe in."

A stream of Aclar came from Kayin, and Rosche only smirked wider.

"Okay, Gered. Should we set terms?" His laugh announced he already knew the outcome of the fight. Either way, the loser wasn't walking away.

"Might as well."

"Let me guess. You and your little drifter get to go free?"

Gered dared lower his rifle slightly. "No. I want the Barracks."

Rosche went still, and murmurs stirred through the units. Laramie sucked in a breath.

"The Barracks?"

"Afraid you might lose after all?" Gered tilted a smile.

Rosche stirred, the sneer curling his lip again. "I accept. The Tlengin had a way of settling things, didn't they?"

Gered's fingers clenched around the rifle. "They did," he confirmed. "Weapon of choice?"

The sneer widened. "Knives."

The word pummeled Gered in the gut, and the rifle muzzle bobbled. Satisfaction hardened across Rosche's face.

It took every ounce of strength for Gered to say evenly, "Agreed."

He lowered the rifle and unholstered the handgun from his

right thigh, flicking the safety off. The place they stood was relatively clear except for some smaller stones scattered about.

"Kayin, mark off ten yards and set it down."

Rosche handed off a pistol to the Unit Three leader, the rider moving opposite Kayin. They each set down the guns on a diagonal from each other. Shifting the rifle in his hands, Gered took out his other handgun.

"Laramie. Put it even with Rosche's." His voice didn't waver under the cold sweeping over him at the thought of holding a knife.

She carefully took it and set it down. Another rider followed Rosche's order and finished the last corner of the square. Gered handed his rifle to Kayin. The traveler gave him a nod as he slung the strap over his shoulder.

"Gered, talk to me. What's this challenge?" Laramie was back at his side, panic lurking just under her tight expression.

At the Barracks, it might have been settled like the fights in the arena, over when the opponent tapped out. But that wasn't the Tlengin way.

"Tlengin ritual challenge. Fight to the death with weapons of choice."

It was always going to end in death.

A curse hissed from Laramie. "So what's with the guns?"

"Last resort."

He slowly unzipped his jacket, sliding it off and tossing it to the ground. The dustscarf went next. Rosche undid his jacket, then with a show, unstrapped his vest and tossed it aside like he was graciously putting them on even footing.

The warlord then pulled his large hunting knife and flicked a thumb along the edge, not breaking Gered's stare.

"Laramie." His voice wobbled finally. "Can I borrow a knife?"

Her touch on his arm brought him turning to meet her wide eyes.

"Marcus …" Her whisper threatened to undo him.

He willed iron back into his trembling joints. This was for survival. For Laramie and Kayin. For Dayo and Gioia. All of Unit Four, including the trainees one ride away from being inducted into the gangs.

"Please?"

Unwillingness slowed her hand to the bigger of her two knives. But she unsheathed it and held it, blade down, between them. His fingers closed around hers.

"Marcus …" Her eyes searched his.

"Just because I hate them doesn't mean I don't know how to use one." A humorless smile touched his lips, but his fingers shook against hers.

"Are you sure?"

The Itan settled him. He cupped his other hand over hers, gently freeing the knife into his palm.

"Trust me, *sassena.*" Sister.

Her lips pressed tight together, and a hand touched his cheek, tilting his head down to tap his forehead against hers.

"Okay." Laramie drew one more shaky breath, then stepped back, hand on her pistol and shoulders squared.

He worked his hand around the knife hilt, bringing it into something more comfortable.

"Touching," Rosche sneered as he stepped into the square.

Gered reached up to tap the medal under his shirt before he strode forward to meet Rosche one last time.

CHAPTER THIRTY-EIGHT

Rosche stalked forward and Gered circled, still trying to convince himself it was okay to even be holding the knife. The warlord matched his pace, stalking around and around.

"So why wait to challenge until now, Gered?" Rosche asked.

The familiarity of someone opposite him, ready to fight, riders watching with silent wagers passing between them, helped settle him. This was just another challenge. Another opponent to face down.

"Didn't see anything worth challenging for until now."

A muscle in Rosche's jaw twitched. He might rule through fear, but he was still just a man.

"So what were the last five years, then?"

Gered lifted a shoulder, forcing more of the walls up around his heart again. "If the Tlengin had an ounce of patience, they would have taken you down."

"But they didn't. Not saying much for yourself there."

Gered shifted the knife again. "I'm not Tlengin." One more step. "And I'm not a dusting viper either."

Rosche charged and Gered twisted away from his slash. With every stab, strike, and slash, his muscles remembered purposefully forgotten lessons learned under Severi's eye.

The sun burned down, dust kicking up under their boots as they strove back and forth.

Gered grabbed Rosche's arm, twisting it and whipping his knife down toward Rosche's elbow. Rosche battered his strike off course, crowding in close. Still holding Rosche's hand, Gered kept a reverse grip on the knife and stabbed toward the warlord's shoulder.

A knee up into his gut sent him stumbling back. Rosche yanked free and stabbed toward Gered. He blocked three successive strikes aimed at his stomach, chest, and neck, retaliating with sweeping strikes which drove Rosche back out of his space.

They fell back to circling each other, panting hard.

The sneer had long vanished from Rosche's face, replaced with grim determination. He closed again, swiping up. Gered pivoted, trying for his own thrust. It barely made it through, nicking Rosche's arm and drawing a thin line of blood.

An enraged roar burst from the warlord and, as if the flowing blood somehow lent strength, he came after Gered with redoubled intensity. Extra power filled each punch, each strike, until finally his knife slashed Gered's side.

Gered stumbled back, focus wavering at the feeling of blood soaking through his shirt. Rosche bulled forward, blocking Gered's thrusts and slashes.

His foot twisted over a rock, knocking him off-balance. Rosche leaped to take advantage. Gered desperately stabbed forward. The warlord swung out of the way, grabbing his wrist and wrenching in a twisting motion.

A scream ripped from Gered as his shoulder was torn from the socket. The knife fell from his nerveless grip and he went to his knees. Rosche released him and kicked him in the chest.

Gered tumbled to the ground, coarse grass and stones digging into his back. A wheezing gasp escaped, and only raw adrenaline helped cover up most of the pain rushing from his shoulder.

Rosche fell toward him, knife raised. Gered jerked a knee up, the impact of Rosche against his leg jamming through his hip. Rosche strained against him, unable to reach his chest for the best killing strike. Short a weapon, Gered grasped at the ground.

Hand closing around a small stone, Gered swung. At such close quarters, he couldn't miss, and the rock impacted Rosche's forehead.

The warlord fell away, half-stunned and bleeding. A pained gasp escaping, Gered rolled, starting to push up with his good arm. But Rosche was stirring, coming up to his feet quicker. His boot impacted Gered's stomach, flinging him back down.

He rolled, tucking his knees back up and kicking up into Rosche's stomach as the warlord loomed over him. Rosche staggered back.

Gered looked for his knife. Rosche was now between him and the blade. But he had a closer weapon. And not much time.

Half-scrambling to his feet, he slipped and stumbled the five feet to the corner of the square. He dove forward as Rosche's bellow sounded behind him. Hand closing around the pistol's grip, he twisted on the ground, brought the gun up, and fired.

Rosche staggered to a halt, arm upraised, prepared to throw the knife. Red blossomed over his chest. Three panting breaths tore through Gered. His arm shook, the gun wobbling with it. Rosche tried to take a step forward. The knife dropped. His knee buckled and he toppled to the ground.

Gered pushed painfully to his feet, injured arm tucked low against his waist. Silence followed as he limped toward the fallen warlord.

Rosche lay on his back, wheezing gasps breaking through bloody lips. He stared up at Gered, rage and confusion warring in his eyes. His lips moved like he wanted to say something.

Heart hardened, Gered raised the gun one last time and pulled the trigger. Rosche died like he'd killed so many times. Perfect shot through the head.

Gered's hand trembled as it fell back to his side, realizing only then he'd grabbed the warlord's pistol. Rosche stared sightlessly up at the sky, and Gered fell back a step from the sight.

Movement to his right sent alertness screaming back through him. Whipping the gun back up, he stared down the barrel at Moshe.

"Easy, Gered."

"About dusting time you got here." Gered's hand started shaking again as he lowered the gun.

A faint smile cracked Moshe's face. "This was your idea of stalling? Straight up challenging him?"

Gered cleared his throat. "Worked, didn't it?"

Moshe spared Rosche's body a glance. "Maybe. We're not quite out of this yet."

Gered cast a glance past him to see Unit Three's leader raising his gun. Dredging up the hardness he'd held for so long as a unit leader, he stalked forward.

"Drop it, Shaw."

Shaw spread his hands, but fight still simmered in the set of his jaw. His unit didn't look too pleased either. The half of Moshe's unit who'd been at the bridge looked to their leader for some sort of guidance.

Gered dared look to Four. He found Dayo first, his friend watching him with something like awe. Then to the rest, who looked back with the same trust they would have if he were still wearing the red jacket. Swallowing hard again, Gered called, "Four, you with me?"

"You know it, boss," Sani replied. Nods answered.

Gered jerked his head. "Muster up."

Unit Four pushed their way from among Unit Three whose guns had all fallen to their sides.

"Good call," Moshe muttered.

Four made their way to stand with him. The two trainees came with them, casting wide-eyed looks at him before ducking heads and hurrying to the back of the group. Gioia kept slightly angled away. Dayo paused at his side until Gered shook himself and wrapped his arm, gun and all, around Dayo's shoulders, yanking him into a hug.

"You okay?"

Dayo gently tapped his uninjured shoulder. "Think it cracked a rib or two this time."

"I thought he killed you." The words wobbled dangerously.

Pulling away, Dayo knocked a fist against his chest. "Stuck with me for a bit longer, *kamé*."

A smile threatened. "Good."

Dayo's mouth twitched. "What's your plan here? No offense, but you'll make a terrible warlord."

Gered wryly arched an eyebrow. "Thanks."

Moshe leaned closer. "Got some trucks incoming, finally." He jerked his chin toward the road. Four transpo trucks lumbered to a halt across the bridge.

Stepping forward, Gered twitched his gun, bringing Dayo up with him.

"Drop the guns and stand down."

Shaw looked at him incredulously.

"You want to try and outfight the military, Shaw?" Gered snarled.

"Why should I listen to you, traitor?" Shaw sneered back.

"Rosche staked the Barracks, and I just killed him. I can name a new unit leader just as easily as he could, so what's it gonna be?"

Not all of Unit Three held Shaw's reluctance. Some were already setting guns down on the ground. Shaw finally relented and did the same. Moshe's unit followed suit.

"What about us, boss?" Sani asked.

Gered looked back over his shoulder. "Hands away from guns. Let this play out."

Soldiers were sweeping in a broad line toward them, weapons raised. In the time it took them to make their careful way over, the last of the adrenaline faded, allowing the pain from his dislocated shoulder to hit Gered hard.

The knife wound had clotted around his shirt and bits of dirt. He fought against the need to sit down and focused on taking one breath after another.

Captain Ramses lowered his gun in surprise when he saw Rosche lying dead and the units disarmed.

"All yours, Captain," Gered said.

"Traitor!" Shaw snarled at him as the soldiers pushed in and began cuffing riders.

Unit Four edged nervously as some soldiers came toward them, but Captain Ramses extended a hand.

"This Four?" he asked Gered, who forced a nod. "They're good," he told the soldiers.

Moshe stepped forward with Ramses, heading toward some of his own riders. Some were uncuffed. Moshe had words with the others, and only a few nodded and were subsequently released. The rest stayed in cuffs.

Ramses and Moshe came back to Gered.

"There's a base about forty-five minutes from here. We'll load up, head there, and sort everyone's situation. Your unit can keep weapons and get more comfortable quarters if they promise to behave," Ramses said, the look he swept over Four barely trusting.

"They will," Gered said around his jaw clenched against the pain. Ramses still looked doubtful as he turned away and started giving the orders. Gered clicked the safety on and shifted the gun so he held the barrel and extended it to Moshe.

"Take the dusting thing," he said.

"You don't want it?" Moshe paused, hand touching the pistol's grip. Gered shook his head vehemently. He had plenty of ways to remember Rosche. He didn't need a physical one.

"It'll give you more pull when you head back to the Barracks carrying his guns." He surrendered it to Moshe's hold.

"Sit down for a minute, Gered," Moshe said. "We'll get everyone loaded up." He turned over Rosche's gun in his hands for several moments before giving Gered another nod.

"What's going on?" Sani pressed. The rest of Four fidgeted restlessly as they watched the other units being moved by the soldiers. "You knew about this, Dayo?" Faint accusation coated the rider's voice.

"I did. Moshe asked me to keep it under wraps," Dayo said. "Long story short, Gered and the drifter agreed to play bait, and Moshe's been working with the army the whole time he's been in. Now Rosche is out of the way, they're planning to head into the territory."

A low whistle cut from Sani. But none of Four looked upset.

The trainees looked relieved. And Gioia. She stared at the ground, hands in her back pockets, not looking at him. It made his heart ache worse than his shoulder.

Dayo nudged his arm and looked past him. He turned to see Laramie and Kayin waiting a few paces away. He lurched forward a step and Laramie met him, hauling him into a hug so tight he winced.

She released him, eyes watery and mouth working a moment before she hugged him again. Once Laramie stepped back, Kayin offered him a hand. Gered clasped it, and the traveler pulled him forward to tap his good shoulder.

Another wave of pain swept over Gered, bringing nausea with it. Kayin caught him.

"Sit down." He guided Gered over to the nearest tree and helped lower him to the ground. Dayo followed, glaring at Kayin.

Gered tipped his head back against the tree, willing the world to stay in focus. "Think you could do something for this shoulder, Dayo?"

Dayo grunted as he took a knee. "Was already planning on it." He began to press around the joint until Gered almost punched him. "Sorry, don't have anything with me."

"But I do," a new voice interrupted. A soldier stood a few feet away, medic patch on his armored vest. "Captain Ramses sent me over."

Dayo hadn't lost the guarded look. Laramie and Kayin stayed close, and it made Gered feel a little more at ease. When Gered didn't object, Dayo waved the medic over.

"What are we looking at?" the soldier asked.

"Dislocated shoulder and at least one laceration."

"Getting professional on me?" Gered asked.

Dayo rolled his eyes. "Give him all the pain meds. He gets more stupid when he's really hurting."

The medic chuckled and dug out a bottle of pills and a water bottle from his pack. He handed the water and two pills over to Gered. After he finished off most of the water and they waited a few minutes, Dayo moved for his arm again.

The medic braced a hand against Gered's chest, keeping him pinned against the tree. Gered gripped the soldier's arm to steady himself. Dayo settled hands around the joint.

"Ready?" And then not waiting for Gered's reply, he maneuvered it back in place.

Gered groaned, the meds not masking all the pain. "I take it back, I hate you."

Dayo thumped his chest. "Serves you right for leaving us."

The medic slowly released his hold on Gered, who kept his jaw clenched as Dayo gently rotated his shoulder, making sure it moved as it should.

Digging in his pack again, the medic produced a bandage roll. "About all I got on me for a sling. You'll want something for a day or so to let the joint settle."

He handed it off to Dayo, along with a bandage kit for the cut, and left. Laramie crouched down, resting a hand on his shoulder.

"You okay?"

It took a moment for Gered to nod. He'd killed again, but at least this time it had been on his terms. This time, he had protected people instead of hurting them. It would still sit raw inside him for a while, but it was going to be the last time.

"How's the family?" he asked.

"Fine. Connor surrendered without a fight," Laramie said.

"Good." Relief swept through him.

"Kayin and I are gonna go get our bikes. We'll grab yours too." She set his pistols down at his side, and he smiled his thanks. She tapped his shoulder and disappeared into the woods.

"Dayo." Gioia's quiet voice drew his attention forward. She still wasn't quite looking at him. Her name froze on his tongue.

"Moshe said we could ride our bikes … wherever we're going."

"Okay." Dayo nodded. "I'll grab mine here in a sec."

She paused a moment more, eyes flicking to Gered before she backed away and waved Unit Four to follow. Gered tracked her path, heart cracking.

"Give her some time," Dayo said quietly. "It's been a rough time all around."

"I'm so sorry, Dayo."

"I know," Dayo reassured as he unrolled the bandage. "But she needs to hear it too."

Gered stared down at his hands, letting Dayo lift his arm up to begin forming the sling around it. "Think she'll let me talk to her?"

"She'll come around. I just punched you a few times, but she'll need to work to it in her own way."

"Since when are you so smart?" Gered mustered a lighter tone.

"Since I quit drinking and hanging around you all the time." Dayo tied off the sling. "Now stay here." He glared until Gered gave a mock salute.

He disappeared into the woods to retrieve his bike, leaving Gered leaning against the tree. Soldiers moved about with quick efficiency, escorting riders to the transpo trucks, others driving motorcycles over to load into other trucks. Some bundled Rosche's body into a canvas wrapping and carted him off.

Laramie and Kayin brought the bikes back in silence, waiting with him as Four did the same, though this time the unit kept a little distance.

Laramie's attention wavered only once when a young rider came over to her.

"Hey, Axel!" She wrapped him up in a hug before holding him at arm's length. "You okay?"

The kid nodded, looking a little overwhelmed. Gered half-smiled. There was no tattoo on his wrist yet, though after Springer there should have been. Moshe must have been trying to keep him clear of anything permanent until it all shook out.

Axel glanced past her, fidgeting as he took a half-step forward. "Gered … sir…"

A faint smile stirred. "Hey, kid."

"I'm really glad you both are okay," Axel blurted and backed away to where Moshe stood. Gered gave him a nod.

"I think you're not-so-secretly a softie." Laramie's teasing voice drew his gaze up.

"Whatever you think, drifter." He gingerly tucked his arm a little closer to his chest, and she flashed a soft smile.

Finally, Ramses came over with another soldier to announce they were ready to go. He offered Gered a place in a truck, which he took. The bullets in his bike had put it in need of some work before it could be drivable again.

Gered pulled himself up into the rear seat. He sank back against the stiff cushions, keeping his rifle beside him. Movement at the other door announced Laramie climbing in to sit next to him. She offered a slight smile.

He leaned his head back, wincing only a little as the truck lurched into motion. The pain meds started to weigh his eyelids down. The swaying eventually lulled them closed, and safe between his rifle and his sister, he let himself slip off into sleep.

CHAPTER THIRTY-NINE

Laramie's hand on his arm brought him back to consciousness. The transpo truck had stopped in the open courtyard of a broad compound. It took a second for his mind to catch up and realize they weren't back at the Barracks. Low buildings ran in a long U-shape, facing off with some taller structures that were probably command centers of some sort. A radio tower stood in the far corner, rising up above the tall pines surrounding the walls.

Gered pushed the door open and slid slowly to the ground, his boots hitting bricked ground. He reached back and took out his rifle, settling it over his uninjured shoulder. Laramie came to stand next to him, hands hanging loose next to her weapons.

"Lodie!" Kayin pulled his bike in where a soldier directed and killed the engine. He came to stand next to them, resting his shoulder against Laramie's and touching his forehead to hers for a second.

It made Gered's heart ache even more for the distance Gioia was holding. He needed to find some way to talk to her.

Unit Four rumbled in behind the next transpo truck, and four more soldiers directed them to a place next to Kayin's bike. They slowly doffed helmets and turned off motorcycles.

Moshe strode over and conferred with Dayo. A bit of pride stirred in Gered as Dayo nodded and confidently gave some orders. The riders began to fall in, and Moshe came toward Gered.

"Ramses wants to go ahead and debrief with you and Four right now. Get everything settled and make any adjustments we need. I'd also like to talk with them as well."

The captain waved them toward one of the command buildings and made no argument when Laramie and Kayin followed. Boots echoed off the tiled entryway where a broad Natux flag took up one wall. Framed pictures hung opposite, groups of soldiers, some in formal uniforms, others in more relaxed gear and grinning out at the passersby.

Ramses led the way under a wide arched door and down a longer hallway into a more formal room with narrow tables and chairs in rows. He headed up to the front of the room where Moshe joined him.

Unit Four slowly filed in to take seats. Gioia hung close to Dayo. Gered took a chair in the back. Laramie and Kayin slid in with him.

"All right, listen up," Ramses began. "The Natux military made a deal with Gered, working with him to help bring Rosche down. His only request was that you, as his former unit, would be able to walk free out of all this."

Some stirred, glancing back over their shoulders to him. Gered scraped a thumb over the grain of the table.

"But this is not where it ends." He gestured to Moshe.

"It's no secret I'm ex-army." Moshe crossed his arms. "I just kept in touch while at the Barracks. Taking Rosche down was the reason I went into the territory and worked myself up to where I am. Second half of the plan that went down today is for me to take my unit back, take care of Barns, and let the military in to start opening up the territory again. Anyone have issues with that?"

Heads shook all around. Gioia's shoulders hunched a little where she slouched in the chair, trying to stay careless. Gered jerked his eyes from her.

"All right. As part of the deal with Gered, any records you have on the outside can be scrubbed clean. You all get a fresh start wherever. But I could also use some backup when I head back."

Gered sat a little taller. Moshe held up a hand to forestall him.

"I'd ask you to head in with me, Gered, but I think I already know your answer."

His heart staggered. Was this where they made him go anyway? He'd just killed Rosche. They couldn't let him go.

"You held up your end, so you're out." Moshe nodded when he didn't make an immediate answer. Relief swept through him. "But I'm leaving it up to anyone else. I know some of you have family back there"—he looked to the trainees— "or might have some sort of personal stake in it all." He glanced at Gioia, whose head tipped down.

"I'm headed back in forty-eight hours. You have until then to decide."

Ramses took over again. "Like he said, records will be scrubbed no matter what you decide. But we will be keeping some sort of tabs on you all, at least for a bit." He offered an apologetic tilt of the head. "That's the way it's gotta be. You've got forty-eight hours here. You'll get a section of the barracks to yourselves and access to the mess hall. We'll reconvene when it's time to hear everyone's decision."

With one last nod, he strode from the room with Moshe.

Another soldier filled the doorway in their place.

"Follow me when you're ready," he said.

Sani slowly gained his feet, turning to face Gered. "You staked for us?"

The rest of the unit rearranged. Dec sat on a table, the two trainees clustered close to him. He looked older than Gered remembered. Tamar propped a boot up on the table and leaned back in his chair. Benj crossed his arms. Ray propped a shoulder up against the wall.

Dayo's lighter spun in his hand, and Gioia still hadn't turned.

Gered pressed his hand flat against the table. "It was the least I could do after leaving you all behind like that."

Sani scoffed lightly. "You had a chance and you took it."

"Doesn't mean it was right. I didn't think about what I was leaving behind." Gered swept a look to all of the unit.

"Felt like you screwed us over," Benj said.

"We've ridden after plenty of runaways. Didn't think we'd have to go after you ourselves," Tamar said, frowning. Several glances were thrown at Sani. One of Dayo's glares seared toward the rider, and Gered wondered what had gone down in the unit.

"We would have gone with you," Dec piped up, his hands loosely clasped as he leaned on his knees.

A lump formed in Gered's chest. "What?"

The younger rider quirked a puzzled frown.

Ray shook his head. "We all know what you did for us. Keeping us at Four. It was a decent enough life. But that's not the only reason we stuck around."

Laramie's knee nudged his, and he jerked a look at her. She raised an eyebrow with an "I told you so" look.

"I ..." Gered cleared his throat. "I've never really thought I was worth something like that."

Five pairs of eyes stared at him with some incredulity, and wide-eyed confusion filled the trainees' faces.

"Don't worry, I already told him he was an idiot," Dayo said wryly.

Gered eased a small smile.

"You need to get out of your own head." Dec shook his head.

"I'm trying," Gered reassured.

"Good." Ray pushed away from the wall. "Now, where can I get a drink around here?" He addressed the soldier, who obligingly waved them out the door.

The rest of Four followed, giving Gered slight nods as they passed. Dayo hung back, waiting for Gered to rise to his feet. He hooked a hand over Gered's shoulder.

"Well, that was touching, and emotional, and cathartic."

Gered shifted his jaw to cover a smile. "You gonna go get checked by the medic, or what?"

Dayo rubbed his chest and winced. "Oh yeah, that searing pain is just my ribs and not my heart overwhelmed."

"Did I miss you? Remind me." Gered let Dayo keep his hand there as they made their way down the hall.

Dayo chuckled. They got directions from another soldier, taking them out of the command center and across the courtyard to another low building. Laramie took Gered's rifle and promised to find them in the next few minutes. She and Kayin split off, leaving Gered and Dayo to keep going.

Dayo kept a hand pressed against his chest and the other leaning on Gered.

"You okay?" Gered asked quietly.

"Yeah." He winced. "Kind of taken a beating the last few

weeks, so I'll be glad to finally just sleep it off."

Gered flinched, looking down at the even spacing of the bricks. Dayo jostled his shoulder so he looked up.

"We've been over it all, yeah?"

"Doesn't make me stop regretting it," Gered said.

"I'm not above letting you wallow for a bit longer. But Four kept our reputation, so don't worry."

In the reflective glass of the med center doors, Gered saw they had a tail. He swallowed hard but let Dayo push open the door, afraid to turn and spook Gioia.

The medic from before met them. "Back already?"

"Dayo needs to be checked out," Gered said.

"Got shot point-blank by a crazy warlord. Doesn't make the ribs feel so good." Dayo shrugged and immediately winced.

The medic waved him over to a bed. "You guys are something else. I thought I knew crazy from the war, but this …" He shook his head.

Dayo eased onto the bed and unzipped his jacket. Gered reached out with his good hand and helped him shrug it off.

"Never underestimate adrenaline as a drug." A curse strained from Dayo as the medic unstrapped his vest and he lost its compression.

Sure enough, bruises splotched in darker patches against his black skin. The medic got some new wraps and after a quick diagnostic sweep, wrapped the cracked ribs back up and got some meds.

He turned to Gered next. "Let's check you over again." Practically shoving Gered over to the next bed, he checked over the knife wound, cleaned it again with stinging antiseptic, and bandaged it.

Gered tugged his bloody and ripped shirt back down, leaving

the new sling the medic handed over for a few minutes, and tried not to stare at Gioia leaning up against the wall by the door, hands in her back pockets. The medic turned from cleaning his hands and nodded to her.

"You with these two, or you need something medical?"

Gered darted a glance over as she straightened a little. "With these two."

"All right. You both stick around for a bit, and I'll be back to check in. Feel free to stay if you want." He offered Gioia a smile before leaving the room.

An uncomfortable silence fell once he was gone, something that hadn't happened between the three of them in a long time. Dayo didn't seem inclined to break it like he normally might.

A knock saved it. Laramie poked her head in.

"The medic said you were still in here." She slid in. "Hey, Gioia." Warmth filled her voice. "How you doing?"

"Okay." Gioia still seemed subdued, flicking a glance between Laramie and Gered. "How about you?" She forced a lighter tone. "You both seem to be doing okay."

Laramie looked to Gered in question, and he nodded. She smiled.

"Yeah, though it got a little intense when we figured out he was the brother I thought was dead, so …"

Gioia's head whipped up, and she looked back and forth between Gered and Laramie. Dayo sat back, studying them just as intently.

"Siblings, huh? That makes sense." He nodded.

"Just like that?" Gered asked.

"Come on, you both have no sense of self-preservation."

Laramie chuckled. "You've got a point."

"How…?" Gioia was still staring but her shoulders had relaxed. "Did you know when…?"

"No, we figured it out after Laramie got us out. I don't really remember this part." Gered gestured to Laramie.

"He told me his name," she said simply.

"His name?" Dayo frowned. "You already knew his name."

"Not exactly. And he didn't really know mine either." Laramie tugged her braid over her shoulder and slid hands into her jacket pockets. "Laramie is the name I go by outside the family when I drift. My name's really Melodie."

Gioia and Dayo looked to Gered, something close to hurt in their faces.

"Marcus," he said softly. "Marcus Solfeggietto."

"Then why Gered?" Dayo asked.

"The Tlengin gave me that name after they took me. And I buried Marcus for sixteen years." He worked his hand in and out of a fist. It was just barely comfortable having someone other than Laramie knowing his name, but he needed Dayo and Gioia to know it too.

"That's …" Dayo cleared his throat. "Dust."

Gioia stepped a little closer to Gered. "So …" Her glance still slid back to Laramie.

His sister leaned closer to her. "He's all yours, Gee."

Gioia flushed, and Gered's stomach flipped.

Laramie and Dayo shared a grin. "Dayo, there are some comfortable-looking couches out in the lobby. Come meet my boyfriend."

Dayo slowly gained his feet. Gioia didn't show any sign of running. Dayo looked between both of them and gave a slight nod and a smile before draping an arm over Laramie's shoulders as they headed for the doors.

"Boyfriend, huh? You found someone to tolerate you?"

Laramie's laugh faded as the door closed, and Gered and Gioia were left alone.

CHAPTER FORTY

Gioia edged forward another few steps, hands still in her back pockets. Gered slowly stood, hesitation filling every movement.

"Hi," she said softly.

"Hi." He held back, uncertain of the new ground they stood on. "Gioia … I'm so sorry. For leaving, for …"

But she shook her head. "I chose to stay, Gered. *I* chose it." Her brown eyes held his. "And yeah, I regretted it every single day. Regretted not going with you the first time. Not going when Laramie offered to take me with you two. Seeing you like that, not knowing if you were alive or dead, and then the weeks after with the scrapping and surviving … these last few days … It's been rough." A short, bitter laugh broke from her, holding almost as much as her words. "I hated you a little, hated her too, but I hated myself plenty. So don't blame yourself."

"I haven't stopped since I woke up in the med center outside the territory. Haven't stopped missing you every day." It rushed from him. "I just hated the thought of you still there, and …"

"I'm okay," she reassured and took another step forward. "You made sure I could look after myself. And that's what got me to today."

She extended a hand across the space between them. His

fingers closed around hers and he squeezed once. She squeezed back twice.

He was good. She was good. They were good.

They stood a moment, looking at their hands linked together. Gioia shifted a little, brushing her thumb over the new scar wrapping his wrist. It sent lightning bolts up his arm, but for once, he didn't have to pull away. And it almost scared him.

"So, Marcus, huh?" A soft smile curved her lips. The sound of his name nearly stole his breath away. She tilted a shy look up at him. "I think I like you better as a blond."

He ducked his head, oddly pleased, before fixing his eyes back on her. "Yeah?"

"Yeah." She reached up tentatively, watching him carefully. When he didn't move, she brushed light fingers across his cheek, settling her hand there.

Ignoring the twinge in his right shoulder, he dared to place an arm around her, bringing her a little closer. They never would have dared at the Barracks. Never be this close, a heartbeat away, foreheads almost touching, hearts straining.

"Gioia…" His voice came husky, but he never finished as her lips pressed over his.

He pulled her close, arms wrapped around her like he was afraid she'd be torn away even then. She pushed up on her toes, hand sliding through his longer hair as he kissed her again and again until they pulled apart.

He brushed a thumb across her cheekbone, counting the new freckles the desert sun had created since the last time he'd seen her.

"Come with me," he whispered. "When we leave, Laramie and I are going back to the family. Come with me."

Gioia nodded, eyes bright, a smile spreading over her face. "You will?"

She answered with another kiss, and another piece of him settled into place. Her fingers traced lightly over his left temple, careful of the lingering bruising.

"You look good," she said. "Really good."

A bit of heat flashed across his cheeks. "The bruising sets off my eyes, doesn't it?"

A laugh broke from her, brightening her face. "How did it happen?"

He settled his hand on hers where her fingers still rested against the side of his head. "Getting into fights without backup."

She shook her head. "Breaking your own rules." She *tskd.* "You really must be related to Laramie."

The corner of his mouth curved up.

"I could get used to that," she said. "And this." She kissed him again, slower and deeper. When they finally pulled apart, she rested her forehead against his, eyes closed for a moment. He was more than happy to get used to that, too.

Gioia stirred, fingers touching the chain visible before it disappeared under his shirt.

"What's this?"

She pulled it out with his nod of permission. The medal rested in the palm of her hand. "Matteo. Matthew?" she guessed.

"I've been to church," he admitted. "And talked to the priest once or twice. It's helped with some things."

"Good." She smiled and turned it over to show the small etching on the back. A frown creased between her eyes. "Is this the same as your tattoo?"

He nodded. "Matteo is sacred to the Itan. We had the verse

hanging up in our home."

This time her brows flew up. He'd never mentioned anything like that before. He barely talked about the Tlengin.

She tucked it back under his shirt before sliding her arms around his neck. "I'd like to hear about it sometime, if you want to tell me."

"I think I do."

She smiled, and he drew her closer for another kiss. This time was shorter only because a jab cut through his shoulder, and he pulled back with a short intake of breath.

"You okay?" Her hands hovered above his chest.

"Yeah." But he winced again as he moved his shoulder.

She smiled slightly. "Let's get the sling on. This is probably not what the medic had in mind when he said to take it easy."

"But I like this better." A faint grin tugged his mouth.

She snorted a laugh and moved around him to pick up the sling.

"Me too, but we should probably go see the others. I'm not ready for Dayo's incessant roasting if we stay in too long."

"You have a point."

Gioia helped maneuver his arm into the sling, and the shoulder joint eased in relief. They made their way, hand in hand, to join the others on the couches. Dayo sprawled on one couch, and Laramie sat with Kayin's arm tucked around her on another.

"Finally," Dayo said. "Now I don't have to keep covering for you two."

"Yes, I'm sure it was so hard for you," Gioia retorted.

Gered tapped her hand, and she tapped back twice.

Dayo yawned and settled more comfortably against the cushions. "Just don't be gross in front of me."

They settled next to each other on a third couch facing the others. Gered tucked his right arm up against his stomach to relieve some of the ache coming back.

"How's life been on the outside?" Gioia directed it at Laramie, but she leaned into his shoulder. He brushed his thumb over hers, knowing he'd find a different time to admit to the sleepless nights, the anger, the way it ached to see normal lives going on around him and how he was trying to reach for it himself.

"I converted him to chocolate, you're welcome," Laramie replied and launched into a summary of life for the last few weeks, focusing on the brighter bits. And he decided he'd never get tired of hearing Gioia's open laughter or the feel of her hand in his, occasionally squeezing in a silent code that might mean more than they'd dared to admit yet.

⁓

That night, as Gered settled into the small room he'd been assigned, a soft knock on the door startled him.

He opened the door, surprised to see Gioia there. She shifted between her feet, twisting the hand not shoved in her back pocket, standing so different than she had a few hours before.

"What's wrong?" Wariness fell over him.

"Nothing ... it's not ..." But she looked sick to her stomach.

"Gioia?"

She swallowed hard. "It's just ... I know you never did at the Barracks, and we ..." Her hand balled in a fist. "This afternoon was ... more than good ... But I just need to know what else you might want f-from me."

His gut lurched as her gaze slid past him to look into his room.

"Hey." He stepped out and shut the door firmly behind him. "No. Not that."

Gioia's shoulders crumpled forward in relief, and she rubbed her eyes. "I'm sorry, I just … I thought I might be okay with it, but …" A shudder cut through her.

"Hey." He extended a hand, and she slowly placed her fingers in his. "I will never make you do anything you don't want to do."

"Thank you." The words whispered tremulously from her. "Does it bother you? That he … that I…? He wasn't the only one, you know."

He did, and he hated it.

"The only thing I care about is that he hurt you. And I'd kill him a hundred times over for that alone." He didn't have to force the iron in his voice.

She nodded, scrubbing the heel of her hand under the corner of her eye. "That's romantic." But the laugh accompanying it was shaky.

"Well, I'm known for my passionate declarations."

A more real laugh burst from her, and a small smile lifted the corner of his mouth.

"I think I like Marcus." Her head tipped as she looked at him.

"I'm glad, because he has no idea what he's doing."

She squeezed his hand gently, but he took a moment, staring at their entwined hands, to figure out what he needed to say.

"Everything in my life, from the Tlengin to the Barracks, has been about taking what you want when you want and caring nothing for what's left in the wake. Even if … even if I tried not to be like that, it is still stuck in my head. And I'm finally learning … I don't know … how to be a person again."

Her watery eyes never left his.

"But what if I can't? What if I can't truly leave it all behind? What if we don't work out? Then I've become just another person who has taken something from you."

She sniffed and scraped the heel of her hand under her eye. "This time I might actually want it." But her laugh came bitter.

"Hey." He squeezed her hand gently, and after a moment she tapped back twice.

She lifted her head to meet his eyes, tears still trembling in the corners. "I'm not afraid to be with you. I want to give this a chance. It's just..."

"I know," he said softly.

She edged forward like she was daring herself, and he let her loop her arms around his waist. His arms settled about her shoulders, her head resting against the crook of his neck.

"This okay?" he asked.

She shifted a little, then sighed. "I think so."

They just stood for a moment in the quiet, hearts slowly syncing.

"What if I'm never ready?" she whispered. "What if ..."

"Then we figure it out." He brushed his thumb against her shoulder. "I'll need time, too. I'm just barely getting used to hugs." He tried to make the words lighter.

"You're pretty good at them." She nestled a little closer.

A faint laugh hummed in his chest. "Thanks."

Her back rose and fell with a deeper sigh. "I'm sorry I was too coward to go with you the first time."

"You're not a coward, Gioia."

"Yeah? What do you call being paralyzed every time you see someone? Afraid to speak out because you'll draw attention?"

"Survival," he said softly. "Believe me. I could write a dusting book about it."

Her arms tightened around him.

"You're one of the bravest people I know," he whispered. "And there were so many days you kept me going. You and Dayo."

She sniffed again.

"There's an Itan proverb I remember. 'Courage isn't always just one big act.' Sometimes it's hundreds of small acts. Sometimes it's getting up in the morning. Sometimes it's waking up in the middle of the night and breathing again. You kept fighting. Day after day. And that takes so much courage."

"I hope you remember all that for yourself." Gioia drew back, searching his face.

"I'm trying." He took her hands in his. "Normal still feels so far out of reach most days. Laramie's been helping me work toward it, but it's going to take time." Her fingers tightened around his. "We've all got scars and cracks. So don't be afraid to take the time you need. I'll be there whenever or however you need."

Tears glistened down her cheeks. "Thank you." She pressed a short kiss, full of promise, against his lips before stepping away and making her way back to her room.

CHAPTER FORTY-ONE

Gered undid the bolt holding the brake pad in place. Carefully sliding it out, he set it aside. The early morning sun cast dappled shadows across the bricked courtyard, shifting in time to the gentle sighing of the pines. Dayo slouched on the bench against the wall, heavy paper rustling as he ate a nutrient bar.

The caliper came loose next, and Gered cleaned it off. A burst of laughter brought his attention across the courtyard. Laramie and Gioia strode over side by side, easy laughter following in their wake. The caliper tapped against his thumb as he watched the openness in Gioia's face, the way she wore the borrowed army sweatshirt instead of the unit jacket.

They made their way over, and Laramie leaned over his shoulder. "What are you working on?"

"Brake pads." He returned to work with the borrowed tools from the mechanic bay.

Laramie snorted a laugh. "Again, Dayo?"

The traveler lifted a shoulder. "I've been chasing the two of you all over the lower country. What do you want me to do?"

"Not wear out your brakes?"

Gered allowed a grin as he placed the new pad. "That's a losing battle, Dee."

A fist thumped his shoulder, and he looked up into his sister's grin at the nickname.

"Need help with anything?" she asked.

He looked over the line of Unit Four's motorcycles. "You can probably pick one and start. Willing to bet no one's looked at their bike in weeks."

Gioia moved over to sit with Dayo. "Why are you eating that? They have perfectly good food in the mess."

"I know," Dayo mumbled around a bite of the bar. "I ate it already. I've told Gered repeatedly I get stressed when he leaves me in charge, and he never listens. I've barely eaten in weeks."

Gioia snorted. "Could have fooled me."

Gered's lungs filled with a deep breath as he closed his eyes and focused on the calm that came with a tool in his hand, the sounds of Gioia and Dayo gently bickering, and Laramie's voice chiming in like she'd been part of their group the entire time.

"Toss me a wrench?" Her voice brought his head up to look over the seat of Dayo's bike.

He handed one over. "Kayin get off okay?"

She nodded. "Had to practically shove him down the mountain."

They'd pushed to be able to send someone back to the family to let them know everything was fine. Laramie had loyally volunteered to go, very clearly torn, until Kayin had gently told her to stay and ride back with Gered when the forty-eight hours were up.

Dayo and Gioia wouldn't be free to leave until then, and he wanted to watch Moshe and the rest of the units leave himself.

"They'll be heading back to the main campgrounds, so we'll have a bit longer ride to get home."

"That's okay." He wouldn't mind the ride, so long as there

wasn't anyone chasing them.

"They're coming, right?" Laramie nodded to the pair sitting on the bench.

"Gioia said yes. Still need to talk to Dayo. Not sure how he'd feel about heading back to a family."

Laramie winced. "Didn't think about that." She thumped the wrench against her open palm.

"Don't worry, drifter. I'll see what I can do."

She smiled and turned back to work.

"Incoming." Dayo's low voice jerked him out of the rhythm of work a few minutes later.

"What the hell?" Laramie hissed.

Connor and Corinne sauntered across the courtyard flanked by three soldiers. Gered rose to his feet, still gripping a screwdriver as the pair made for him. Connor kept hands in his pockets, sleeves tucked up around his elbows, his usual careless smirk in place. Corinne had ditched unit dress and wore a tight-fitting tank top despite the morning chill.

"Already back at work?" Connor drawled.

"Shouldn't you be in a cell somewhere?" Laramie snapped.

"Relax, drifter." Corinne flicked sharpened nails at her.

The sardonic tilt to Connor's mouth didn't falter. "Don't worry. We didn't even pull on those travelers. We were all ready to ride Rosche down ourselves until your little army buddies jumped out."

"That what this is?" Gered pointed to the soldiers with the screwdriver.

"Yeah, old Moshe came and offered us the deal. Wish I'd been there to see you kill Rosche." Connor's smile faltered, allowing the coldness to shine brighter in his green eyes. "Sounds like it was something."

"You headed back with Moshe?" Gered kept his mind from the fight with an effort.

"Yeah. They'll have to stop me from burning the damn place down." Corinne smirked. "What about you, Gioia? Coming?" Her sharp eyes swept from Gioia to Gered and back again.

"No, thanks. Don't want to steal your fun," Gioia returned.

"My unit's packing back out, and you're the only mechanic here I trust." Connor didn't look away from Gered. Laramie scoffed.

"I'll take a look," Gered said.

"Thanks." Connor shifted like he meant to leave, then paused. "Sorry about putting that tracker on your bike."

The tip of the screwdriver pressed into Gered's opposite palm. The reason they'd been caught the first time.

"I thought you were crazy to use up your last chance." Connor looked past him for a second, then focused back. "We've always been square, so I thought maybe I'd stick it on but not activate it."

Gered didn't say anything, not breaking Connor's stare.

"But turns out, we all have something we care about, right?" Connor's smile turned bitter, and his eyes shifted a little in Corinne's direction.

"We do," Gered quietly agreed. "I'll take care of the bikes, then we're all squared up, Connor."

The careless tilt came back to the unit leader's head. "Sure thing, Gered. Maybe we'll see you around one of these days." He rocked back on his heel and turned to walk off. Corinne paused a bit longer, her unsettling eyes resting on him.

"Heard you used his own gun," she said.

Gered confirmed with a nod.

"Serves the bastard right." She snorted and backed away, giving an almost civil nod to Gioia before joining Connor and making their way back across the courtyard.

"They're so weird," Laramie muttered.

Gered tapped the screwdriver against his palm. Corinne was right. Rosche had been carrying the bullet for himself the entire time. There might be some sort of poetic justice there if he could just get rid of the feel of the pistol's textured grip against his palm.

Still. He hoped they made it, made some sort of life after the Barracks fell.

Laramie graciously helped him with Five's bikes after they finished with Four, his shoulder aching with a vengeance by the time they returned the tools to the bay.

Ramses caught up with them as they started to head back to the barracks building.

"Glad I could catch you two."

Gered darted a glance around, but it was just the army captain. Laramie's hand dangled by her knife, and he wondered if he was making her more paranoid.

"Been turning this over since we talked at the river bridge, but I wanted to see how it all played out first," Ramses said.

The dread surfaced again in Gered's gut.

"You're both Itan." It was a sort of stated question.

Laramie tilted her head. "Last I checked."

It almost made Gered smile. He wasn't Tlengin or a viper anymore. He was free to be whatever he wanted. And he wanted to be Itan again. A brother. A friend.

Ramses nodded. "There's not many left here in Natux. So the river and transport bridges have been suffering ever since the raids stopped. And not a heck of a lot of Itan wanting to come over from the old country to help out."

Gered stared at the captain, almost afraid to follow the line of reasoning to its end.

"Our engineers have done what they can, but even those with some magic left can't quite figure them out. Don't have the blue." Ramses flicked a finger at their eyes. "So how 'bout it?" He snapped his fists together. "I know you're probably headed back to the travelers, but you both have an open job for life if you ever want to mess around with the bridges. It's just the two of you, and we used to have entire towns dedicated to them, but—"

"I'll do it," Gered burst out. Ramses looked slightly taken aback at the suddenness, but Laramie bumped his arm, a smile growing.

He could be Itan. He could build, repair, and keep up the legacy of their parents and their town. Maybe someday put away the guns.

"I'm game," Laramie said. "I've always wanted a closer look at those bridges."

Ramses broke into a relieved smile. "You just solved so many problems. It might be a full job at first, but you can probably work it into a schedule once primary repairs are done." He shook both their hands. "I'll be in touch once you're settled to get something set up."

They watched him stride away, arms swinging a little freer like they'd lifted some burden.

"You sure?" Gered asked Laramie.

"I'm not going to let you have all the fun." She nudged his shoulder. "Besides, those bridges are huge. And ..." A contemplative look fell over her narrow features. "It might help settle the drifter itch. I don't know, I think I might be getting ready to settle down."

"Yeah?"

A smile grew over her face. "Kayin and I were talking a bit last night. I think I've finally got what I need around me."

"Settling down doesn't sound so bad." He found Gioia waiting across the courtyard for him.

Laramie leaned into his shoulder. "Yeah?" There was a tease in her voice. "You and I can build an awesome transpo truck, and Ade and Temi can help with a caravan. Unless you want to find a house somewhere…"

He jabbed her side with an elbow and crooked a wry smile. "One thing at a time, Dee. We've both still got some things to work through before we're ready for that talk. If ever."

"Hey." She rested an arm on his good shoulder. "That's okay. You've got plenty of family around to help."

"Family doesn't sound so bad either."

Her smile grew. "Good, because Memi and Baba are about one breath away from making cords for you."

His feet paused. "Really?"

She nodded and dug into her pocket, pulling out a trailing leather cord. "And if you don't want them, you're stuck with me anyway. So." She held it out. Blue and lighter grey wove together in a slim braid. "Family?"

A half-smile spread, and he held out his left wrist. She wrapped it around and tied it off, the leather hiding part of the writhing snake tattoo. Laramie produced a second one, and he did the same for her, the new cords settling below her traveler bands.

"Family."

⁓

Four had one last dinner together that night. Dayo had been more than happy to help convince Gered he did belong. Laramie was also given a place at the table. Dayo had dragged her along after she'd tried to get out of it.

"You were almost in Four anyway, drifter. You're part of the team."

But the riders made way for her. The trainees still sat awkwardly at the end of the table. Everyone but Gioia had decided to go back with Moshe. But no one had yet asked Dayo what he was doing. Dec had been uncertain, but he announced over another beer that he wanted to see it all finished before he went and found a cousin somewhere in the lower country. It made him actually look all his nineteen years when he realized he could get out.

As dinner finished, the unit moved to a rec area to spread out and break out more beers. Dayo took one look at the cans and stepped into the cool night air just beyond the broad square of light falling from the open door and pulled out his lighter and a cigarette. He tipped his head back to the vast spread of stars as he exhaled a puff of smoke.

Soft bootsteps coming to stand by him had him regretfully looking at his cigarette. But Gered made a small motion with his hand that stopped Dayo from throwing it away.

Dayo raised an eyebrow. Gered slid hands into jacket pockets and lifted a shoulder.

"Some things aren't bothering me as much recently."

"Yeah?" Dayo took another drag, angling his head away to blow out the smoke, keeping his hand a little extended to keep some distance between it and Gered.

"Work in progress," Gered offered, his boots scuffing against the stones as he settled into a slightly wider stance.

"Seems like you're doing okay."

Gered lifted a shoulder. Dayo flicked ash and considered him from the corner of his eye. There was something different to Gered, or Marcus, though that itself was going to take some getting used to.

"You looked almost spooked after you shot Rosche." Dayo tipped his head to regard Gered better and took another inhale, the smoke helping to steady some of the jittery feeling the sight of the beer had brought on.

Gered's boots scuffed again, and motion stirred through his shoulders, the light from the doorway catching on his softened edges. "I told myself that I didn't want to kill again. And then I did. Even if it was him, and even if it was something different than just shooting him in cold blood. I'm just ... *tired* of killing and blood. I'm never doing it again." His jaw hardened as he stared out into the darkness.

"Good."

The half-smile Gered offered was a little strained.

"I saw you talked with Sani." Dayo tipped some ash away.

"Yeah." Gered looked down at his feet, the toe of his boot nudging the edge of an uneven brick. "Can't really blame him for what he did. I might have done the same thing if Rosche knew how much I cared. Hell, if *I* knew how much I cared."

Dayo almost smiled. He had some aching ribs that said Rosche knew Gered cared at least a little bit.

"I still would have punched him." Dayo tucked the cigarette between his lips.

A faint chuckle came from Gered. He glanced over at Dayo.

"Noticed you didn't say where you were going."

Dayo shrugged. "Haven't decided yet. But back to the Barracks is not high on my list."

Gered worked his jaw, staring back at the ground for a second. "Laramie and I are going back to the family. Gioia's coming, too."

Dayo nodded, holding smoke in until it burned his lungs. It rushed out.

"You choosing to go back and stay?" he asked.

He'd only ever seen such raw understanding from Gered once before. And that had been after Dayo's first kill when he realized there was no going back, and he was well and truly stuck in the gangs.

"Yes." Gered broke away before the look could sear deeper. "It reminds me of … home." There was a bit of longing over the word. "It's … it's got me thinking that maybe I can put away the guns someday."

It prodded at Dayo, and he flung the cigarette down and ground it out. Of course the one place Gered might find something like that was a traveler camp.

"I know a traveler camp is probably not what you want to see."

"Yeah… " Dayo stared out at the walls where the dark shapes of soldiers stood guard at even intervals.

"You know I'm going to ask."

"You damn well better this time." Dayo tilted his head to look at Gered, who half-smiled.

"You gonna come with us?"

He took a breath. He trusted Gered, and there was no way his friend was willingly going into a place that would use him again. Or dump him in some place to be used. No way Laramie would do the same. He hadn't thought he'd ever trust again, but then had come Gered and then Gioia.

Maybe he could give it a try.

"Yeah." Dayo slung his arm over Gered's shoulders. "Don't know if I'll ever want the cords again, but you and Gee, you're family enough for me."

"That was heartwarming." A grin spread over Gered's face. "And emotional, and I might cry."

"Shut up." Dayo shoved him away, but he was chuckling.

Gered knocked a fist against Dayo's shoulder. "Thanks for having my back, *kamé*."

Brother.

Dayo smiled. "Any time."

CHAPTER FORTY-TWO

Gered pulled to a halt at the crest of the hill. Dayo swung in beside him. The others did the same, pulling across the road as they turned to watch the procession of army transpo trucks and unit bikes led by Moshe disappear over the hills—headed west, back to the desert.

Unit Four had taken leave of him and Gioia and Dayo. All of them knew where they could find him if they needed anything. When the last truck vanished, they turned to look at each other through open visors.

"Let's go home." Melodie grinned and snapped her visor shut.

He followed suit and let her take lead to the east.

A slow two-day ride brought them back through the town. Melodie turned down the cutoff to take them out to the family's campgrounds.

Dayo nodded reassurance as they fell in again.

Peace fell over Gered at the sight of the double circle of caravans and the bright yellow one in its place. Figures strode out to meet them as they pulled up to the open space in front of the caravans.

They killed their engines, and he pulled his helmet off, letting Ade and Temi greet their daughter first.

Ade pulled him into her arms next, rocking slightly back and forth. He closed his eyes as his feet settled firm on the ground.

She pulled back and Temi was there. They settled hands on his shoulders, and he knew he'd found his place with them.

"Welcome home, Marcus."

We at Uncommon Universes Press hope you enjoyed this book, Uncommon Reader! Please feel free to post your honest feedback in a review on any major platform.

Scan the QR code or visit uncommonuniverses.com to sign up for the Uncommon Reader Newsletter and get the latest in thrilling book news from UUP (and a 10% off discount on an autographed paperback):

Thank you for reading!

ACKNOWLEDGEMENTS

This series has such a large part of my heart. In many ways, it feels unapologetically *me*. The sort of book I love. Where characters go through hard times, sometimes with that careless smile in place to hide what they really feel, but always with a bit of hope and family and love sprinkled through.

And with books like these, there's always some special thank-yous to add.

My family always, for being supportive in my writing career. My mom, for faithfully preordering and not being afraid to tell me what she thinks of my stories. Or maybe yell at me for leaving her on a cliffhanger. Dad, for reading my books and helping nurture my love of stories by reading to us all when we were kids. And for giving me oil field tips for this series.

To my bestie for being there for me always and keeping me slightly sane during the last few years.

To beta readers Jenni, Selina, Kate, Jessica, and Brittany. And especially to Jenni and Selina for completely embracing this series and encouraging me in so many ways to keep going. Selina, I still can't believe you got Gered's Itan tattoo.

To MJ McGriff for providing a sensitivity read for both books and for loving Gered and Dayo. And for putting up with me when my brain short-circuited and forgot to add you in the acknowledgements for book 1. You're amazing, MJ!!

To the Inkwell—you are such an amazing group of women, and I have so appreciated your support over the last few years. Emily, thanks for the weekly check-ins and general steady encouragement when I hit burnout in the midst of this draft.

To the team at UUP—thanks for loving this story and for

putting up with me and my occasional existential crises and Dory brain. Y'all have been rockstars, and I know my books are in good hands.

It feels weird to thank a place, but I can't finish off Gered and Laramie's story without mentioning again my love of the wilds of west Texas and New Mexico. The hardy mountains and open deserts, sudden rainstorms, hidden arroyos, sweeping mesas, purple sage and mesquite, friendly people who'll throw in behind you without question, and the sense that there's still a bit of untamed wonder out there, waiting to be discovered.

Always, always, to my Creator for having given me a love of stories and the means to tell them.

And to you, reader, for having taken a chance on these books. I hope it'll stick with you long after the last page. Thanks for all the messages, posts, reviews, and sharing about these books. It means the world to me, and it means I can keep creating wild worlds and tenacious characters.

If you loved this story, stick around. I'm not sure Dayo and I are quite done yet.

ABOUT THE AUTHOR

C. M. Banschbach is a native Texan and would make an excellent hobbit if she wasn't so tall. She's an overall dork, ice cream addict, and fangirl. When not writing fantasy stories packed full of adventure and snark, she works as a pediatric Physical Therapist where she happily embraces the fact that she never actually has to grow up. She writes clean YA/MG fantasy-adventure as Claire M. Banschbach.

Connect with her on social media:
Facebook @cmbanschbach
Instagram @cmbanschbach
Twitter @cmbanschbach

OTHER BOOKS BY C. M. BANSCHBACH

The Dragon Keep Chronicles:
Oath of the Outcast
Blood of the Seer

The Drifter Duology :
Then Comes a Drifter
A Name Long Buried

Spirits' Valley Duology:
Greywolf's Heart
Saber's Pride